Jenna Ayoub

# FOREVER HOME™

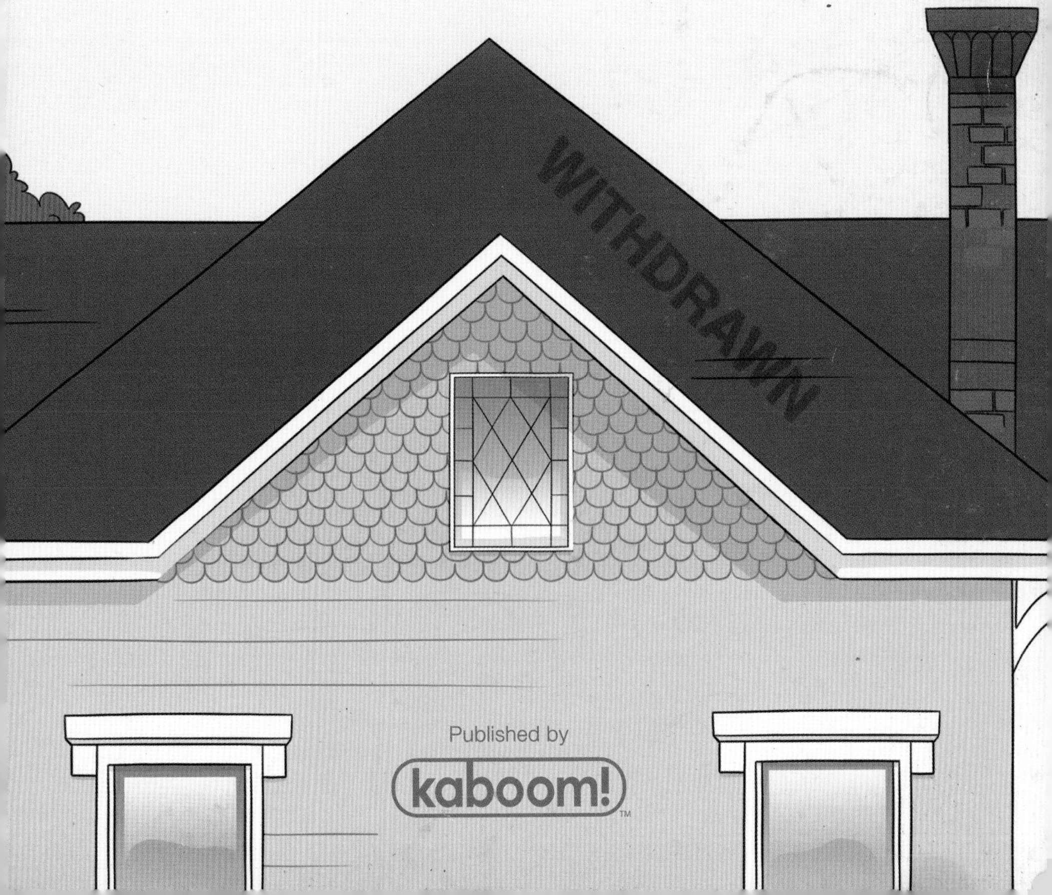



Published by
kaboom!™

Ross Richie .................................................................CEO & Founder
Joy Huffman ...........................................................................................CFO
Matt Gagnon ...............................................................Editor-in-Chief
Filip Sablik .........................President, Publishing & Marketing
Stephen Christy ...................................President, Development
Lance Kreiter ........Vice President, Licensing & Merchandising
Arune Singh ...............................Vice President, Marketing
Bryce Carlson ..... Vice President, Editorial & Creative Strategy
Kate Henning ......................................Director, Operations
Spencer Simpson ...................................Director, Sales
Scott Newman ....................Manager, Production Design
Elyse Strandberg .............................Manager, Finance
Sierra Hahn ......................................Executive Editor
Jeanine Schaefer ............................Executive Editor
Dafna Pleban ..........................................Senior Editor
Shannon Watters .................................Senior Editor
Eric Harburn ...........................................Senior Editor
Sophie Philips-Roberts ....................Associate Editor
Amanda LaFranco ..............................Associate Editor
Jonathan Manning ............................Associate Editor
Gavin Gronenthal ..............................Assistant Editor
Gwen Waller ......................................Assistant Editor

Allyson Gronowitz ...............................Assistant Editor
Ramiro Portnoy ...................................Assistant Editor
Kenzie Rzonca ..................................... Assistant Editor
Shelby Netschke ............................... Editorial Assistant
Michelle Ankley ................................ Design Coordinator
Marie Krupina ...................................Production Designer
Grace Park .......................................Production Designer
Chelsea Roberts ..............................Production Designer
Samantha Knapp ...................Production Design Assistant
José Meza ...........................................Live Events Lead
Stephanie Hocutt ......................Digital Marketing Lead
Esther Kim .................................Marketing Coordinator
Breanna Sarpy ..................... Live Events Coordinator
Amanda Lawson ......................Marketing Assistant
Holly Aitchison ....................Digital Sales Coordinator
Morgan Perry ......................Retail Sales Coordinator
Megan Christopher ............ Operations Coordinator
Rodrigo Hernandez ...........Operations Coordinator
Zipporah Smith ..................Operations Assistant
Jason Lee ................................ Senior Accountant
Sabrina Lesin .....................Accounting Assistant

FOREVER HOME, February 2021. Published by KaBOOM!,
a division of Boom Entertainment, Inc. Forever Home is ™ &
© 2021 Jenna Ayoub. All rights reserved. KaBOOM!™ and the
KaBOOM! logo are trademarks of Boom Entertainment,
Inc., registered in various countries and categories. All characters, events, and institutions
depicted herein are fictional. Any similarity between any of the names, characters,
persons, events, and/or institutions in this publication to actual names, characters,
and persons, whether living or dead, events, and/or institutions is unintended
and purely coincidental. KaBOOM! does not read or accept unsolicited
submissions of ideas, stories, or artwork.

BOOM! Studios, 5670 Wilshire Boulevard, Suite 400, Los
Angeles, CA 90036-5679. Printed in China. First Printing.

ISBN: 978-1-68415-603-0,
eISBN: 978-1-64668-015-3

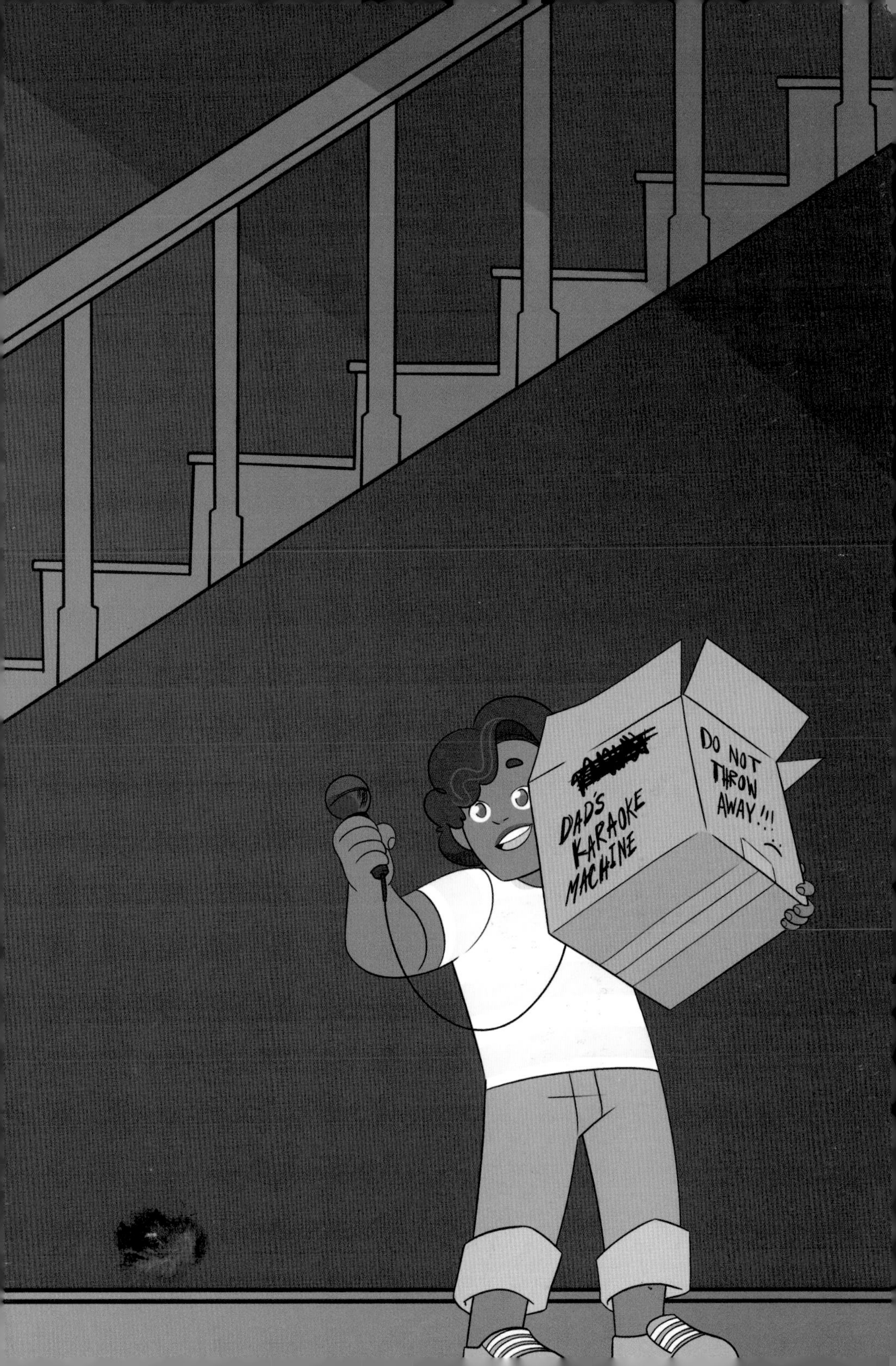
DAD'S KARAOKE MACHINE
DO NOT THROW AWAY!!!

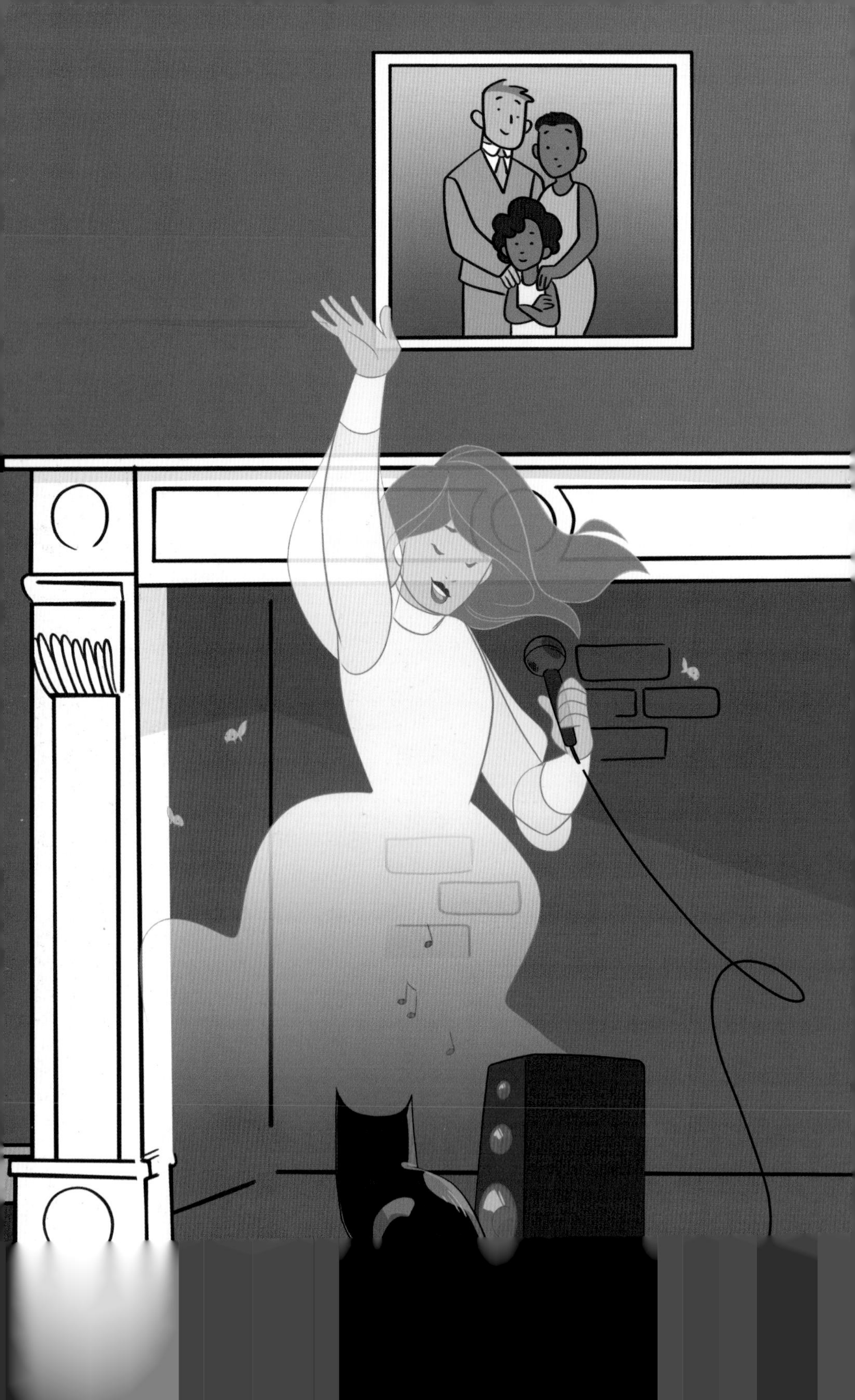

# FOREVER HOME ™

## Written & Illustrated by
Jenna Ayoub

## Cover by
Jenna Ayoub

**Designer**
Chelsea Roberts

**Assistant Editor**
Michael Moccio

**Associate Editor**
Jonathan Manning

**Editor**
Bryce Carlson

***Forever Home* created by**
Jenna Ayoub

**Special Thanks**
Whitney Leopard

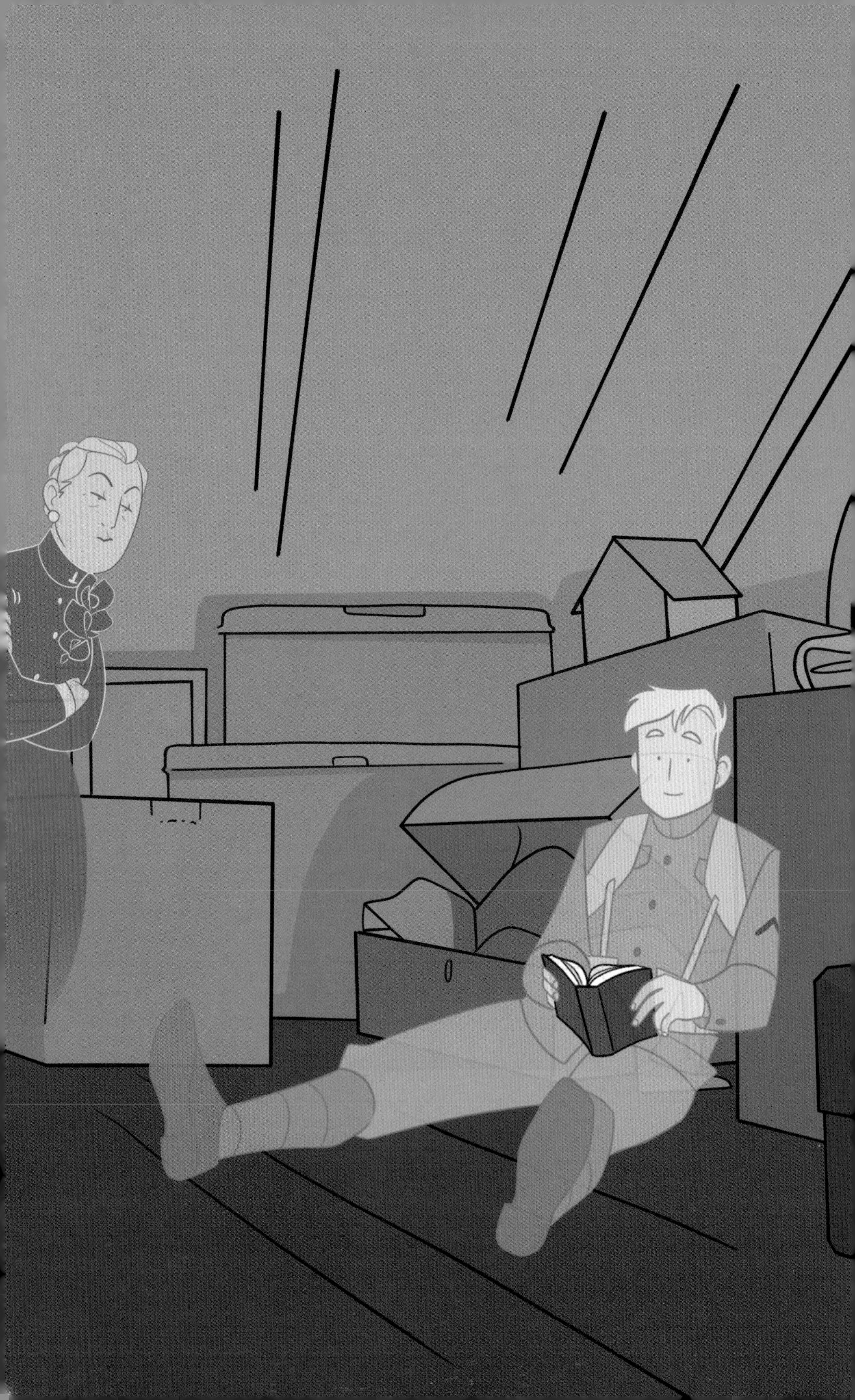

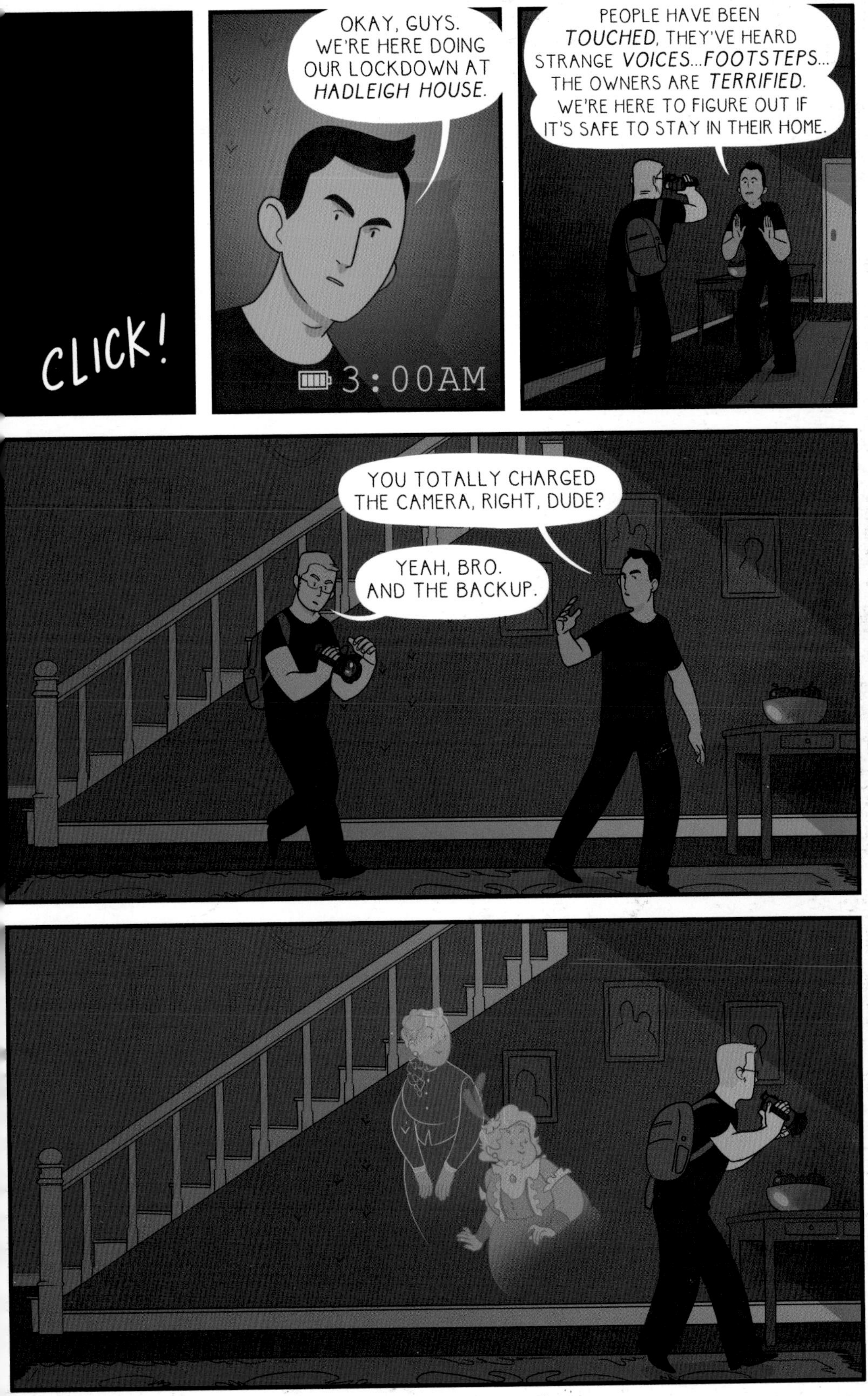
CLICK!
OKAY, GUYS. WE'RE HERE DOING OUR LOCKDOWN AT *HADLEIGH HOUSE*.
3:00AM
PEOPLE HAVE BEEN *TOUCHED*, THEY'VE HEARD STRANGE *VOICES*...*FOOTSTEPS*... THE OWNERS ARE *TERRIFIED*. WE'RE HERE TO FIGURE OUT IF IT'S SAFE TO STAY IN THEIR HOME.
YOU TOTALLY CHARGED THE CAMERA, RIGHT, DUDE?
YEAH, BRO. AND THE BACKUP.

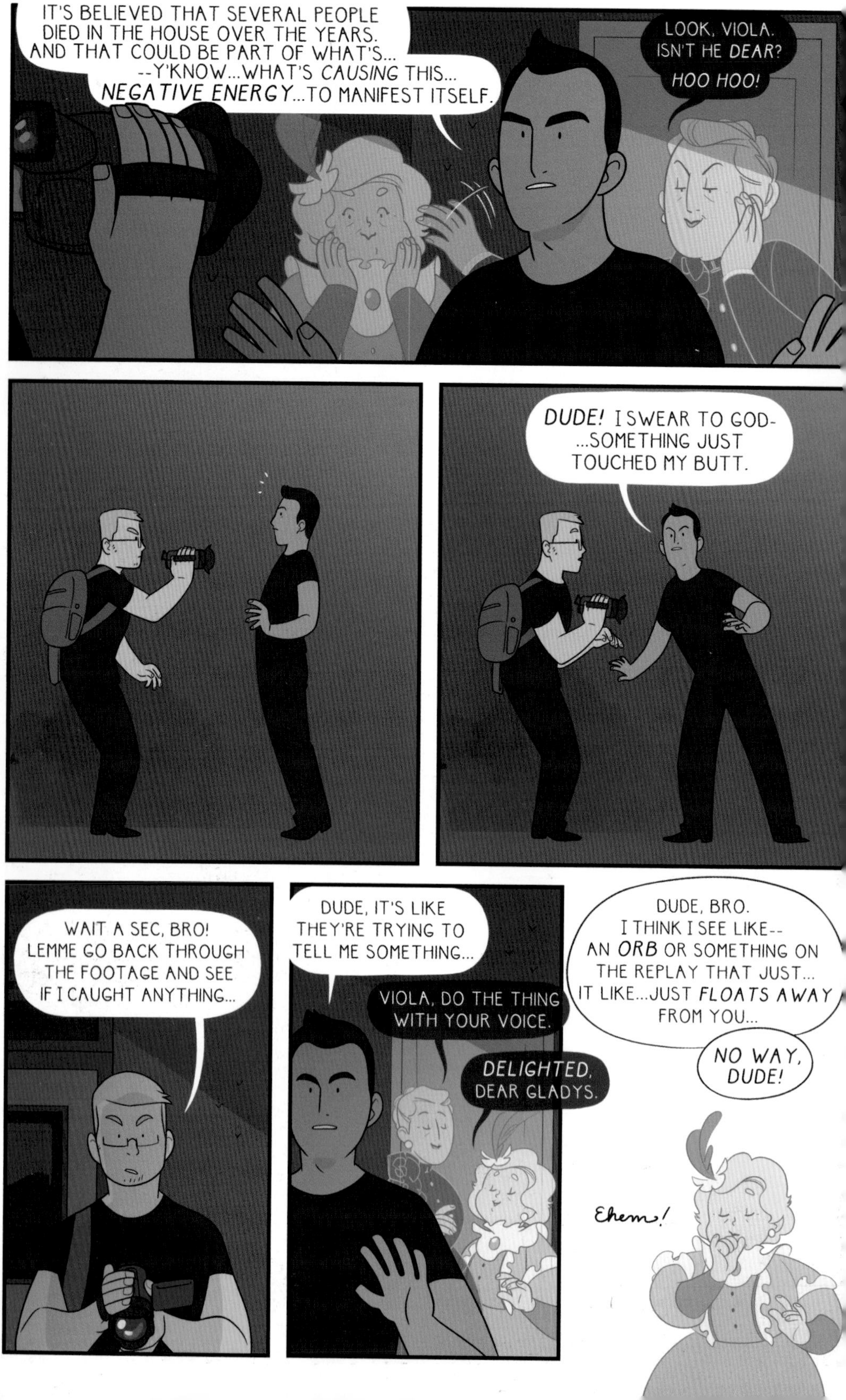
IT'S BELIEVED THAT SEVERAL PEOPLE DIED IN THE HOUSE OVER THE YEARS. AND THAT COULD BE PART OF WHAT'S... --Y'KNOW...WHAT'S CAUSING THIS... NEGATIVE ENERGY...TO MANIFEST ITSELF.
LOOK, VIOLA. ISN'T HE DEAR?
HOO HOO!
DUDE! I SWEAR TO GOD- ...SOMETHING JUST TOUCHED MY BUTT.
WAIT A SEC, BRO! LEMME GO BACK THROUGH THE FOOTAGE AND SEE IF I CAUGHT ANYTHING...
DUDE, IT'S LIKE THEY'RE TRYING TO TELL ME SOMETHING...
VIOLA, DO THE THING WITH YOUR VOICE.
DELIGHTED, DEAR GLADYS.
DUDE, BRO. I THINK I SEE LIKE-- AN ORB OR SOMETHING ON THE REPLAY THAT JUST... IT LIKE...JUST FLOATS AWAY FROM YOU...
NO WAY, DUDE!
Ehem!

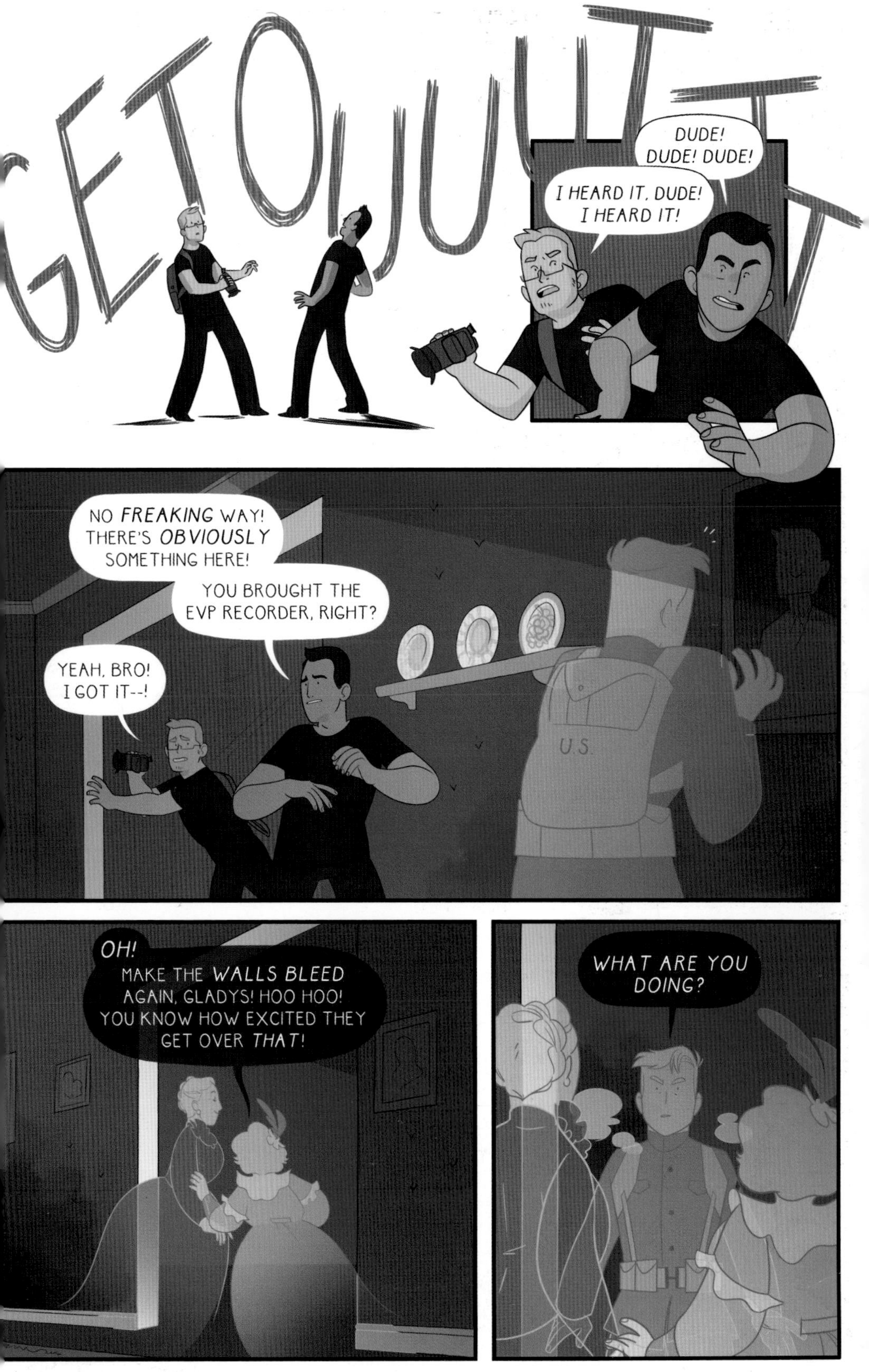
GET OUUUT
DUDE! DUDE! DUDE!
I HEARD IT, DUDE! I HEARD IT!
NO FREAKING WAY! THERE'S OBVIOUSLY SOMETHING HERE!
YOU BROUGHT THE EVP RECORDER, RIGHT?
YEAH, BRO! I GOT IT--!
U.S.
OH!
MAKE THE WALLS BLEED AGAIN, GLADYS! HOO HOO! YOU KNOW HOW EXCITED THEY GET OVER THAT!
WHAT ARE YOU DOING?

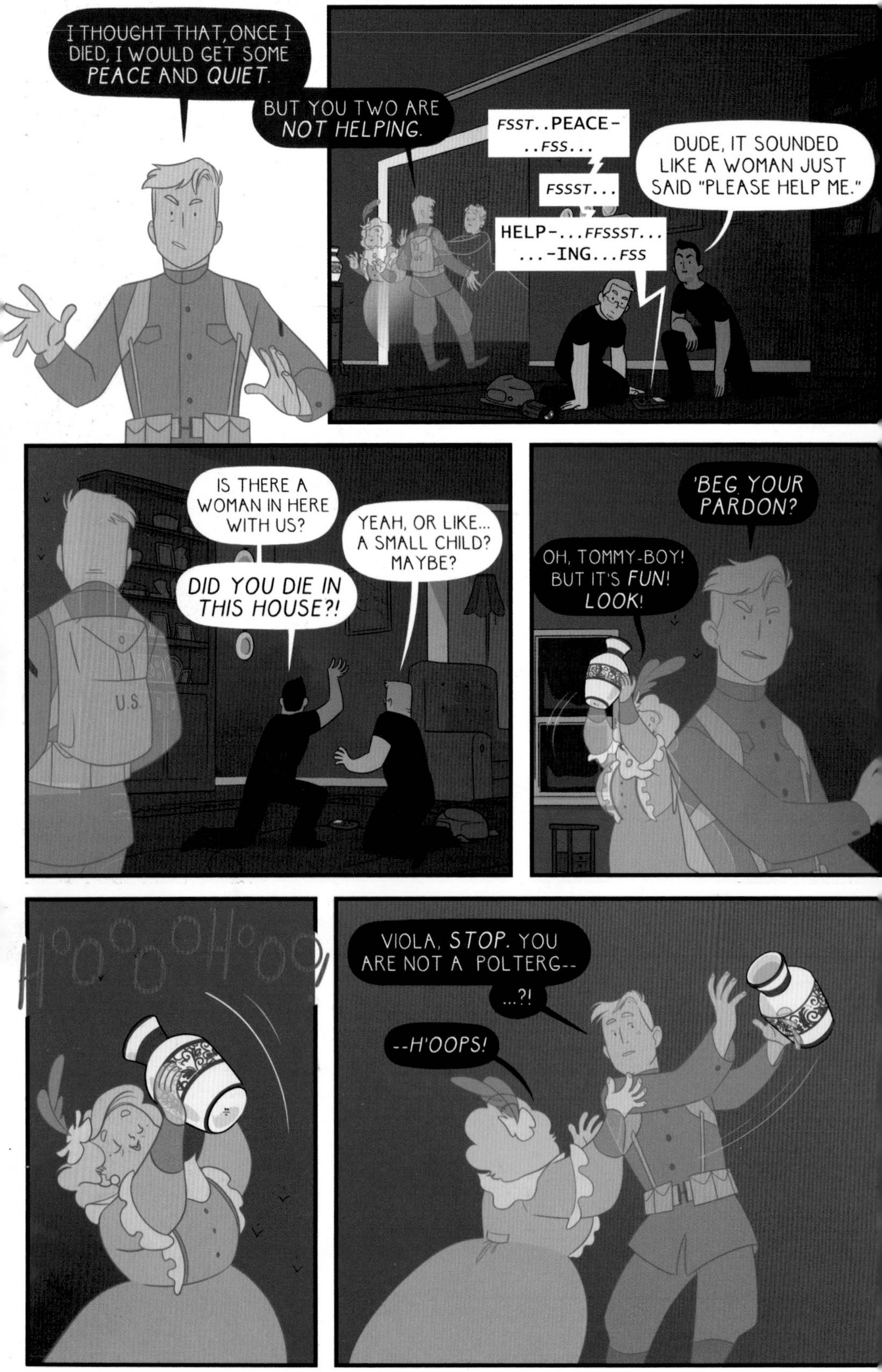
I THOUGHT THAT, ONCE I DIED, I WOULD GET SOME *PEACE* AND *QUIET*.
BUT YOU TWO ARE *NOT HELPING*.
FSST..PEACE- ..FSS...
FSSST...
HELP-...FFSSST... ...-ING...FSS
DUDE, IT SOUNDED LIKE A WOMAN JUST SAID "PLEASE HELP ME."
IS THERE A WOMAN IN HERE WITH US?
*DID YOU DIE IN THIS HOUSE?!*
YEAH, OR LIKE... A SMALL CHILD? MAYBE?
'BEG YOUR PARDON?
OH, TOMMY-BOY! BUT IT'S *FUN*! *LOOK*!
HOOOOOHOOO
VIOLA, *STOP*. YOU ARE NOT A POLTERG--
...?!
--H'OOPS!

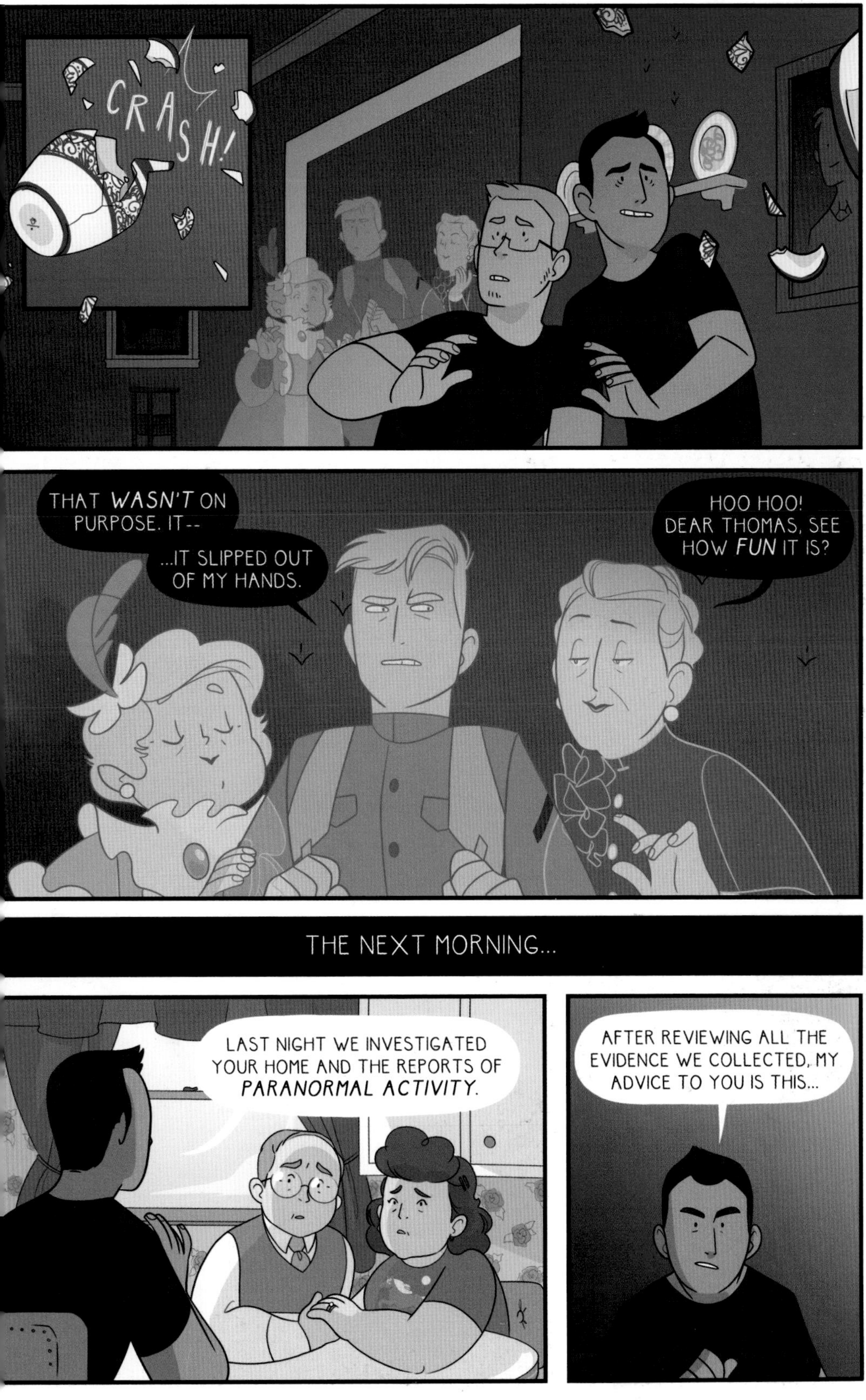
CRASH!
THAT *WASN'T* ON PURPOSE. IT--
...IT SLIPPED OUT OF MY HANDS.
HOO HOO! DEAR THOMAS, SEE HOW *FUN* IT IS?
THE NEXT MORNING...
LAST NIGHT WE INVESTIGATED YOUR HOME AND THE REPORTS OF *PARANORMAL ACTIVITY*.
AFTER REVIEWING ALL THE EVIDENCE WE COLLECTED, MY ADVICE TO YOU IS THIS...

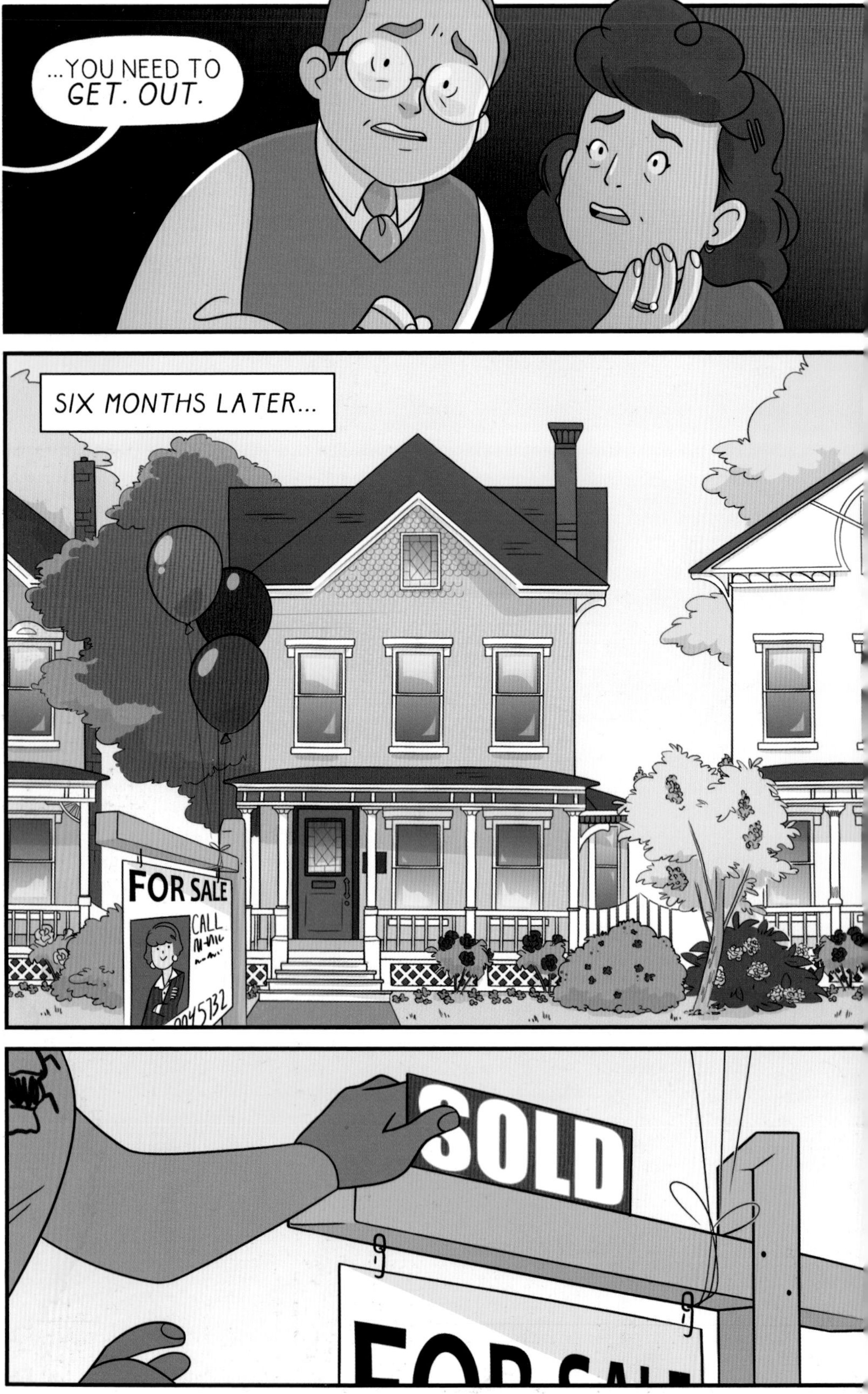
...YOU NEED TO *GET. OUT.*
SIX MONTHS LATER...
FOR SALE
CALL
SOLD

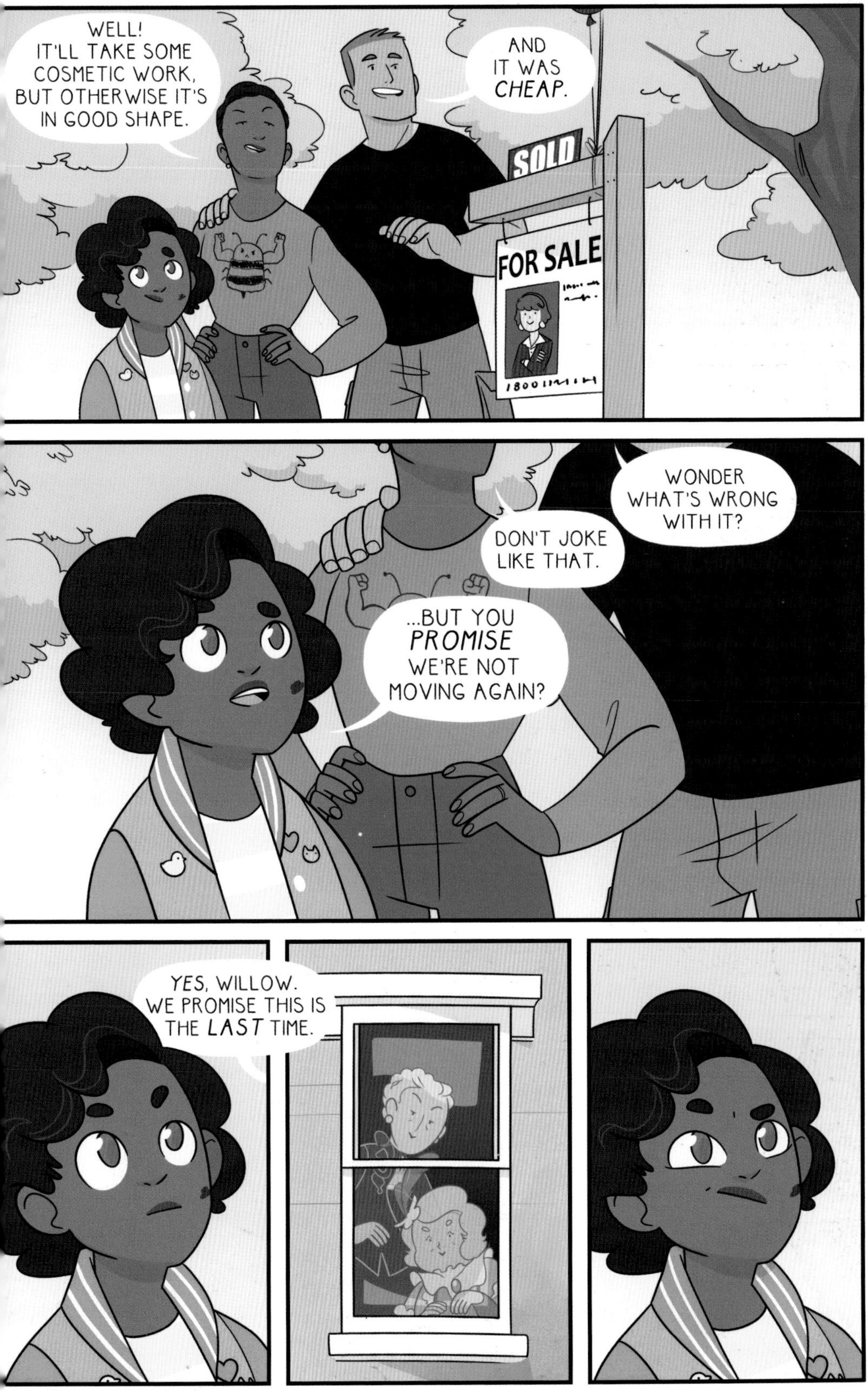
WELL! IT'LL TAKE SOME COSMETIC WORK, BUT OTHERWISE IT'S IN GOOD SHAPE.
AND IT WAS *CHEAP*.
SOLD
FOR SALE
WONDER WHAT'S WRONG WITH IT?
DON'T JOKE LIKE THAT.
...BUT YOU *PROMISE* WE'RE NOT MOVING AGAIN?
*YES*, WILLOW. WE PROMISE THIS IS THE *LAST* TIME.

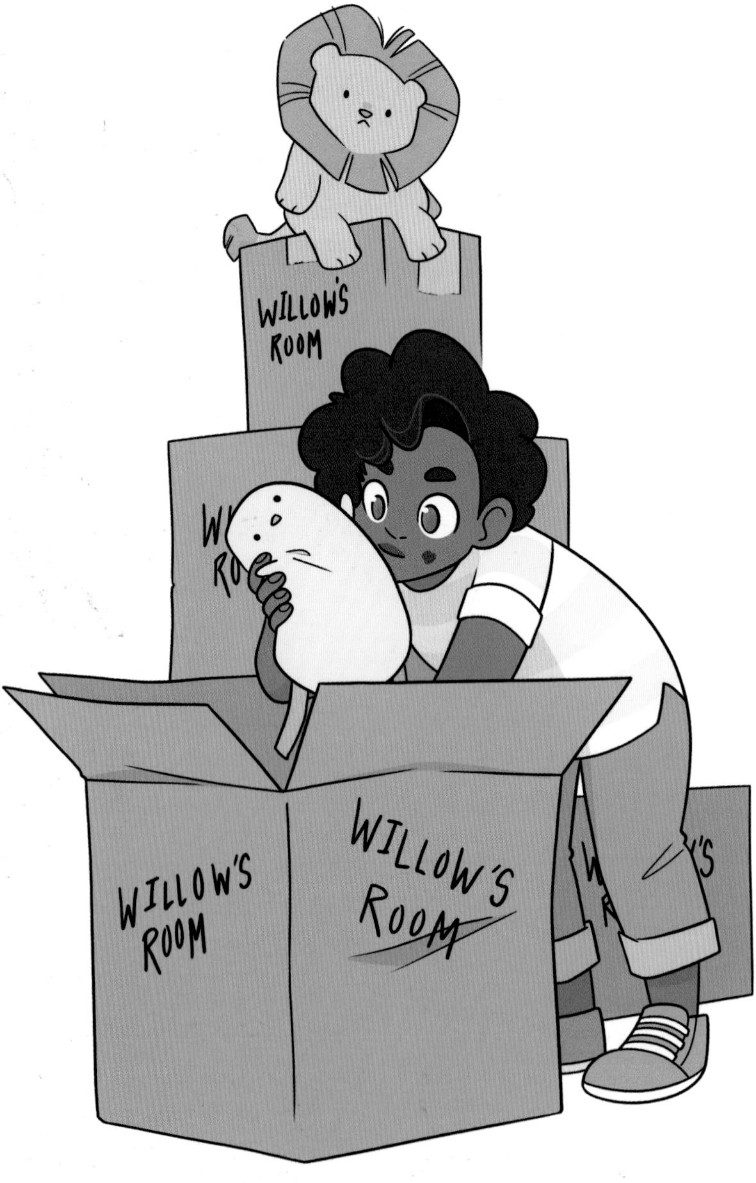
WILLOW'S ROOM
WILLOW'S ROOM
WILLOW'S ROOM

Y PARENTS ALWAYS
LL ME NOT TO BE
RAID OF THE DARK...
CREEEAAAAK
BECAUSE IF THE "MONSTERS" CAN BE SCARY...
ThOoOmAaAaSsSs... HEEEEELP...I-I CAN'T FIND MY EEEEAAARRRIIINGSSSSS...

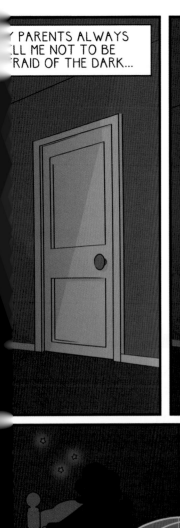

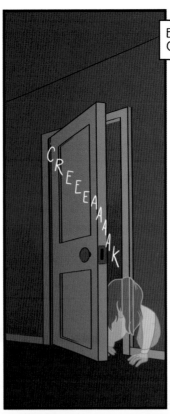

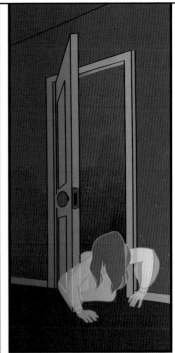

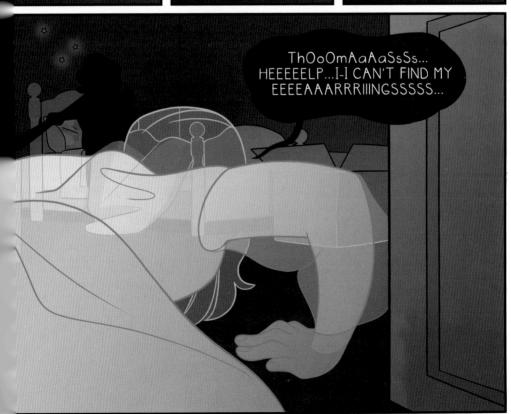

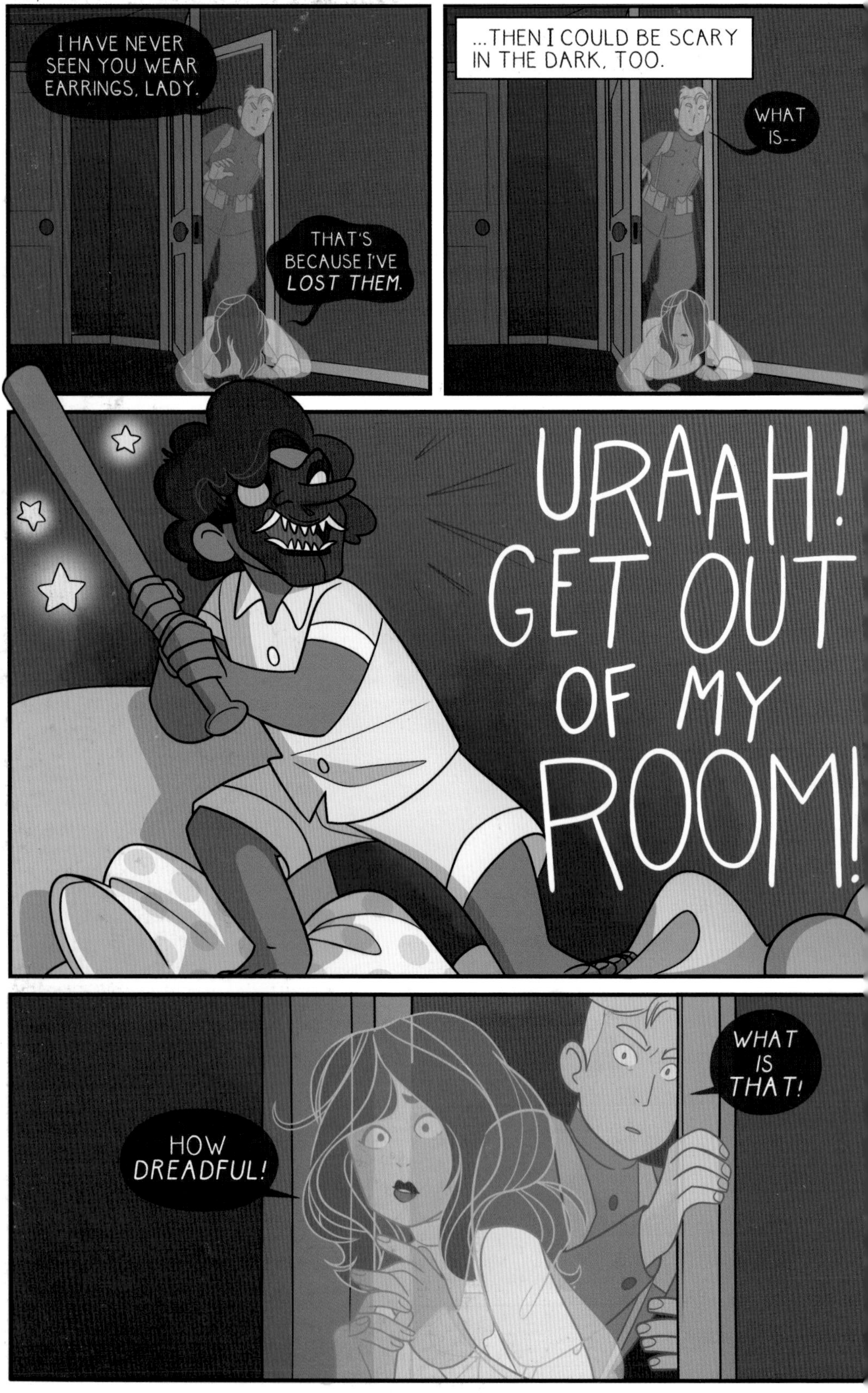
I HAVE NEVER SEEN YOU WEAR EARRINGS, LADY.
THAT'S BECAUSE I'VE *LOST THEM.*
...THEN I COULD BE SCARY IN THE DARK, TOO.
WHAT IS--
URAAH! GET OUT OF MY ROOM!
WHAT IS THAT!
HOW *DREADFUL!*

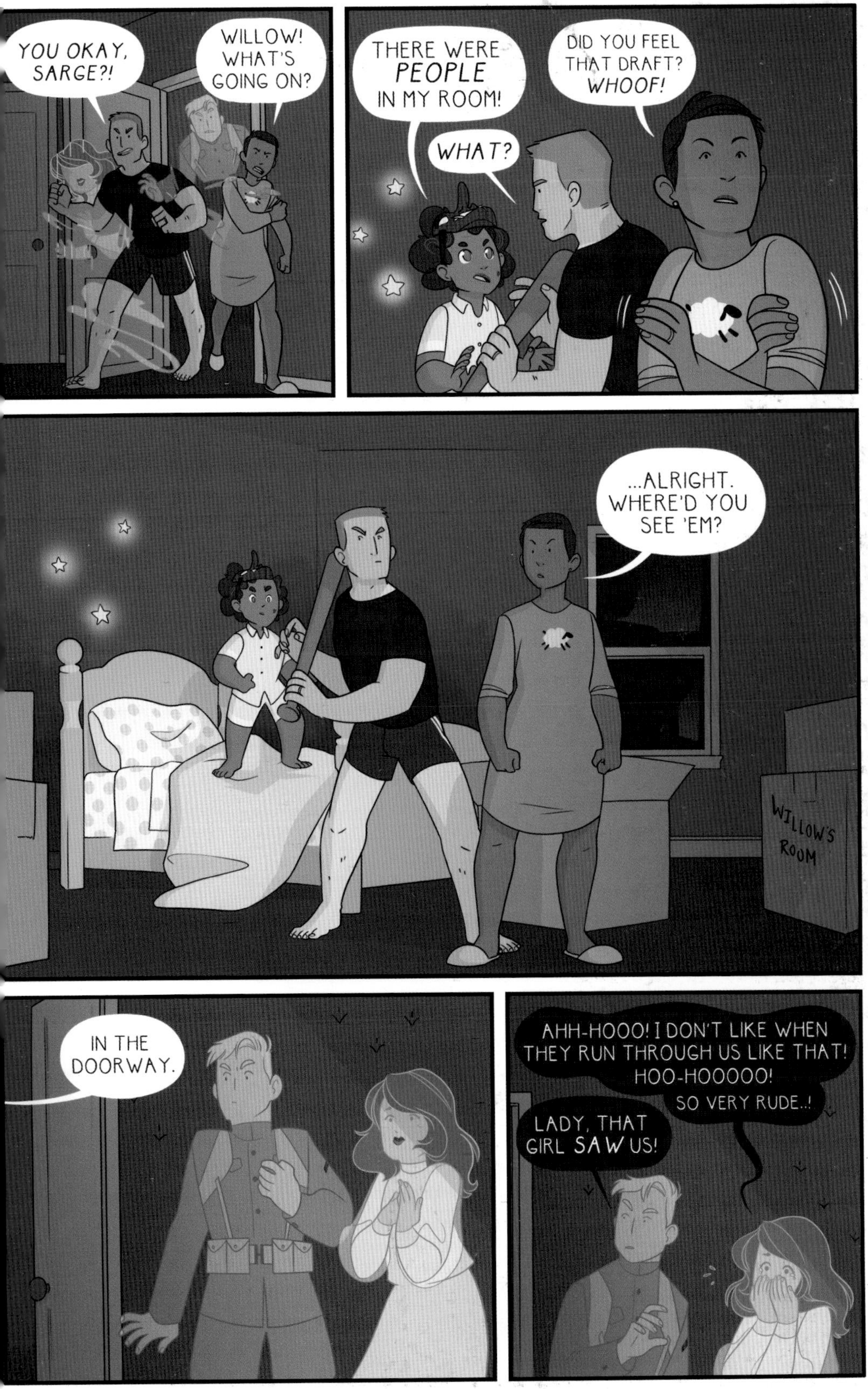
YOU OKAY, SARGE?!
WILLOW! WHAT'S GOING ON?
THERE WERE PEOPLE IN MY ROOM!
WHAT?
DID YOU FEEL THAT DRAFT? WHOOF!
...ALRIGHT. WHERE'D YOU SEE 'EM?
WILLOW'S ROOM
IN THE DOORWAY.
AHH-HOOO! I DON'T LIKE WHEN THEY RUN THROUGH US LIKE THAT! HOO-HOOOOO!
SO VERY RUDE..!
LADY, THAT GIRL SAW US!

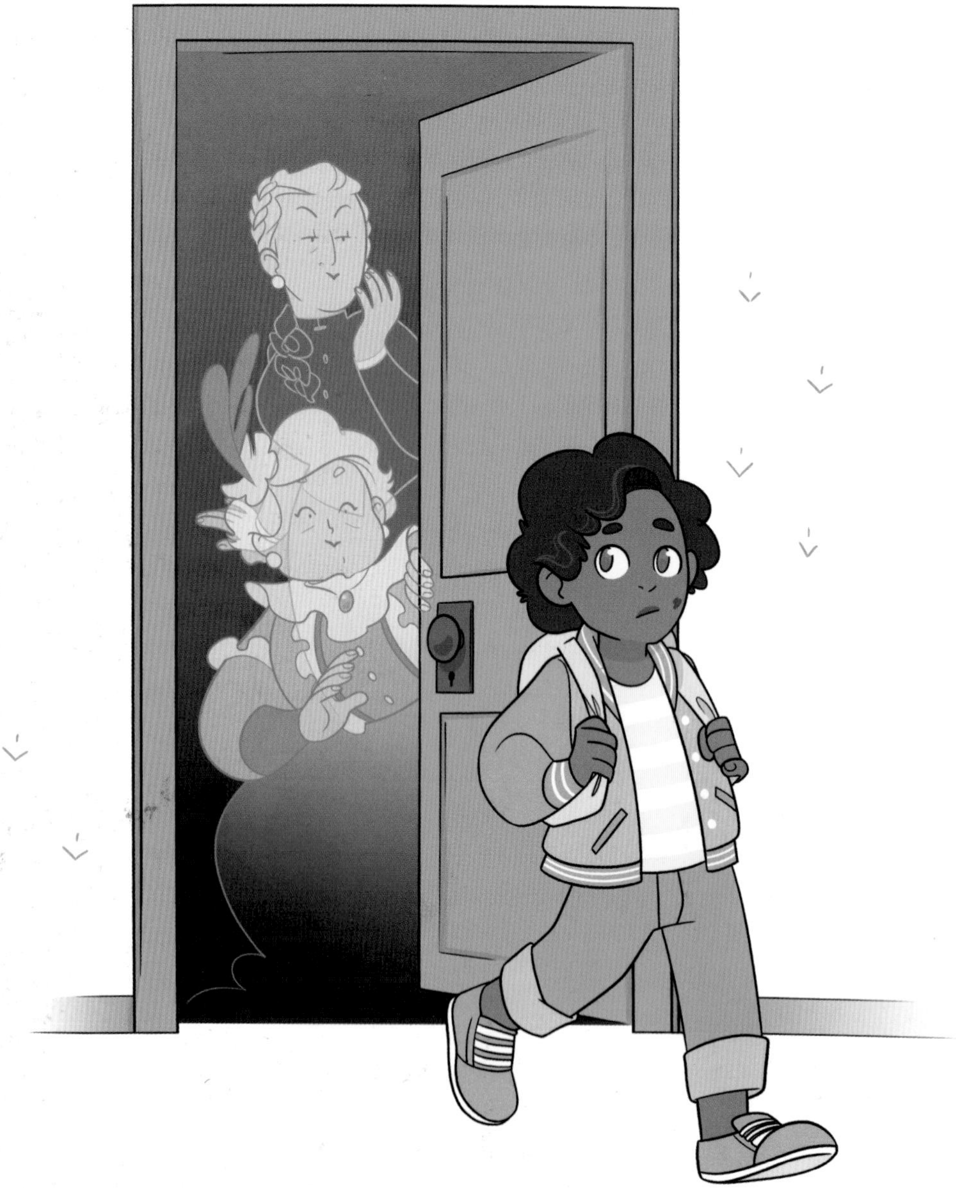

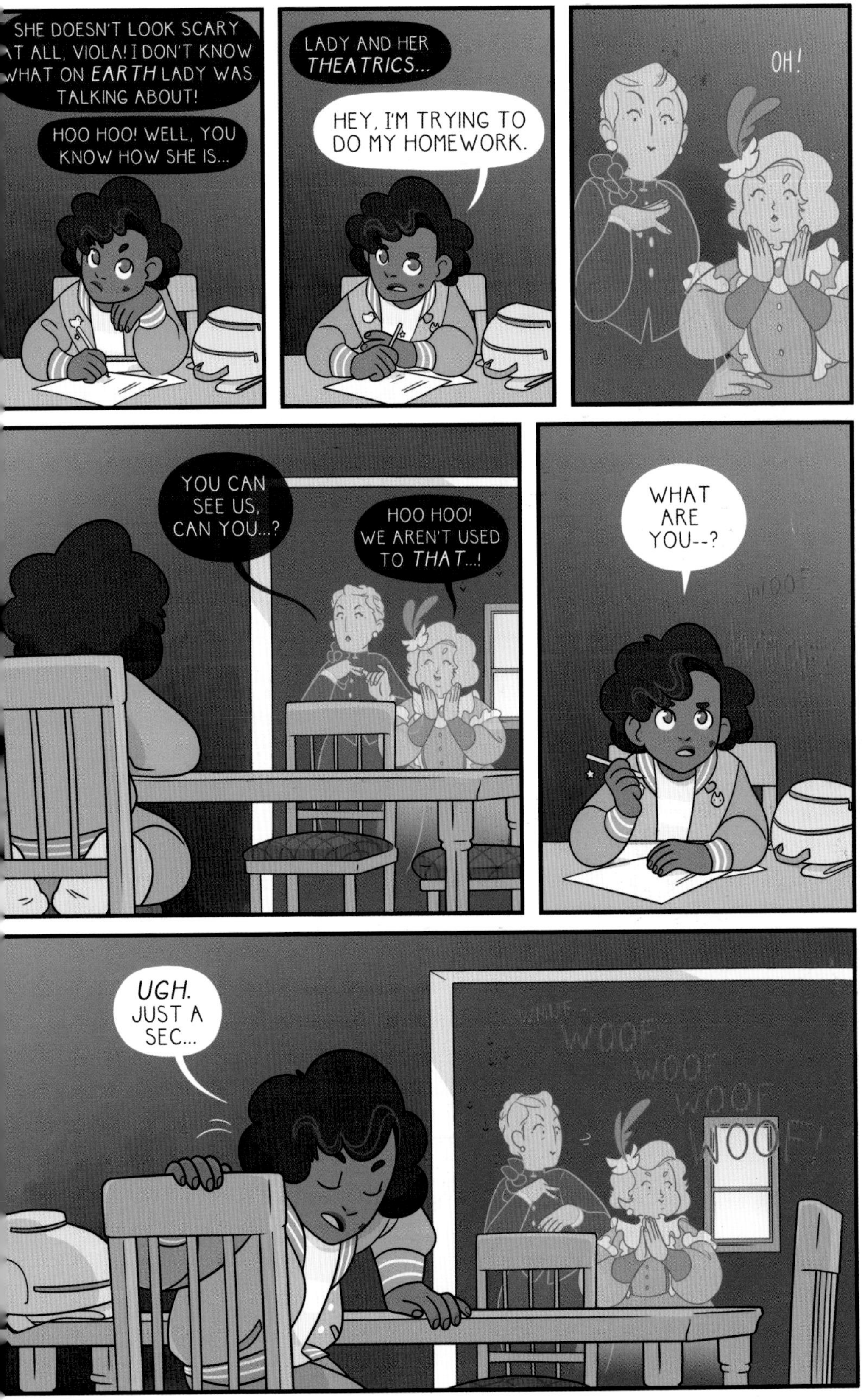
SHE DOESN'T LOOK SCARY AT ALL, VIOLA! I DON'T KNOW WHAT ON *EARTH* LADY WAS TALKING ABOUT!
HOO HOO! WELL, YOU KNOW HOW SHE IS...
LADY AND HER *THEATRICS*...
HEY, I'M TRYING TO DO MY HOMEWORK.
OH!
YOU CAN SEE US, CAN YOU...?
HOO HOO! WE AREN'T USED TO *THAT*...!
WHAT ARE YOU--?
*UGH.* JUST A SEC...
WOOF
WOOF
WOOF
WOOF!

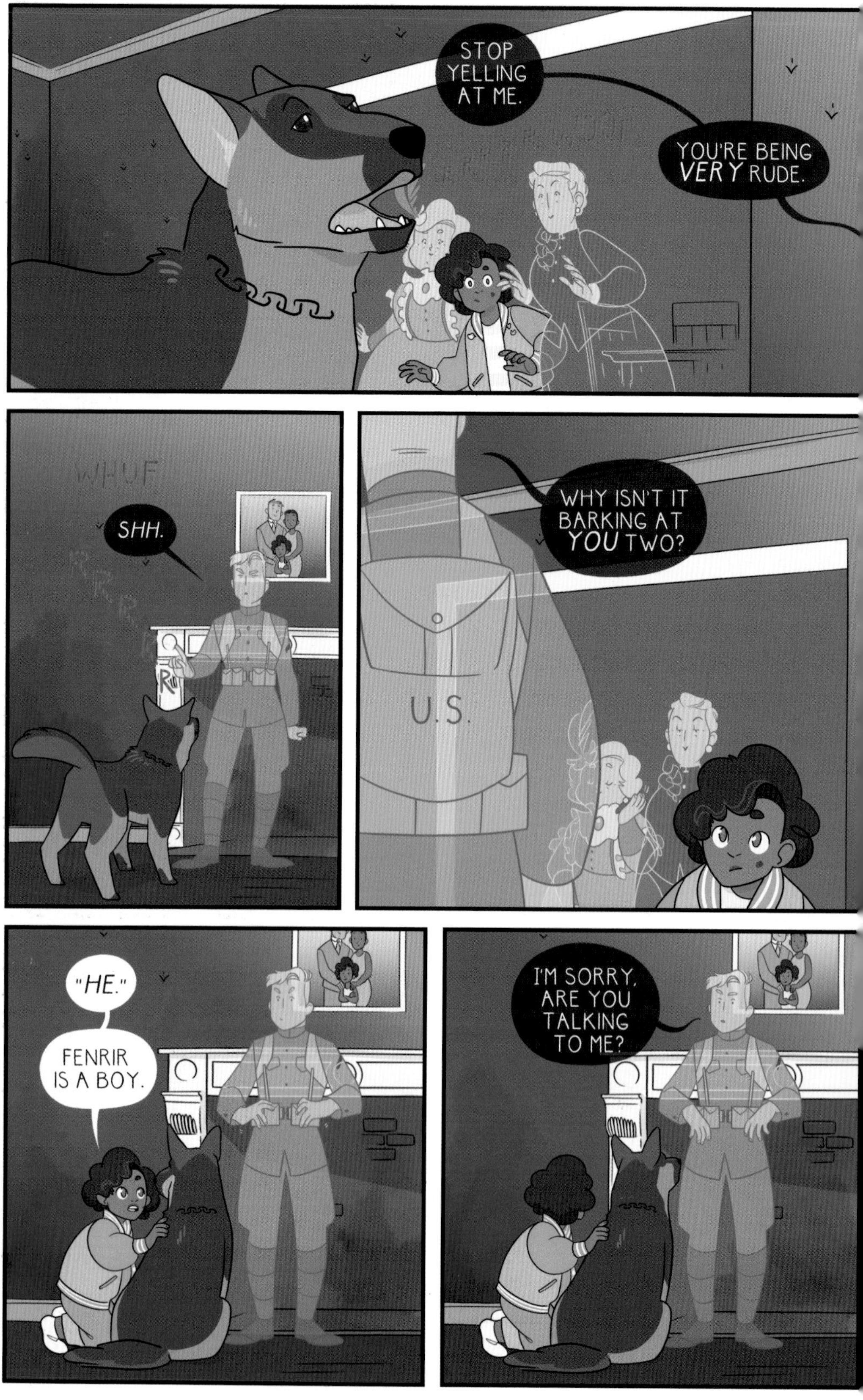
STOP YELLING AT ME.
YOU'RE BEING VERY RUDE.
WHUF
SHH.
WHY ISN'T IT BARKING AT YOU TWO?
U.S.
"HE."
FENRIR IS A BOY.
I'M SORRY, ARE YOU TALKING TO ME?

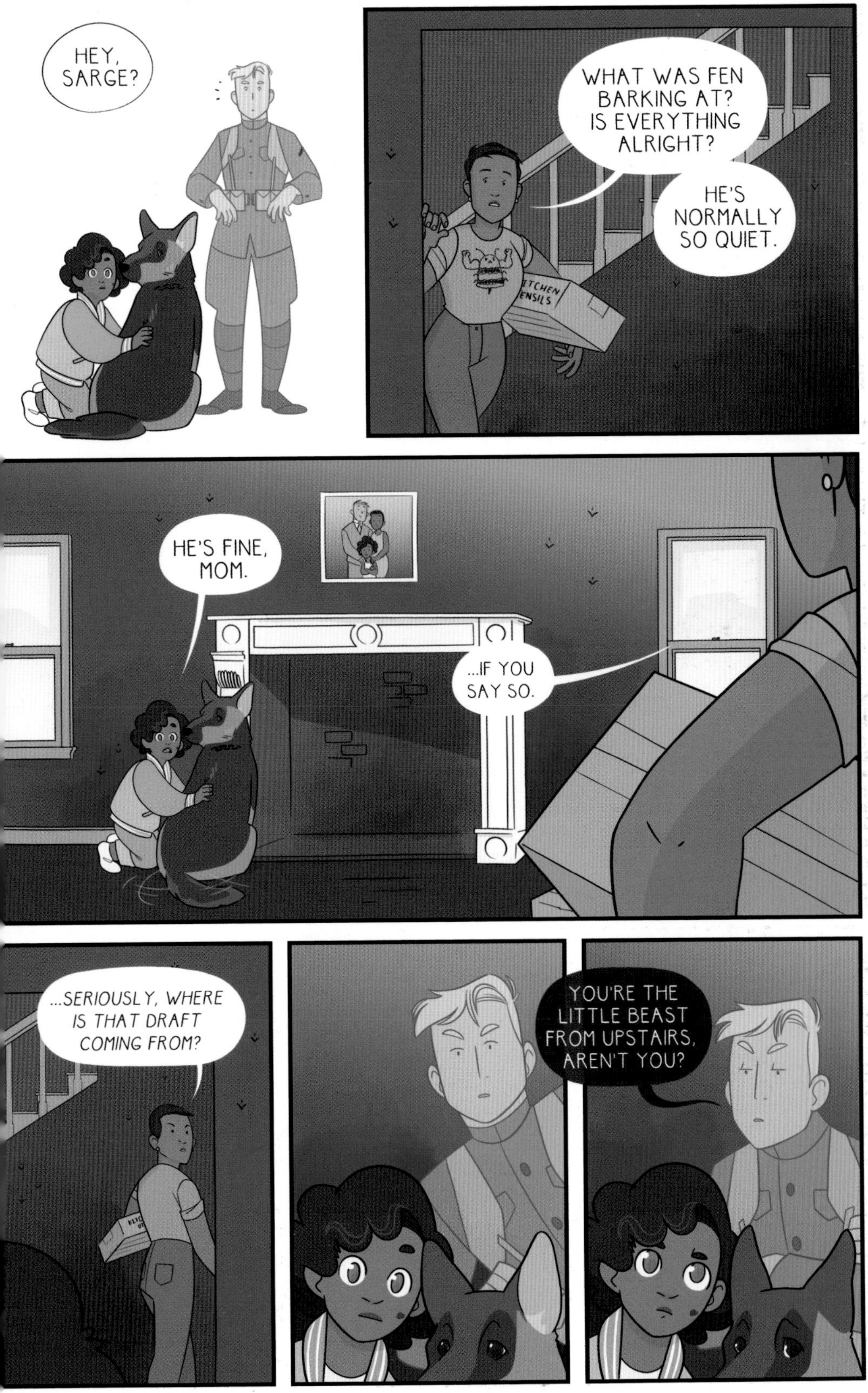
HEY, SARGE?
WHAT WAS FEN BARKING AT? IS EVERYTHING ALRIGHT?
HE'S NORMALLY SO QUIET.
KITCHEN UTENSILS
HE'S FINE, MOM.
...IF YOU SAY SO.
...SERIOUSLY, WHERE IS THAT DRAFT COMING FROM?
YOU'RE THE LITTLE BEAST FROM UPSTAIRS, AREN'T YOU?

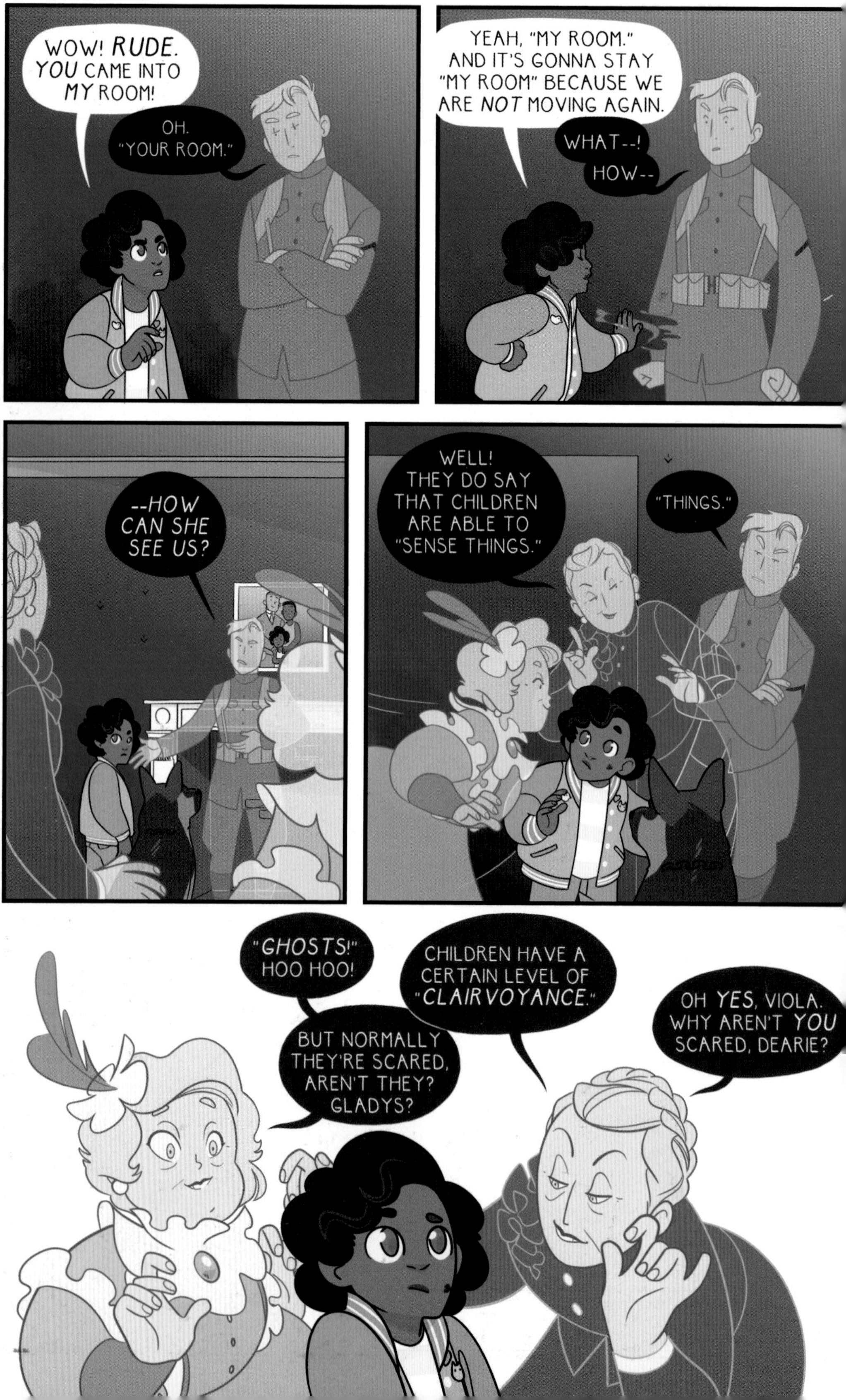
WOW! RUDE. YOU CAME INTO MY ROOM!
OH. "YOUR ROOM."
YEAH, "MY ROOM." AND IT'S GONNA STAY "MY ROOM" BECAUSE WE ARE NOT MOVING AGAIN.
WHAT--!
HOW--
--HOW CAN SHE SEE US?
WELL! THEY DO SAY THAT CHILDREN ARE ABLE TO "SENSE THINGS."
"THINGS."
"GHOSTS!" HOO HOO!
CHILDREN HAVE A CERTAIN LEVEL OF "CLAIRVOYANCE."
BUT NORMALLY THEY'RE SCARED, AREN'T THEY? GLADYS?
OH YES, VIOLA. WHY AREN'T YOU SCARED, DEARIE?

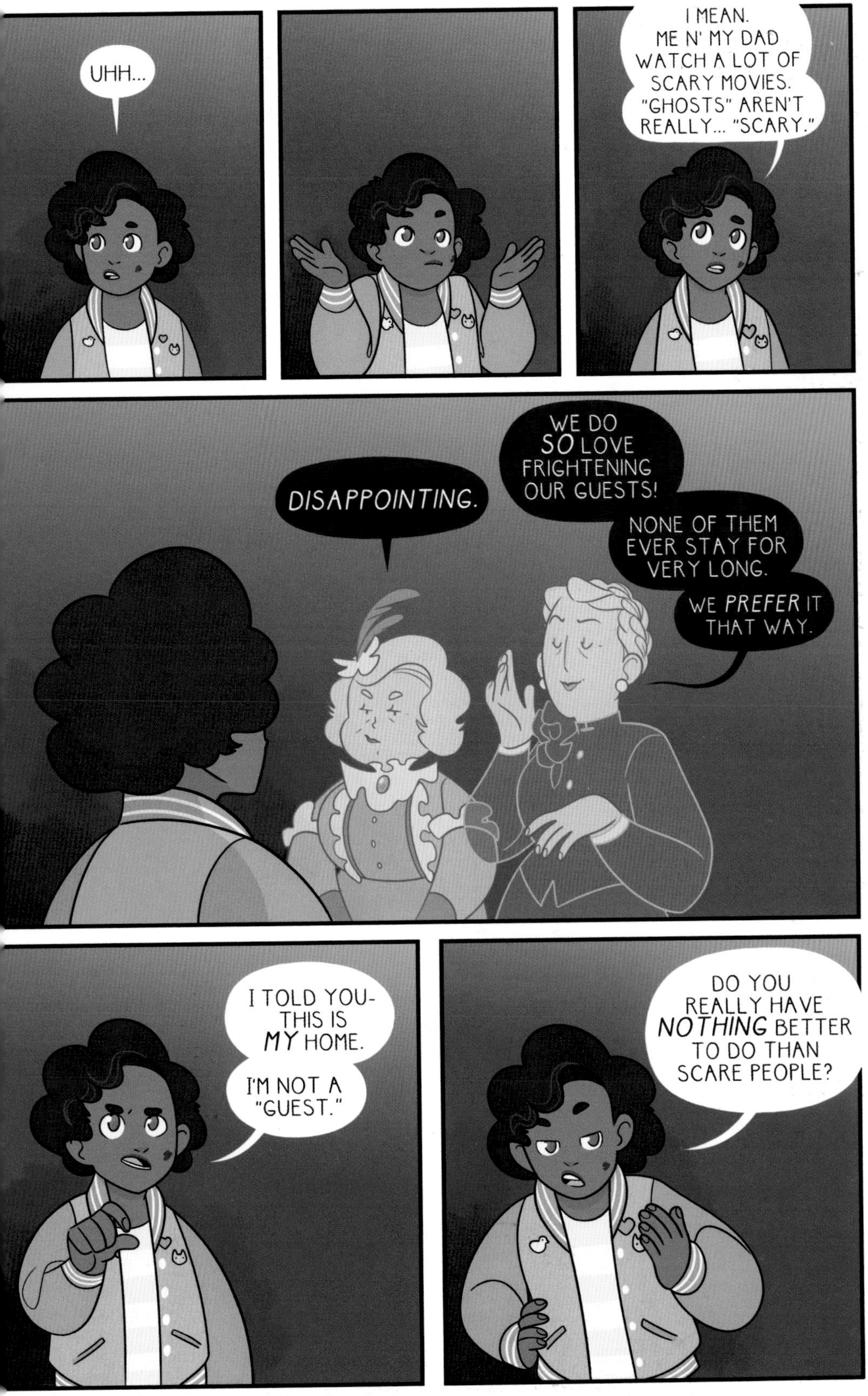
UHH...
I MEAN. ME N' MY DAD WATCH A LOT OF SCARY MOVIES. "GHOSTS" AREN'T REALLY... "SCARY."
DISAPPOINTING.
WE DO *SO* LOVE FRIGHTENING OUR GUESTS!
NONE OF THEM EVER STAY FOR VERY LONG.
WE *PREFER* IT THAT WAY.
I TOLD YOU- THIS IS *MY* HOME.
I'M NOT A "GUEST."
DO YOU REALLY HAVE *NOTHING* BETTER TO DO THAN SCARE PEOPLE?

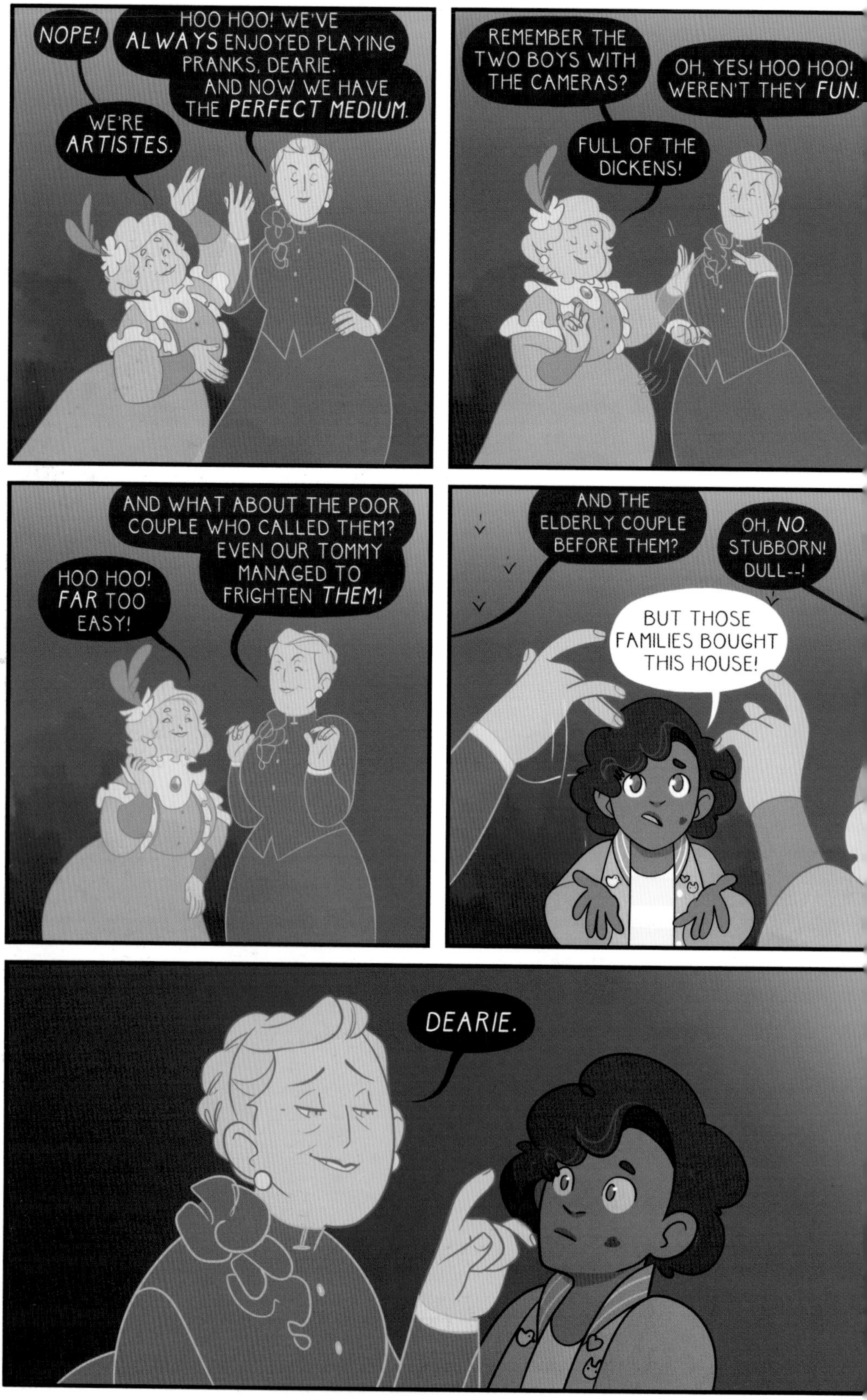
NOPE!
HOO HOO! WE'VE ALWAYS ENJOYED PLAYING PRANKS, DEARIE.
AND NOW WE HAVE THE PERFECT MEDIUM.
WE'RE ARTISTES.
REMEMBER THE TWO BOYS WITH THE CAMERAS?
OH, YES! HOO HOO! WEREN'T THEY FUN.
FULL OF THE DICKENS!
AND WHAT ABOUT THE POOR COUPLE WHO CALLED THEM?
EVEN OUR TOMMY MANAGED TO FRIGHTEN THEM!
HOO HOO! FAR TOO EASY!
AND THE ELDERLY COUPLE BEFORE THEM?
OH, NO. STUBBORN! DULL--!
BUT THOSE FAMILIES BOUGHT THIS HOUSE!
DEARIE.

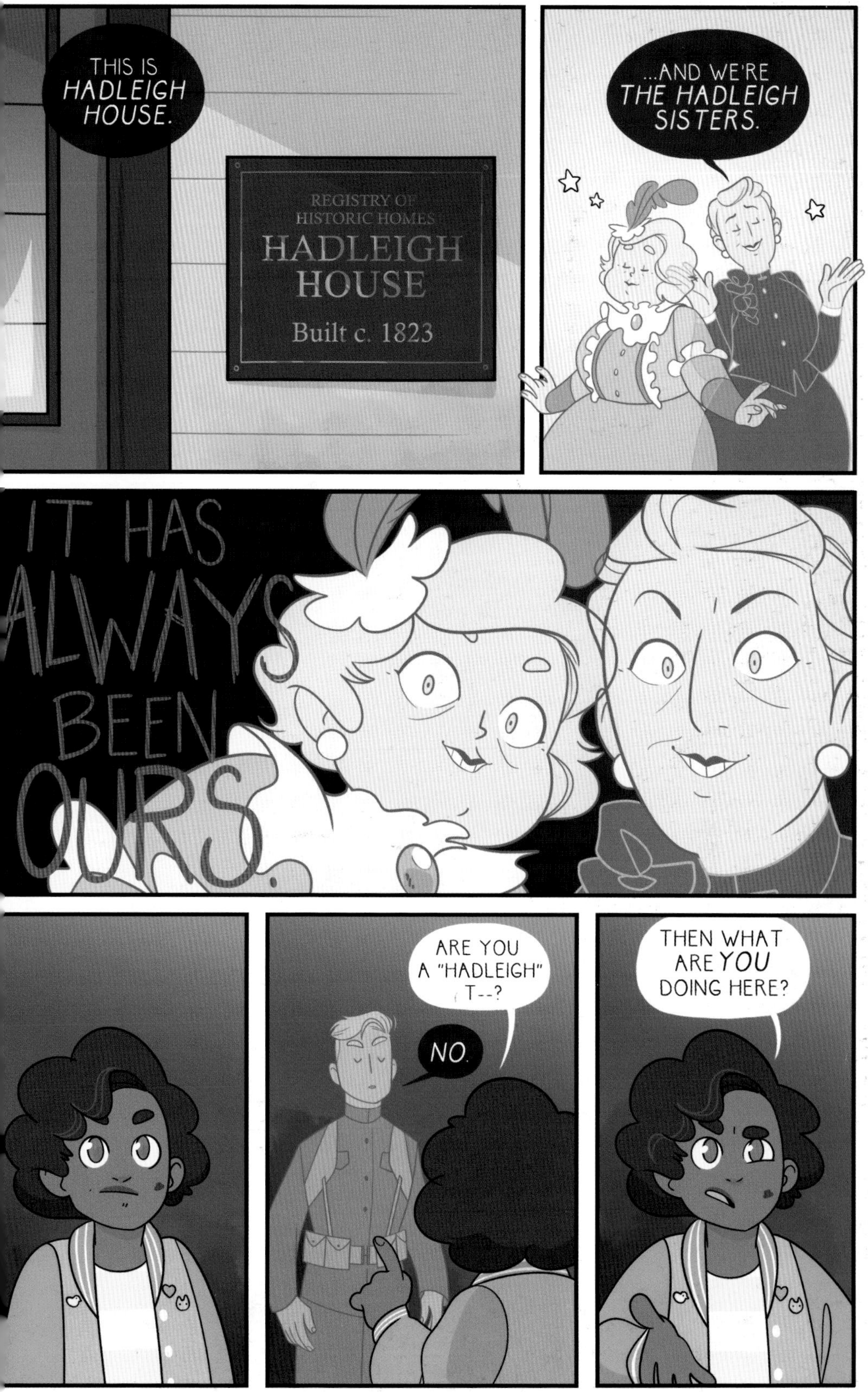
THIS IS HADLEIGH HOUSE.
REGISTRY OF HISTORIC HOMES
HADLEIGH HOUSE
Built c. 1823
...AND WE'RE THE HADLEIGH SISTERS.
IT HAS ALWAYS BEEN OURS
ARE YOU A "HADLEIGH" T--?
NO.
THEN WHAT ARE YOU DOING HERE?

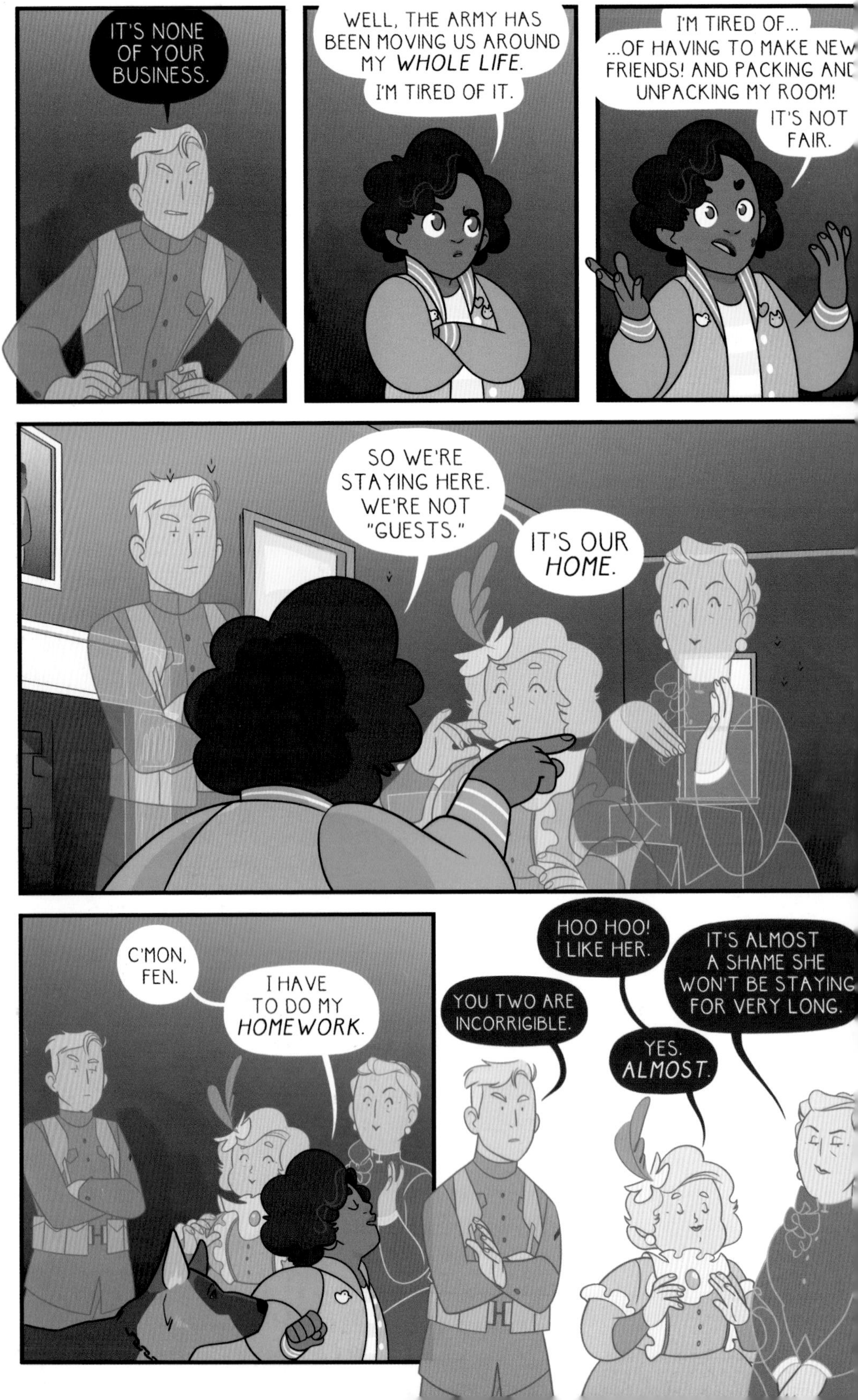
IT'S NONE OF YOUR BUSINESS.
WELL, THE ARMY HAS BEEN MOVING US AROUND MY *WHOLE LIFE*.
I'M TIRED OF IT.
I'M TIRED OF...
...OF HAVING TO MAKE NEW FRIENDS! AND PACKING AND UNPACKING MY ROOM!
IT'S NOT FAIR.
SO WE'RE STAYING HERE. WE'RE NOT "GUESTS."
IT'S OUR *HOME*.
C'MON, FEN.
I HAVE TO DO MY *HOMEWORK*.
YOU TWO ARE INCORRIGIBLE.
HOO HOO! I LIKE HER.
IT'S ALMOST A SHAME SHE WON'T BE STAYING FOR VERY LONG.
YES. *ALMOST*.

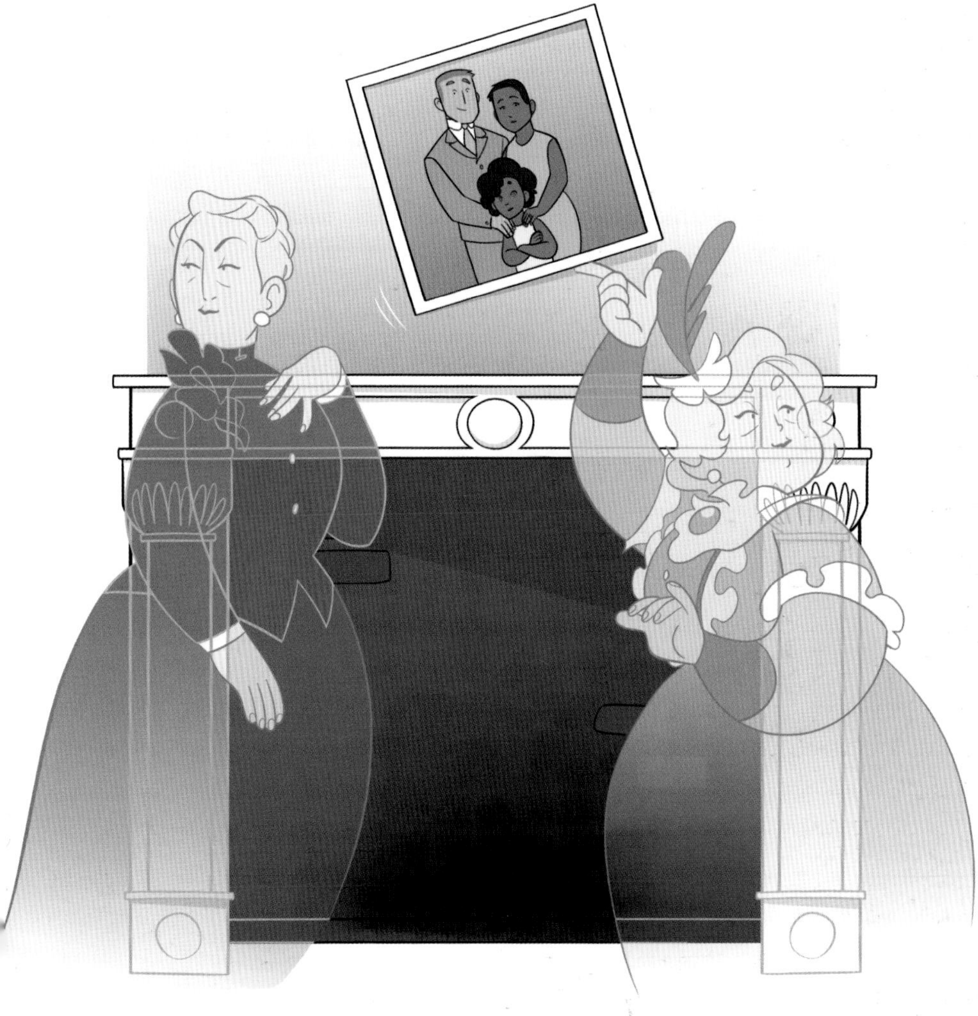

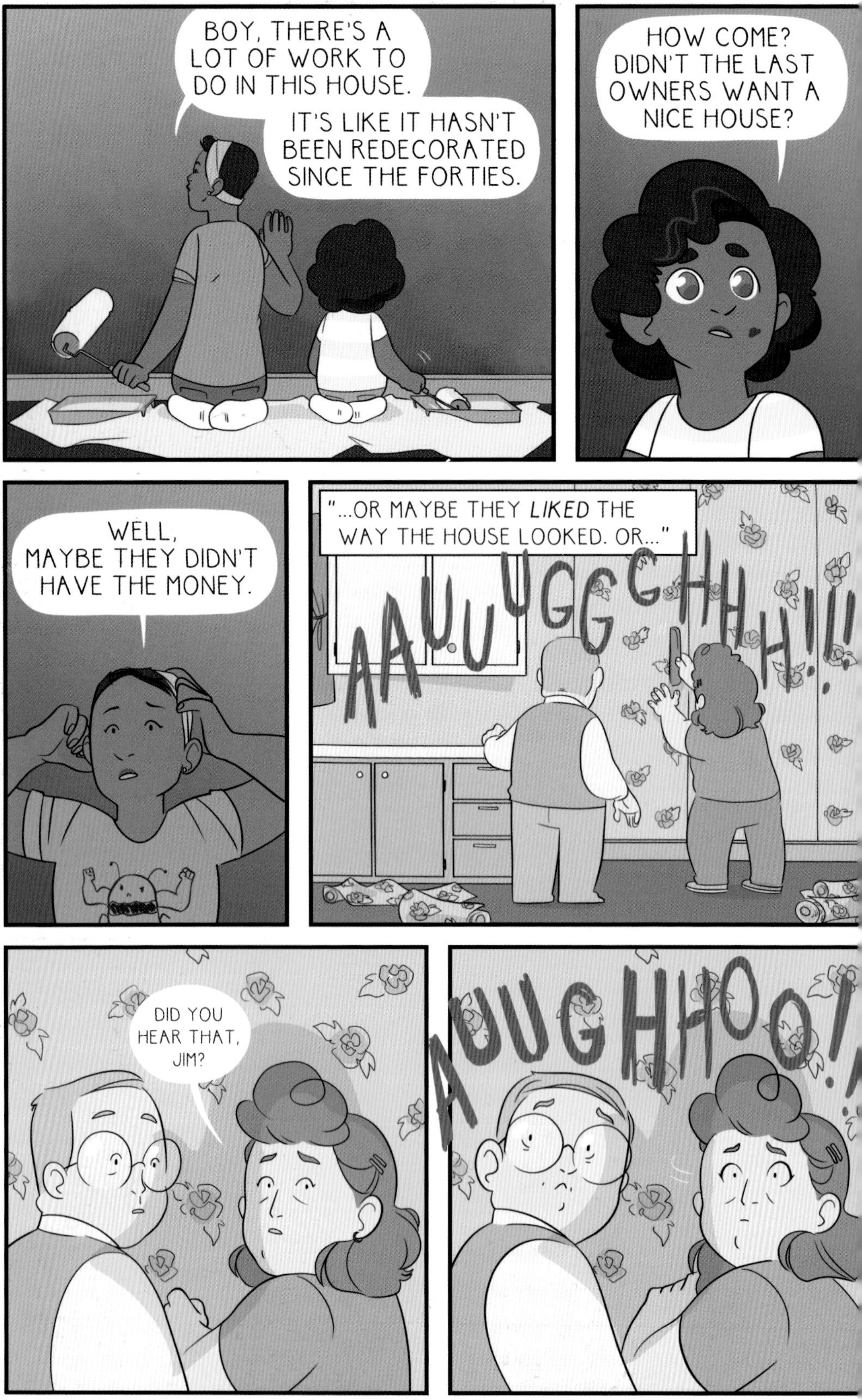
BOY, THERE'S A LOT OF WORK TO DO IN THIS HOUSE.
IT'S LIKE IT HASN'T BEEN REDECORATED SINCE THE FORTIES.
HOW COME? DIDN'T THE LAST OWNERS WANT A NICE HOUSE?
WELL, MAYBE THEY DIDN'T HAVE THE MONEY.
"...OR MAYBE THEY *LIKED* THE WAY THE HOUSE LOOKED. OR..."
AAUUGGCHHH!!!
DID YOU HEAR THAT, JIM?
AUUGHHOO!!

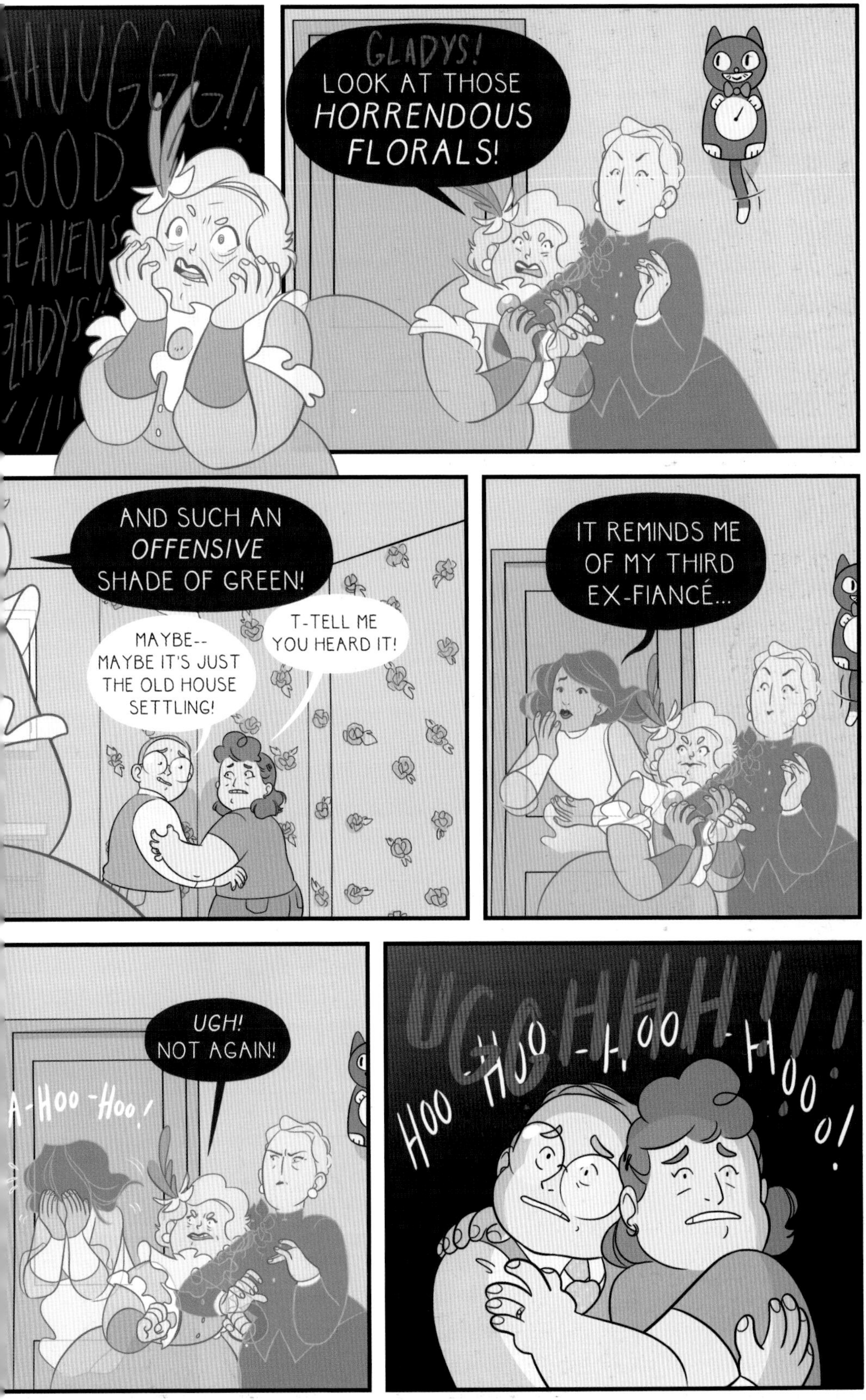

HAUUGGG!! GOOD HEAVENS GLADYS!!
GLADYS! LOOK AT THOSE HORRENDOUS FLORALS!
AND SUCH AN OFFENSIVE SHADE OF GREEN!
MAYBE-- MAYBE IT'S JUST THE OLD HOUSE SETTLING!
T-TELL ME YOU HEARD IT!
IT REMINDS ME OF MY THIRD EX-FIANCÉ...
UGH! NOT AGAIN!
A-HOO-HOO!
UGHHHH!!!
HOO HOO-HOO-HOOo!

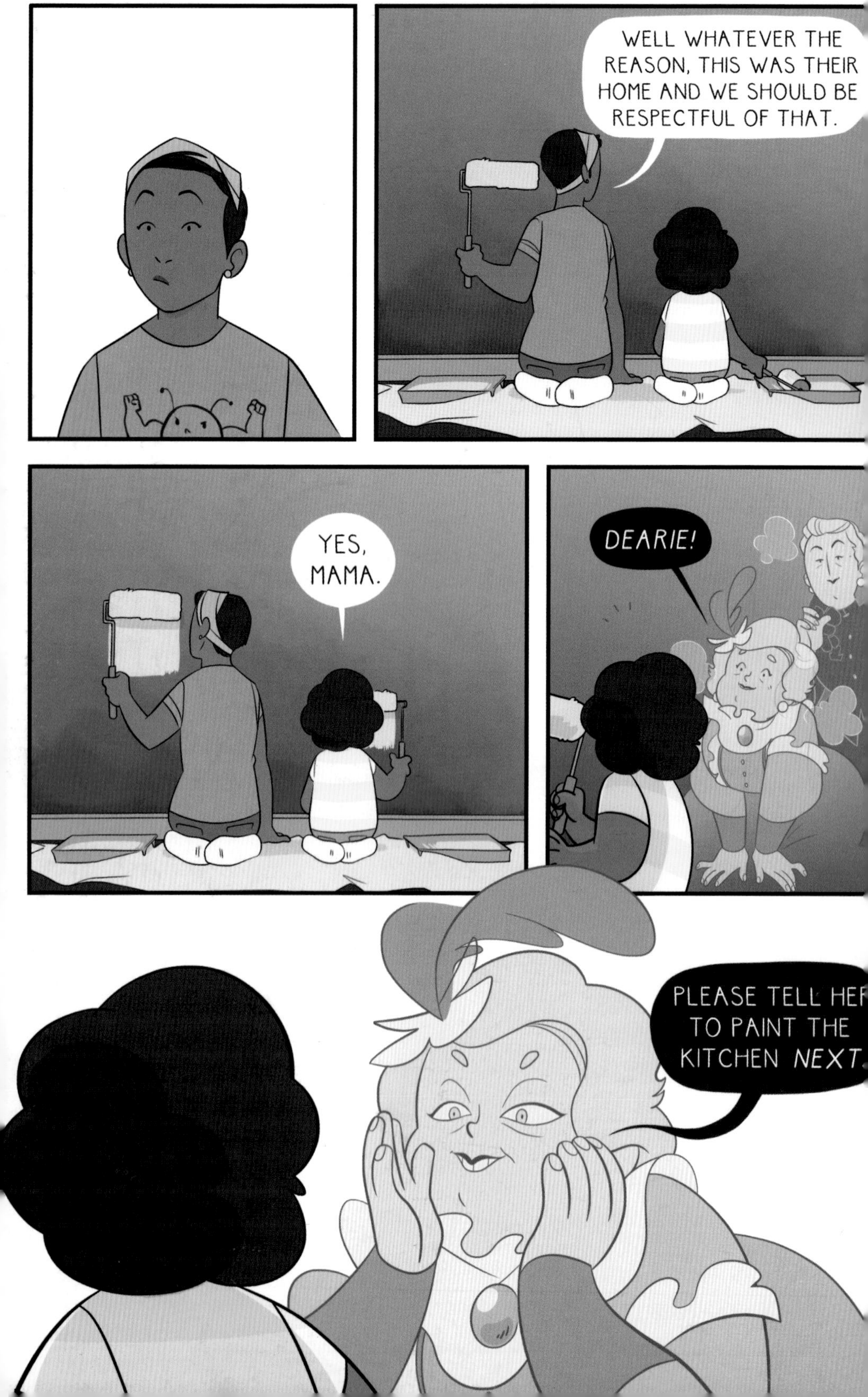
WELL WHATEVER THE REASON, THIS WAS THEIR HOME AND WE SHOULD BE RESPECTFUL OF THAT.
YES, MAMA.
DEARIE!
PLEASE TELL HER TO PAINT THE KITCHEN NEXT.

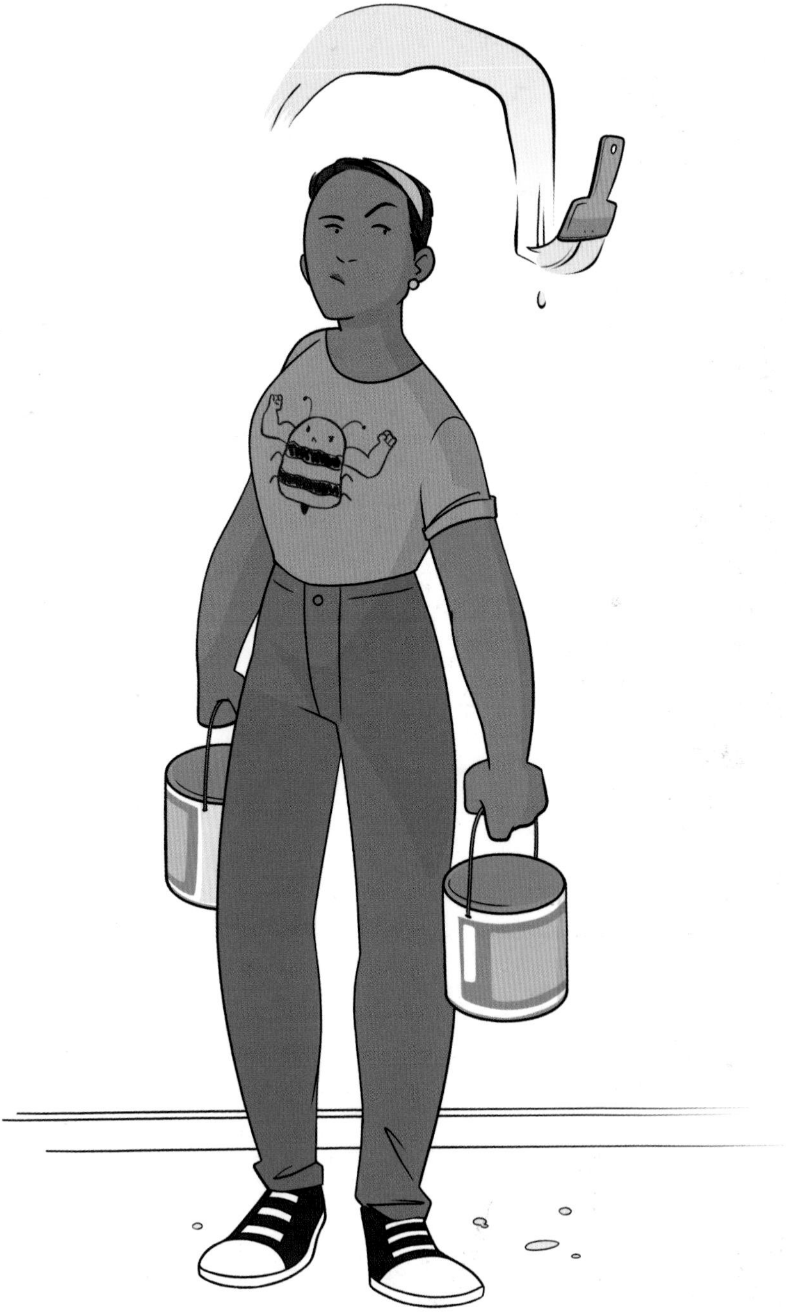

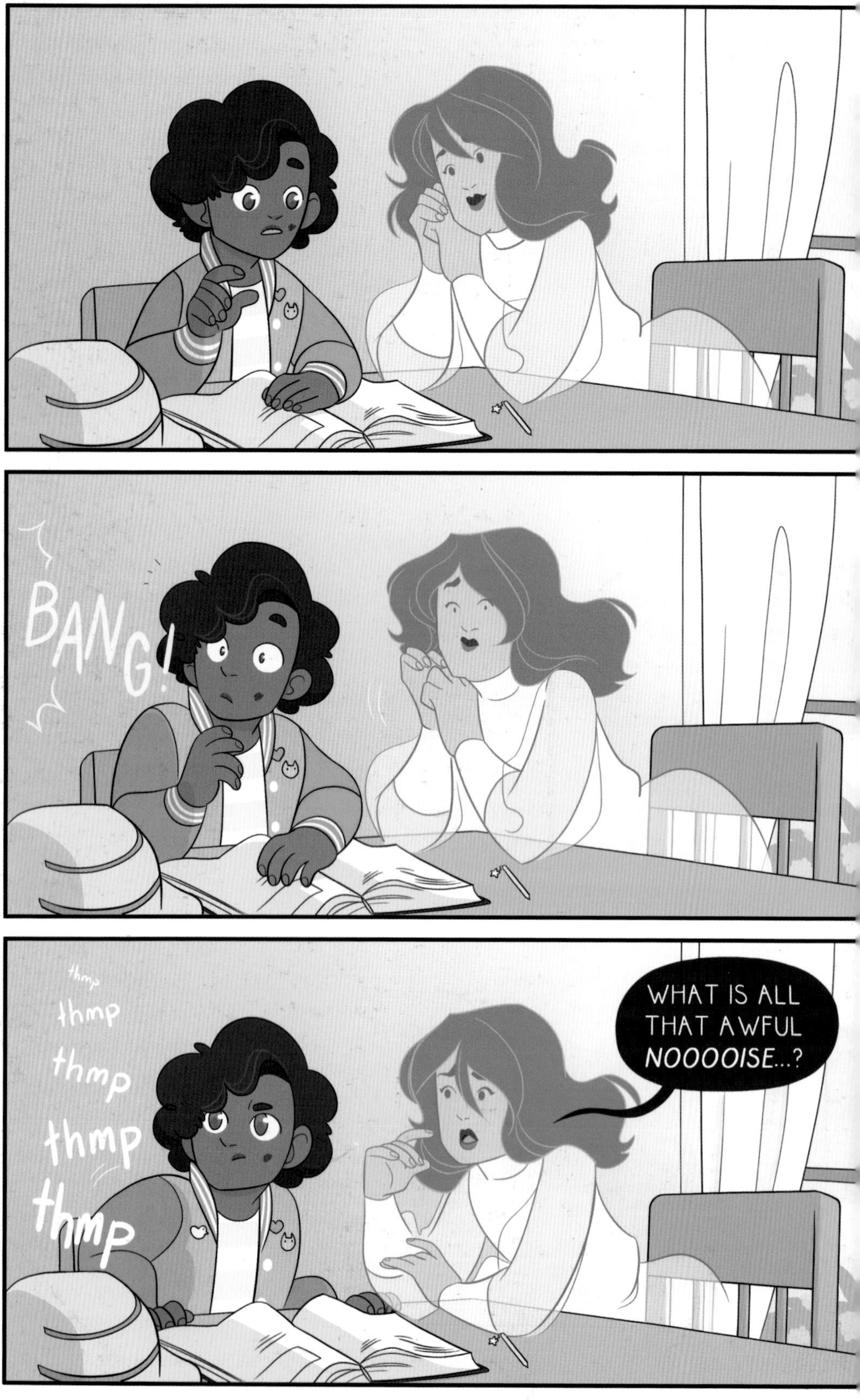
BANG!
thmp
thmp
thmp
thmp
thmp
WHAT IS ALL THAT AWFUL NOOOOISE...?

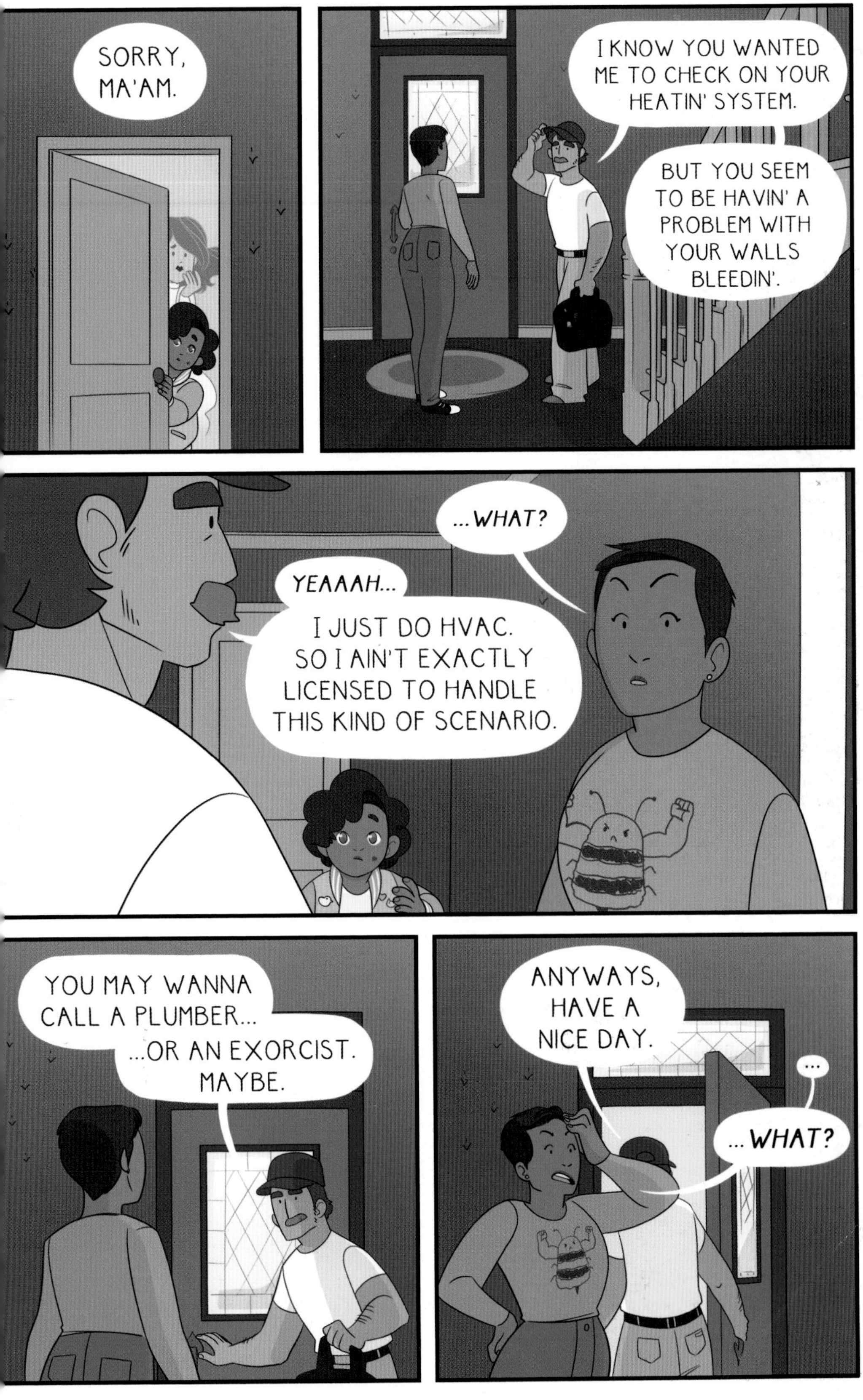
SORRY, MA'AM.
I KNOW YOU WANTED ME TO CHECK ON YOUR HEATIN' SYSTEM.
BUT YOU SEEM TO BE HAVIN' A PROBLEM WITH YOUR WALLS BLEEDIN'.
...WHAT?
YEAAAH...
I JUST DO HVAC. SO I AIN'T EXACTLY LICENSED TO HANDLE THIS KIND OF SCENARIO.
YOU MAY WANNA CALL A PLUMBER...
...OR AN EXORCIST. MAYBE.
ANYWAYS, HAVE A NICE DAY.
...
...WHAT?

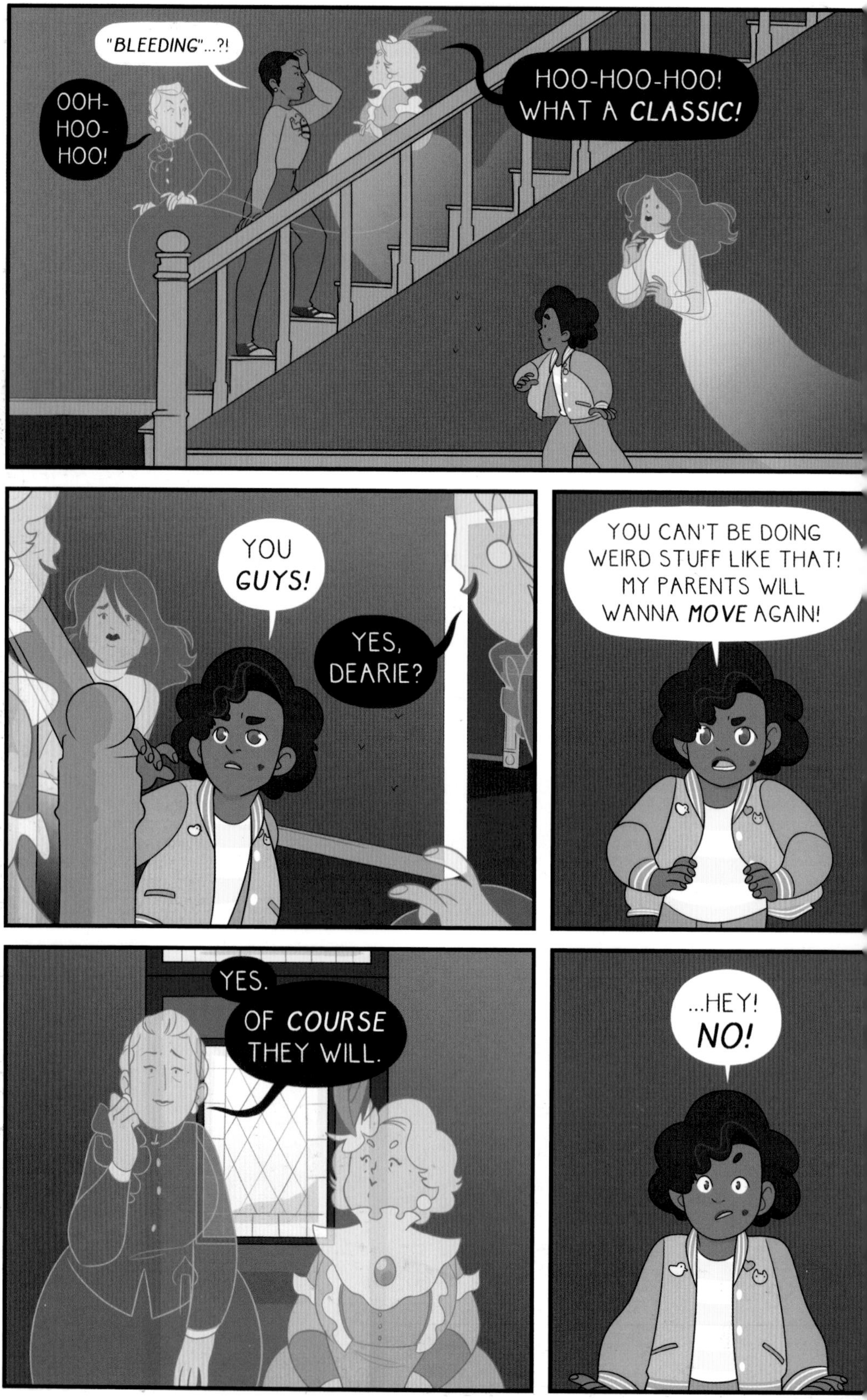
"BLEEDING"...?!
OOH-HOO-HOO!
HOO-HOO-HOO! WHAT A CLASSIC!
YOU GUYS!
YES, DEARIE?
YOU CAN'T BE DOING WEIRD STUFF LIKE THAT! MY PARENTS WILL WANNA MOVE AGAIN!
YES.
OF COURSE THEY WILL.
...HEY! NO!

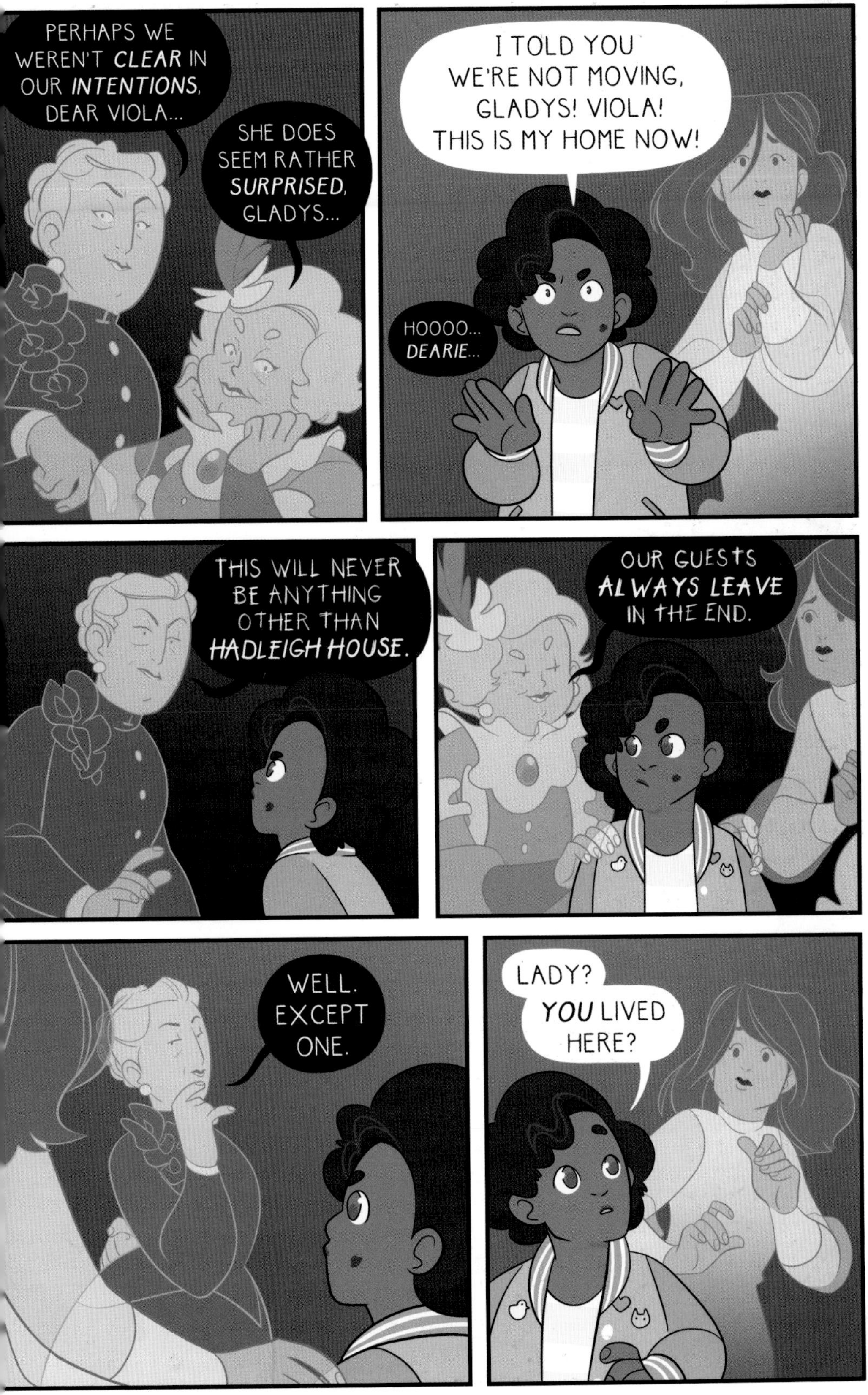
PERHAPS WE WEREN'T CLEAR IN OUR INTENTIONS, DEAR VIOLA...
SHE DOES SEEM RATHER SURPRISED, GLADYS...
I TOLD YOU WE'RE NOT MOVING, GLADYS! VIOLA! THIS IS MY HOME NOW!
HOOOO... DEARIE...
THIS WILL NEVER BE ANYTHING OTHER THAN HADLEIGH HOUSE.
OUR GUESTS ALWAYS LEAVE IN THE END.
WELL. EXCEPT ONE.
LADY? YOU LIVED HERE?

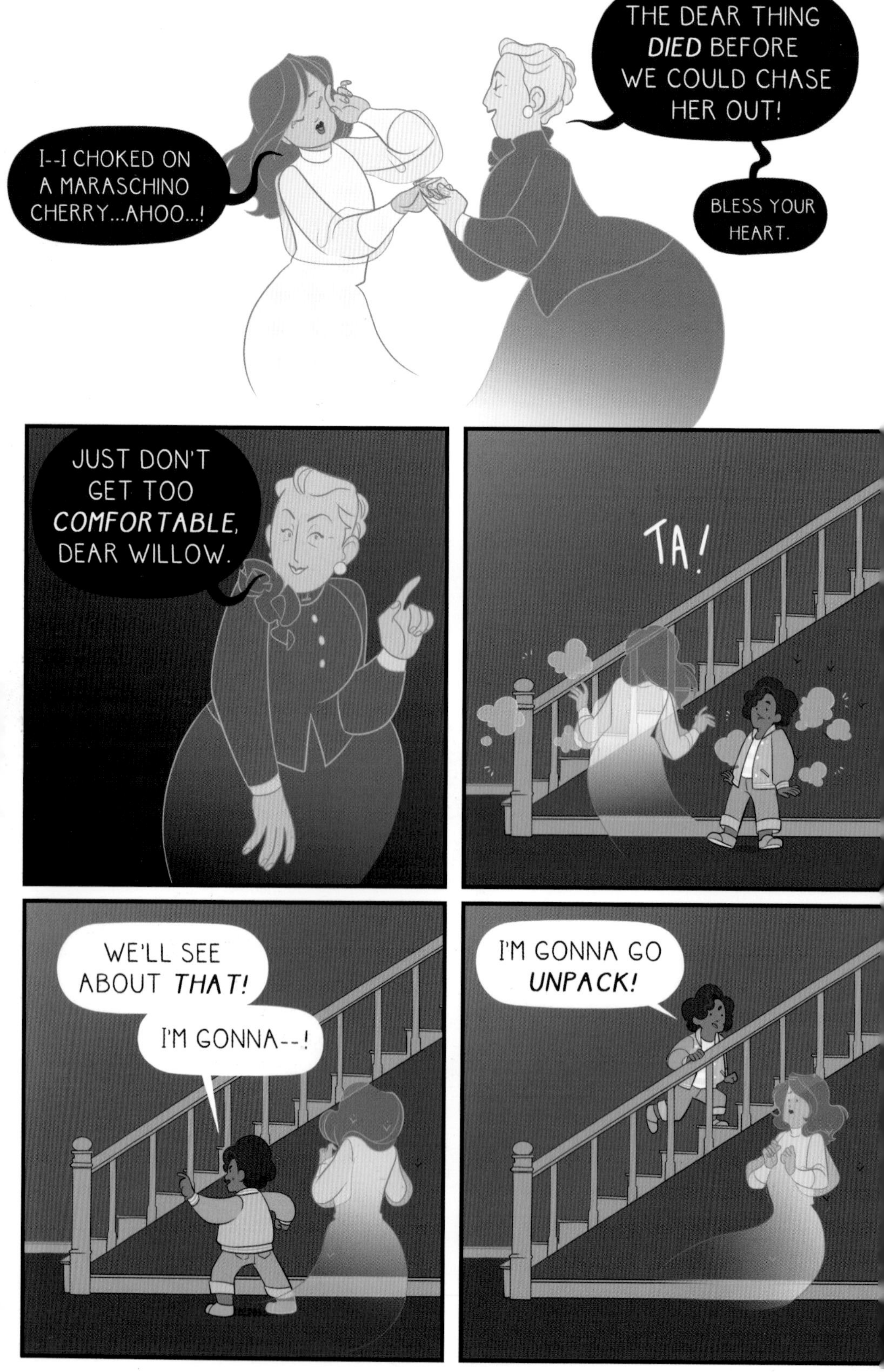
I--I CHOKED ON A MARASCHINO CHERRY...AHOO...!
THE DEAR THING *DIED* BEFORE WE COULD CHASE HER OUT!
BLESS YOUR HEART.
JUST DON'T GET TOO *COMFORTABLE*, DEAR WILLOW.
TA!
WE'LL SEE ABOUT *THAT!*
I'M GONNA--!
I'M GONNA GO *UNPACK!*

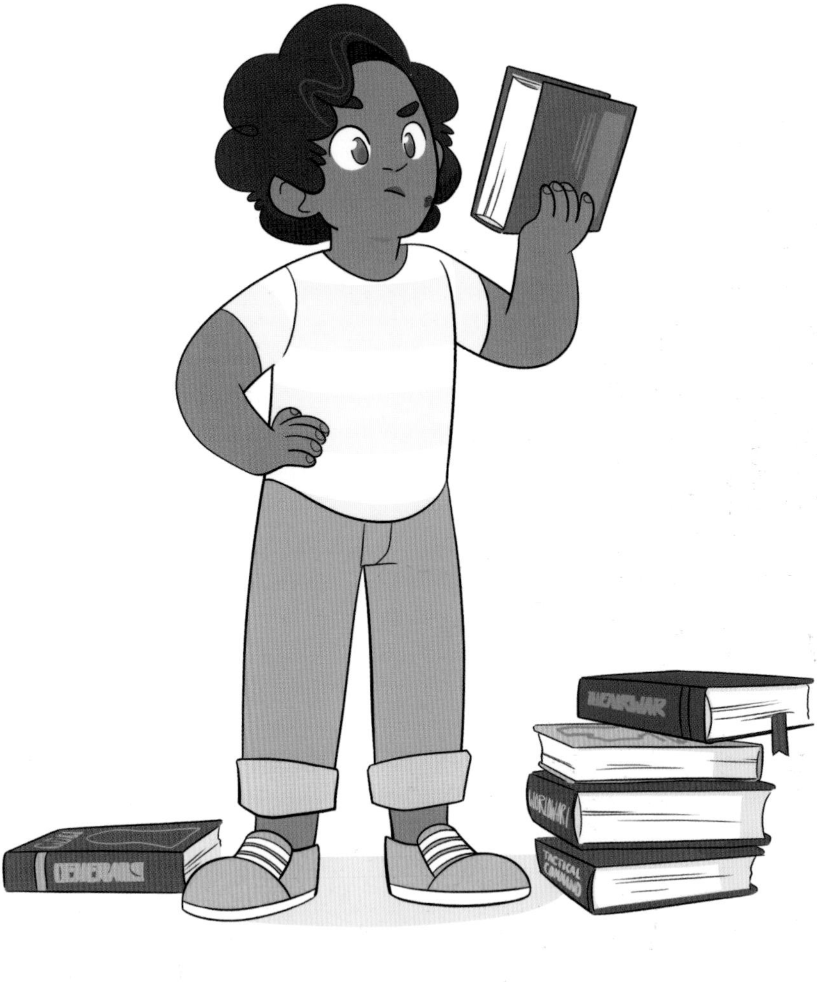
TACTICAL COMMAND

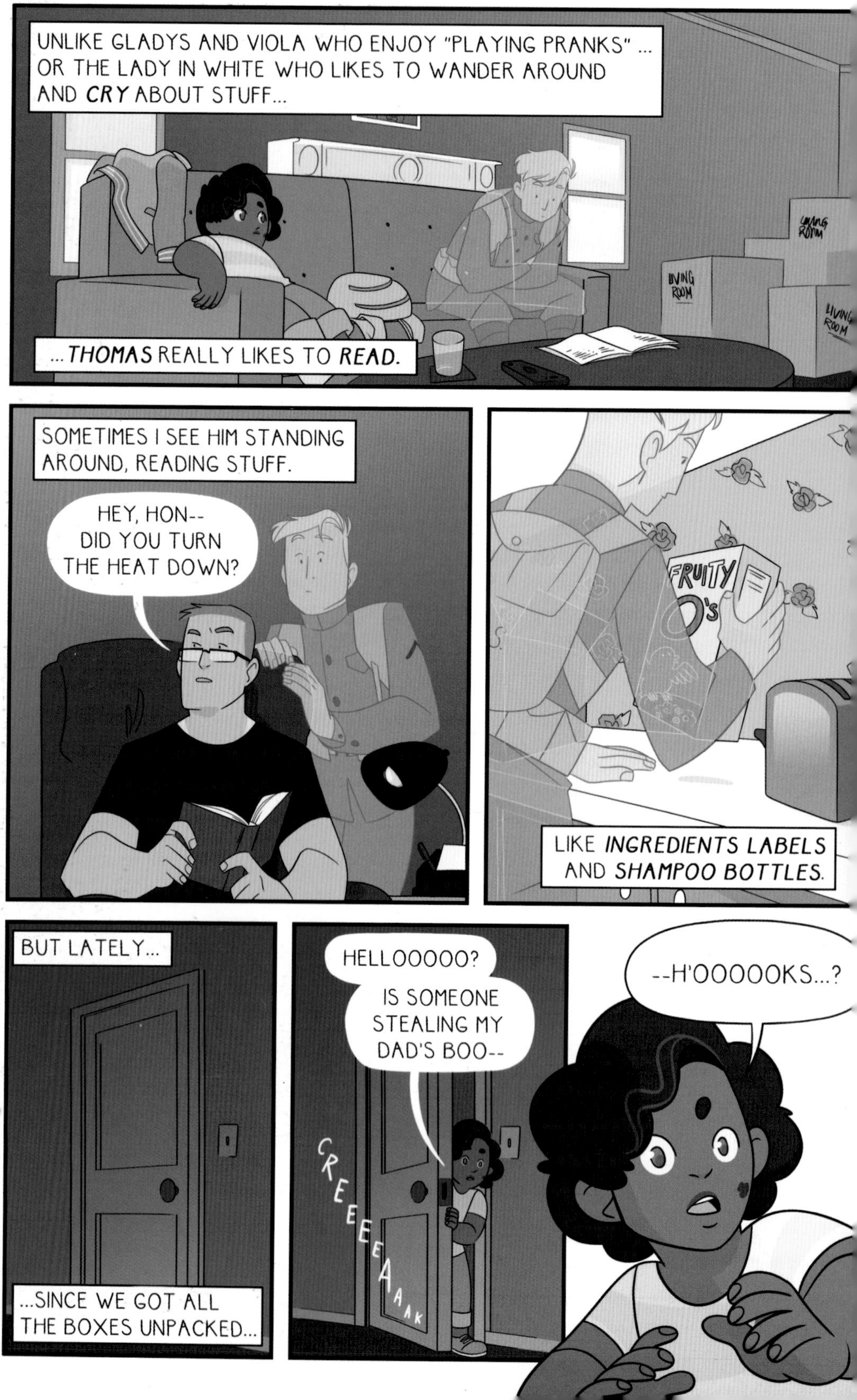
UNLIKE GLADYS AND VIOLA WHO ENJOY "PLAYING PRANKS"... OR THE LADY IN WHITE WHO LIKES TO WANDER AROUND AND CRY ABOUT STUFF...
LIVING ROOM
LIVING ROOM
LIVING ROOM
...THOMAS REALLY LIKES TO READ.
SOMETIMES I SEE HIM STANDING AROUND, READING STUFF.
HEY, HON-- DID YOU TURN THE HEAT DOWN?
FRUITY O'S
LIKE INGREDIENTS LABELS AND SHAMPOO BOTTLES.
BUT LATELY...
...SINCE WE GOT ALL THE BOXES UNPACKED...
HELLOOOOO?
IS SOMEONE STEALING MY DAD'S BOO--
CREEEEAAAK
--H'OOOOOKS...?

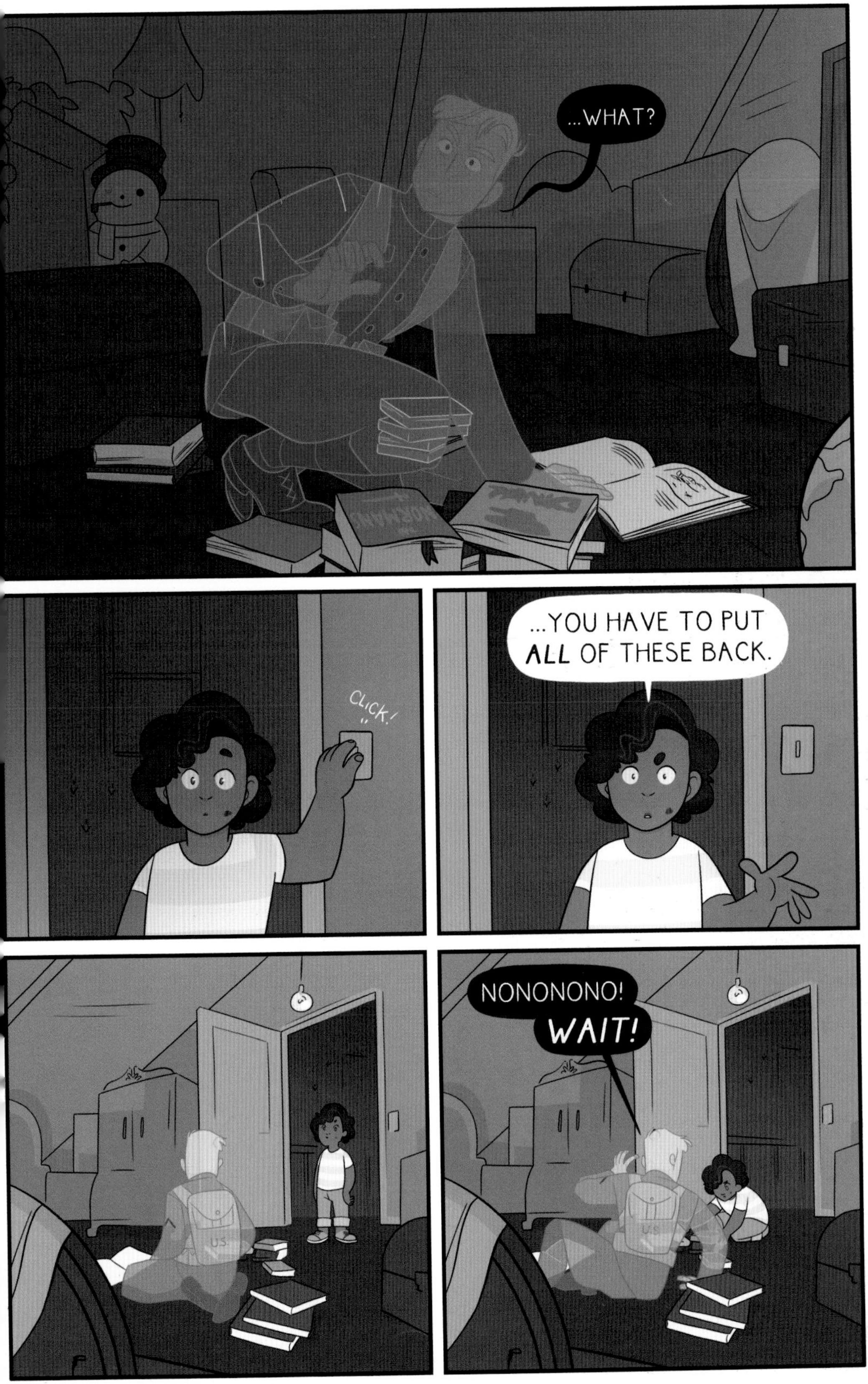
...WHAT?
CLICK!
...YOU HAVE TO PUT ALL OF THESE BACK.
NONONONO!
WAIT!

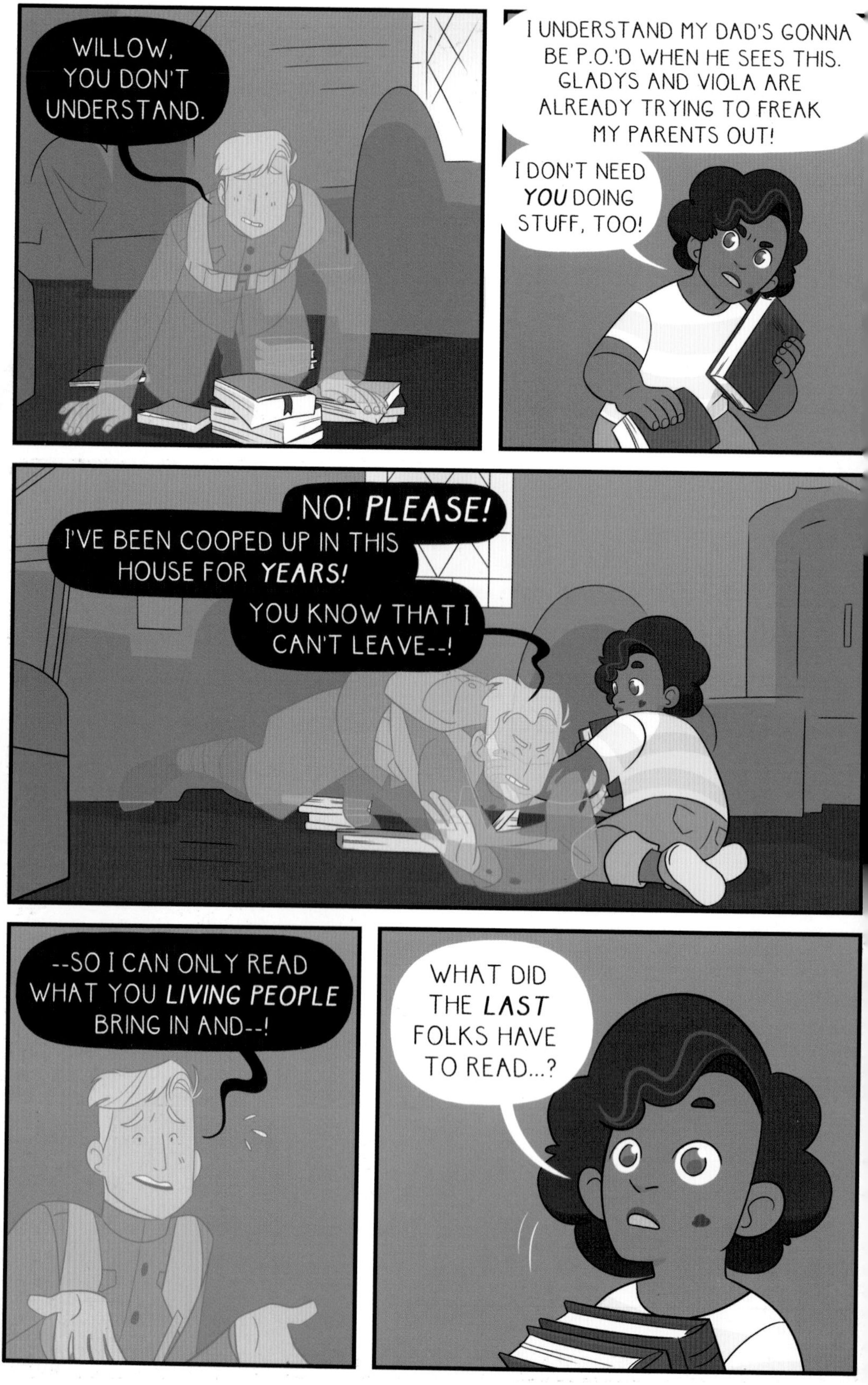
WILLOW, YOU DON'T UNDERSTAND.
I UNDERSTAND MY DAD'S GONNA BE P.O.'D WHEN HE SEES THIS. GLADYS AND VIOLA ARE ALREADY TRYING TO FREAK MY PARENTS OUT!
I DON'T NEED YOU DOING STUFF, TOO!
NO! PLEASE!
I'VE BEEN COOPED UP IN THIS HOUSE FOR YEARS!
YOU KNOW THAT I CAN'T LEAVE--!
--SO I CAN ONLY READ WHAT YOU LIVING PEOPLE BRING IN AND--!
WHAT DID THE LAST FOLKS HAVE TO READ...?

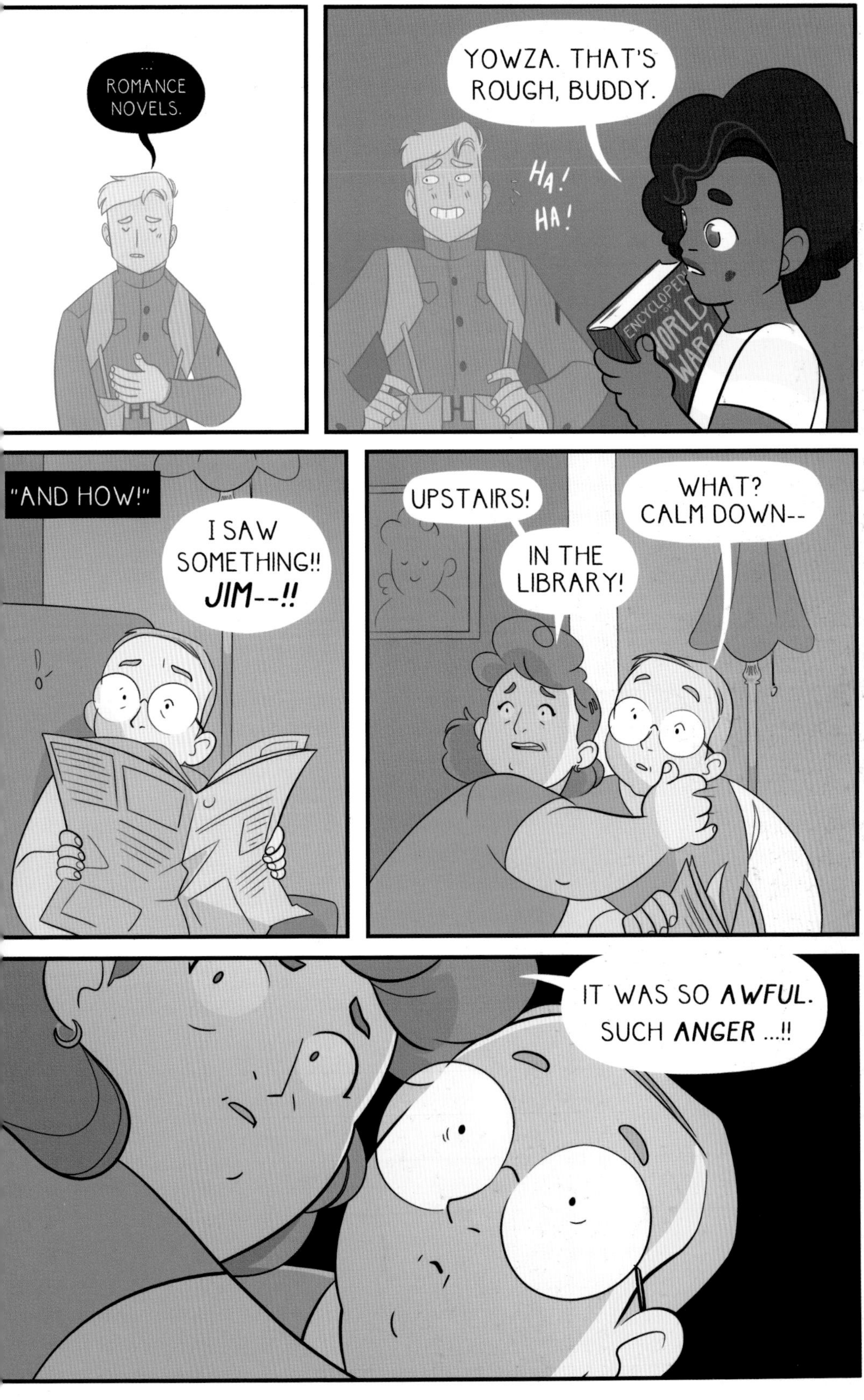
... ROMANCE NOVELS.
YOWZA. THAT'S ROUGH, BUDDY.
HA! HA!
ENCYCLOPEDIA OF WORLD WAR 2
"AND HOW!"
I SAW SOMETHING!! JIM--!!
UPSTAIRS!
IN THE LIBRARY!
WHAT? CALM DOWN--
IT WAS SO AWFUL. SUCH ANGER ...!!

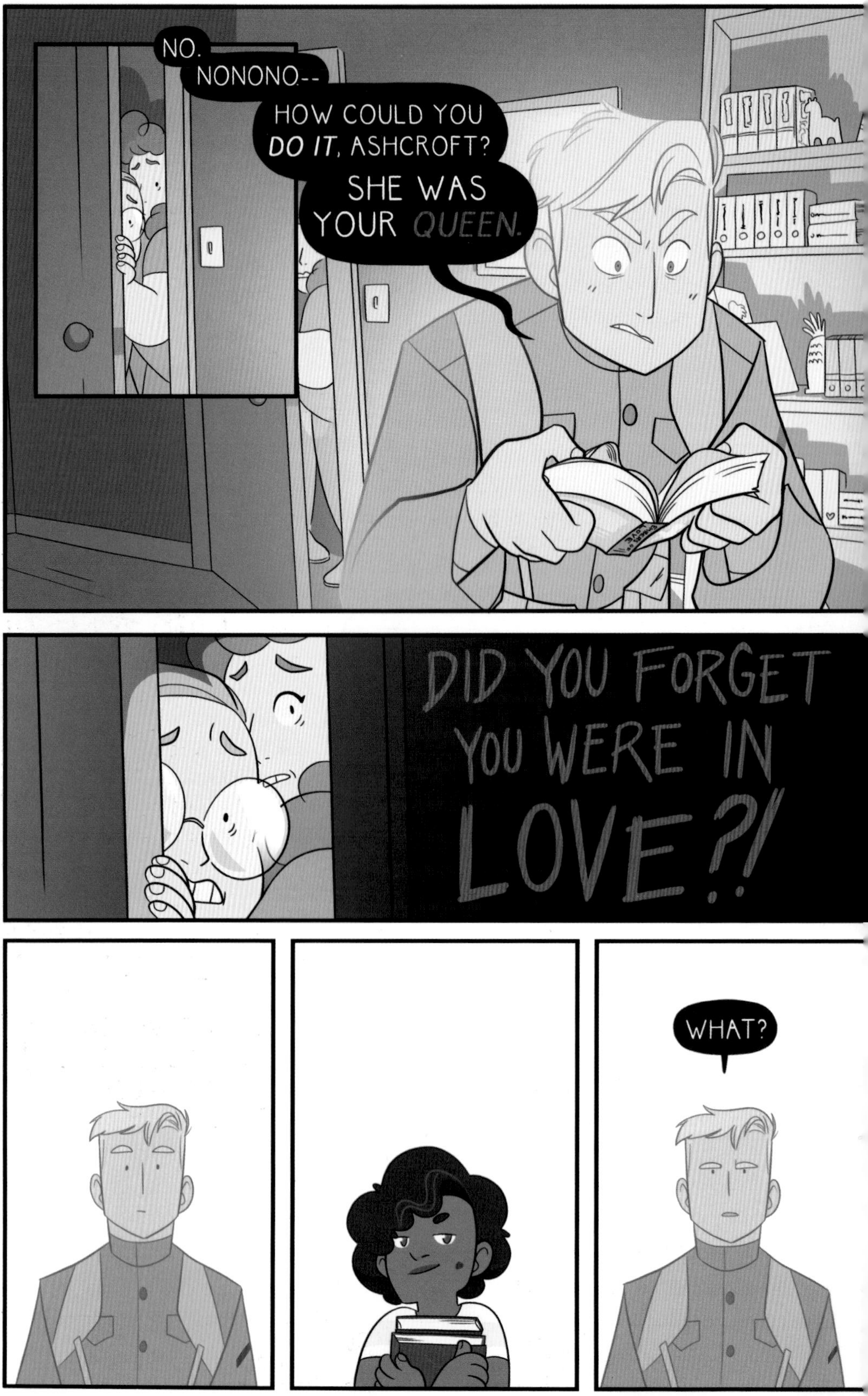
NO.
NONONO--
HOW COULD YOU DO IT, ASHCROFT?
SHE WAS YOUR QUEEN.
DID YOU FORGET YOU WERE IN LOVE?!
WHAT?

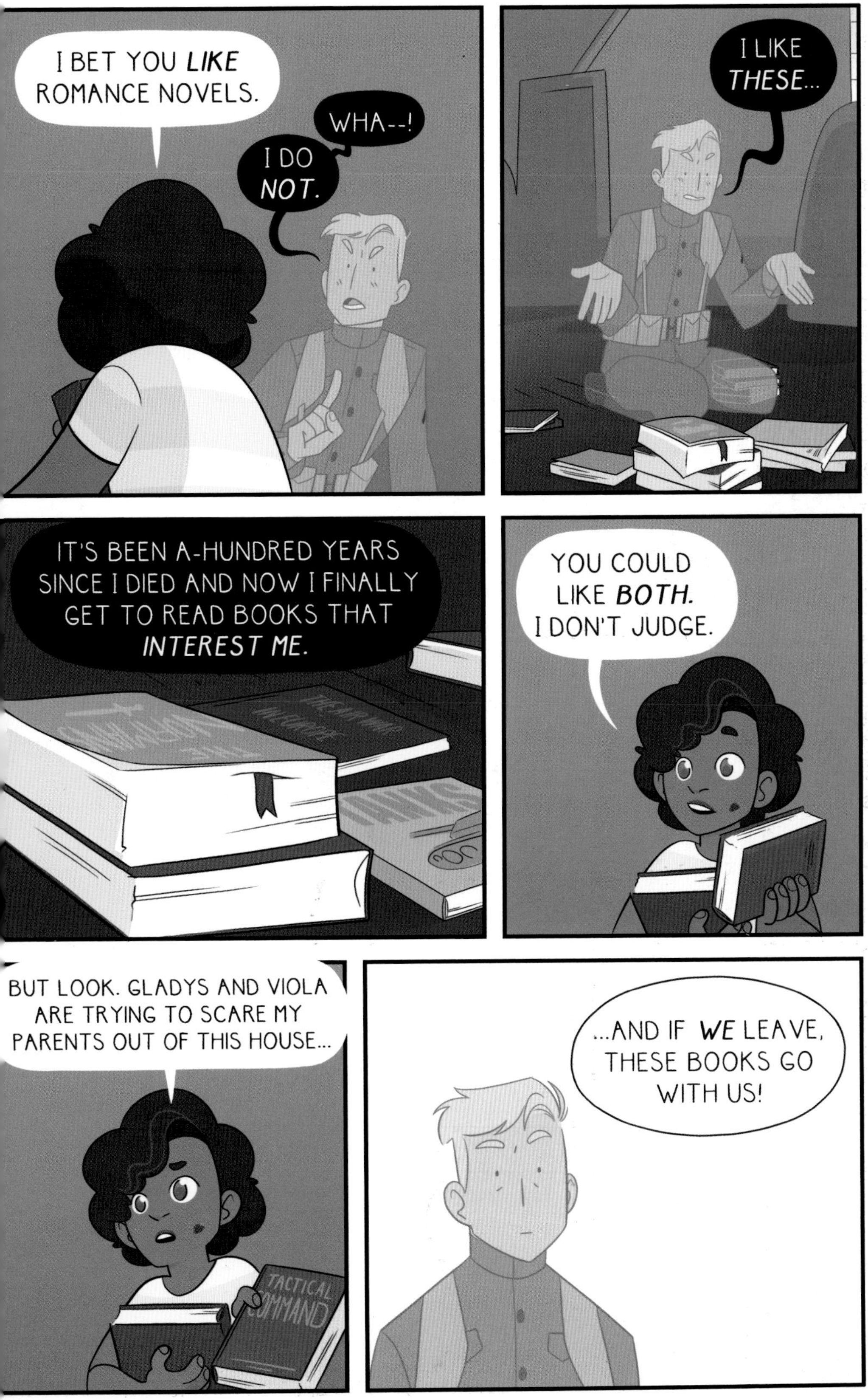
I BET YOU *LIKE* ROMANCE NOVELS.
WHA--!
I DO *NOT.*
I LIKE *THESE...*
IT'S BEEN A-HUNDRED YEARS SINCE I DIED AND NOW I FINALLY GET TO READ BOOKS THAT *INTEREST ME.*
YOU COULD LIKE *BOTH.* I DON'T JUDGE.
BUT LOOK. GLADYS AND VIOLA ARE TRYING TO SCARE MY PARENTS OUT OF THIS HOUSE...
TACTICAL COMMAND
...AND IF *WE* LEAVE, THESE BOOKS GO WITH US!

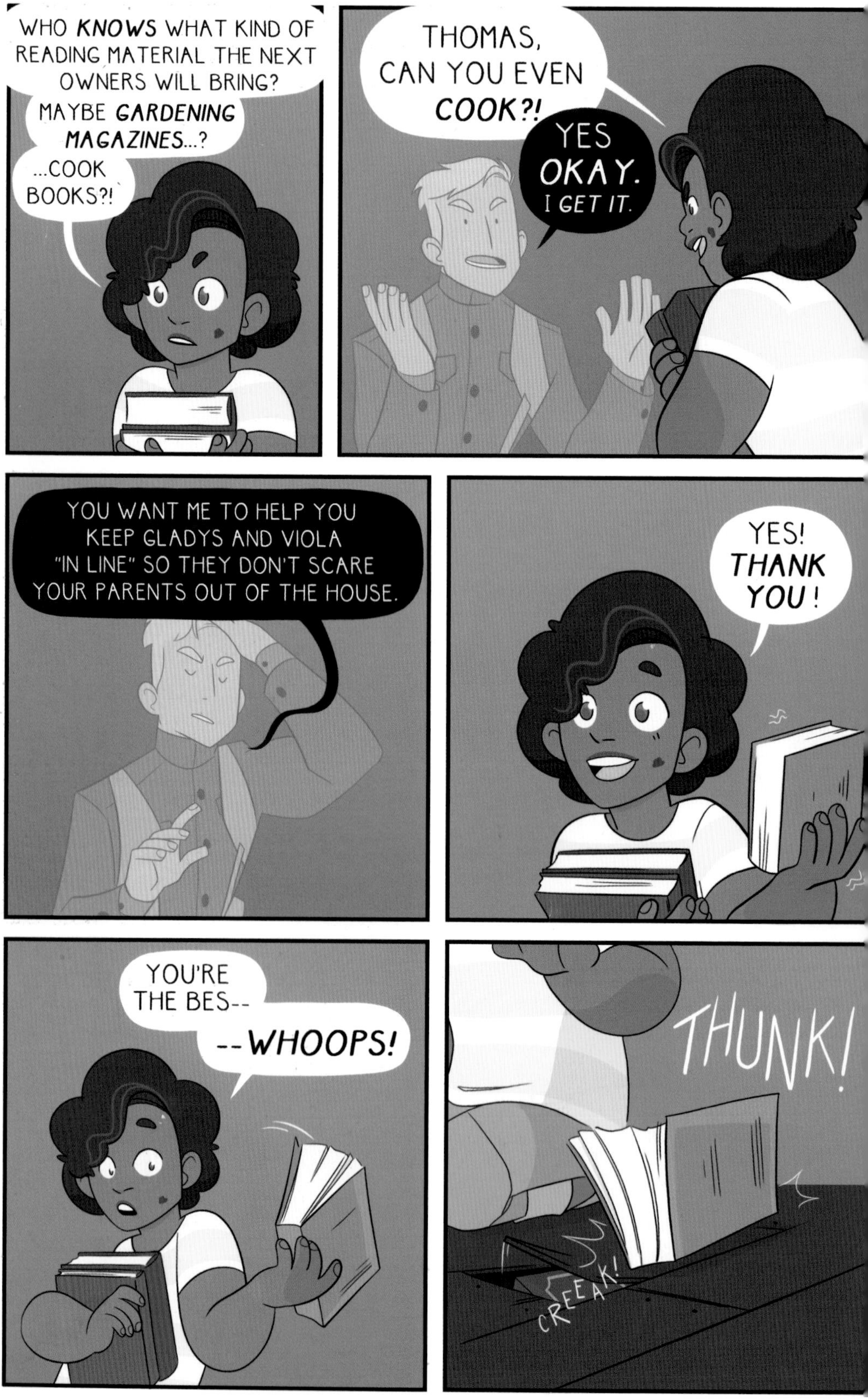
WHO KNOWS WHAT KIND OF READING MATERIAL THE NEXT OWNERS WILL BRING?
MAYBE GARDENING MAGAZINES...?
...COOK BOOKS?!
THOMAS, CAN YOU EVEN COOK?!
YES OKAY. I GET IT.
YOU WANT ME TO HELP YOU KEEP GLADYS AND VIOLA "IN LINE" SO THEY DON'T SCARE YOUR PARENTS OUT OF THE HOUSE.
YES! THANK YOU!
YOU'RE THE BES--
--WHOOPS!
THUNK!
CREEAK!

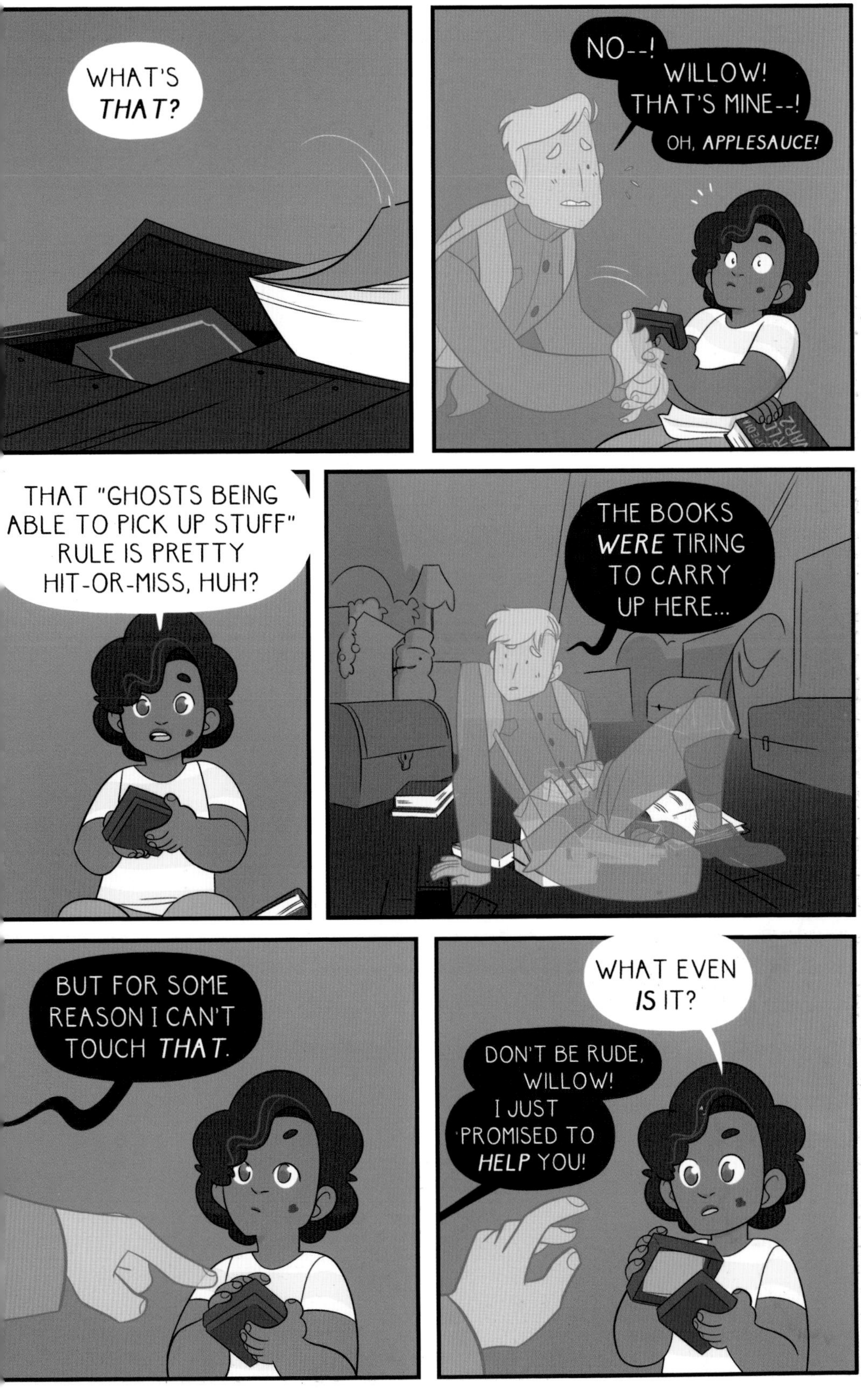
WHAT'S *THAT?*
NO--!
WILLOW! THAT'S MINE--!
OH, *APPLESAUCE!*
THAT "GHOSTS BEING ABLE TO PICK UP STUFF" RULE IS PRETTY HIT-OR-MISS, HUH?
THE BOOKS *WERE* TIRING TO CARRY UP HERE...
BUT FOR SOME REASON I CAN'T TOUCH *THAT*.
WHAT EVEN *IS* IT?
DON'T BE RUDE, WILLOW!
I JUST PROMISED TO *HELP* YOU!

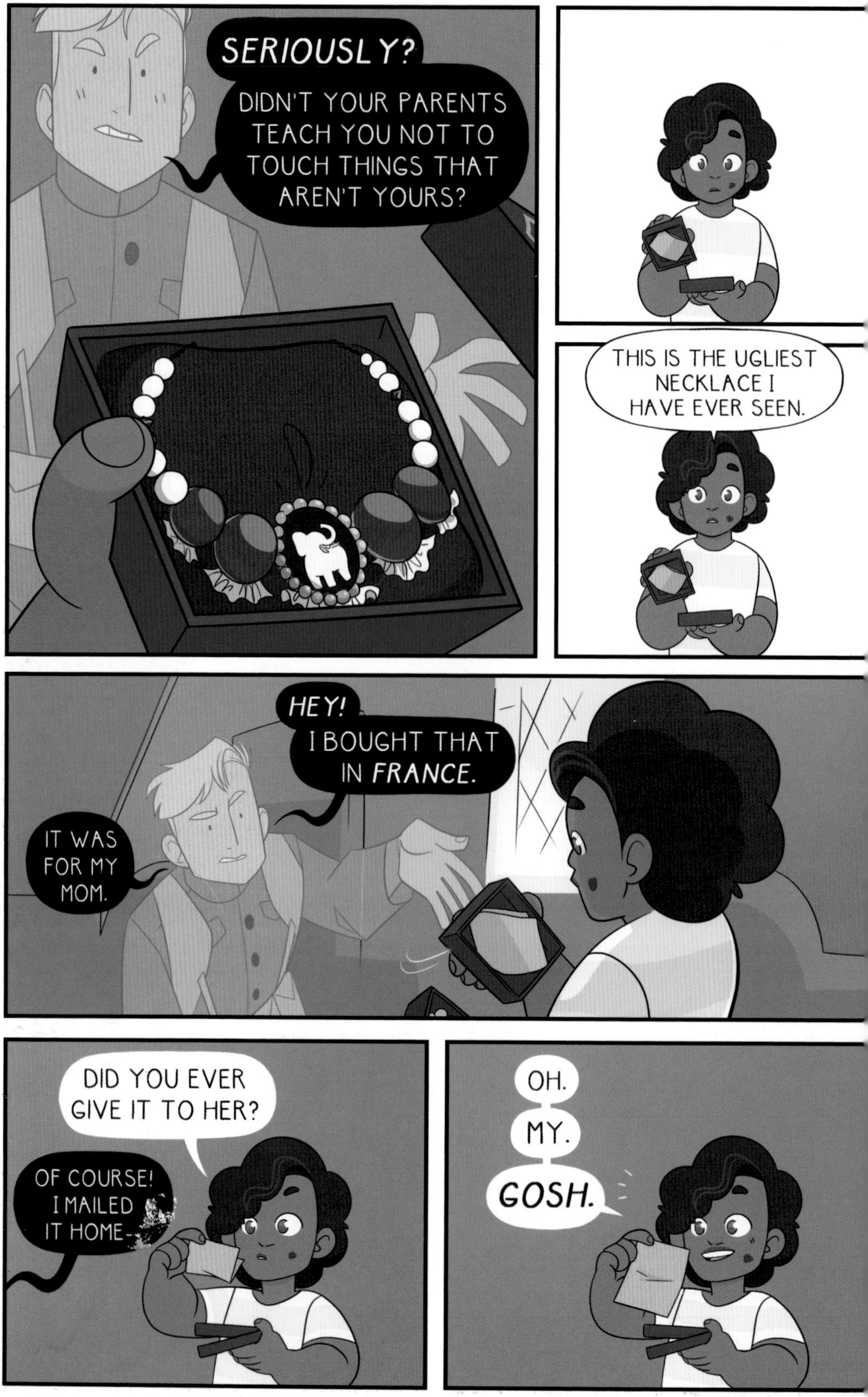
SERIOUSLY?
DIDN'T YOUR PARENTS TEACH YOU NOT TO TOUCH THINGS THAT AREN'T YOURS?
THIS IS THE UGLIEST NECKLACE I HAVE EVER SEEN.
HEY!
I BOUGHT THAT IN FRANCE.
IT WAS FOR MY MOM.
DID YOU EVER GIVE IT TO HER?
OF COURSE! I MAILED IT HOME-
OH.
MY.
GOSH.

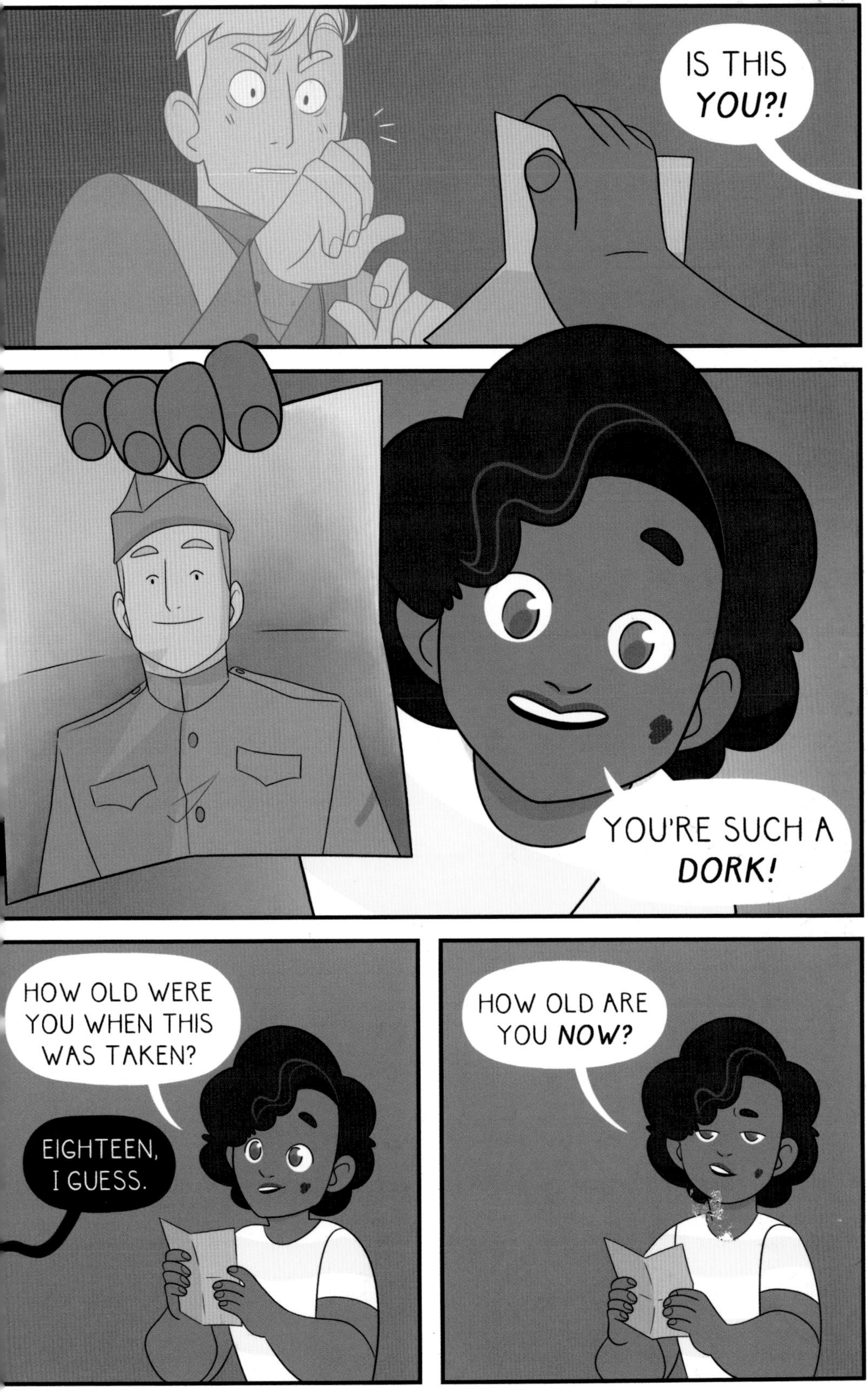
IS THIS *YOU?!*
YOU'RE SUCH A *DORK!*
HOW OLD WERE YOU WHEN THIS WAS TAKEN?
EIGHTEEN, I GUESS.
HOW OLD ARE YOU *NOW?*

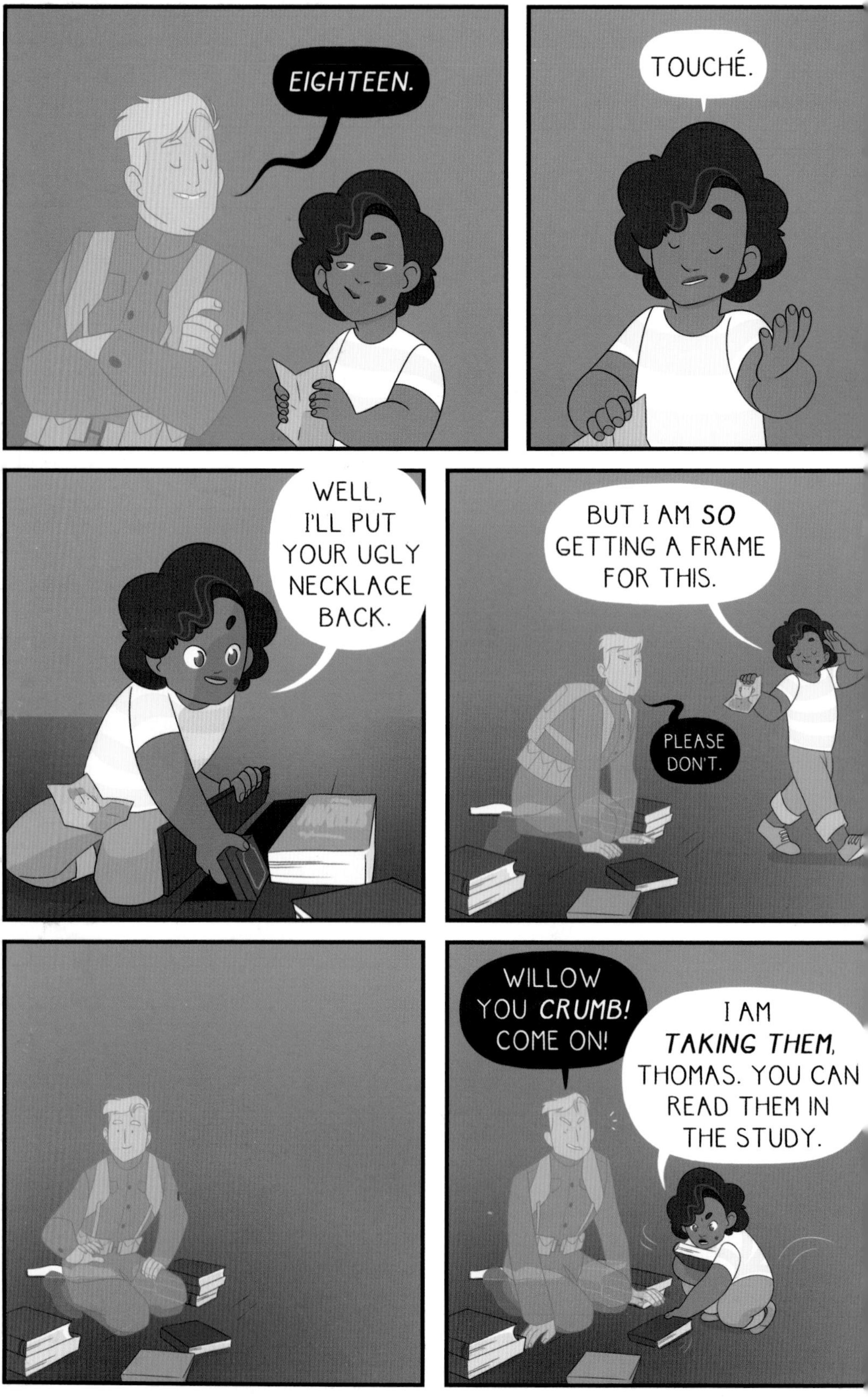
EIGHTEEN.
TOUCHÉ.
WELL, I'LL PUT YOUR UGLY NECKLACE BACK.
BUT I AM SO GETTING A FRAME FOR THIS.
PLEASE DON'T.
WILLOW YOU CRUMB! COME ON!
I AM TAKING THEM, THOMAS. YOU CAN READ THEM IN THE STUDY.

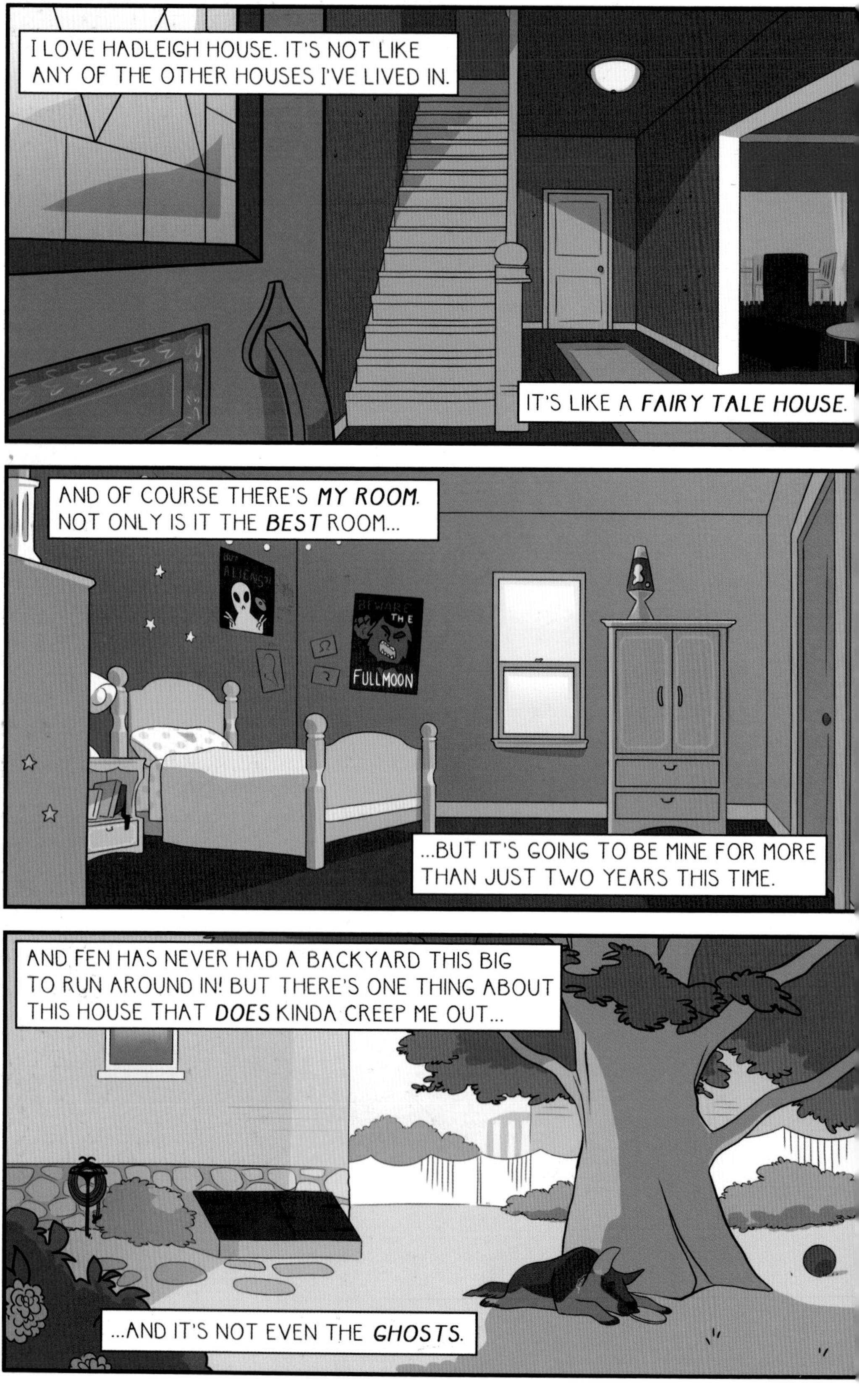
I LOVE HADLEIGH HOUSE. IT'S NOT LIKE ANY OF THE OTHER HOUSES I'VE LIVED IN.
IT'S LIKE A *FAIRY TALE HOUSE*.
AND OF COURSE THERE'S *MY ROOM*. NOT ONLY IS IT THE *BEST* ROOM...
ALIENS?!
BEWARE THE
FULLMOON
...BUT IT'S GOING TO BE MINE FOR MORE THAN JUST TWO YEARS THIS TIME.
AND FEN HAS NEVER HAD A BACKYARD THIS BIG TO RUN AROUND IN! BUT THERE'S ONE THING ABOUT THIS HOUSE THAT *DOES* KINDA CREEP ME OUT...
...AND IT'S NOT EVEN THE *GHOSTS*.

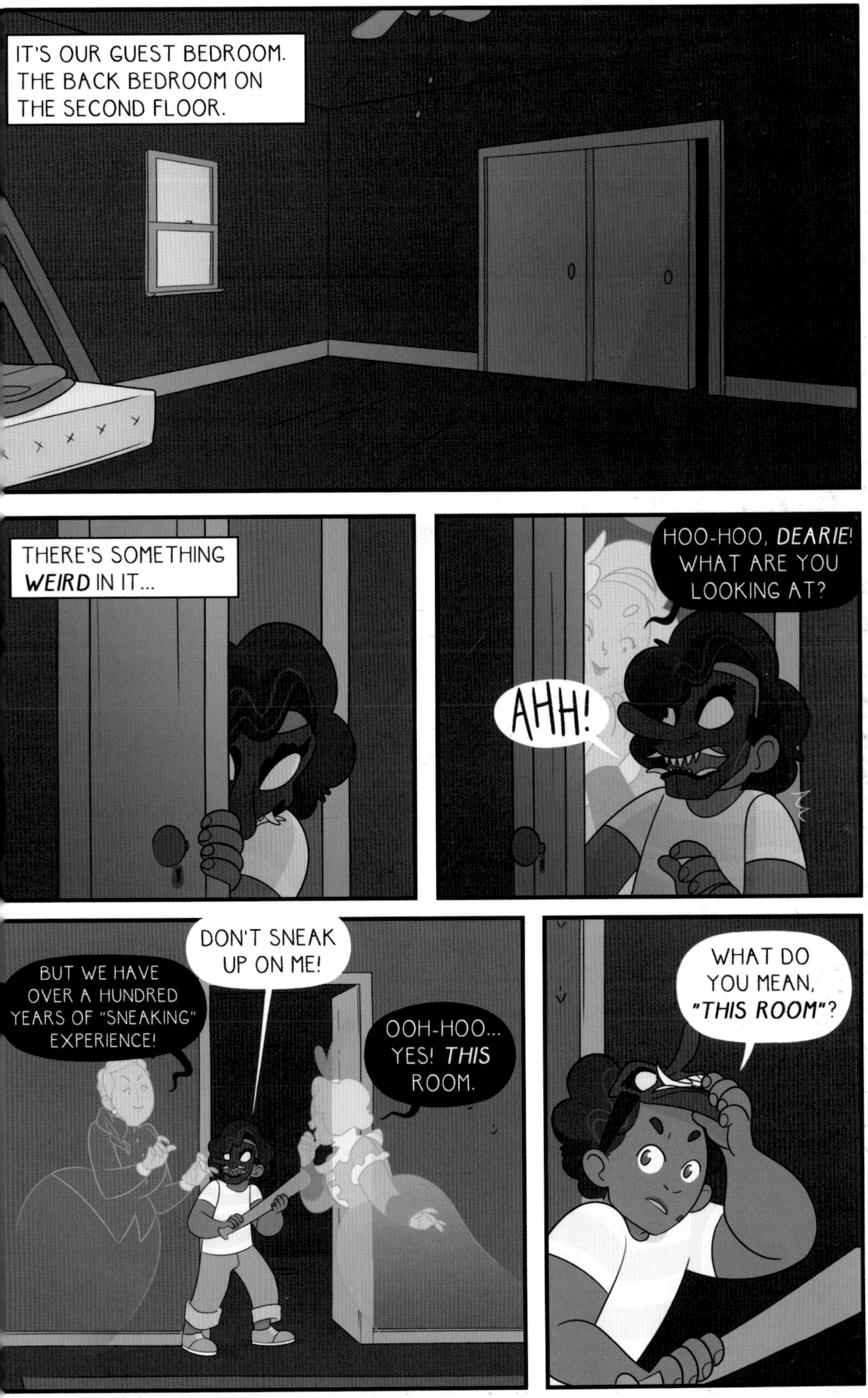

IT'S OUR GUEST BEDROOM. THE BACK BEDROOM ON THE SECOND FLOOR.
THERE'S SOMETHING **WEIRD** IN IT...
HOO-HOO, **DEARIE**! WHAT ARE YOU LOOKING AT?
AHH!
BUT WE HAVE OVER A HUNDRED YEARS OF "SNEAKING" EXPERIENCE!
DON'T SNEAK UP ON ME!
OOH-HOO... YES! **THIS** ROOM.
WHAT DO YOU MEAN, **"THIS ROOM"**?

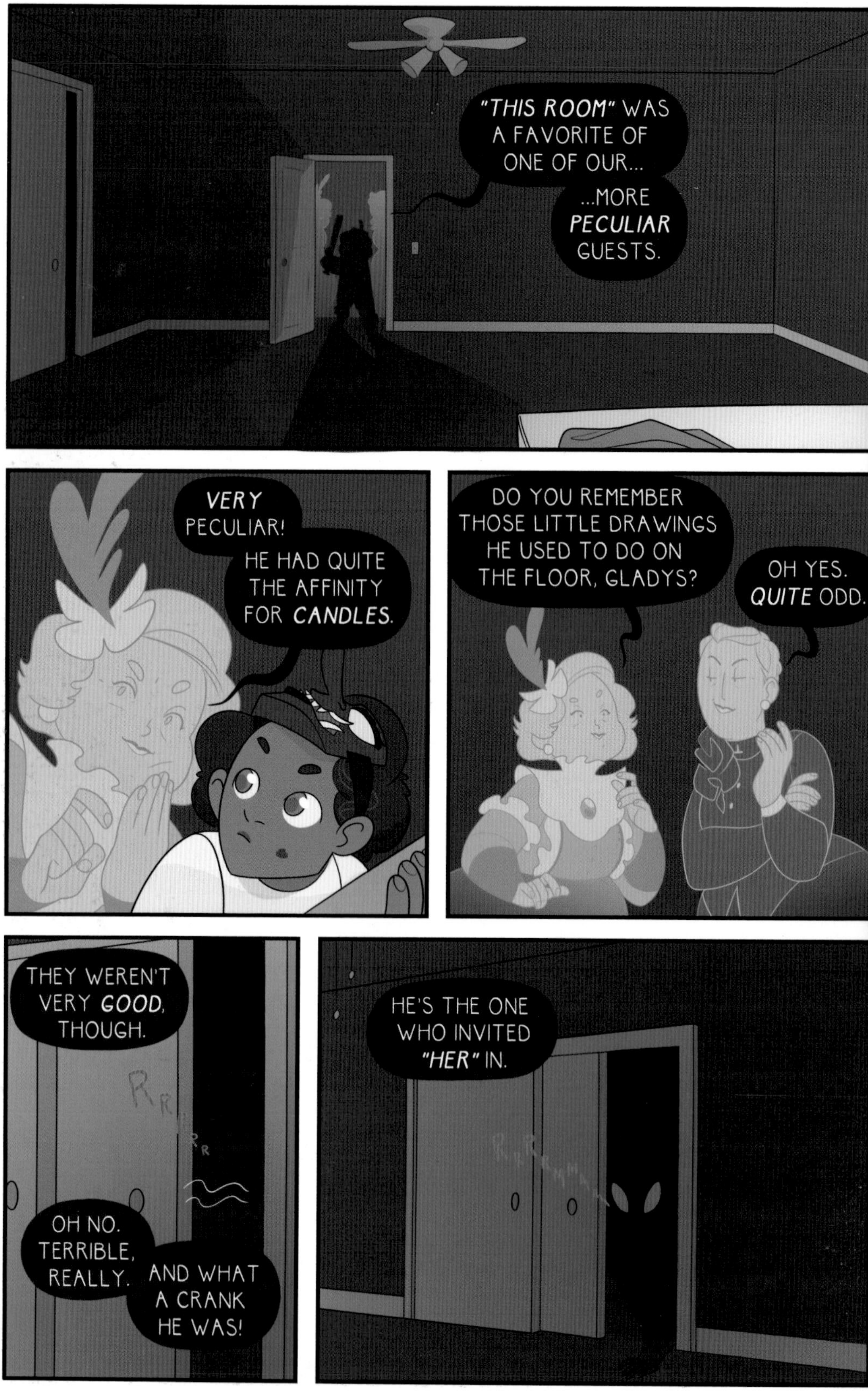
"THIS ROOM" WAS A FAVORITE OF ONE OF OUR...
...MORE PECULIAR GUESTS.
VERY PECULIAR!
HE HAD QUITE THE AFFINITY FOR CANDLES.
DO YOU REMEMBER THOSE LITTLE DRAWINGS HE USED TO DO ON THE FLOOR, GLADYS?
OH YES. QUITE ODD.
THEY WEREN'T VERY GOOD, THOUGH.
OH NO. TERRIBLE, REALLY.
AND WHAT A CRANK HE WAS!
HE'S THE ONE WHO INVITED "HER" IN.

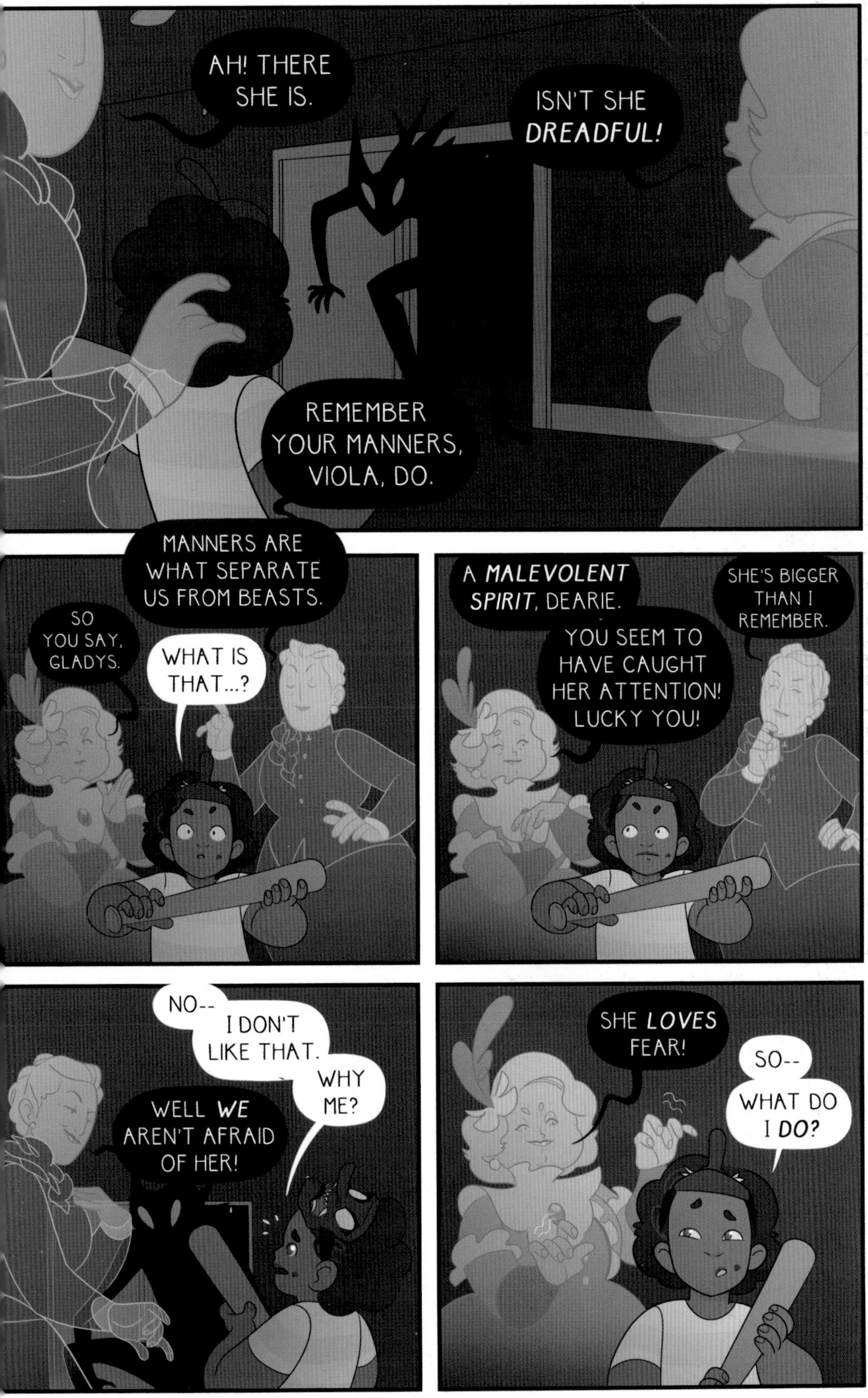

AH! THERE SHE IS.
ISN'T SHE *DREADFUL!*
REMEMBER YOUR MANNERS, VIOLA, DO.
MANNERS ARE WHAT SEPARATE US FROM BEASTS.
SO YOU SAY, GLADYS.
WHAT IS THAT...?
A *MALEVOLENT SPIRIT*, DEARIE.
SHE'S BIGGER THAN I REMEMBER.
YOU SEEM TO HAVE CAUGHT HER ATTENTION! LUCKY YOU!
NO--
I DON'T LIKE THAT.
WHY ME?
WELL *WE* AREN'T AFRAID OF HER!
SHE *LOVES* FEAR!
SO--
WHAT DO I *DO?*

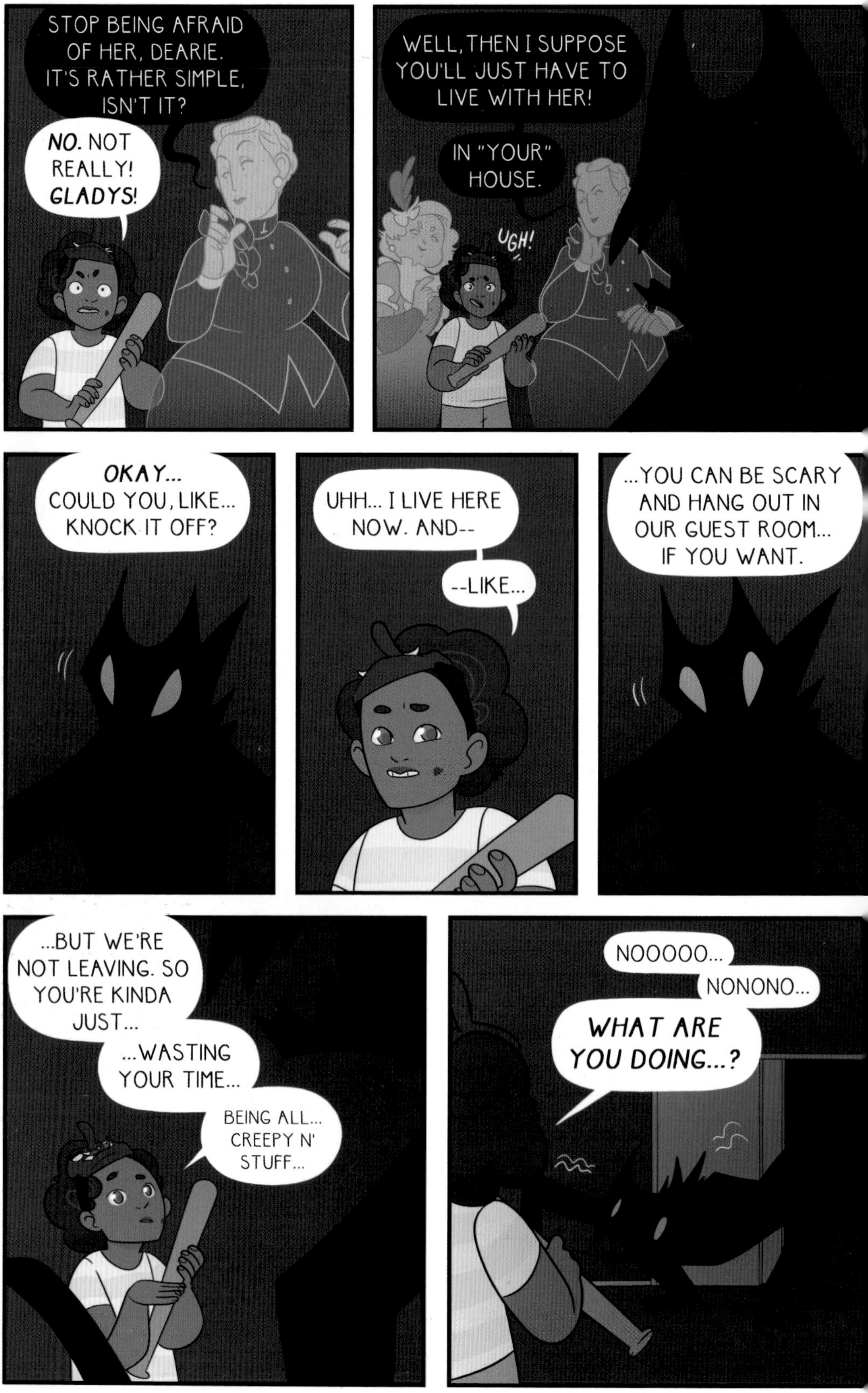
STOP BEING AFRAID OF HER, DEARIE. IT'S RATHER SIMPLE, ISN'T IT?
NO. NOT REALLY! GLADYS!
WELL, THEN I SUPPOSE YOU'LL JUST HAVE TO LIVE WITH HER!
IN "YOUR" HOUSE.
UGH!
OKAY... COULD YOU, LIKE... KNOCK IT OFF?
UHH... I LIVE HERE NOW. AND--
--LIKE...
...YOU CAN BE SCARY AND HANG OUT IN OUR GUEST ROOM... IF YOU WANT.
...BUT WE'RE NOT LEAVING. SO YOU'RE KINDA JUST...
...WASTING YOUR TIME...
BEING ALL... CREEPY N' STUFF...
NOOOOO...
NONONO...
WHAT ARE YOU DOING...?

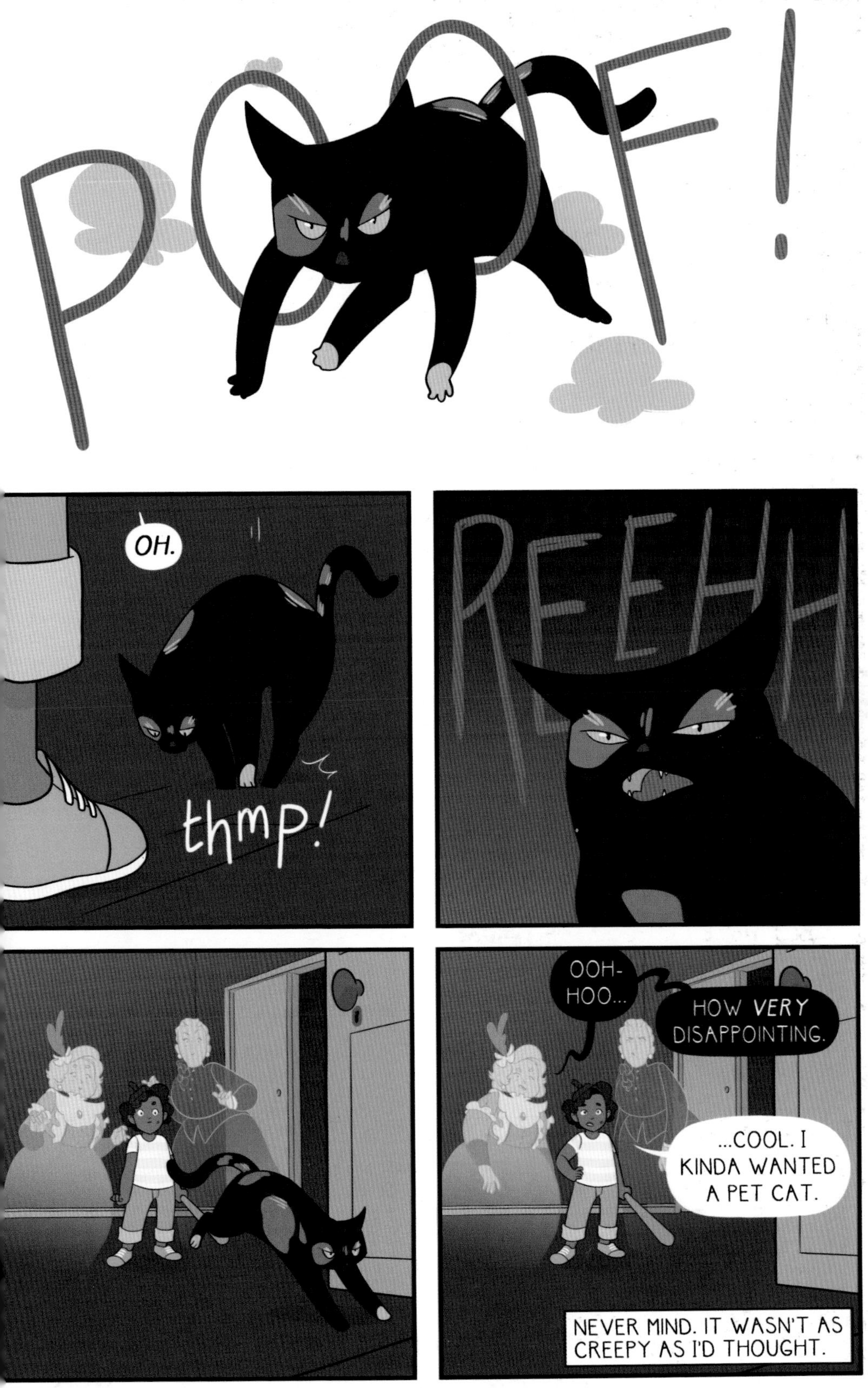
POOF!
OH.
thmp!
REEHH
OOH-HOO...
HOW VERY DISAPPOINTING.
...COOL. I KINDA WANTED A PET CAT.
NEVER MIND. IT WASN'T AS CREEPY AS I'D THOUGHT.

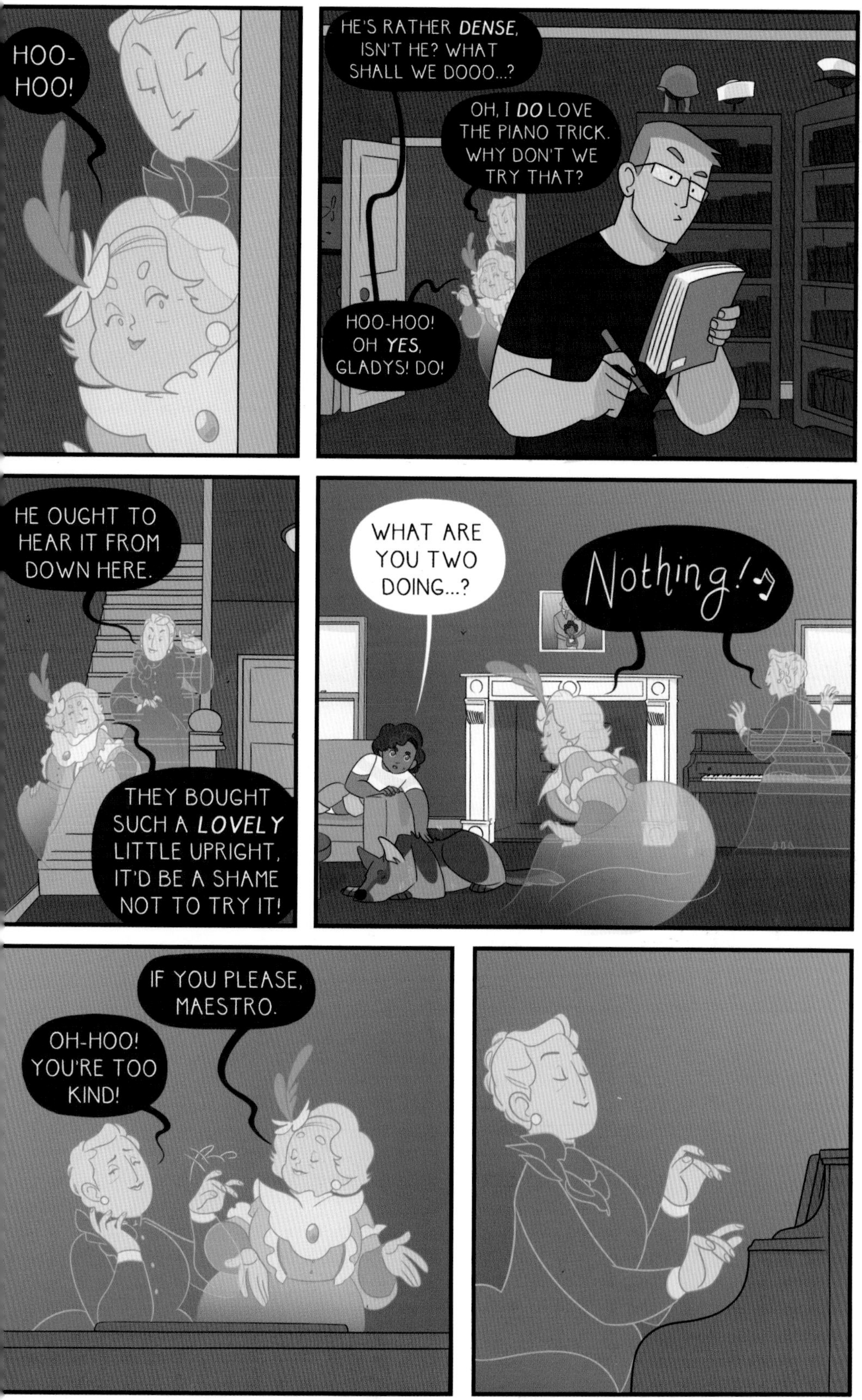
HOO-HOO!
HE'S RATHER DENSE, ISN'T HE? WHAT SHALL WE DOOO...?
OH, I DO LOVE THE PIANO TRICK. WHY DON'T WE TRY THAT?
HOO-HOO! OH YES, GLADYS! DO!
HE OUGHT TO HEAR IT FROM DOWN HERE.
THEY BOUGHT SUCH A LOVELY LITTLE UPRIGHT, IT'D BE A SHAME NOT TO TRY IT!
WHAT ARE YOU TWO DOING...?
Nothing!
IF YOU PLEASE, MAESTRO.
OH-HOO! YOU'RE TOO KIND!

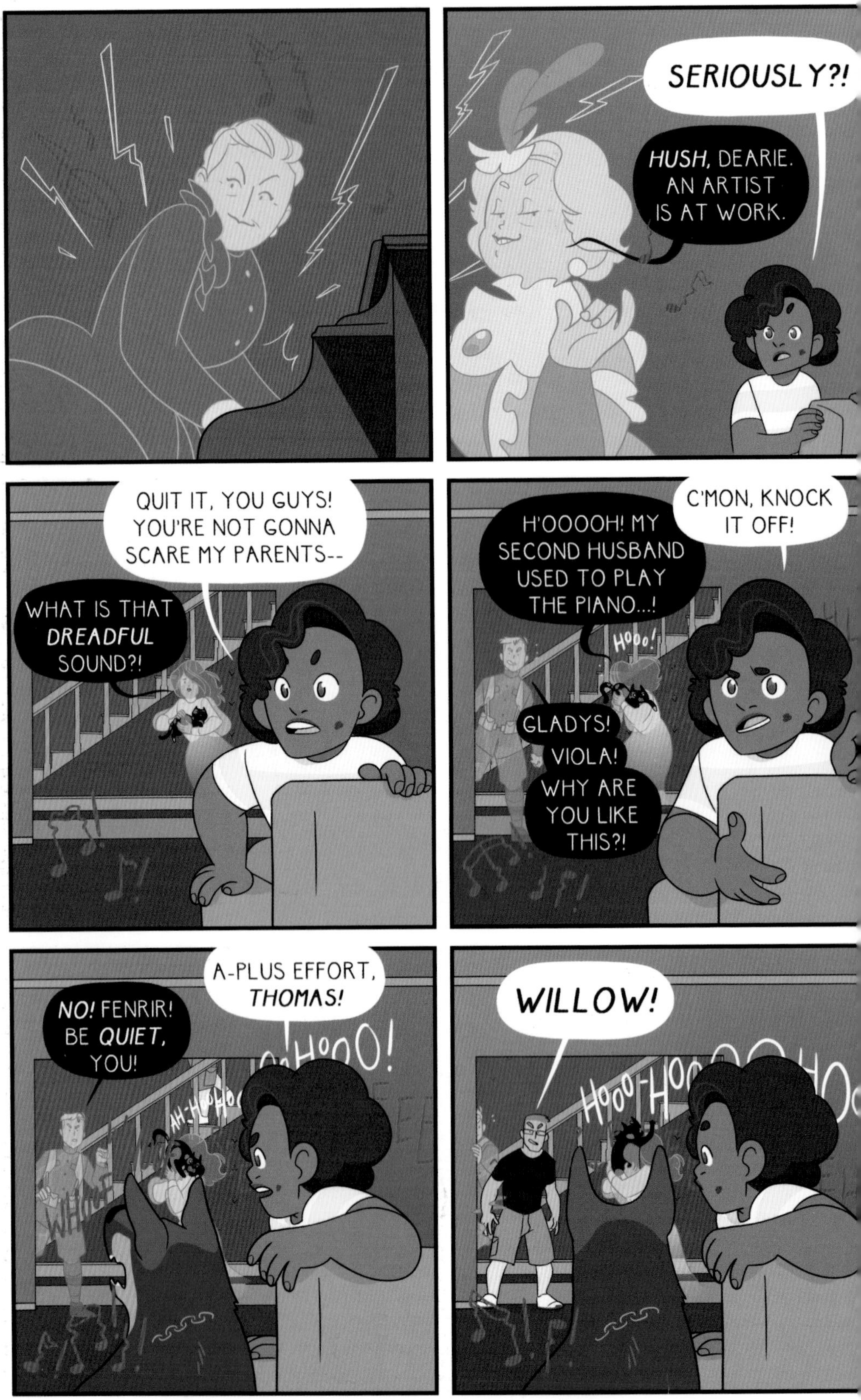
SERIOUSLY?!
HUSH, DEARIE. AN ARTIST IS AT WORK.
QUIT IT, YOU GUYS! YOU'RE NOT GONNA SCARE MY PARENTS--
WHAT IS THAT DREADFUL SOUND?!
C'MON, KNOCK IT OFF!
H'OOOOH! MY SECOND HUSBAND USED TO PLAY THE PIANO...!
HOOO!
GLADYS!
VIOLA!
WHY ARE YOU LIKE THIS?!
A-PLUS EFFORT, THOMAS!
NO! FENRIR! BE QUIET, YOU!
HOOO!
AH-HOOHOO
WILLOW!
HOOO-HOOOOOHOO

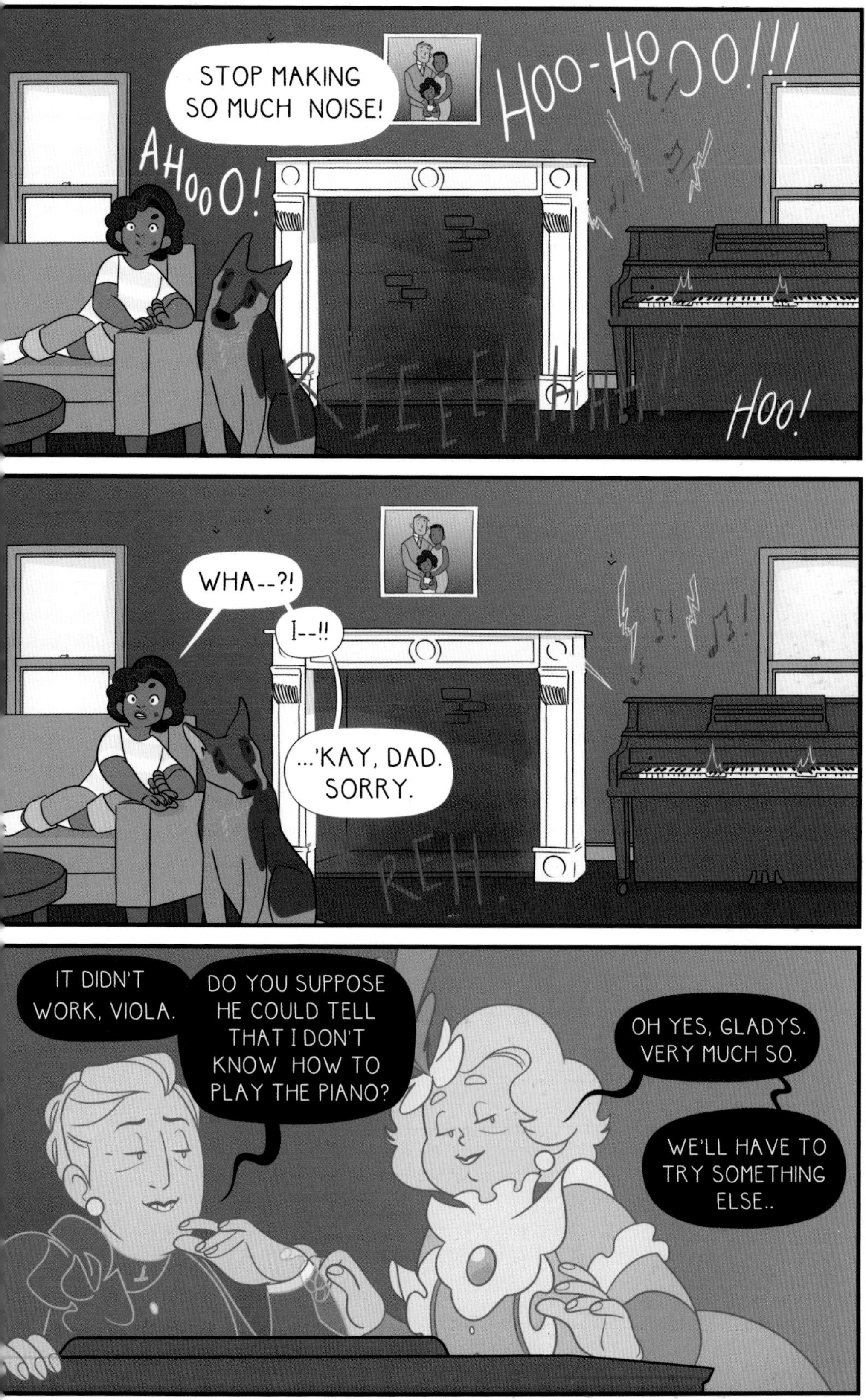
STOP MAKING SO MUCH NOISE!
AHOOO!
HOO-HOOOO!!!
HOO!
WHA--?!
I--!!
...'KAY, DAD. SORRY.
REH
IT DIDN'T WORK, VIOLA.
DO YOU SUPPOSE HE COULD TELL THAT I DON'T KNOW HOW TO PLAY THE PIANO?
OH YES, GLADYS. VERY MUCH SO.
WE'LL HAVE TO TRY SOMETHING ELSE..

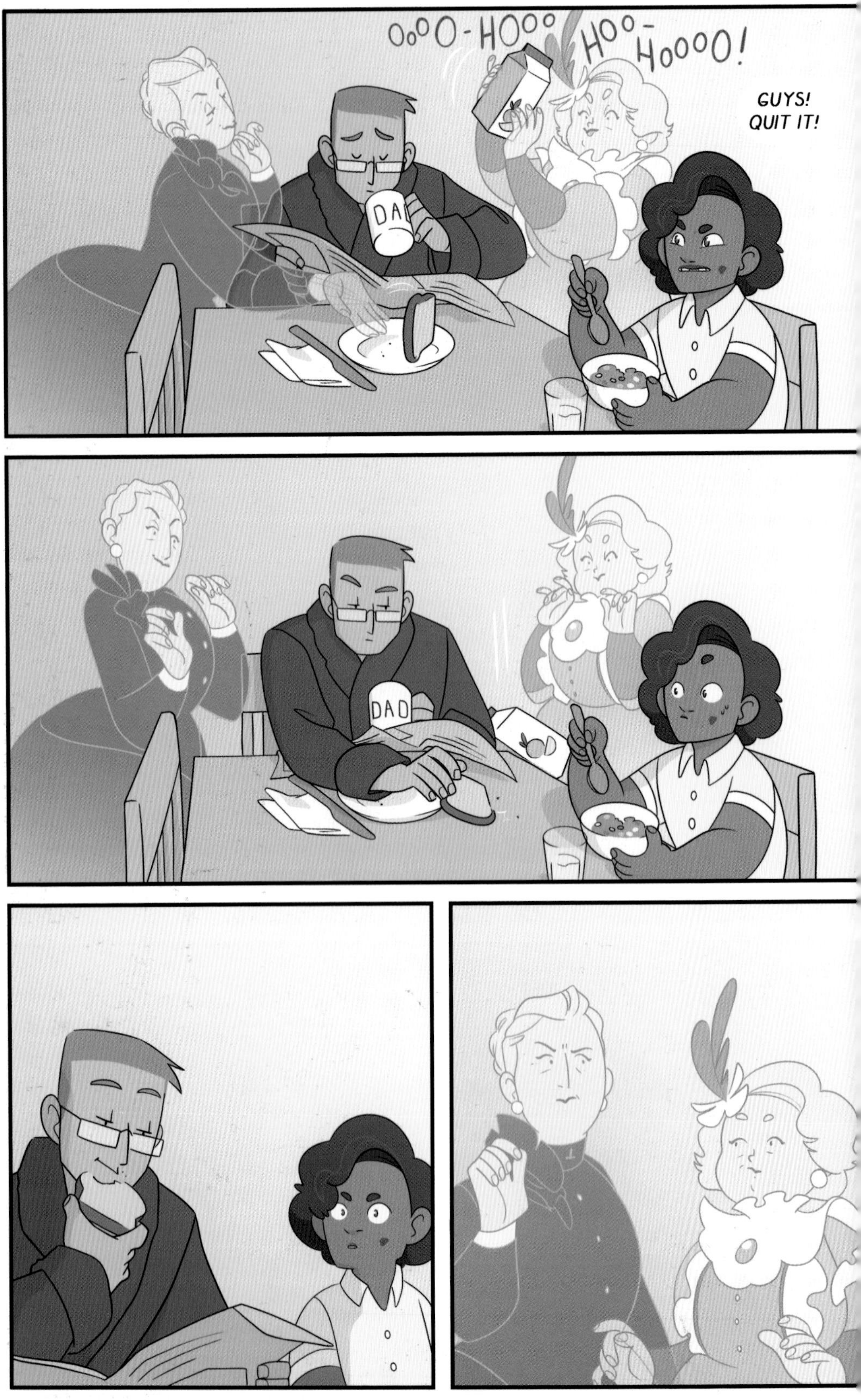
OoOO-HOOO HOO-HOOOO!
GUYS! QUIT IT!
DAD
DAD

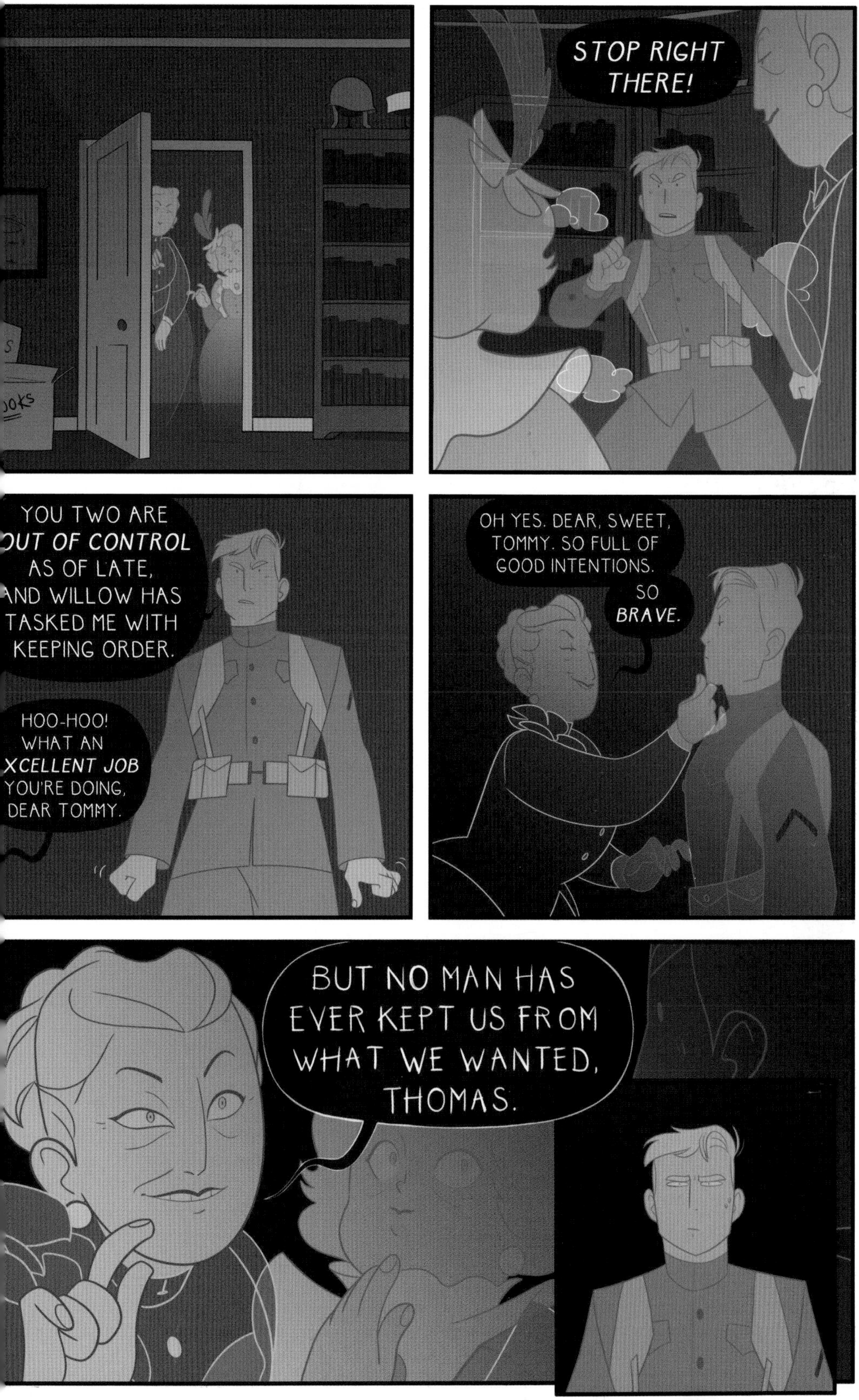

STOP RIGHT THERE!
YOU TWO ARE OUT OF CONTROL AS OF LATE, AND WILLOW HAS TASKED ME WITH KEEPING ORDER.
HOO-HOO! WHAT AN EXCELLENT JOB YOU'RE DOING, DEAR TOMMY.
OH YES. DEAR, SWEET, TOMMY. SO FULL OF GOOD INTENTIONS.
SO BRAVE.
BUT NO MAN HAS EVER KEPT US FROM WHAT WE WANTED, THOMAS.

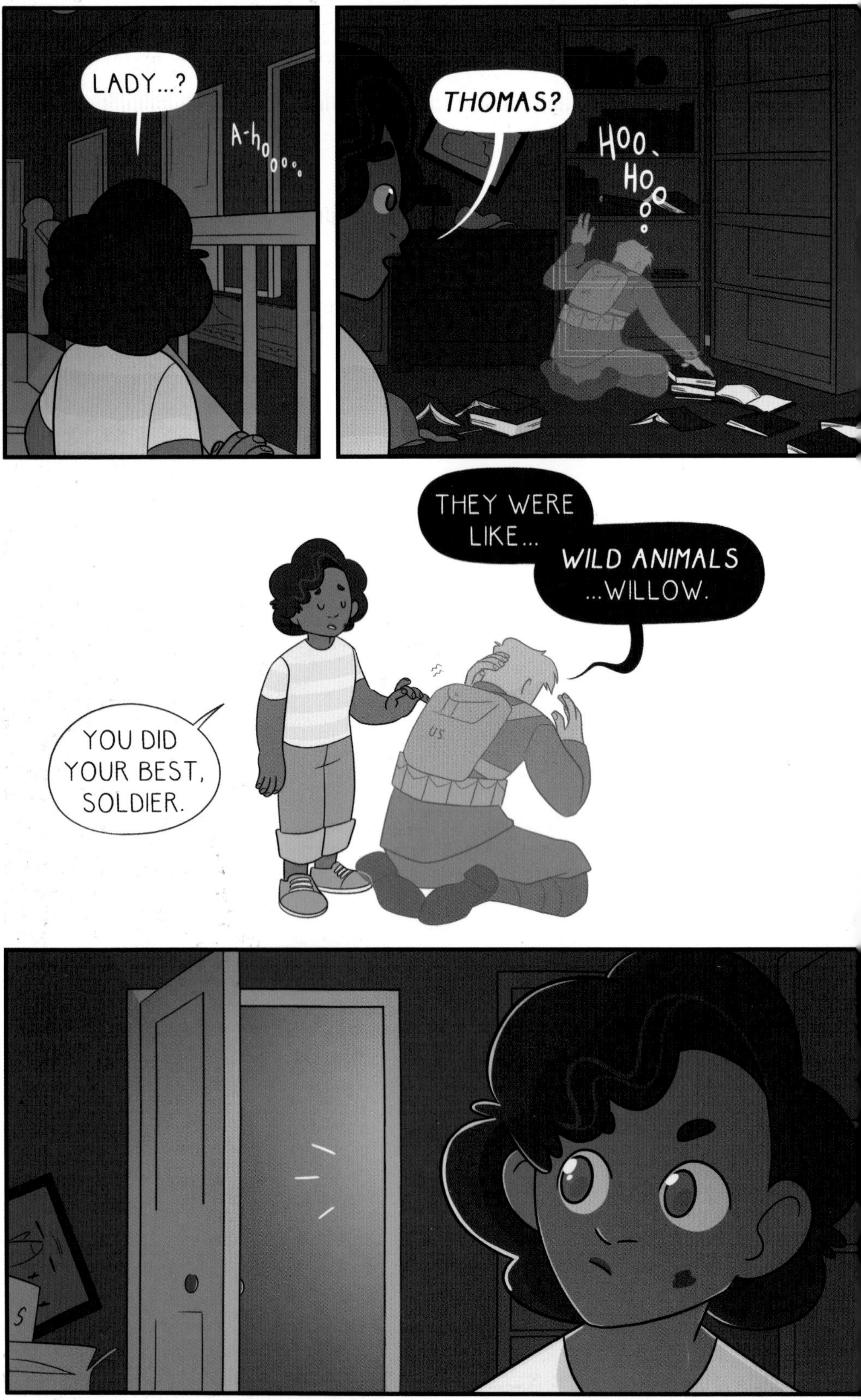
LADY...?
A-hooooo
THOMAS?
HOO HOOooo
THEY WERE LIKE...
WILD ANIMALS ...WILLOW.
YOU DID YOUR BEST, SOLDIER.
US

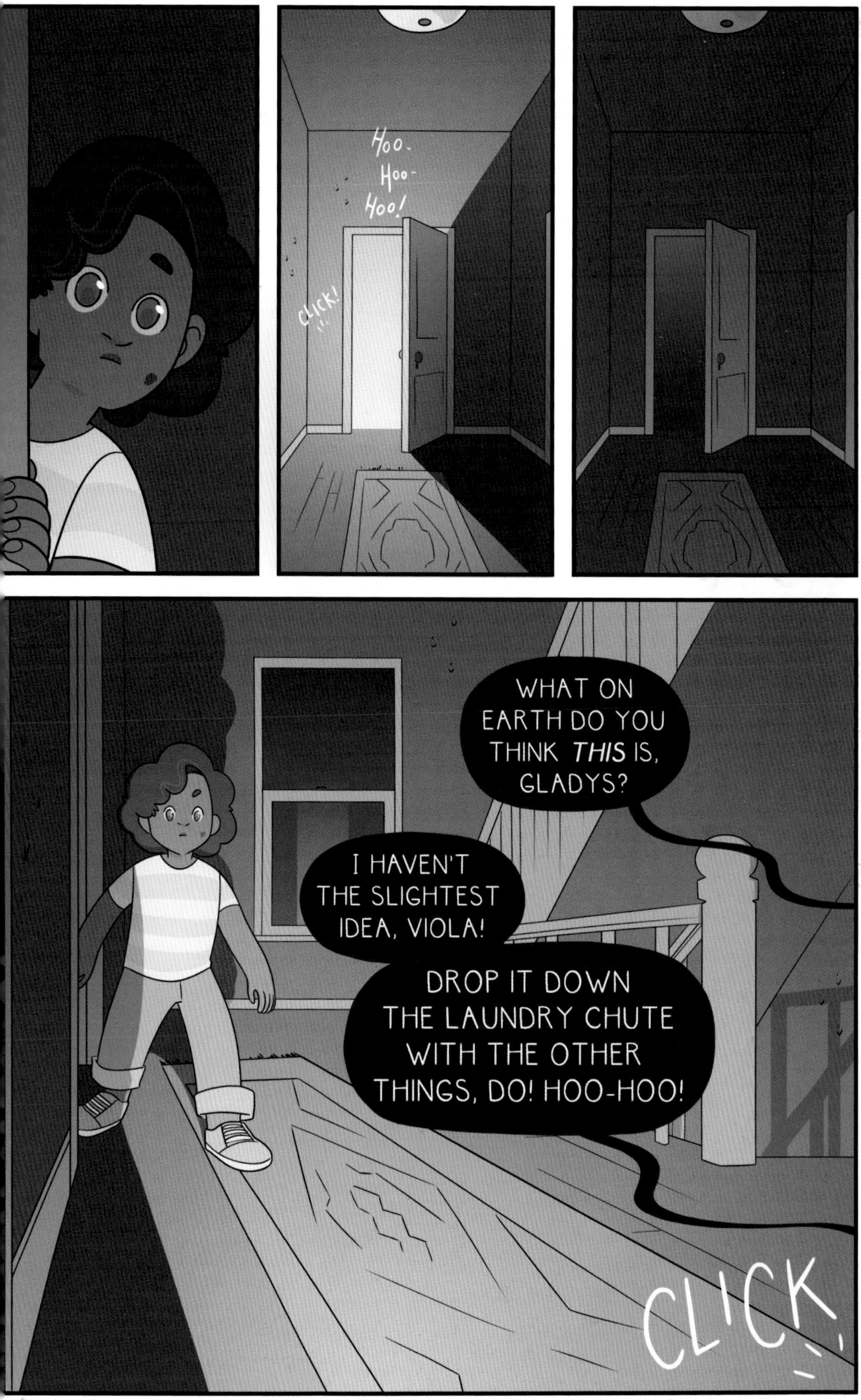
HOO-
HOO-
HOO!
CLICK!
WHAT ON EARTH DO YOU THINK *THIS* IS, GLADYS?
I HAVEN'T THE SLIGHTEST IDEA, VIOLA!
DROP IT DOWN THE LAUNDRY CHUTE WITH THE OTHER THINGS, DO! HOO-HOO!
CLICK

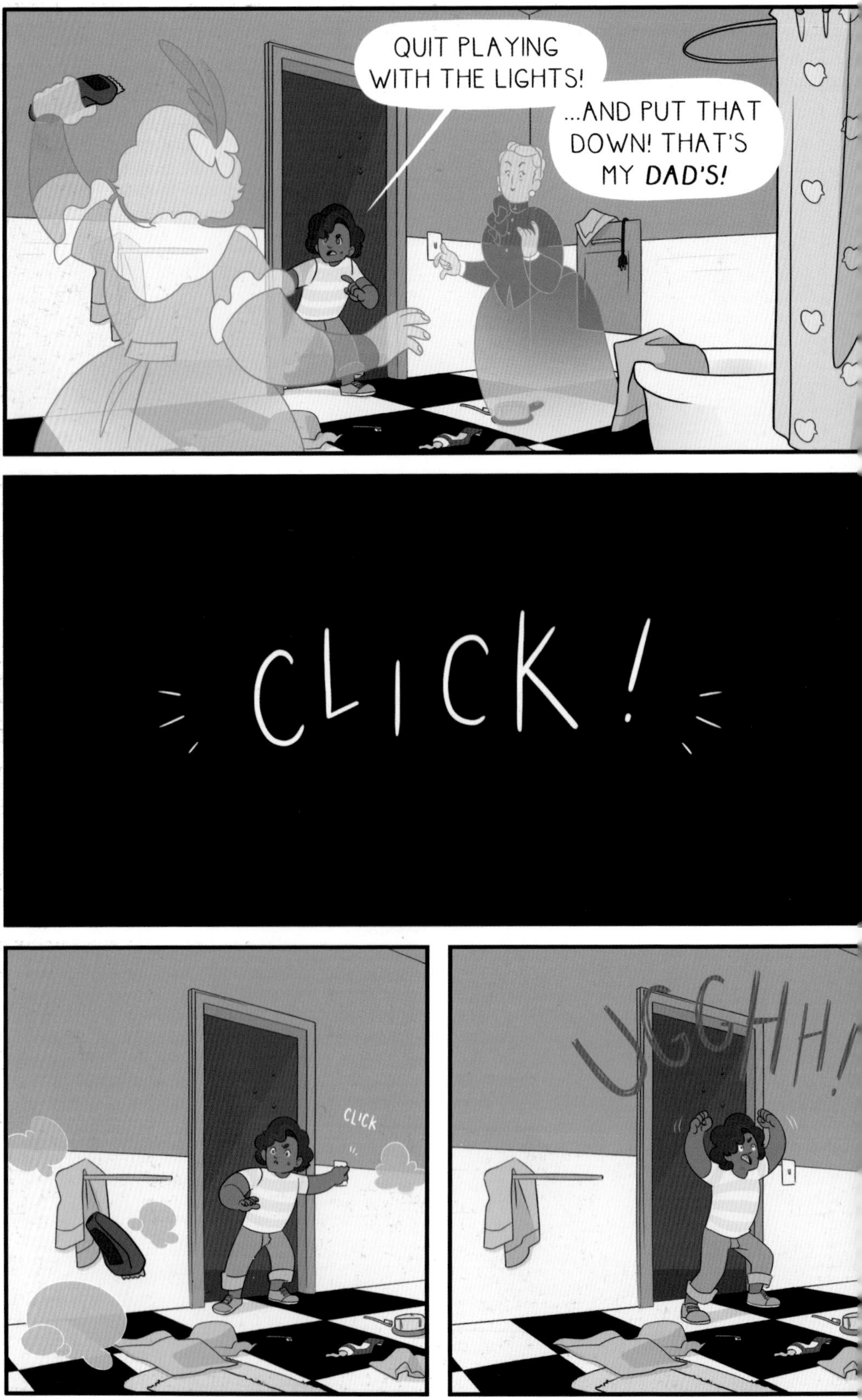
QUIT PLAYING WITH THE LIGHTS!
...AND PUT THAT DOWN! THAT'S MY **DAD'S!**
CLICK!
CLICK
UGGHH!

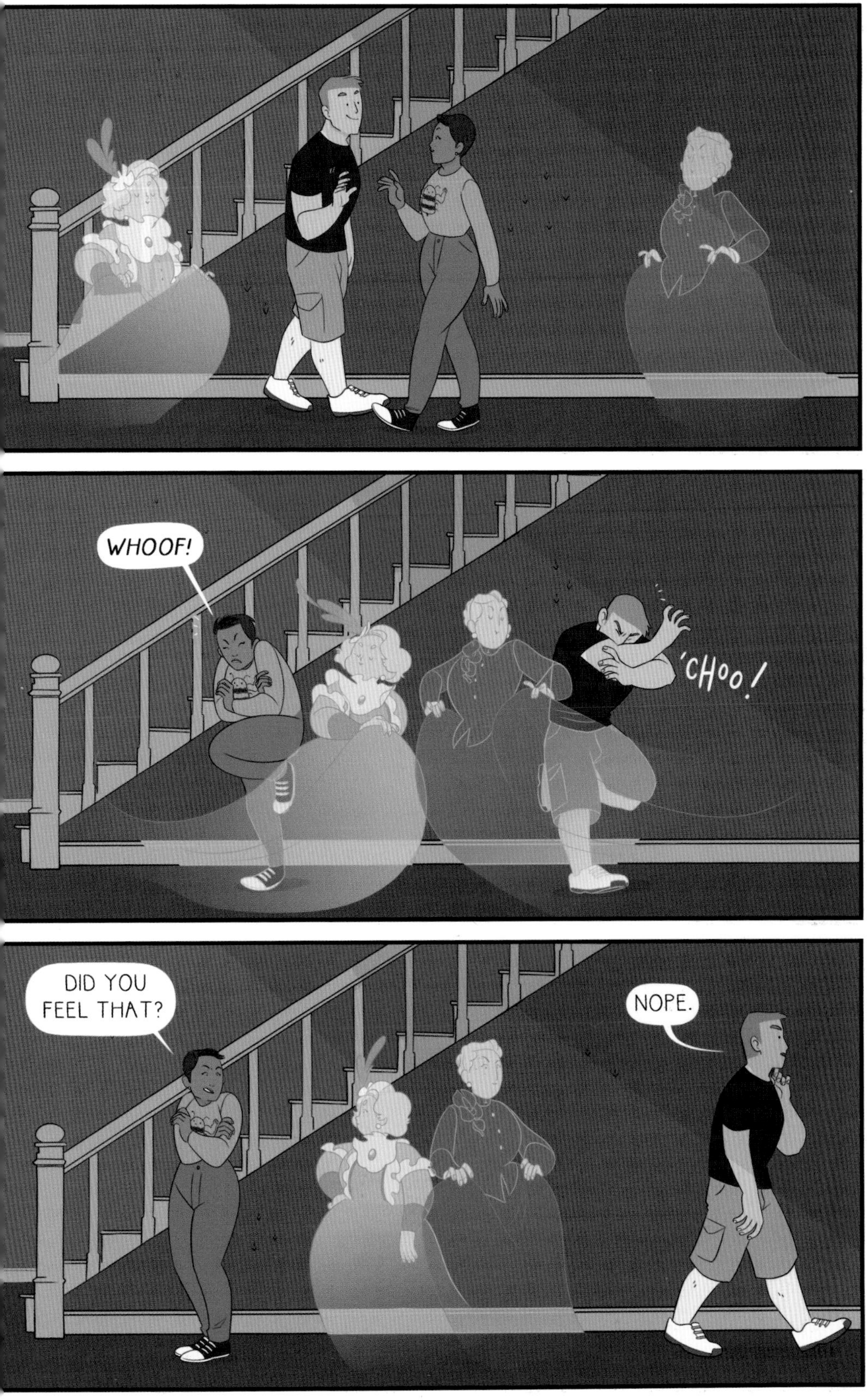
WHOOF!
'CHOO!
DID YOU FEEL THAT?
NOPE.

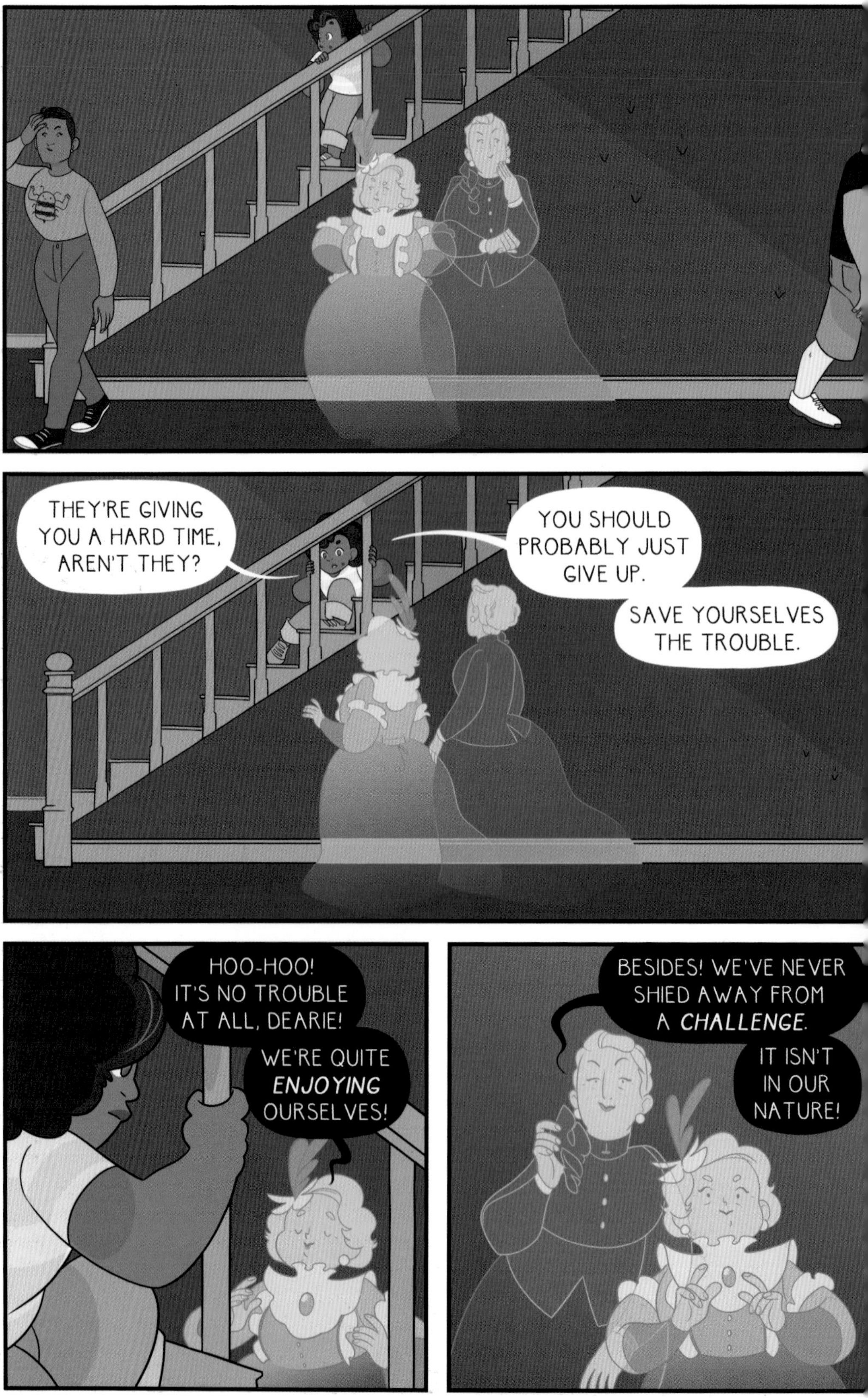
THEY'RE GIVING YOU A HARD TIME, AREN'T THEY?
YOU SHOULD PROBABLY JUST GIVE UP.
SAVE YOURSELVES THE TROUBLE.
HOO-HOO! IT'S NO TROUBLE AT ALL, DEARIE!
WE'RE QUITE *ENJOYING* OURSELVES!
BESIDES! WE'VE NEVER SHIED AWAY FROM A *CHALLENGE*.
IT ISN'T IN OUR NATURE!

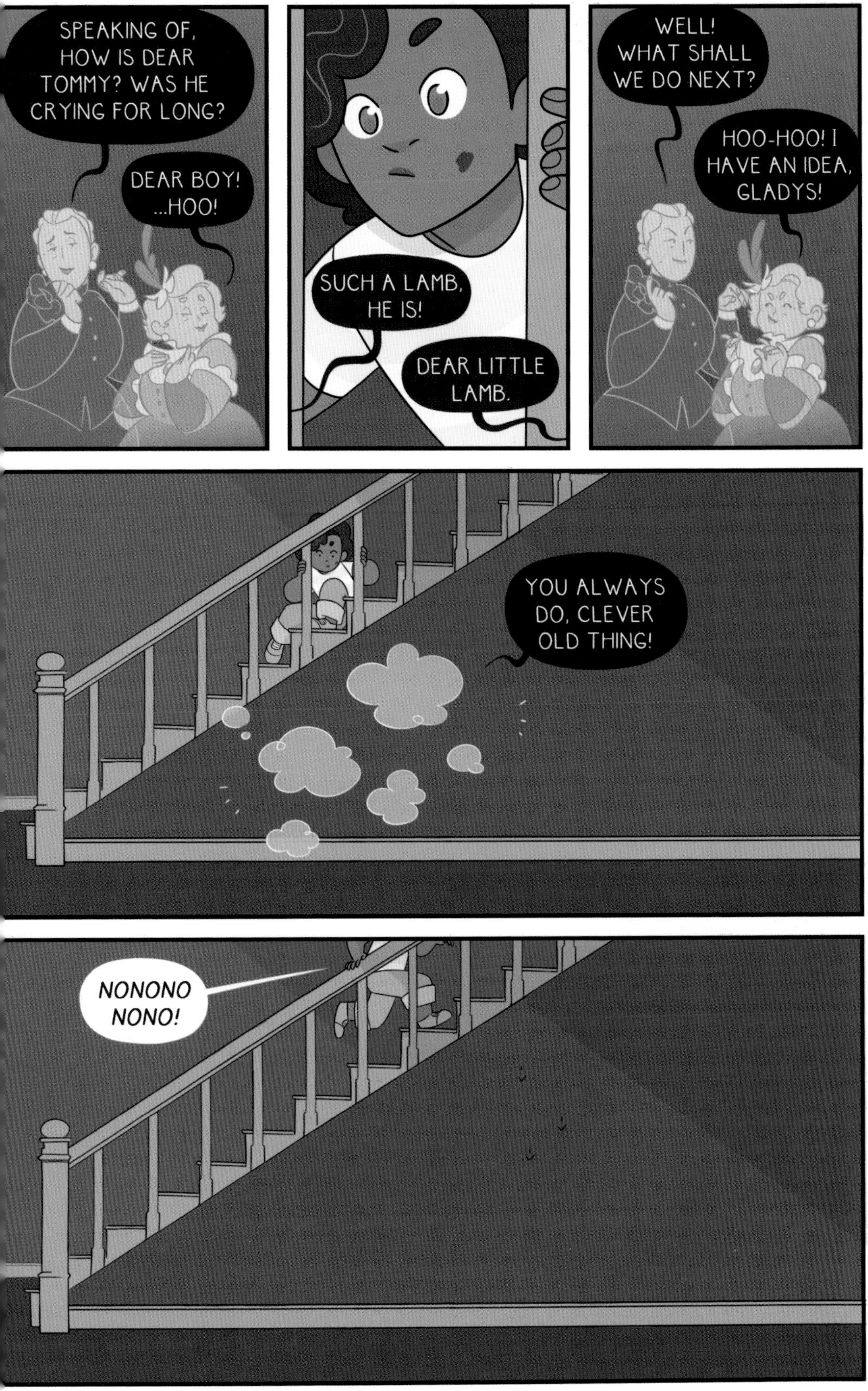
SPEAKING OF, HOW IS DEAR TOMMY? WAS HE CRYING FOR LONG?
DEAR BOY! ...HOO!
SUCH A LAMB, HE IS!
DEAR LITTLE LAMB.
WELL! WHAT SHALL WE DO NEXT?
HOO-HOO! I HAVE AN IDEA, GLADYS!
YOU ALWAYS DO, CLEVER OLD THING!
NONONO NONO!

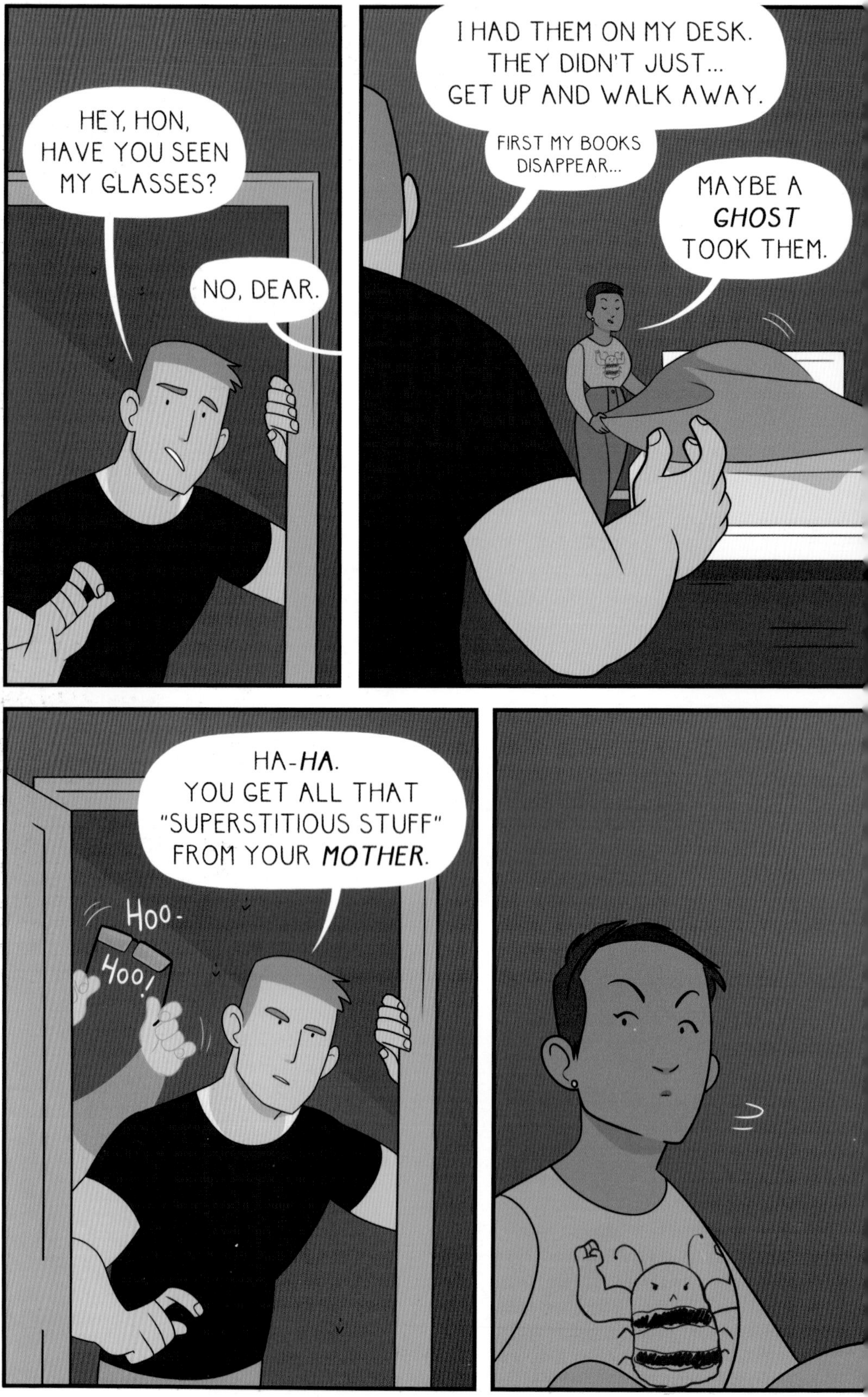
HEY, HON, HAVE YOU SEEN MY GLASSES?
NO, DEAR.
I HAD THEM ON MY DESK. THEY DIDN'T JUST... GET UP AND WALK AWAY.
FIRST MY BOOKS DISAPPEAR...
MAYBE A *GHOST* TOOK THEM.
HA-*HA*. YOU GET ALL THAT "SUPERSTITIOUS STUFF" FROM YOUR ***MOTHER***.
HOO-
HOO!

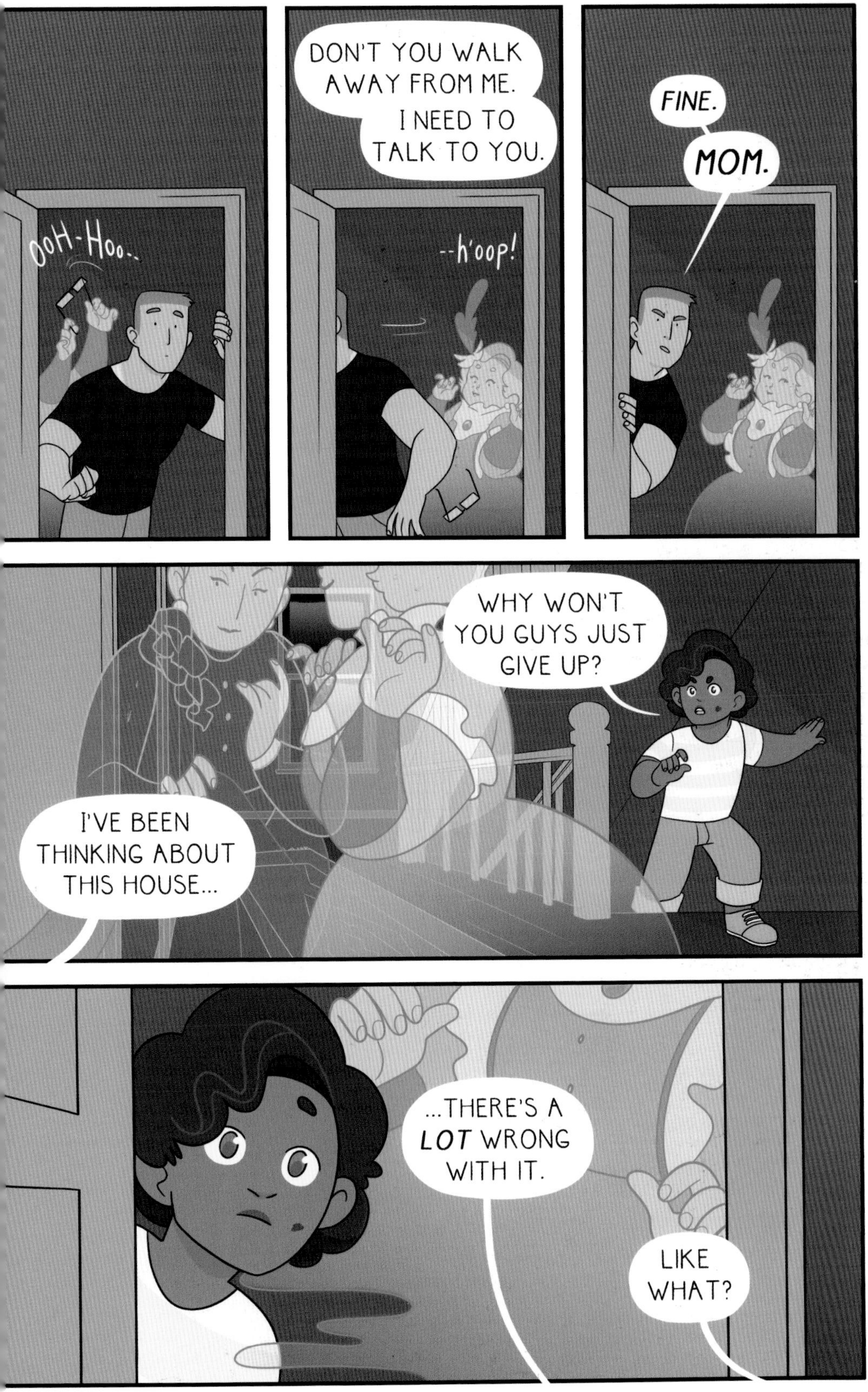
OOH-HOO...
DON'T YOU WALK AWAY FROM ME.
I NEED TO TALK TO YOU.
--h'oop!
FINE.
MOM.
WHY WON'T YOU GUYS JUST GIVE UP?
I'VE BEEN THINKING ABOUT THIS HOUSE...
...THERE'S A LOT WRONG WITH IT.
LIKE WHAT?

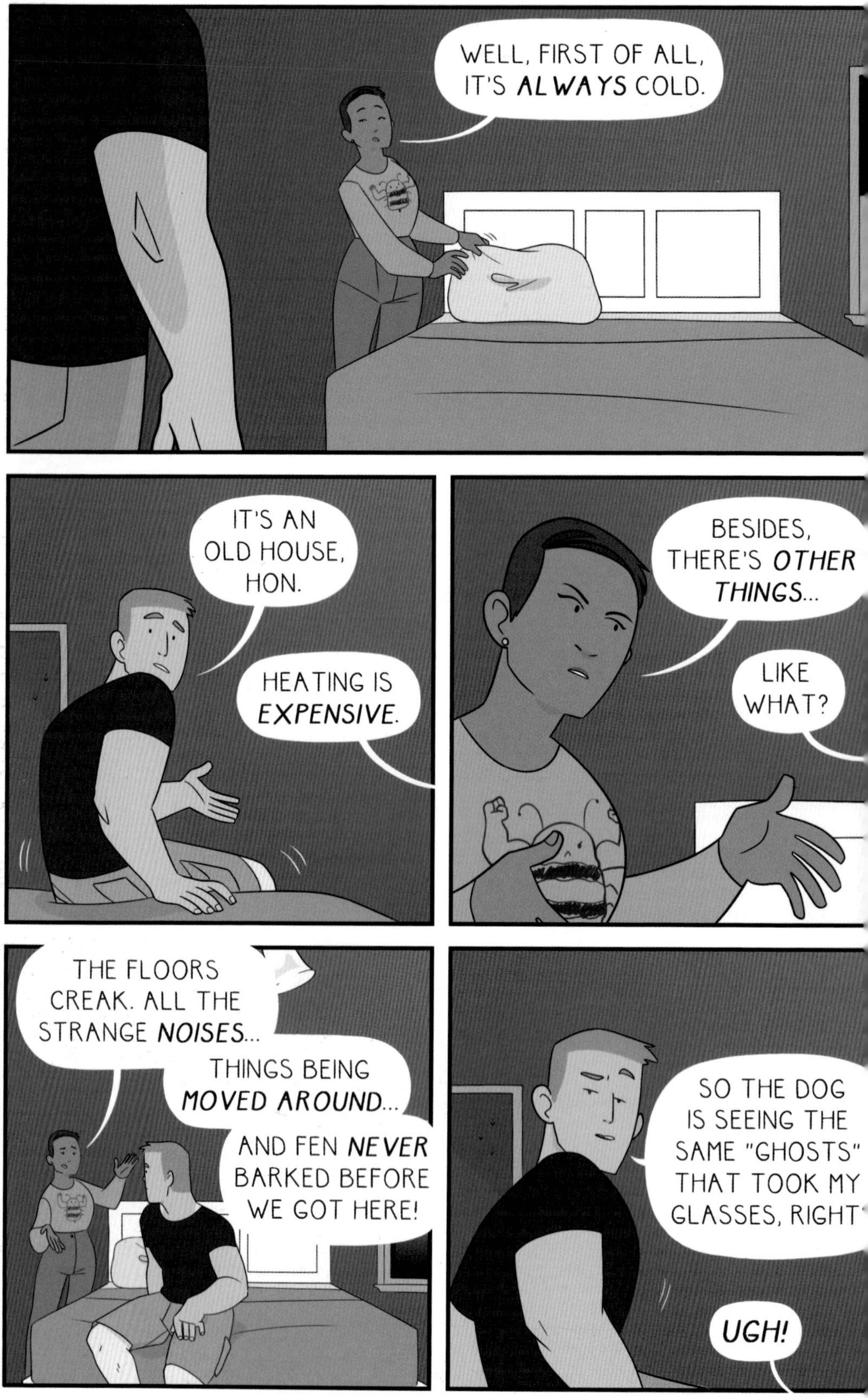
WELL, FIRST OF ALL, IT'S ALWAYS COLD.
IT'S AN OLD HOUSE, HON.
HEATING IS EXPENSIVE.
BESIDES, THERE'S OTHER THINGS...
LIKE WHAT?
THE FLOORS CREAK. ALL THE STRANGE NOISES...
THINGS BEING MOVED AROUND...
AND FEN NEVER BARKED BEFORE WE GOT HERE!
SO THE DOG IS SEEING THE SAME "GHOSTS" THAT TOOK MY GLASSES, RIGHT
UGH!

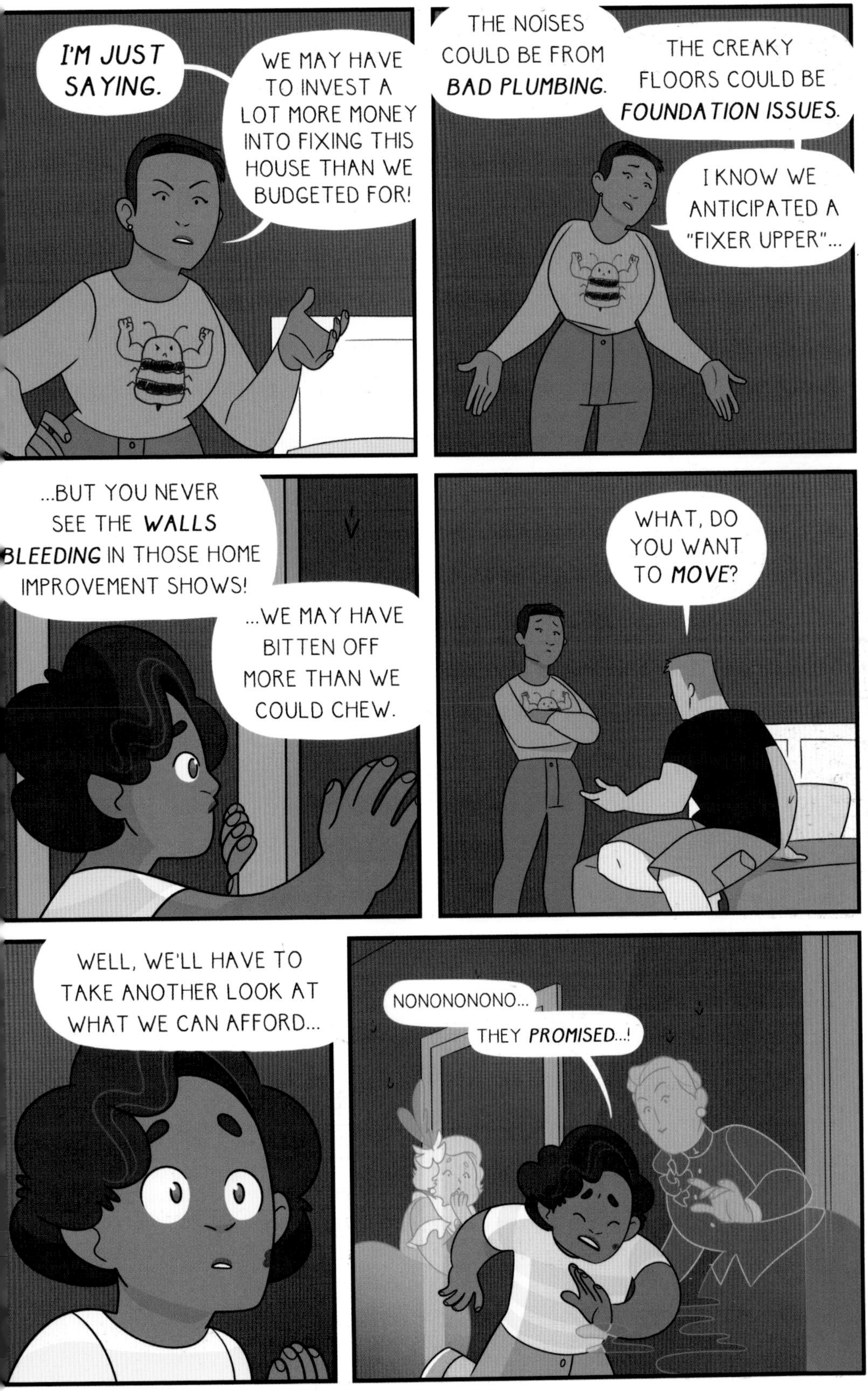
I'M JUST SAYING.
WE MAY HAVE TO INVEST A LOT MORE MONEY INTO FIXING THIS HOUSE THAN WE BUDGETED FOR!
THE NOISES COULD BE FROM BAD PLUMBING.
THE CREAKY FLOORS COULD BE FOUNDATION ISSUES.
I KNOW WE ANTICIPATED A "FIXER UPPER"...
...BUT YOU NEVER SEE THE WALLS BLEEDING IN THOSE HOME IMPROVEMENT SHOWS!
...WE MAY HAVE BITTEN OFF MORE THAN WE COULD CHEW.
WHAT, DO YOU WANT TO MOVE?
WELL, WE'LL HAVE TO TAKE ANOTHER LOOK AT WHAT WE CAN AFFORD...
NONONONONO...
THEY PROMISED...!

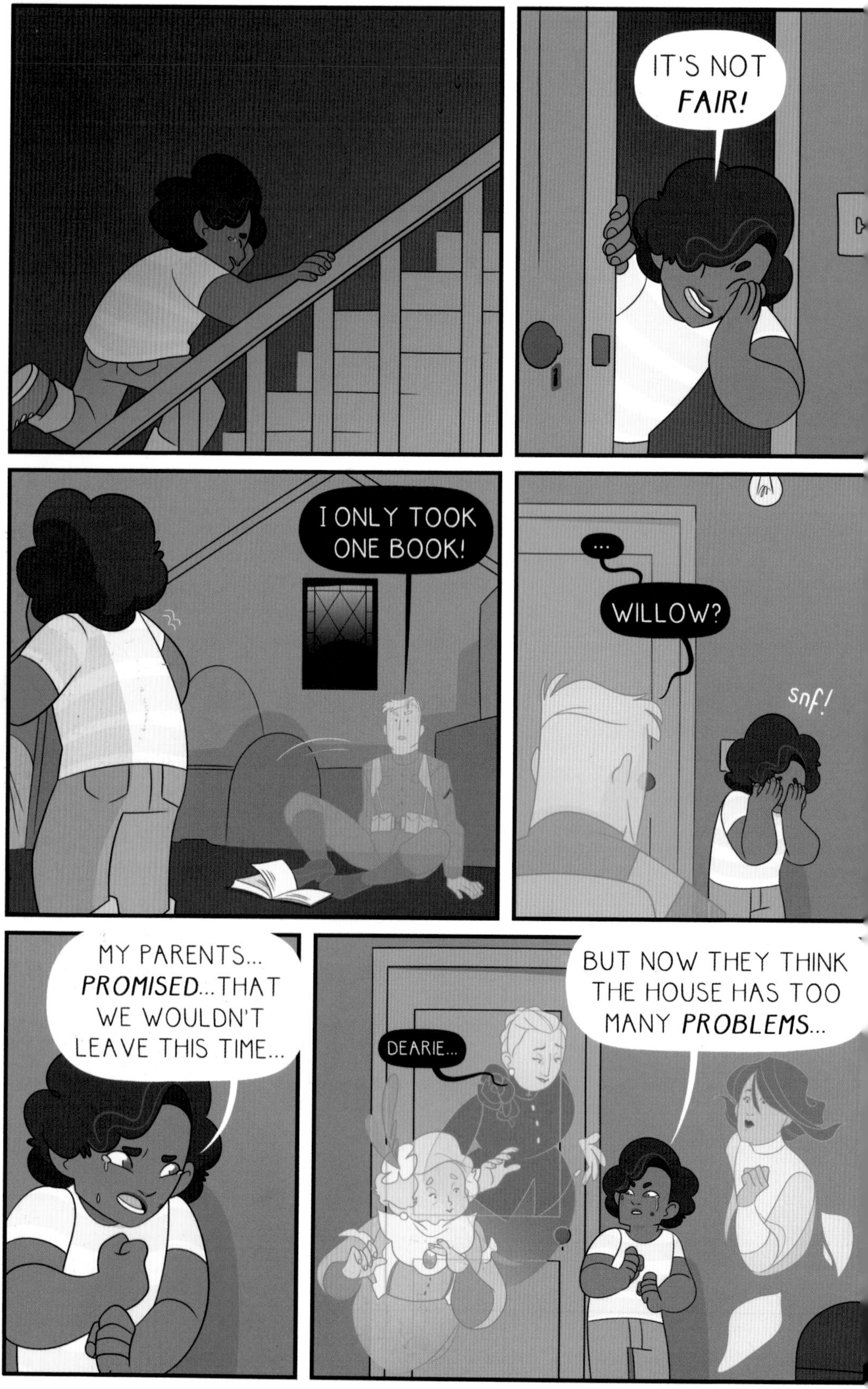
IT'S NOT *FAIR!*
I ONLY TOOK ONE BOOK!
...
WILLOW?
snf!
MY PARENTS... *PROMISED*... THAT WE WOULDN'T LEAVE THIS TIME...
DEARIE...
BUT NOW THEY THINK THE HOUSE HAS TOO MANY *PROBLEMS*...

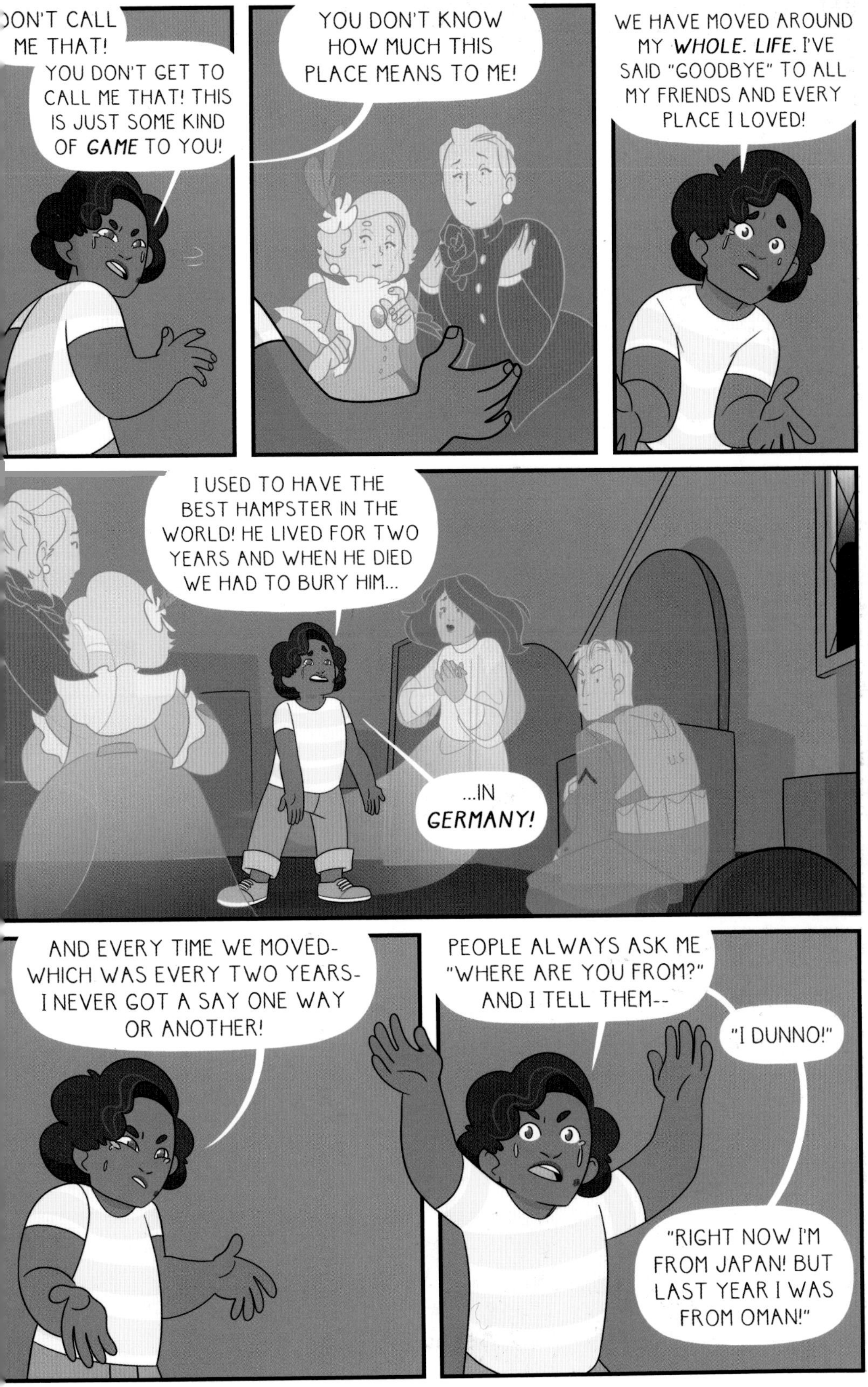

DON'T CALL ME THAT!
YOU DON'T GET TO CALL ME THAT! THIS IS JUST SOME KIND OF *GAME* TO YOU!
YOU DON'T KNOW HOW MUCH THIS PLACE MEANS TO ME!
WE HAVE MOVED AROUND MY *WHOLE. LIFE.* I'VE SAID "GOODBYE" TO ALL MY FRIENDS AND EVERY PLACE I LOVED!
I USED TO HAVE THE BEST HAMPSTER IN THE WORLD! HE LIVED FOR TWO YEARS AND WHEN HE DIED WE HAD TO BURY HIM...
...IN *GERMANY!*
U.S.
AND EVERY TIME WE MOVED- WHICH WAS EVERY TWO YEARS- I NEVER GOT A SAY ONE WAY OR ANOTHER!
PEOPLE ALWAYS ASK ME "WHERE ARE YOU FROM?" AND I TELL THEM--
"I DUNNO!"
"RIGHT NOW I'M FROM JAPAN! BUT LAST YEAR I WAS FROM OMAN!"

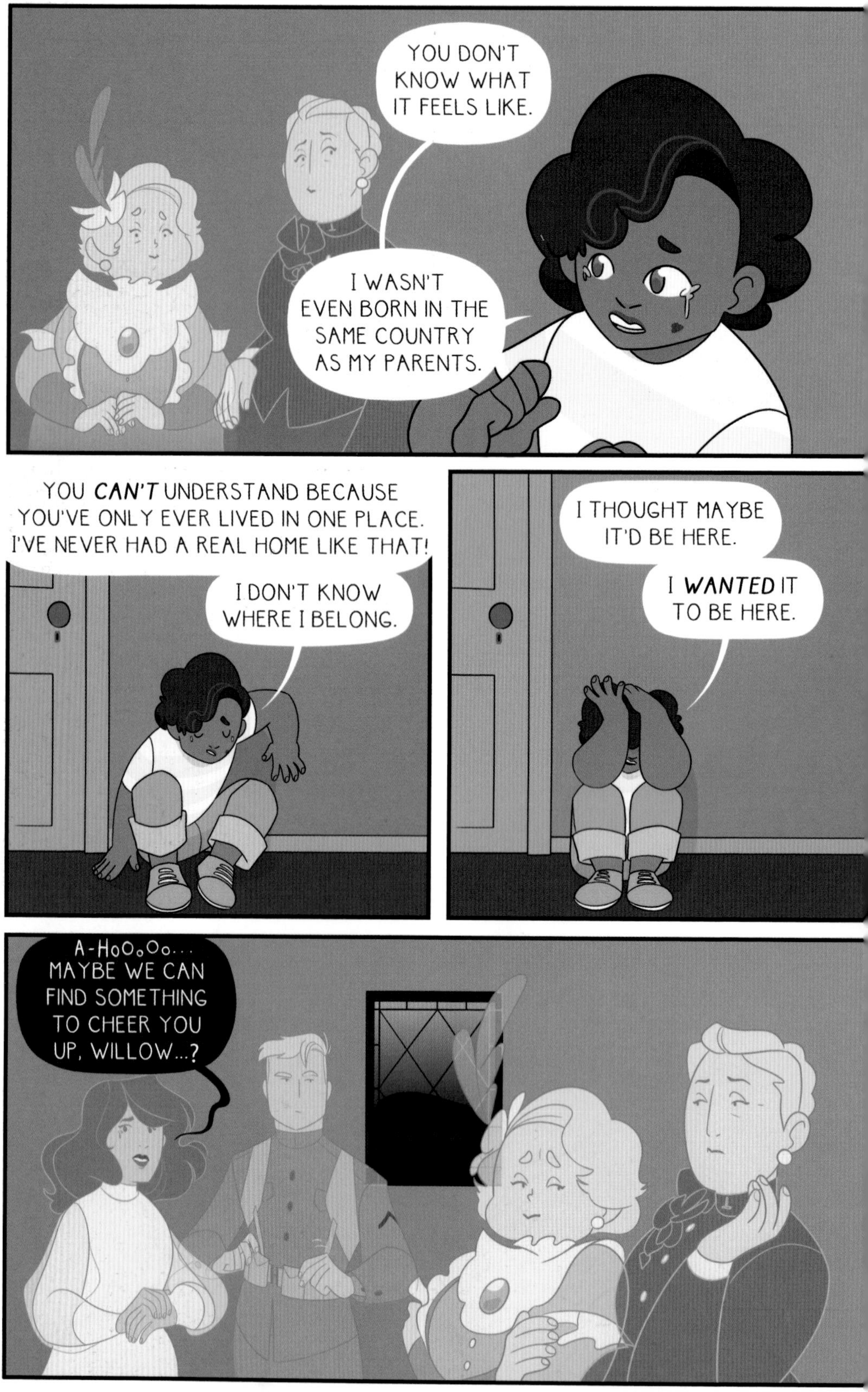

YOU DON'T KNOW WHAT IT FEELS LIKE.
I WASN'T EVEN BORN IN THE SAME COUNTRY AS MY PARENTS.
YOU **CAN'T** UNDERSTAND BECAUSE YOU'VE ONLY EVER LIVED IN ONE PLACE. I'VE NEVER HAD A REAL HOME LIKE THAT!
I DON'T KNOW WHERE I BELONG.
I THOUGHT MAYBE IT'D BE HERE.
I **WANTED** IT TO BE HERE.
A-HoOoOo... MAYBE WE CAN FIND SOMETHING TO CHEER YOU UP, WILLOW...?

fwpp!
OOOOH...DEAD GOLDFISH...
HOW NICE...
Shff
shff
H'OOOOH... MY THIRD HUSBAND GAVE THESE TO ME FOR OUR WEDDING...
WHAT HAPPENED TO ALL OF YOUR "HUSBANDS" AND "FIANCÉS," LADY?
HOO-HOO!
DID YOU KILL THEM?

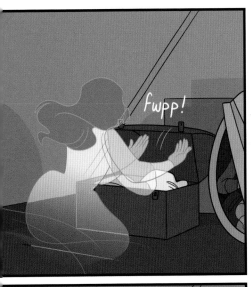

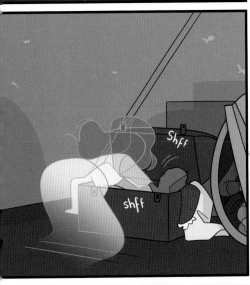

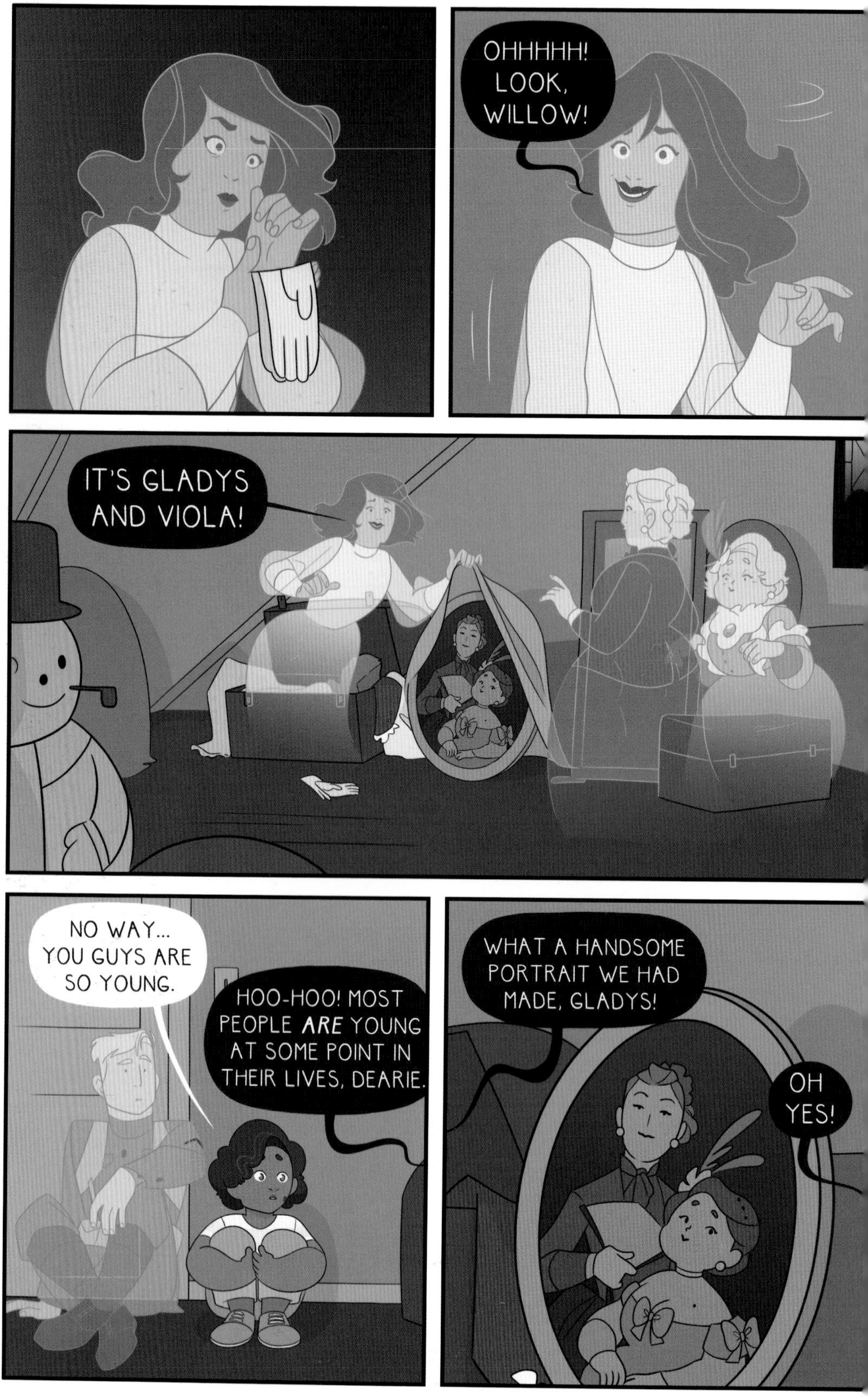
OHHHHH! LOOK, WILLOW!
IT'S GLADYS AND VIOLA!
NO WAY... YOU GUYS ARE SO YOUNG.
HOO-HOO! MOST PEOPLE *ARE* YOUNG AT SOME POINT IN THEIR LIVES, DEARIE.
WHAT A HANDSOME PORTRAIT WE HAD MADE, GLADYS!
OH YES!

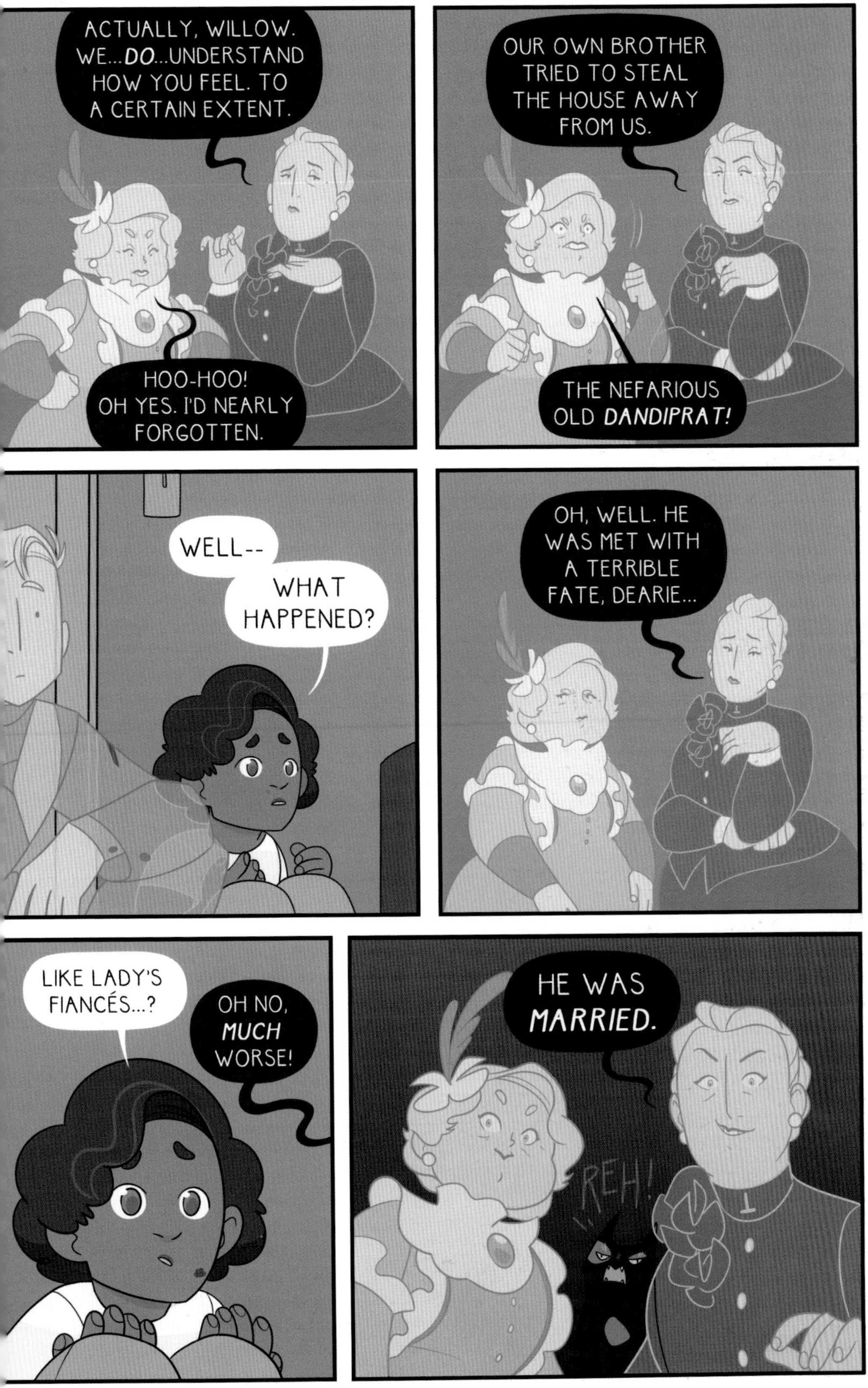
ACTUALLY, WILLOW. WE...DO...UNDERSTAND HOW YOU FEEL. TO A CERTAIN EXTENT.
HOO-HOO! OH YES. I'D NEARLY FORGOTTEN.
OUR OWN BROTHER TRIED TO STEAL THE HOUSE AWAY FROM US.
THE NEFARIOUS OLD DANDIPRAT!
WELL--
WHAT HAPPENED?
OH, WELL. HE WAS MET WITH A TERRIBLE FATE, DEARIE...
LIKE LADY'S FIANCÉS...?
OH NO, MUCH WORSE!
HE WAS MARRIED.
REH!

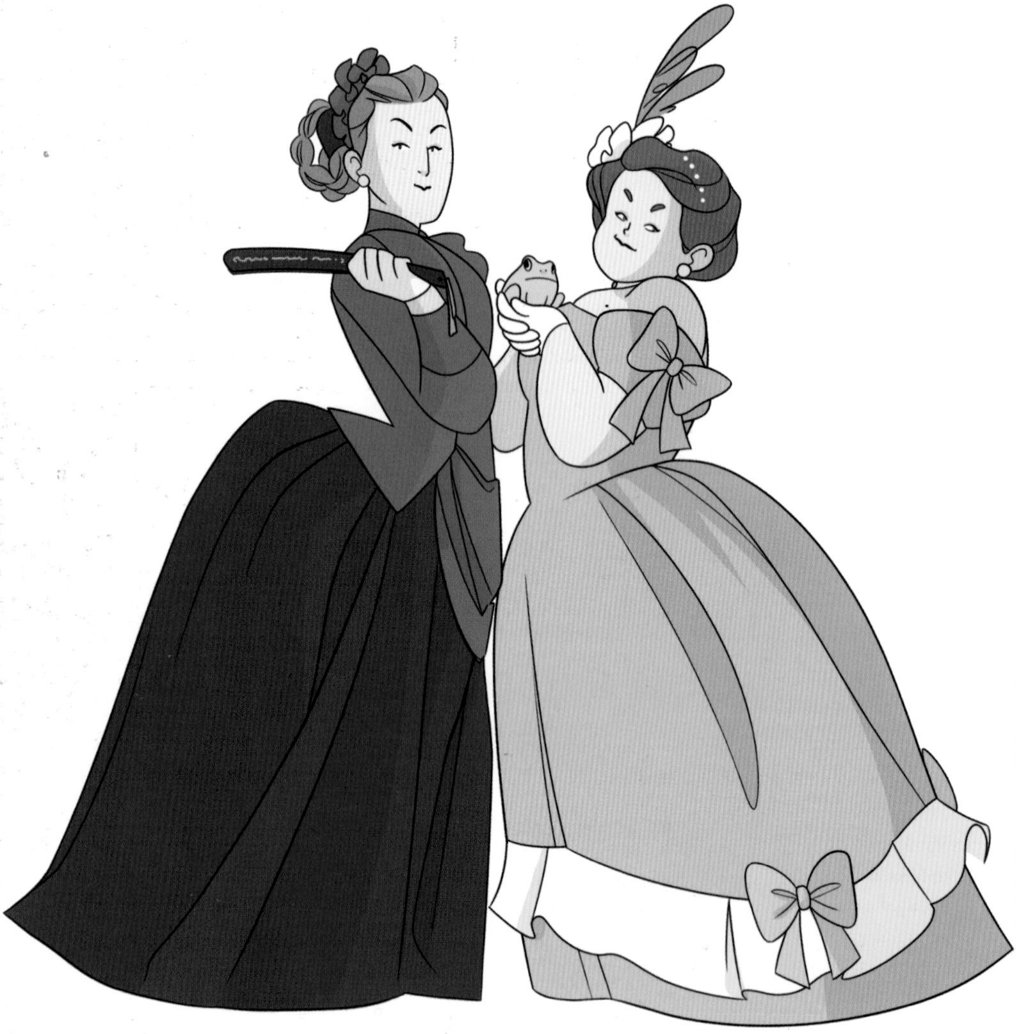

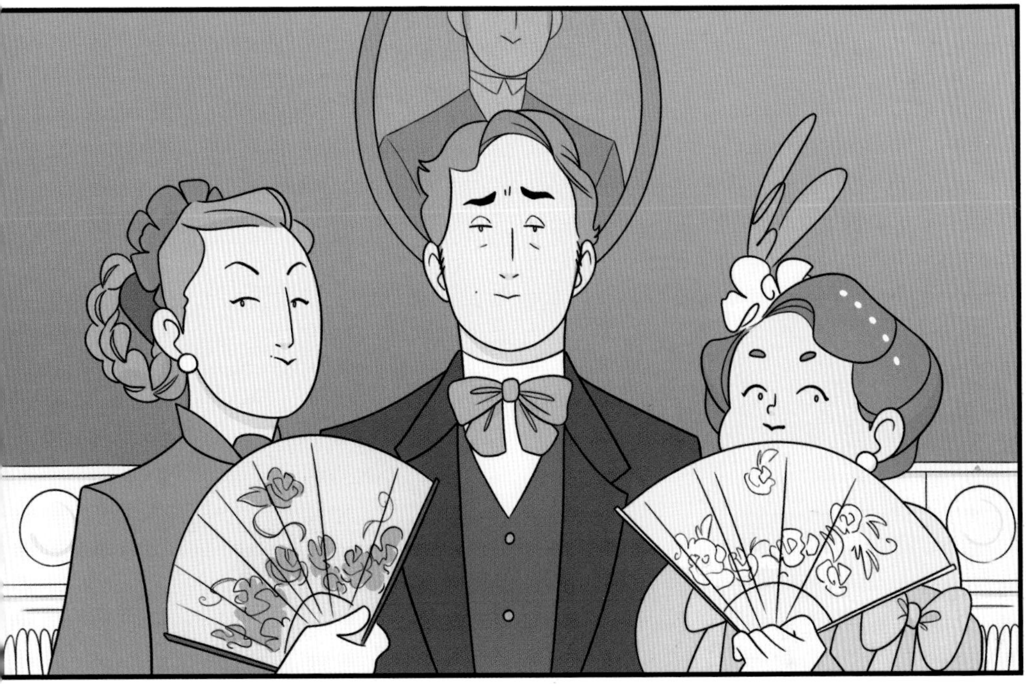

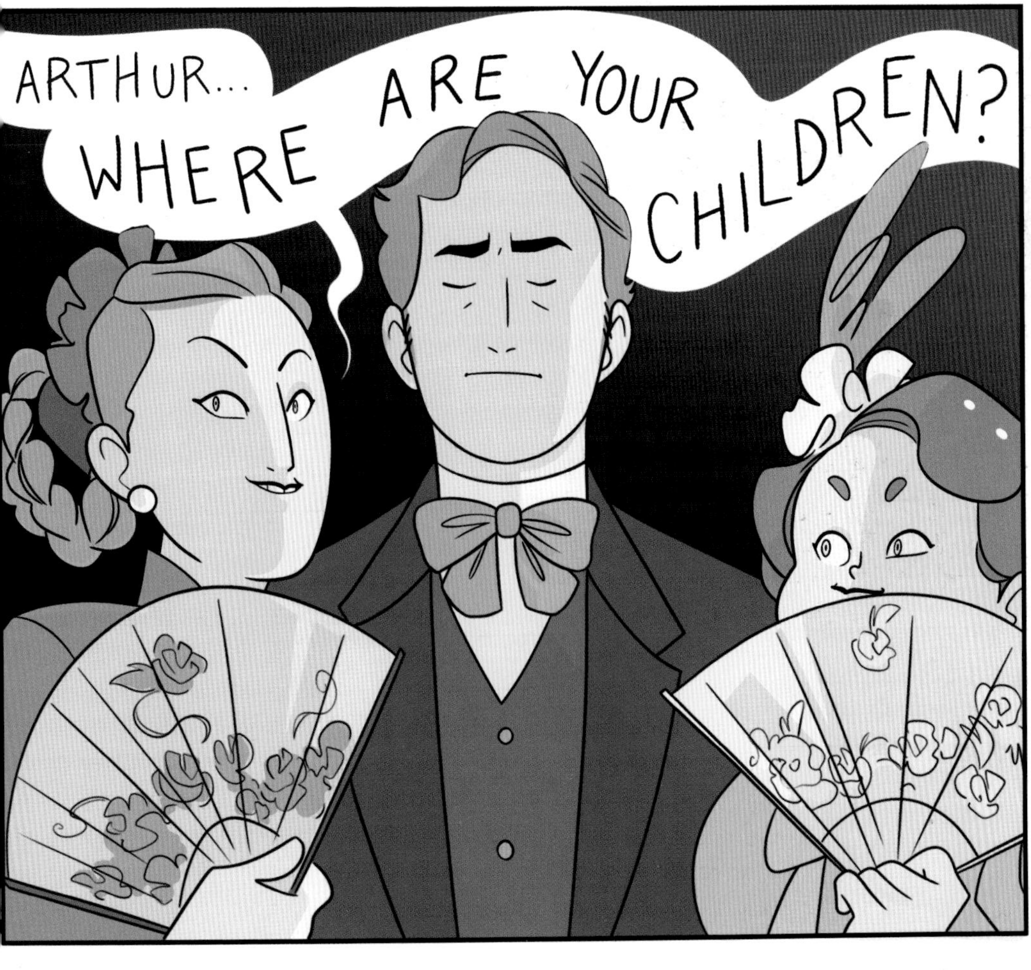
ARTHUR...
WHERE ARE YOUR CHILDREN?

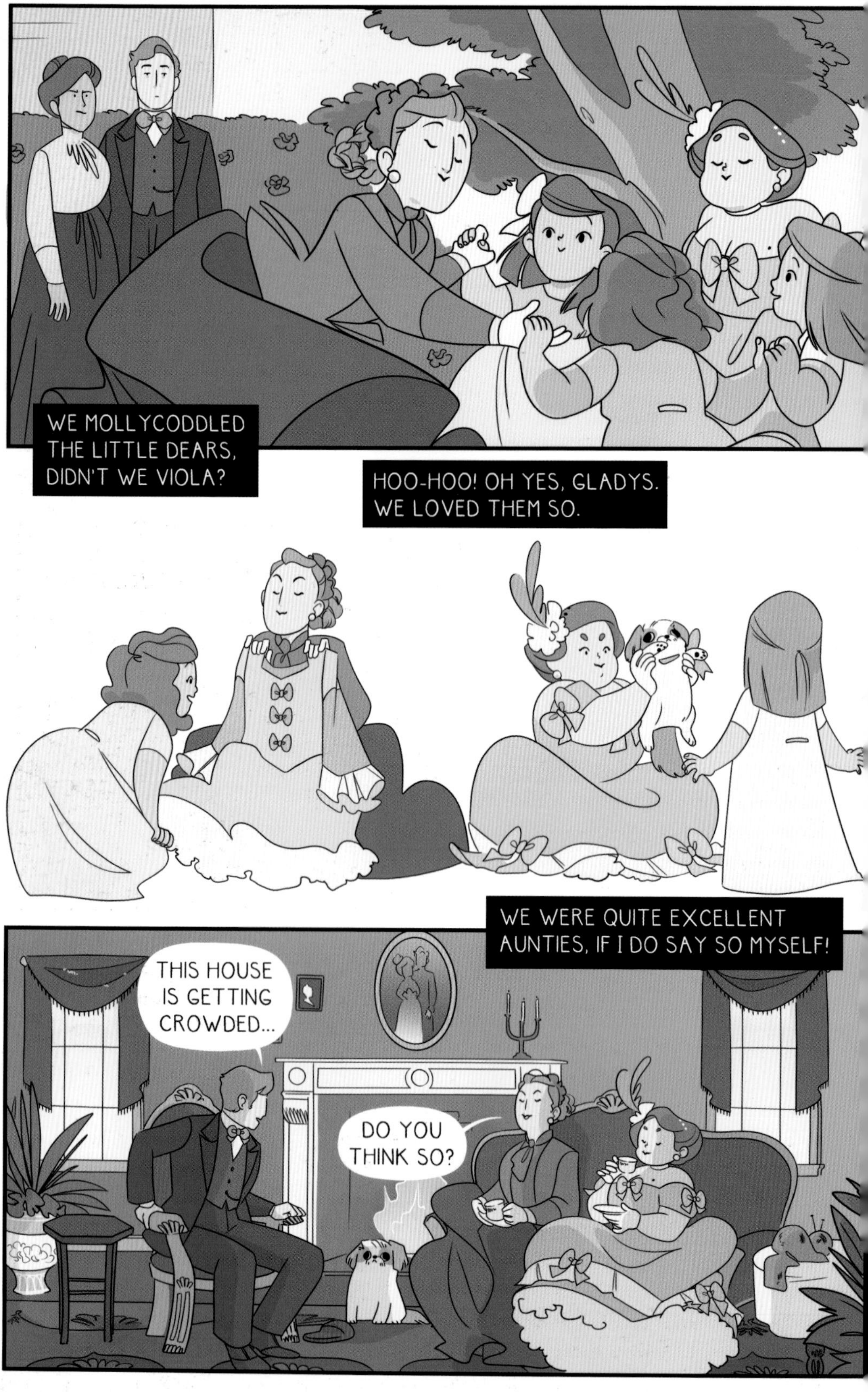

WE MOLLYCODDLED THE LITTLE DEARS, DIDN'T WE VIOLA?
HOO-HOO! OH YES, GLADYS. WE LOVED THEM SO.
WE WERE QUITE EXCELLENT AUNTIES, IF I DO SAY SO MYSELF!
THIS HOUSE IS GETTING CROWDED...
DO YOU THINK SO?

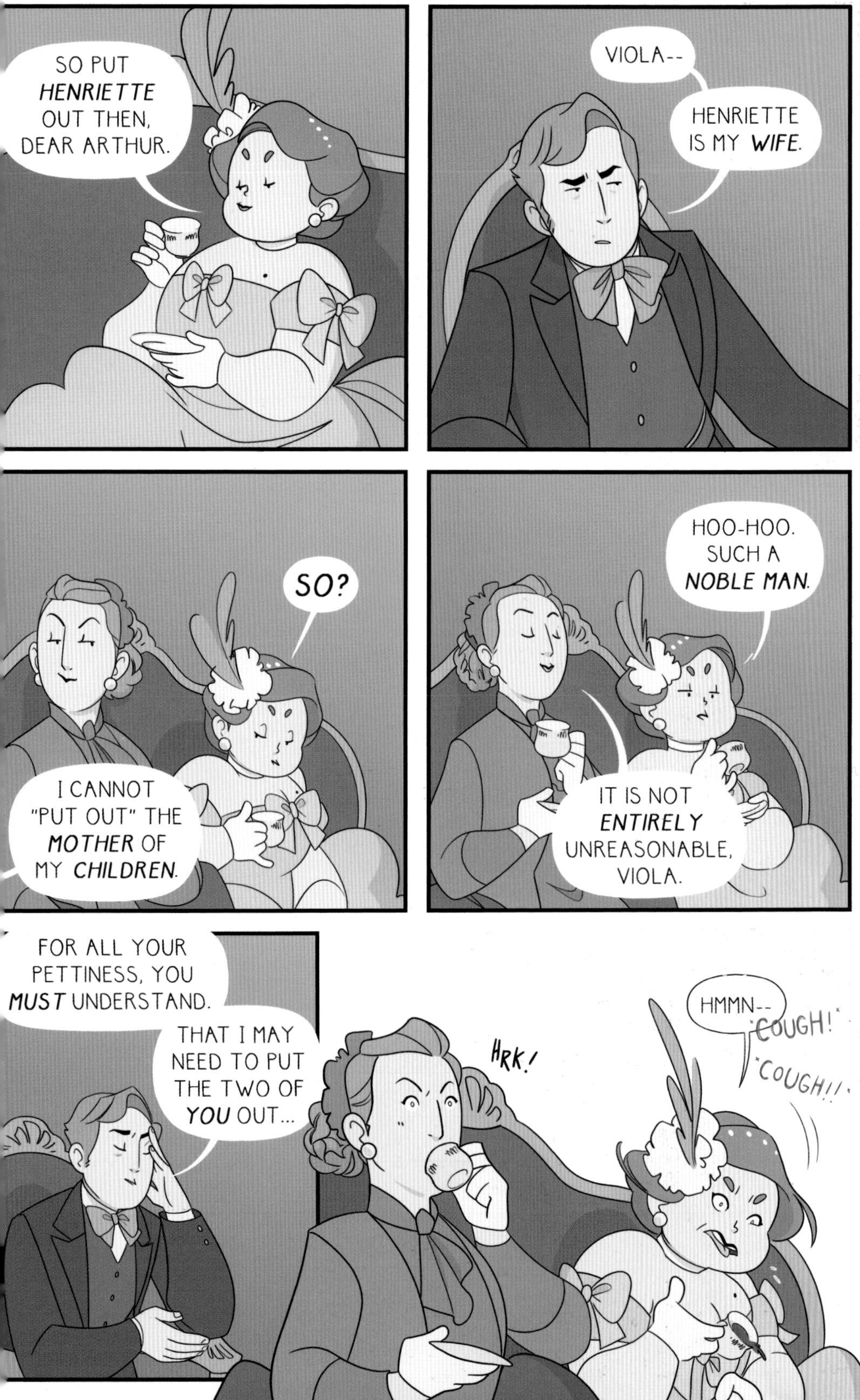
SO PUT HENRIETTE OUT THEN, DEAR ARTHUR.
VIOLA--
HENRIETTE IS MY WIFE.
SO?
I CANNOT "PUT OUT" THE MOTHER OF MY CHILDREN.
HOO-HOO. SUCH A NOBLE MAN.
IT IS NOT ENTIRELY UNREASONABLE, VIOLA.
FOR ALL YOUR PETTINESS, YOU MUST UNDERSTAND.
THAT I MAY NEED TO PUT THE TWO OF YOU OUT...
HRK!
HMMN--
COUGH!
COUGH!!

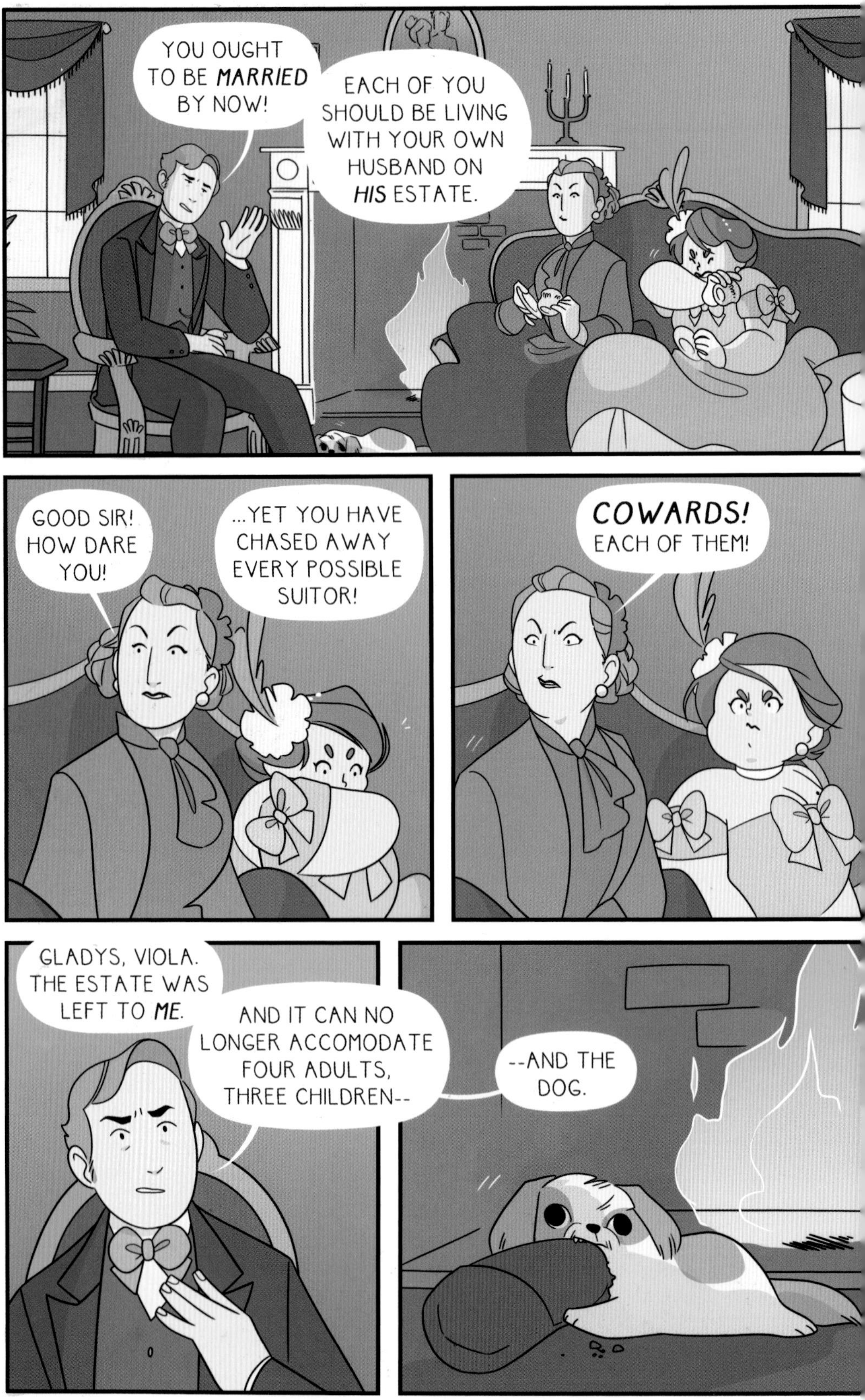
YOU OUGHT TO BE MARRIED BY NOW!
EACH OF YOU SHOULD BE LIVING WITH YOUR OWN HUSBAND ON HIS ESTATE.
GOOD SIR! HOW DARE YOU!
...YET YOU HAVE CHASED AWAY EVERY POSSIBLE SUITOR!
COWARDS! EACH OF THEM!
GLADYS, VIOLA. THE ESTATE WAS LEFT TO ME.
AND IT CAN NO LONGER ACCOMODATE FOUR ADULTS, THREE CHILDREN--
--AND THE DOG.

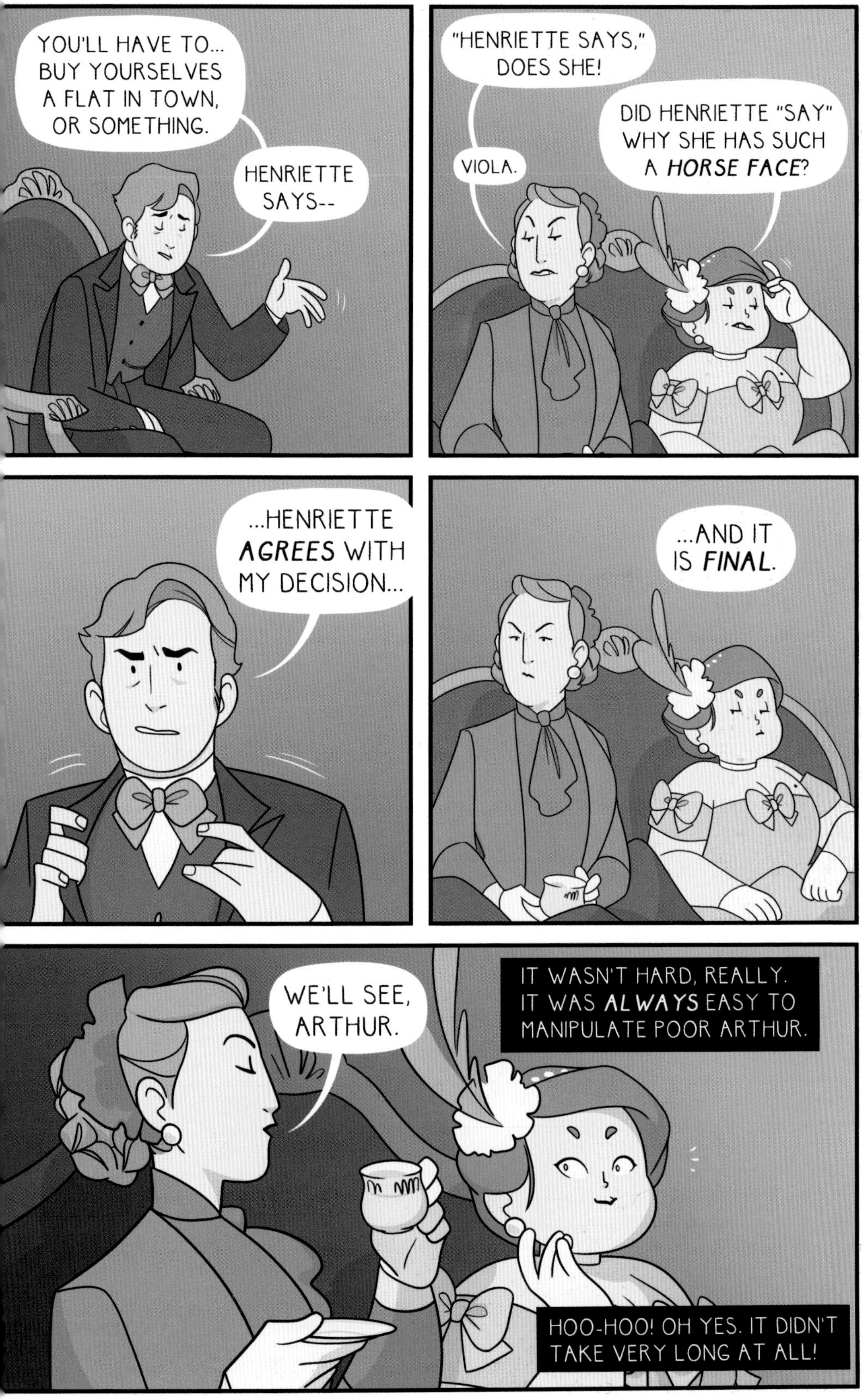
YOU'LL HAVE TO... BUY YOURSELVES A FLAT IN TOWN, OR SOMETHING.
HENRIETTE SAYS--
"HENRIETTE SAYS," DOES SHE!
VIOLA.
DID HENRIETTE "SAY" WHY SHE HAS SUCH A HORSE FACE?
...HENRIETTE AGREES WITH MY DECISION...
...AND IT IS FINAL.
WE'LL SEE, ARTHUR.
IT WASN'T HARD, REALLY. IT WAS ALWAYS EASY TO MANIPULATE POOR ARTHUR.
HOO-HOO! OH YES. IT DIDN'T TAKE VERY LONG AT ALL!

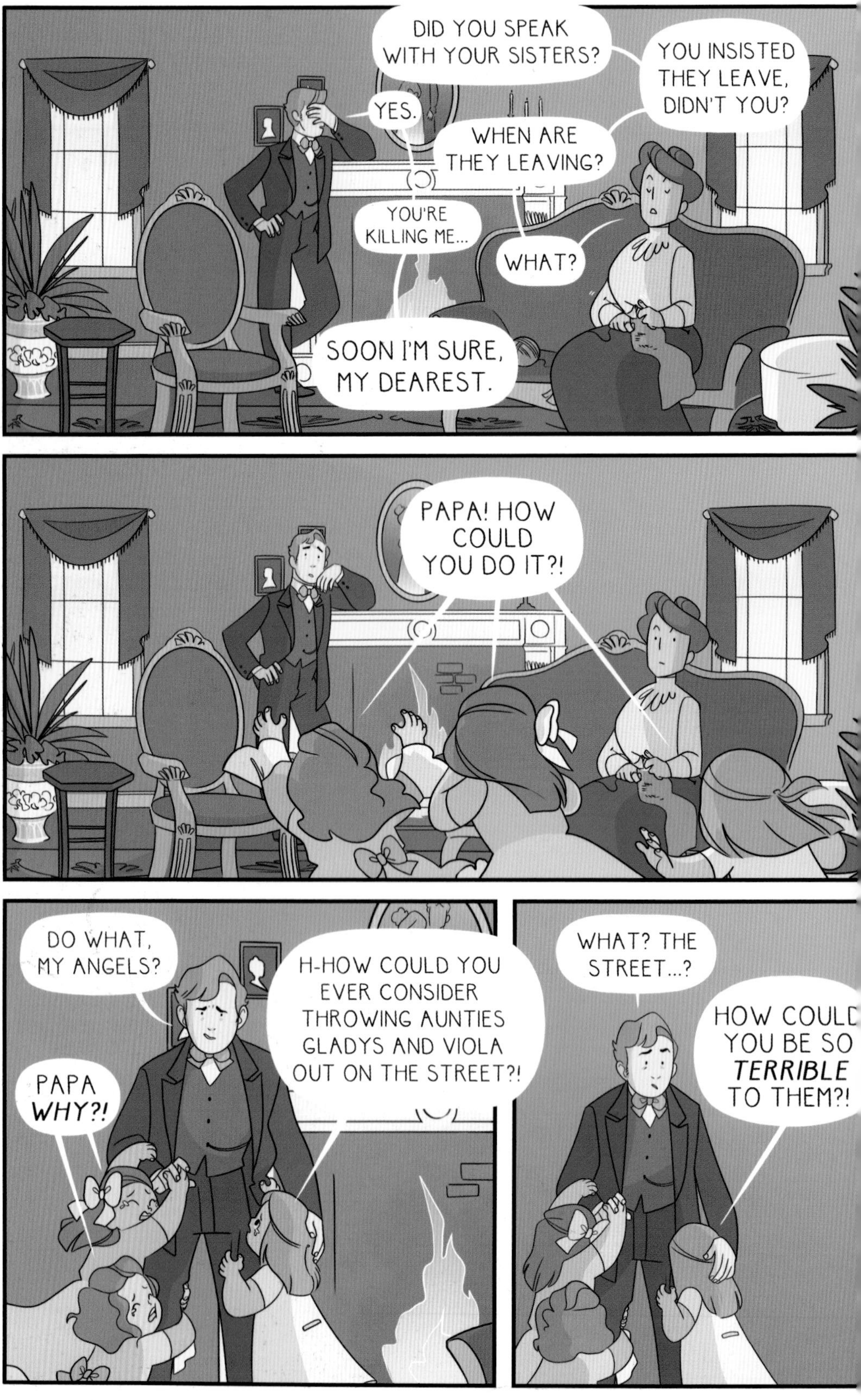

DID YOU SPEAK WITH YOUR SISTERS?
YES.
YOU INSISTED THEY LEAVE, DIDN'T YOU?
WHEN ARE THEY LEAVING?
YOU'RE KILLING ME...
WHAT?
SOON I'M SURE, MY DEAREST.
PAPA! HOW COULD YOU DO IT?!
DO WHAT, MY ANGELS?
PAPA *WHY?!*
H-HOW COULD YOU EVER CONSIDER THROWING AUNTIES GLADYS AND VIOLA OUT ON THE STREET?!
WHAT? THE STREET...?
HOW COULD YOU BE SO *TERRIBLE* TO THEM?!

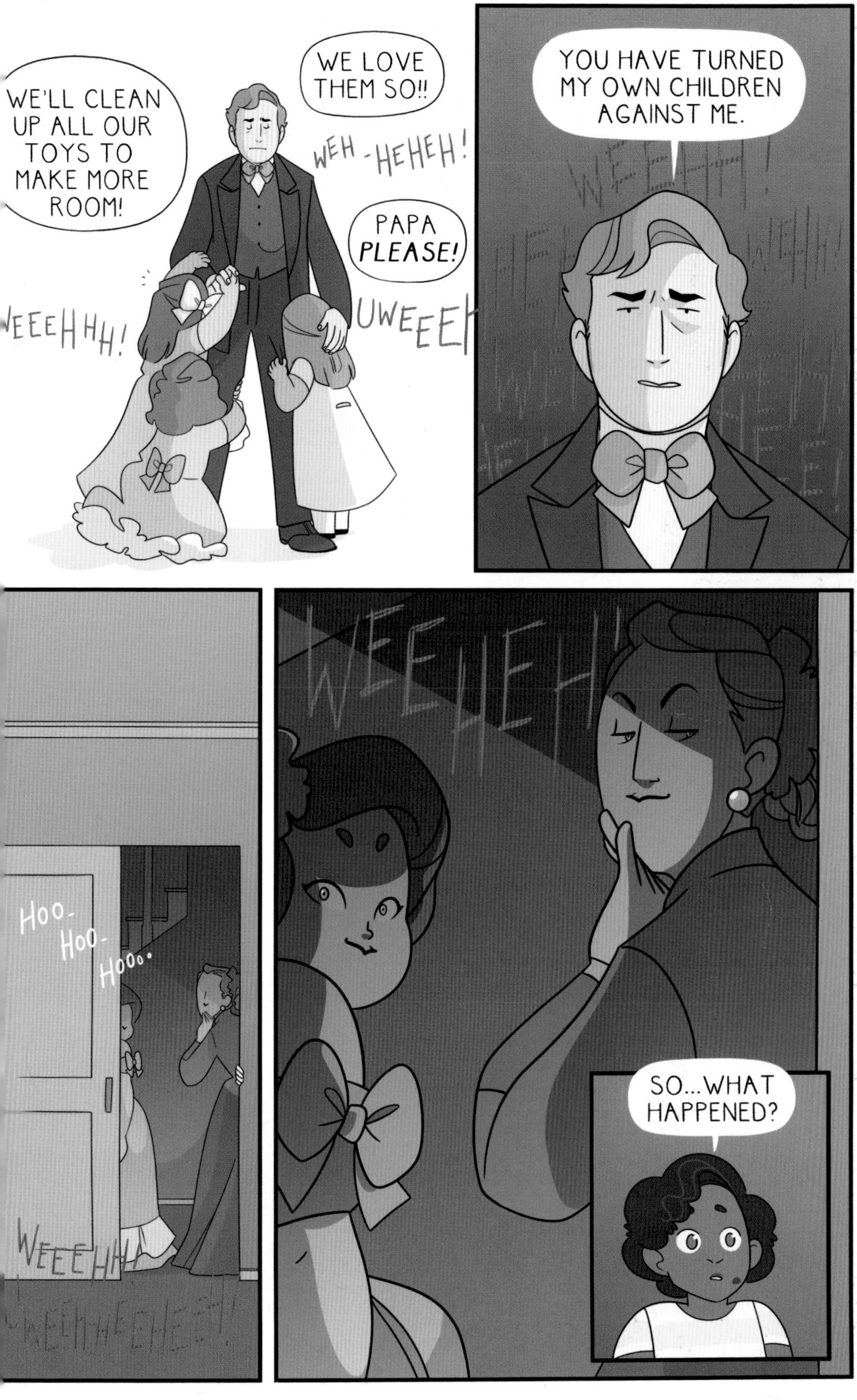
WE'LL CLEAN UP ALL OUR TOYS TO MAKE MORE ROOM!
WE LOVE THEM SO!!
WEH-HEHEH!
PAPA PLEASE!
EEEHHHH!
UWEEEH
YOU HAVE TURNED MY OWN CHILDREN AGAINST ME.
HOO-HOO-HOOo..
WEEEHH!
WEEHEH!
SO...WHAT HAPPENED?

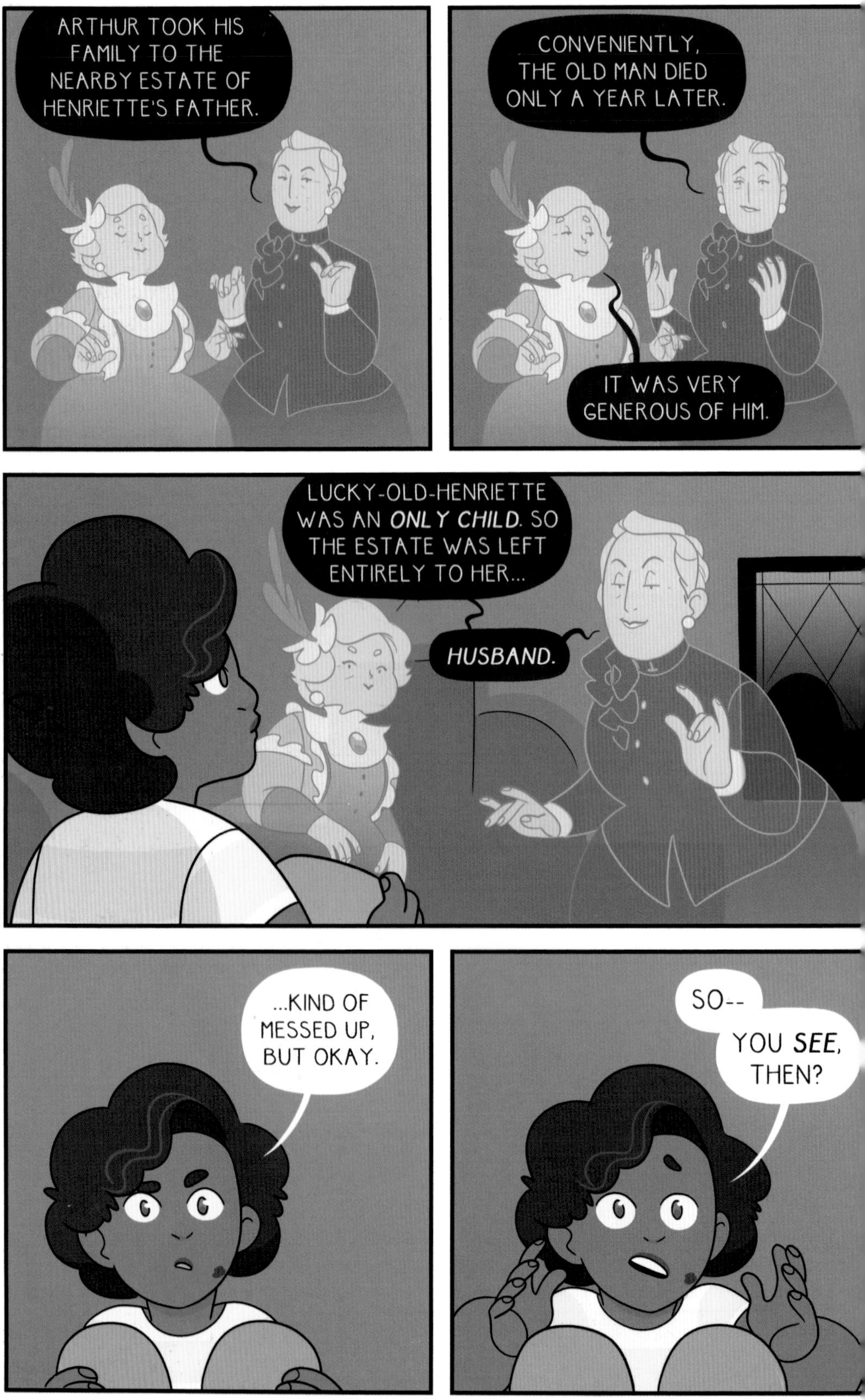
ARTHUR TOOK HIS FAMILY TO THE NEARBY ESTATE OF HENRIETTE'S FATHER.
CONVENIENTLY, THE OLD MAN DIED ONLY A YEAR LATER.
IT WAS VERY GENEROUS OF HIM.
LUCKY-OLD-HENRIETTE WAS AN *ONLY CHILD*. SO THE ESTATE WAS LEFT ENTIRELY TO HER...
*HUSBAND*.
...KIND OF MESSED UP, BUT OKAY.
SO--
YOU *SEE*, THEN?

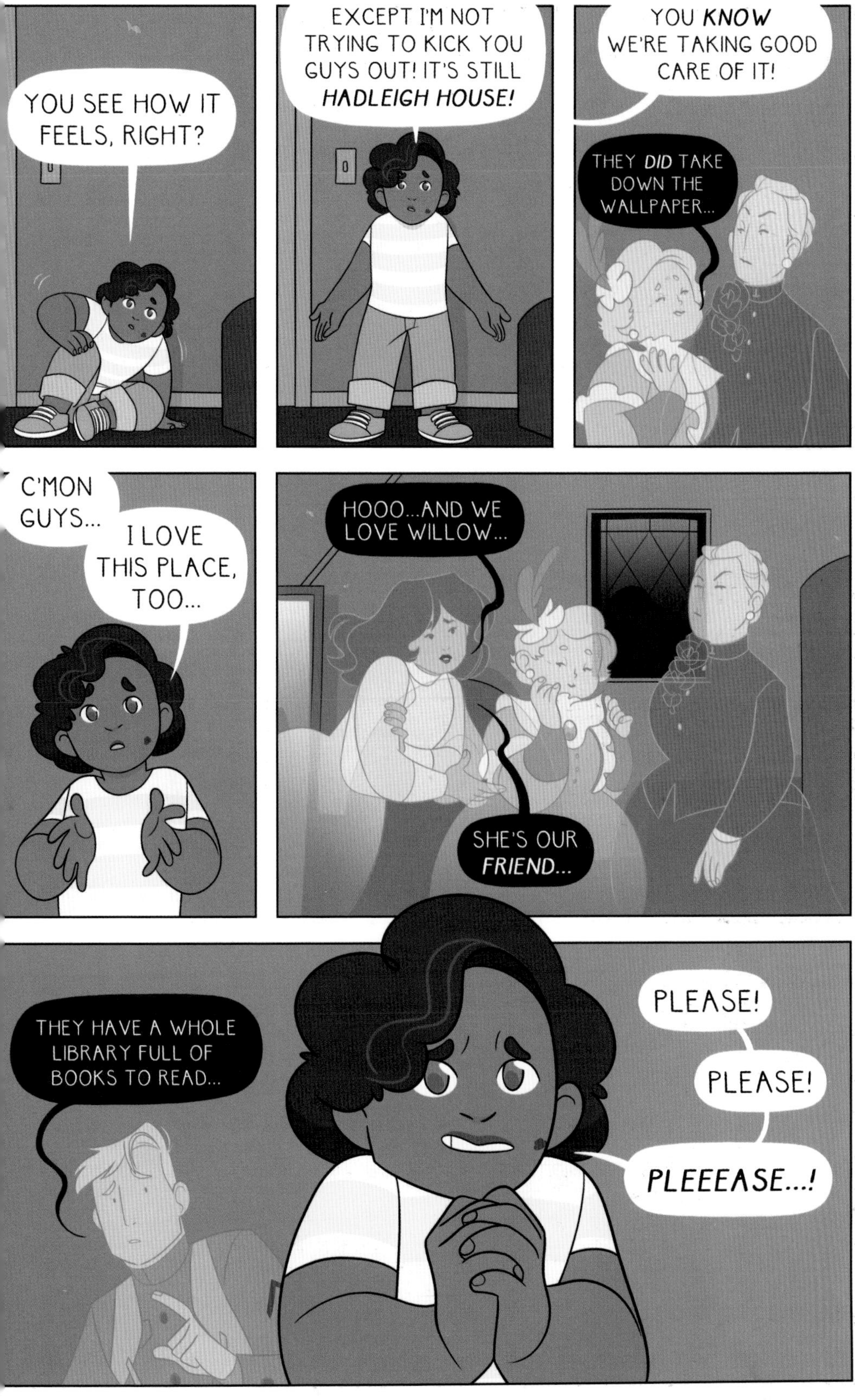
YOU SEE HOW IT FEELS, RIGHT?
EXCEPT I'M NOT TRYING TO KICK YOU GUYS OUT! IT'S STILL *HADLEIGH HOUSE!*
YOU *KNOW* WE'RE TAKING GOOD CARE OF IT!
THEY *DID* TAKE DOWN THE WALLPAPER...
C'MON GUYS...
I LOVE THIS PLACE, TOO...
HOOO...AND WE LOVE WILLOW...
SHE'S OUR *FRIEND*...
THEY HAVE A WHOLE LIBRARY FULL OF BOOKS TO READ...
PLEASE!
PLEASE!
*PLEEEASE...!*

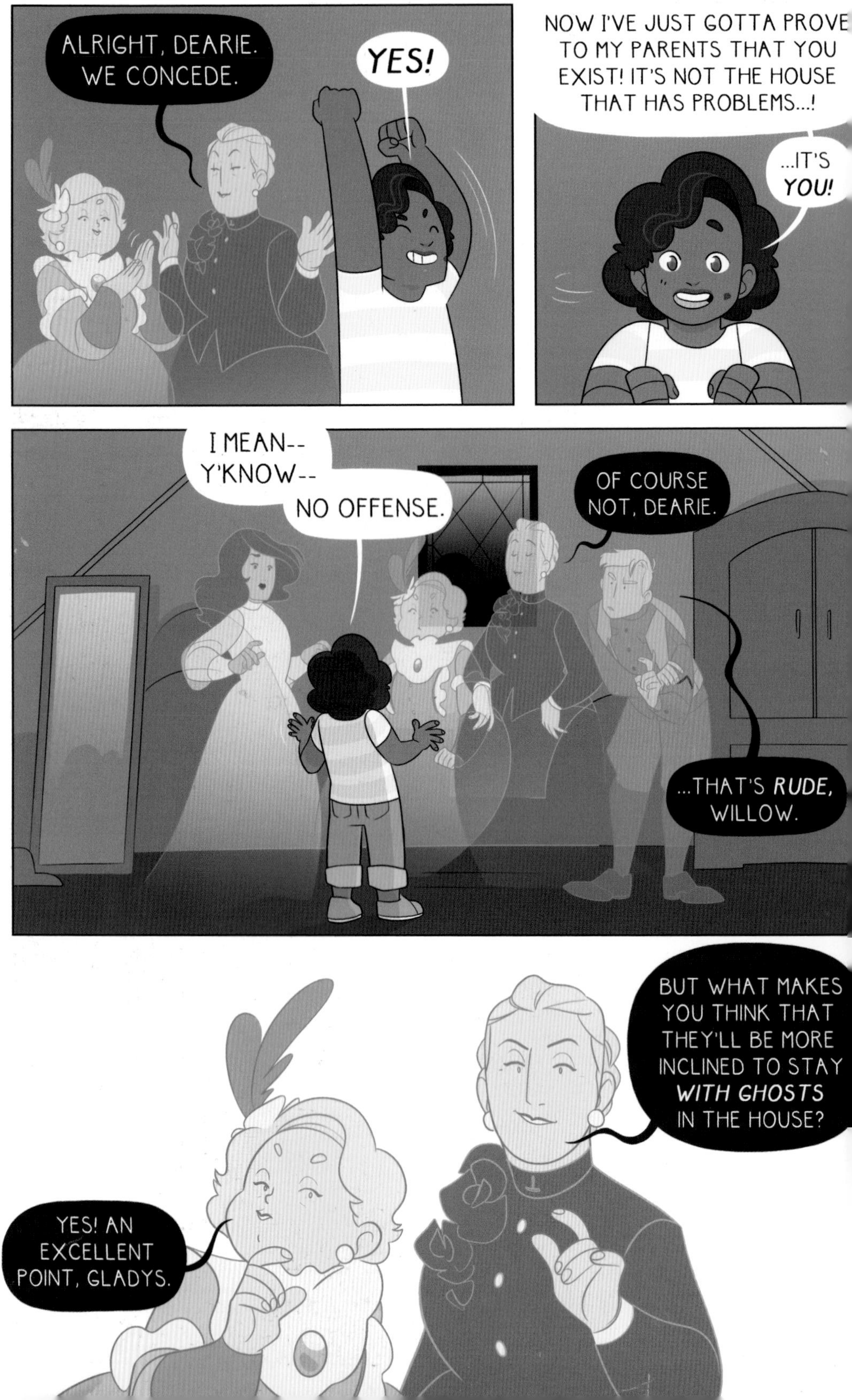
ALRIGHT, DEARIE. WE CONCEDE.
YES!
NOW I'VE JUST GOTTA PROVE TO MY PARENTS THAT YOU EXIST! IT'S NOT THE HOUSE THAT HAS PROBLEMS...!
...IT'S YOU!
I MEAN-- Y'KNOW-- NO OFFENSE.
OF COURSE NOT, DEARIE.
...THAT'S RUDE, WILLOW.
BUT WHAT MAKES YOU THINK THAT THEY'LL BE MORE INCLINED TO STAY WITH GHOSTS IN THE HOUSE?
YES! AN EXCELLENT POINT, GLADYS.

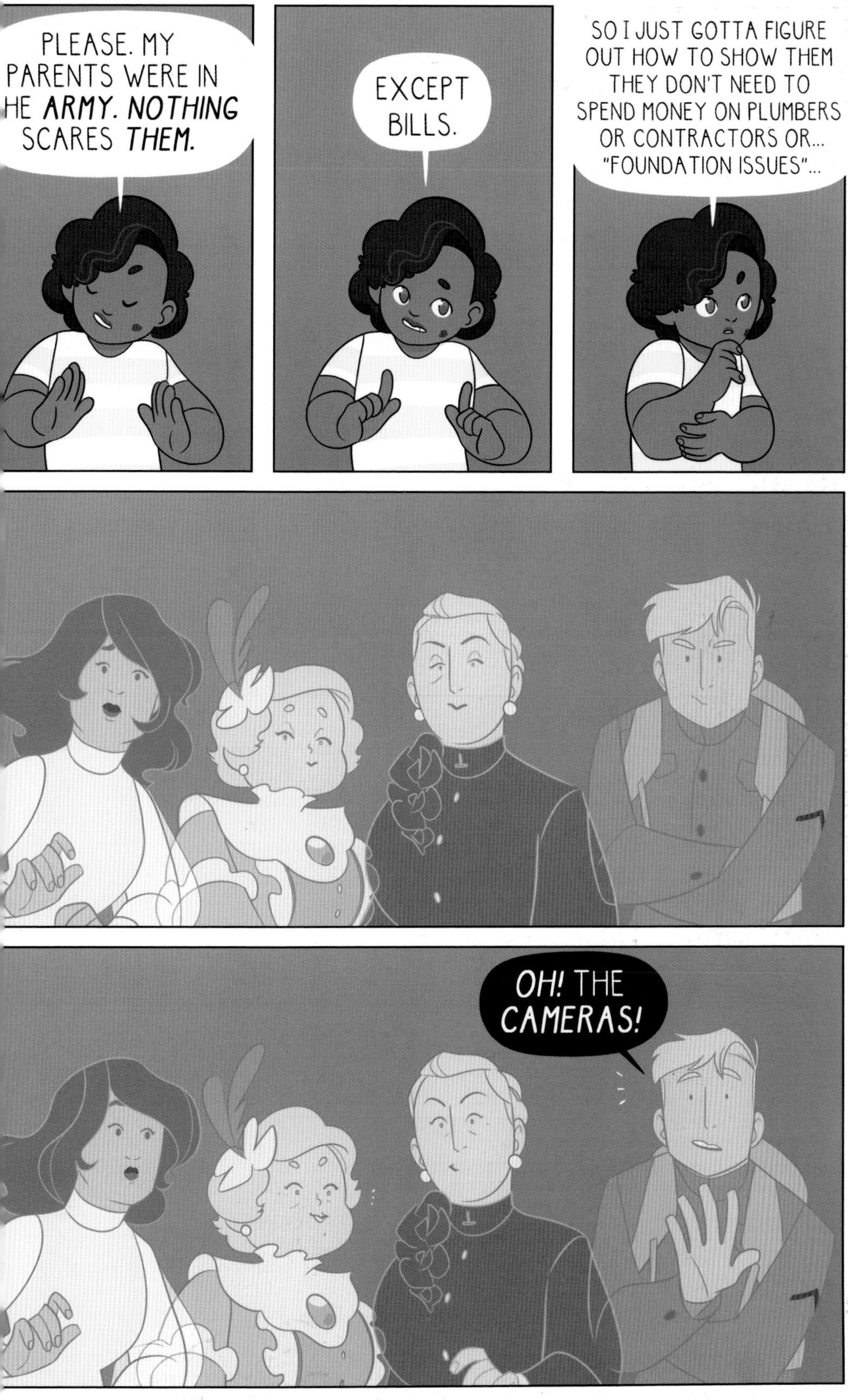
PLEASE. MY PARENTS WERE IN HE ARMY. NOTHING SCARES THEM.
EXCEPT BILLS.
SO I JUST GOTTA FIGURE OUT HOW TO SHOW THEM THEY DON'T NEED TO SPEND MONEY ON PLUMBERS OR CONTRACTORS OR... "FOUNDATION ISSUES"...
OH! THE CAMERAS!

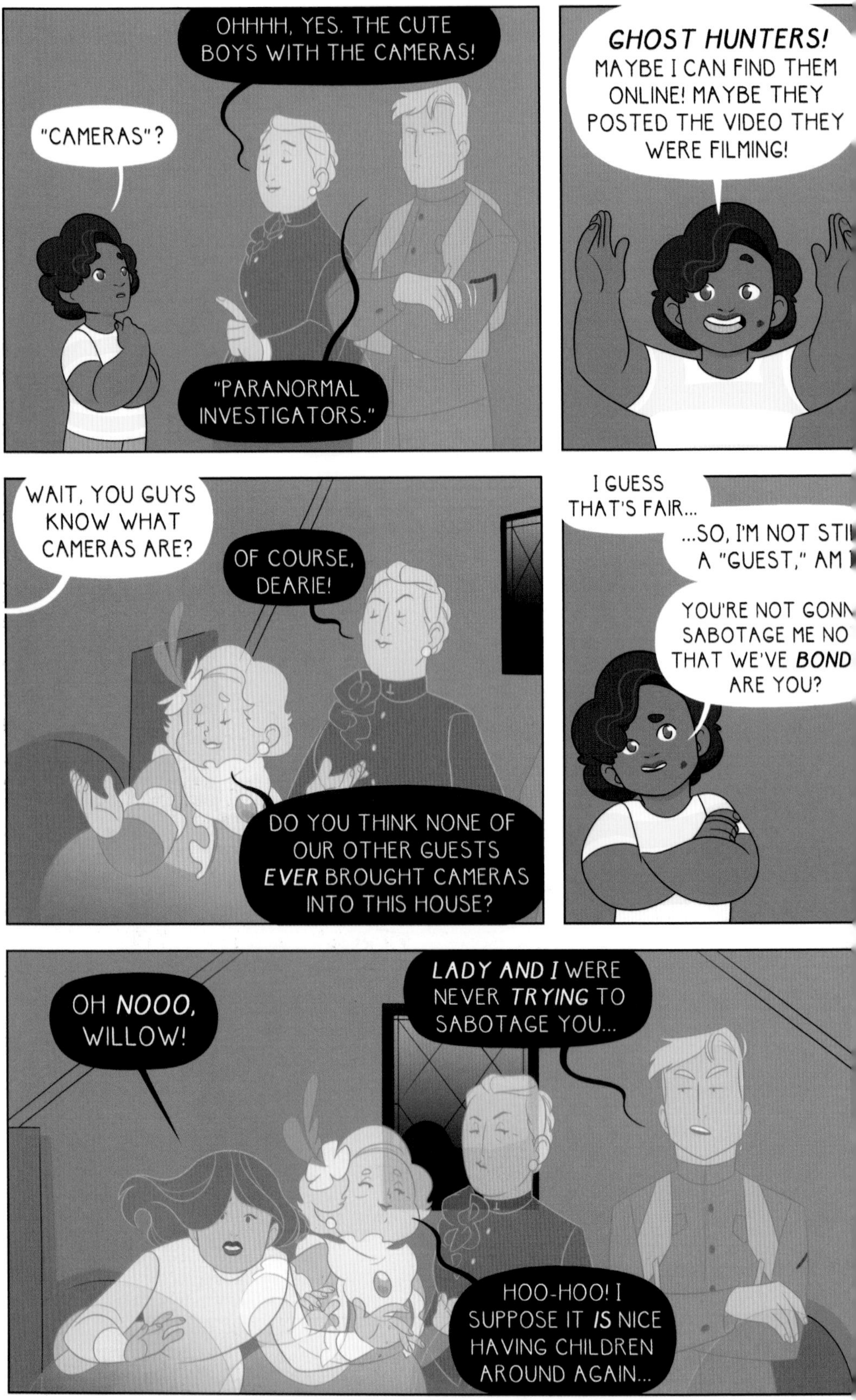
OHHHH, YES. THE CUTE BOYS WITH THE CAMERAS!
"CAMERAS"?
"PARANORMAL INVESTIGATORS."
*GHOST HUNTERS!* MAYBE I CAN FIND THEM ONLINE! MAYBE THEY POSTED THE VIDEO THEY WERE FILMING!
WAIT, YOU GUYS KNOW WHAT CAMERAS ARE?
OF COURSE, DEARIE!
DO YOU THINK NONE OF OUR OTHER GUESTS *EVER* BROUGHT CAMERAS INTO THIS HOUSE?
I GUESS THAT'S FAIR...
...SO, I'M NOT STI
A "GUEST," AM
YOU'RE NOT GONN
SABOTAGE ME NO
THAT WE'VE *BOND*
ARE YOU?
OH *NOOO,* WILLOW!
*LADY AND I* WERE NEVER *TRYING* TO SABOTAGE YOU...
HOO-HOO! I SUPPOSE IT *IS* NICE HAVING CHILDREN AROUND AGAIN...

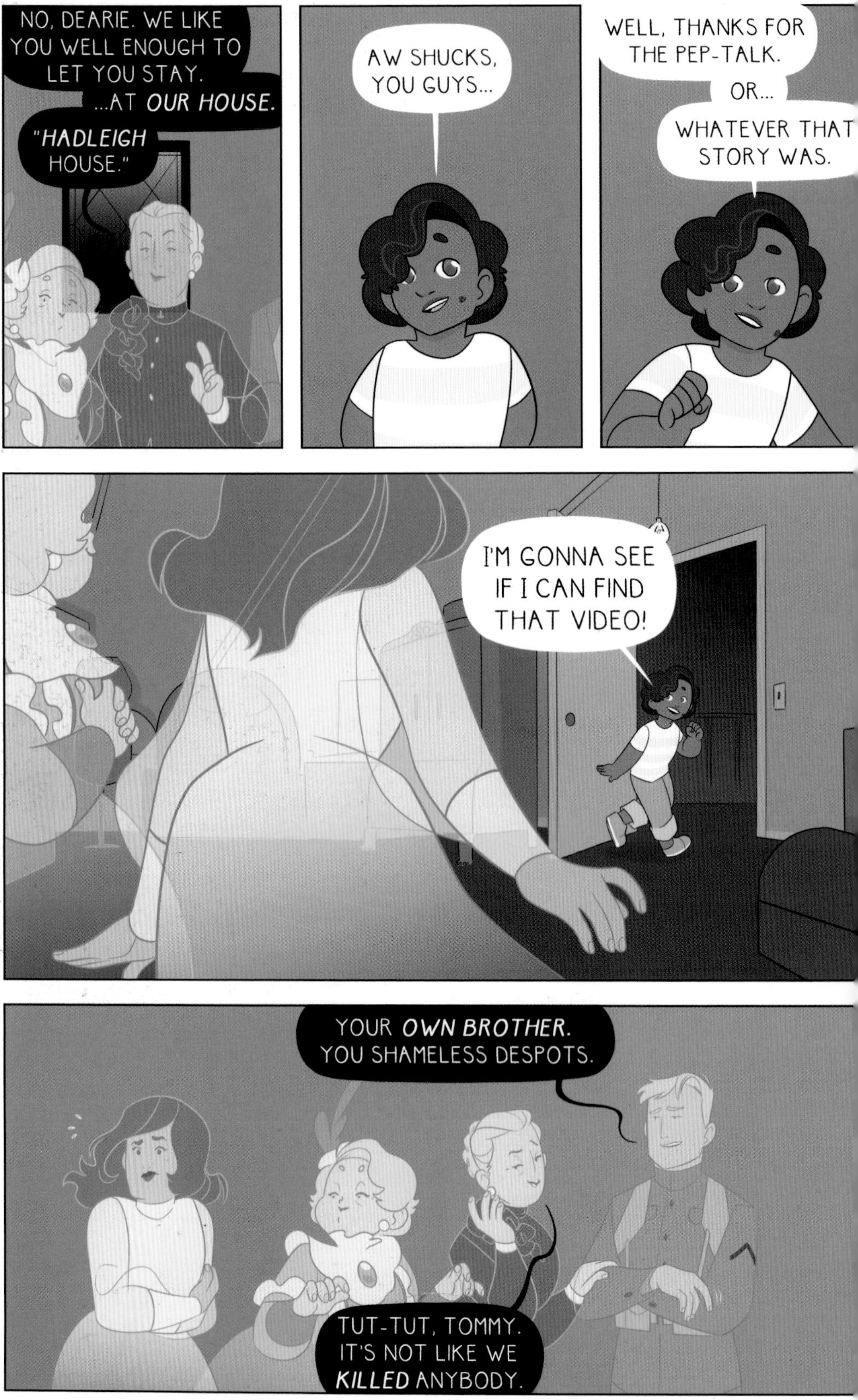
NO, DEARIE. WE LIKE YOU WELL ENOUGH TO LET YOU STAY.
...AT OUR HOUSE.
"HADLEIGH HOUSE."
AW SHUCKS, YOU GUYS...
WELL, THANKS FOR THE PEP-TALK.
OR...
WHATEVER THAT STORY WAS.
I'M GONNA SEE IF I CAN FIND THAT VIDEO!
YOUR OWN BROTHER. YOU SHAMELESS DESPOTS.
TUT-TUT, TOMMY. IT'S NOT LIKE WE KILLED ANYBODY.

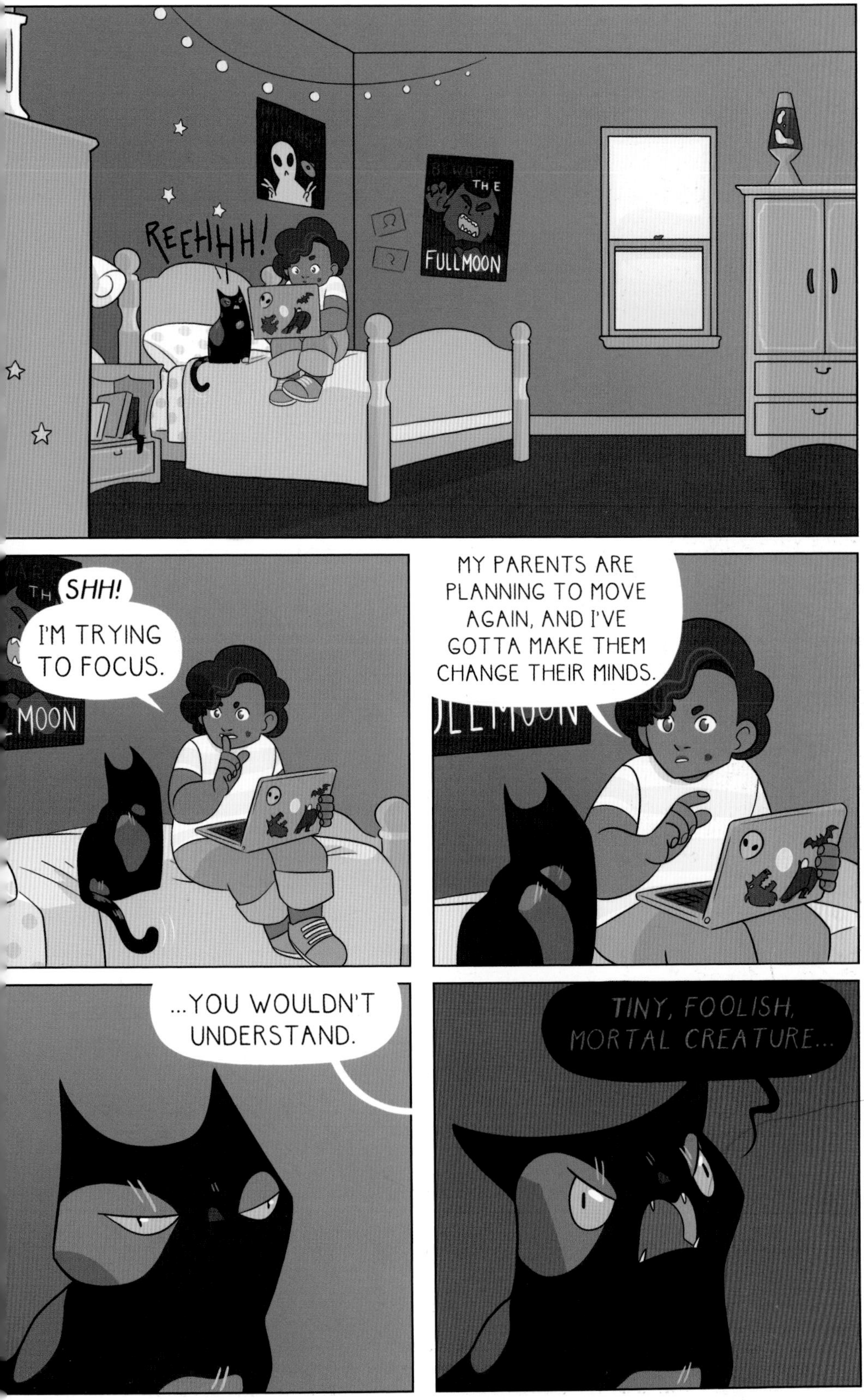
REEHHHH!
THE
FULLMOON
SHH!
I'M TRYING TO FOCUS.
MY PARENTS ARE PLANNING TO MOVE AGAIN, AND I'VE GOTTA MAKE THEM CHANGE THEIR MINDS.
...YOU WOULDN'T UNDERSTAND.
TINY, FOOLISH, MORTAL CREATURE...

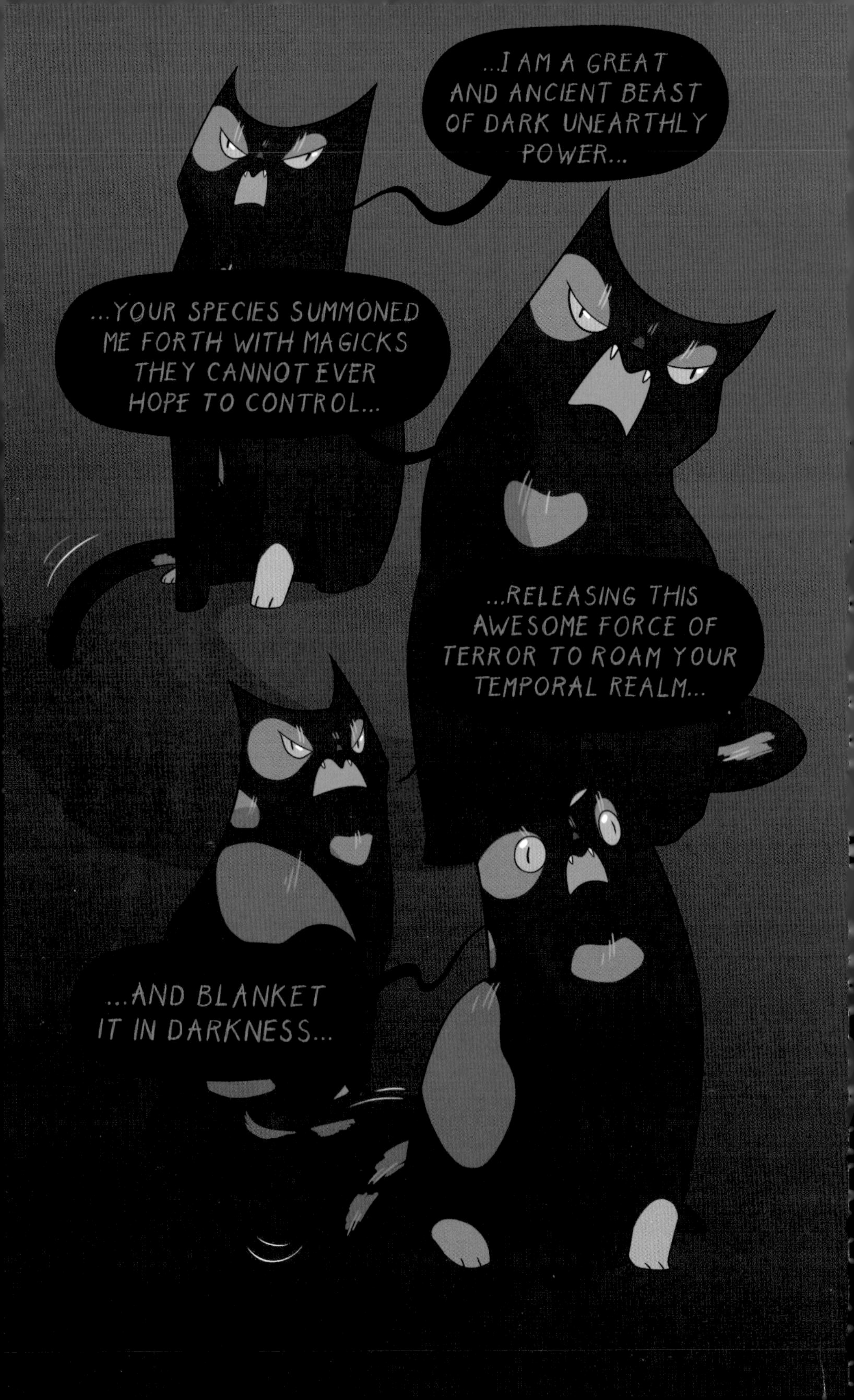
...I AM A GREAT AND ANCIENT BEAST OF DARK UNEARTHLY POWER...
...YOUR SPECIES SUMMONED ME FORTH WITH MAGICKS THEY CANNOT EVER HOPE TO CONTROL...
...RELEASING THIS AWESOME FORCE OF TERROR TO ROAM YOUR TEMPORAL REALM...
...AND BLANKET IT IN DARKNESS...

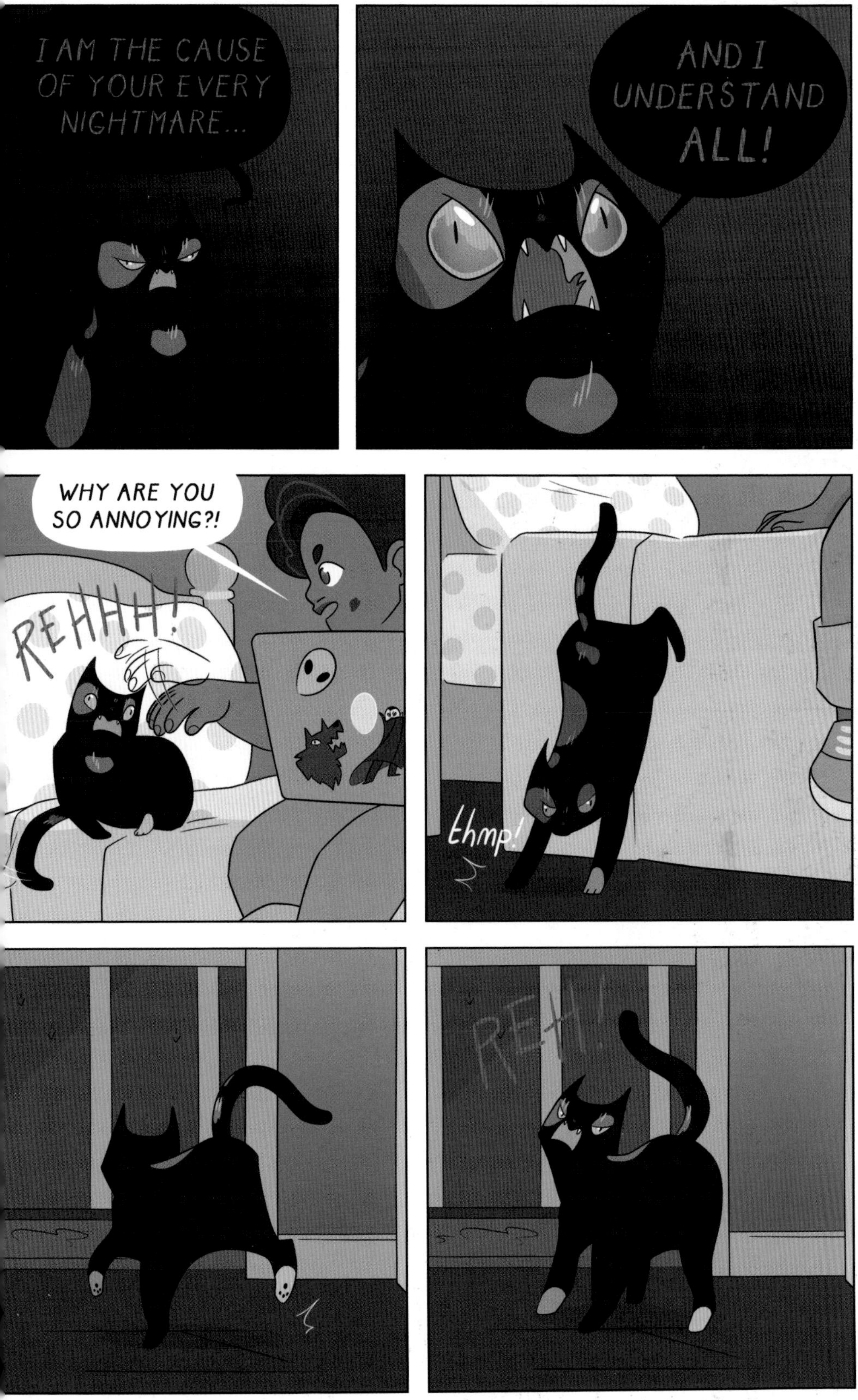
I AM THE CAUSE OF YOUR EVERY NIGHTMARE...
AND I UNDERSTAND ALL!
WHY ARE YOU SO ANNOYING?!
REHHH!
thmp!
REH!

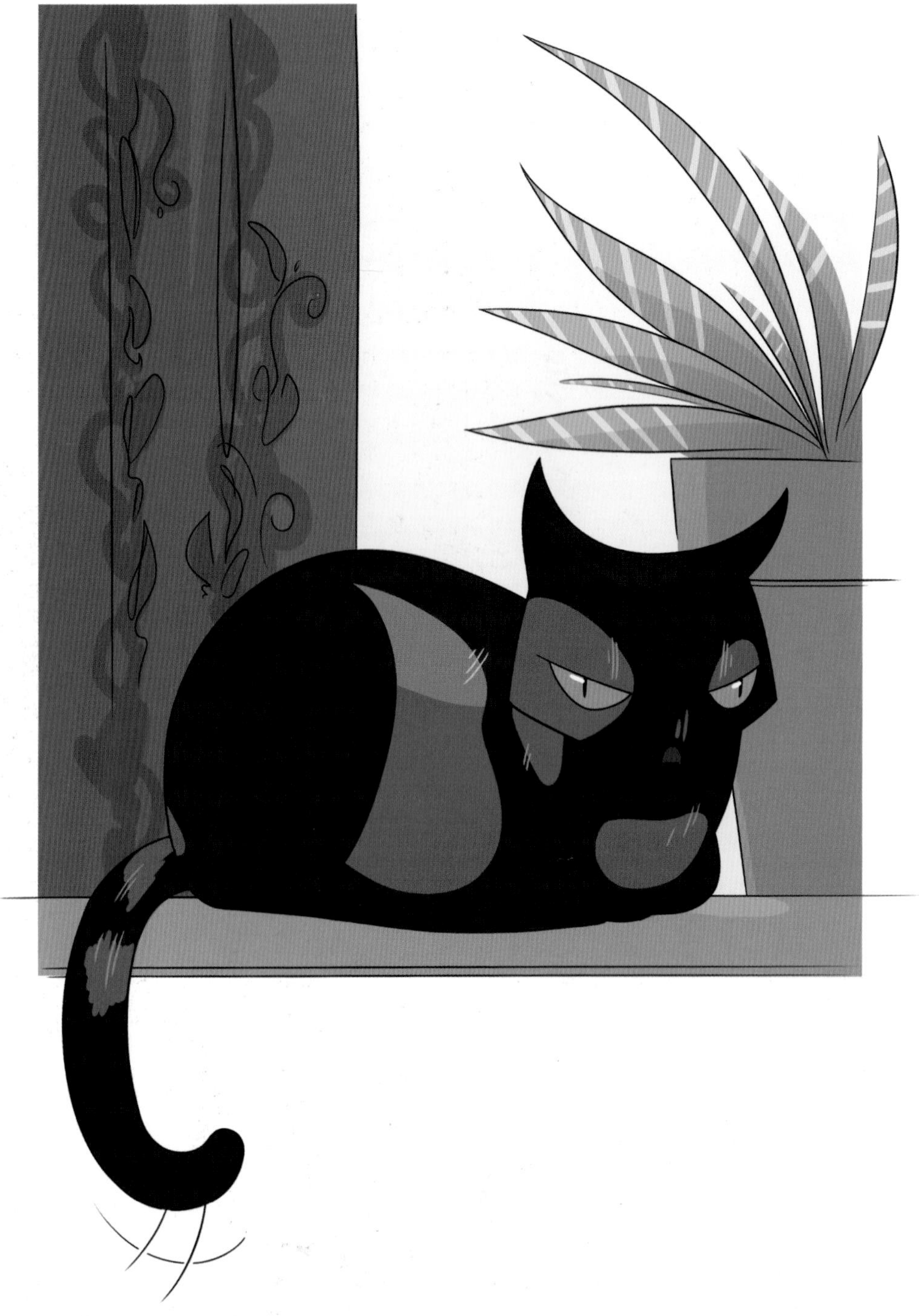

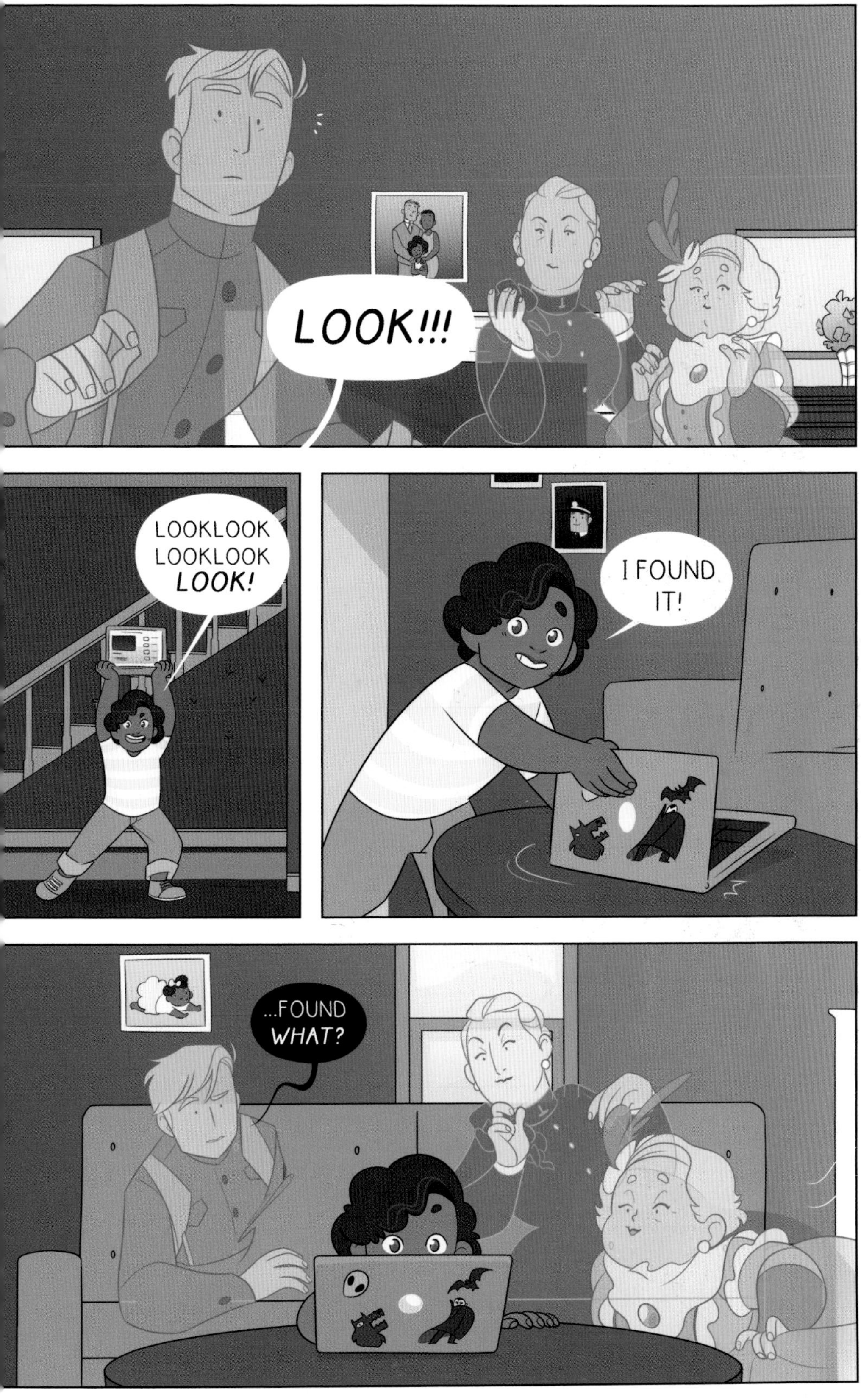
LOOK!!!
LOOKLOOK
LOOKLOOK
LOOK!
I FOUND
IT!
...FOUND
WHAT?

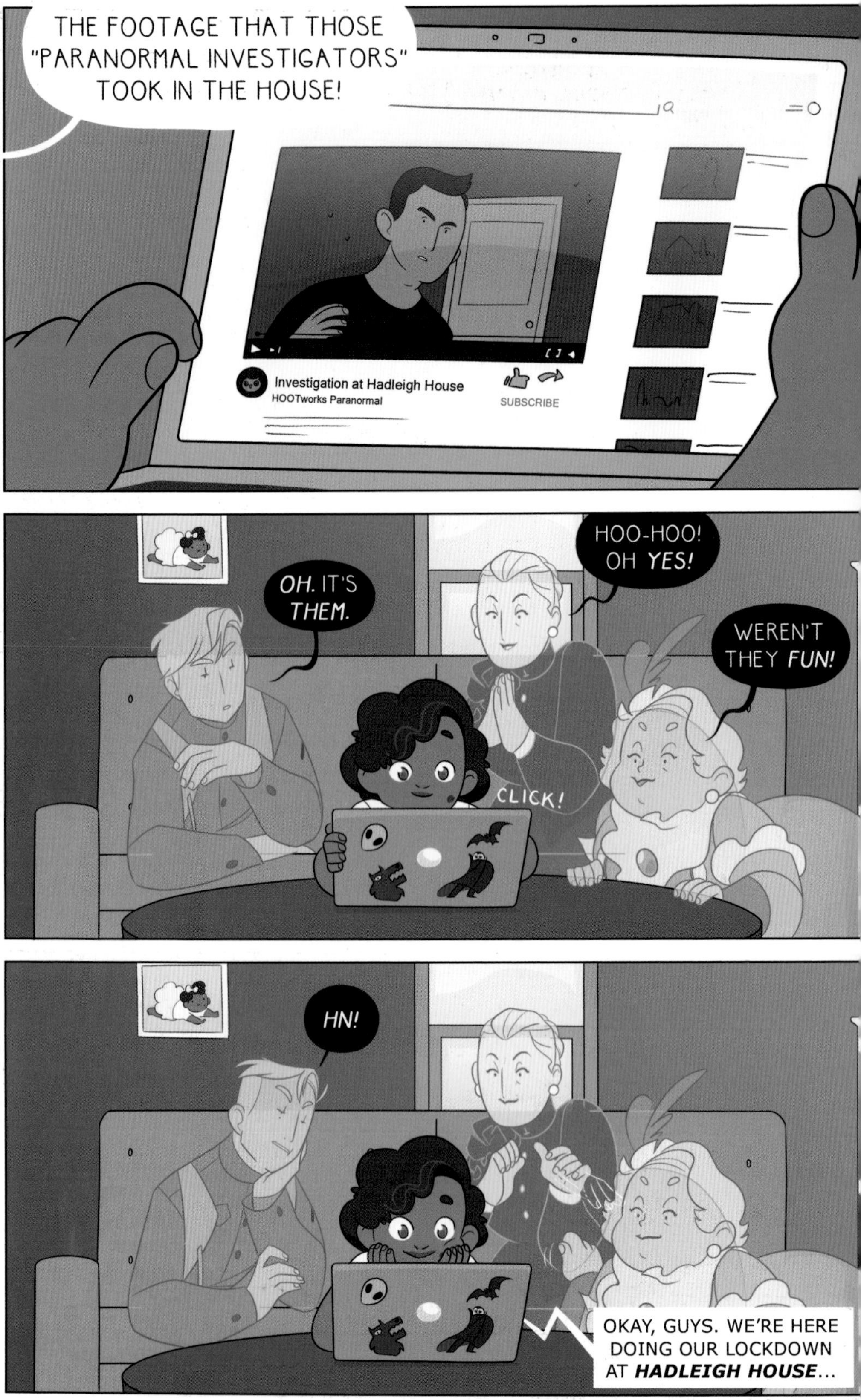

THE FOOTAGE THAT THOSE "PARANORMAL INVESTIGATORS" TOOK IN THE HOUSE!
Investigation at Hadleigh House
HOOTworks Paranormal
SUBSCRIBE
OH. IT'S THEM.
HOO-HOO! OH YES!
WEREN'T THEY FUN!
CLICK!
HN!
OKAY, GUYS. WE'RE HERE DOING OUR LOCKDOWN AT HADLEIGH HOUSE...

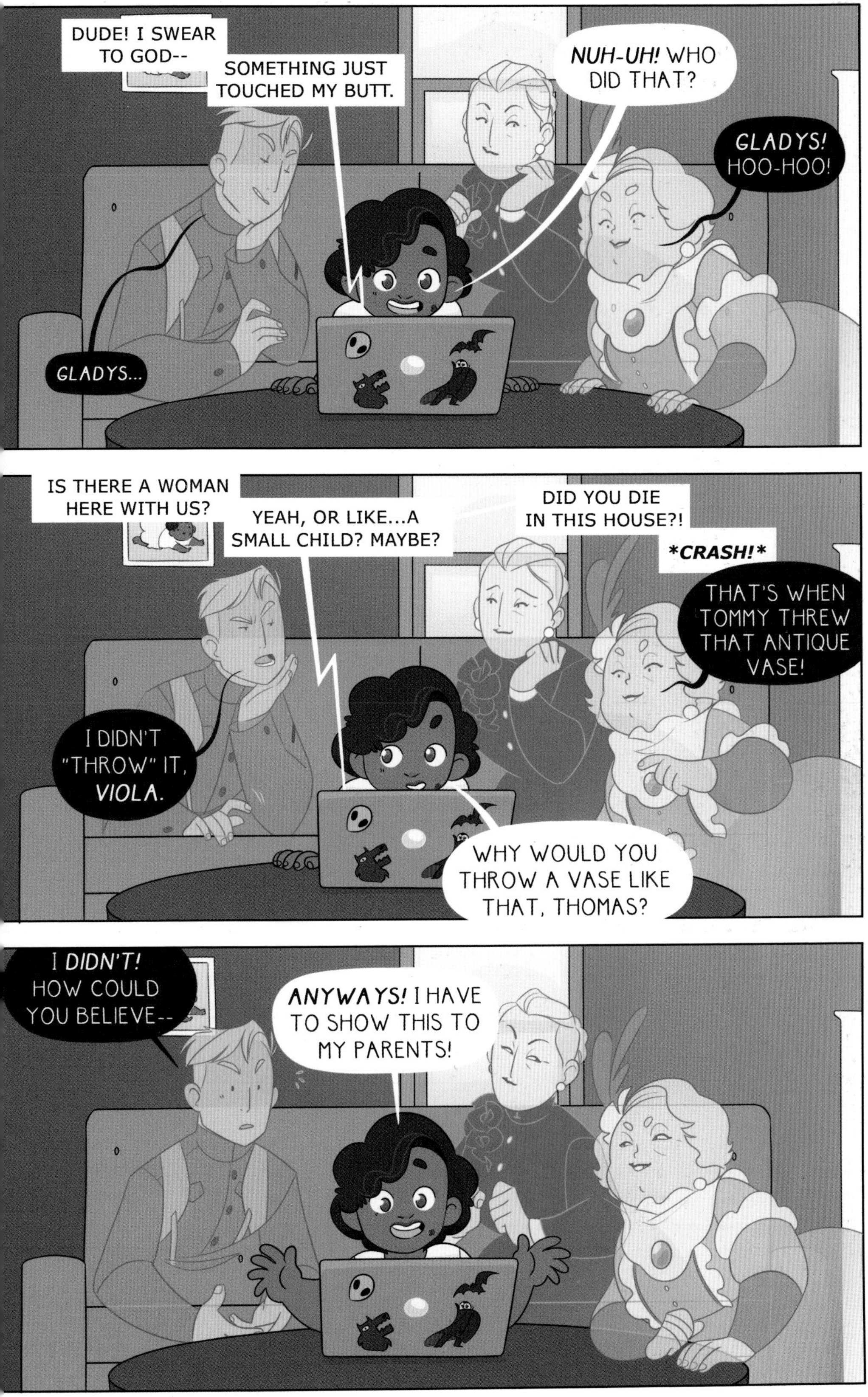
DUDE! I SWEAR TO GOD--
SOMETHING JUST TOUCHED MY BUTT.
NUH-UH! WHO DID THAT?
GLADYS! HOO-HOO!
GLADYS...
IS THERE A WOMAN HERE WITH US?
YEAH, OR LIKE...A SMALL CHILD? MAYBE?
DID YOU DIE IN THIS HOUSE?!
*CRASH!*
THAT'S WHEN TOMMY THREW THAT ANTIQUE VASE!
I DIDN'T "THROW" IT, VIOLA.
WHY WOULD YOU THROW A VASE LIKE THAT, THOMAS?
I DIDN'T! HOW COULD YOU BELIEVE--
ANYWAYS! I HAVE TO SHOW THIS TO MY PARENTS!

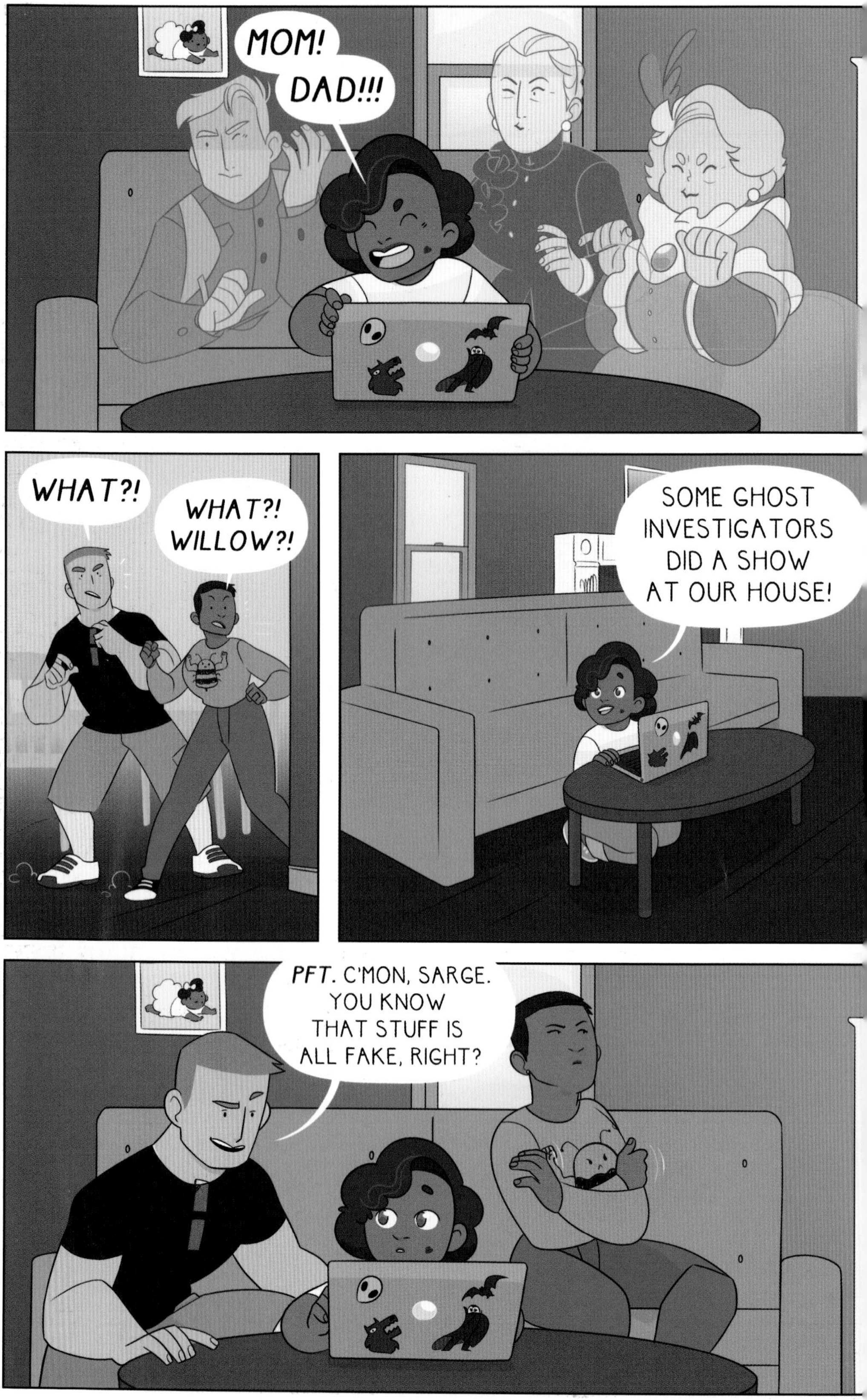
MOM!
DAD!!!
WHAT?!
WHAT?! WILLOW?!
SOME GHOST INVESTIGATORS DID A SHOW AT OUR HOUSE!
PFT. C'MON, SARGE. YOU KNOW THAT STUFF IS ALL FAKE, RIGHT?

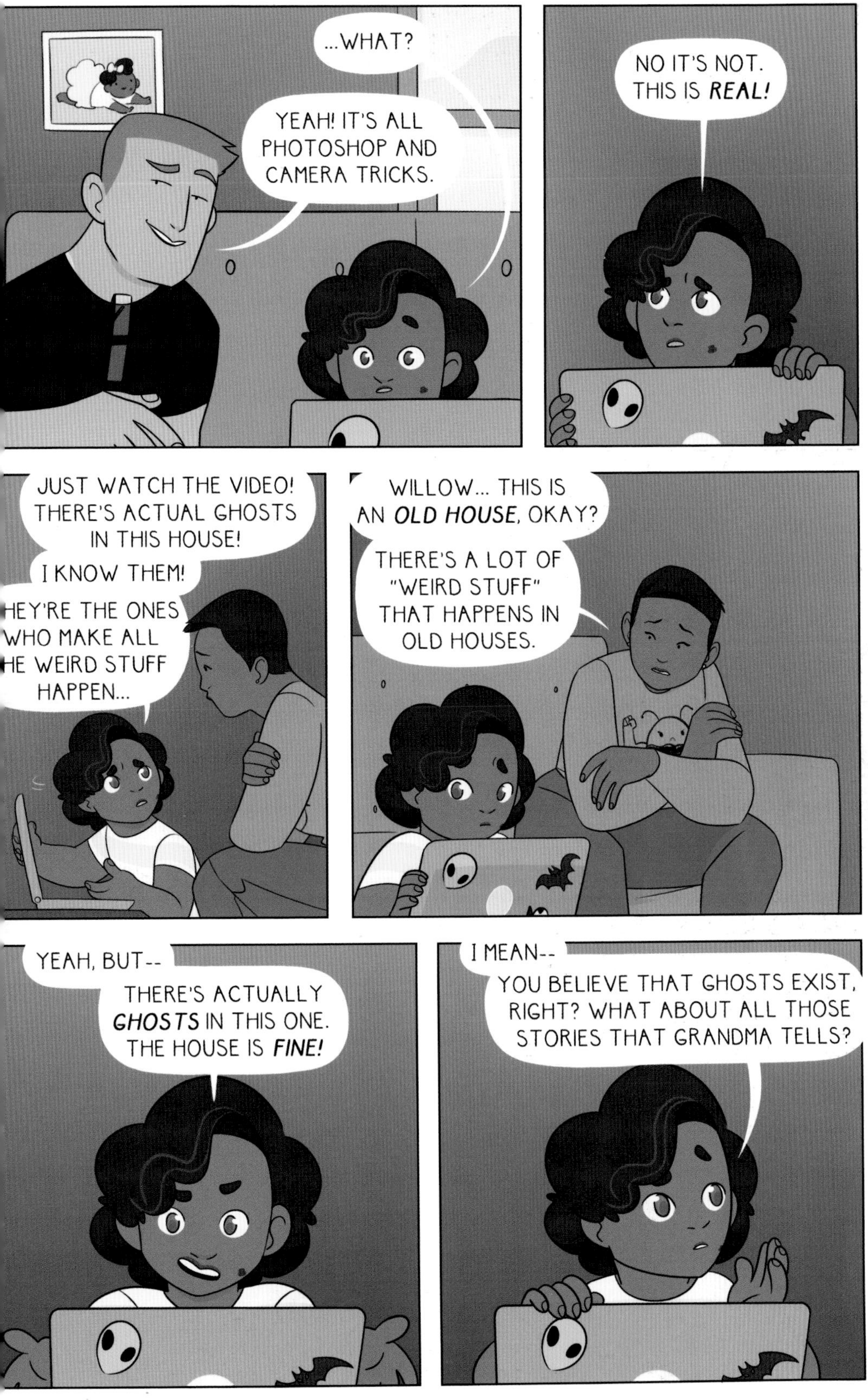
...WHAT?
YEAH! IT'S ALL PHOTOSHOP AND CAMERA TRICKS.
NO IT'S NOT. THIS IS *REAL!*
JUST WATCH THE VIDEO! THERE'S ACTUAL GHOSTS IN THIS HOUSE!
I KNOW THEM!
HEY'RE THE ONES WHO MAKE ALL HE WEIRD STUFF HAPPEN...
WILLOW... THIS IS AN *OLD HOUSE*, OKAY?
THERE'S A LOT OF "WEIRD STUFF" THAT HAPPENS IN OLD HOUSES.
YEAH, BUT--
THERE'S ACTUALLY *GHOSTS* IN THIS ONE. THE HOUSE IS *FINE!*
I MEAN--
YOU BELIEVE THAT GHOSTS EXIST, RIGHT? WHAT ABOUT ALL THOSE STORIES THAT GRANDMA TELLS?

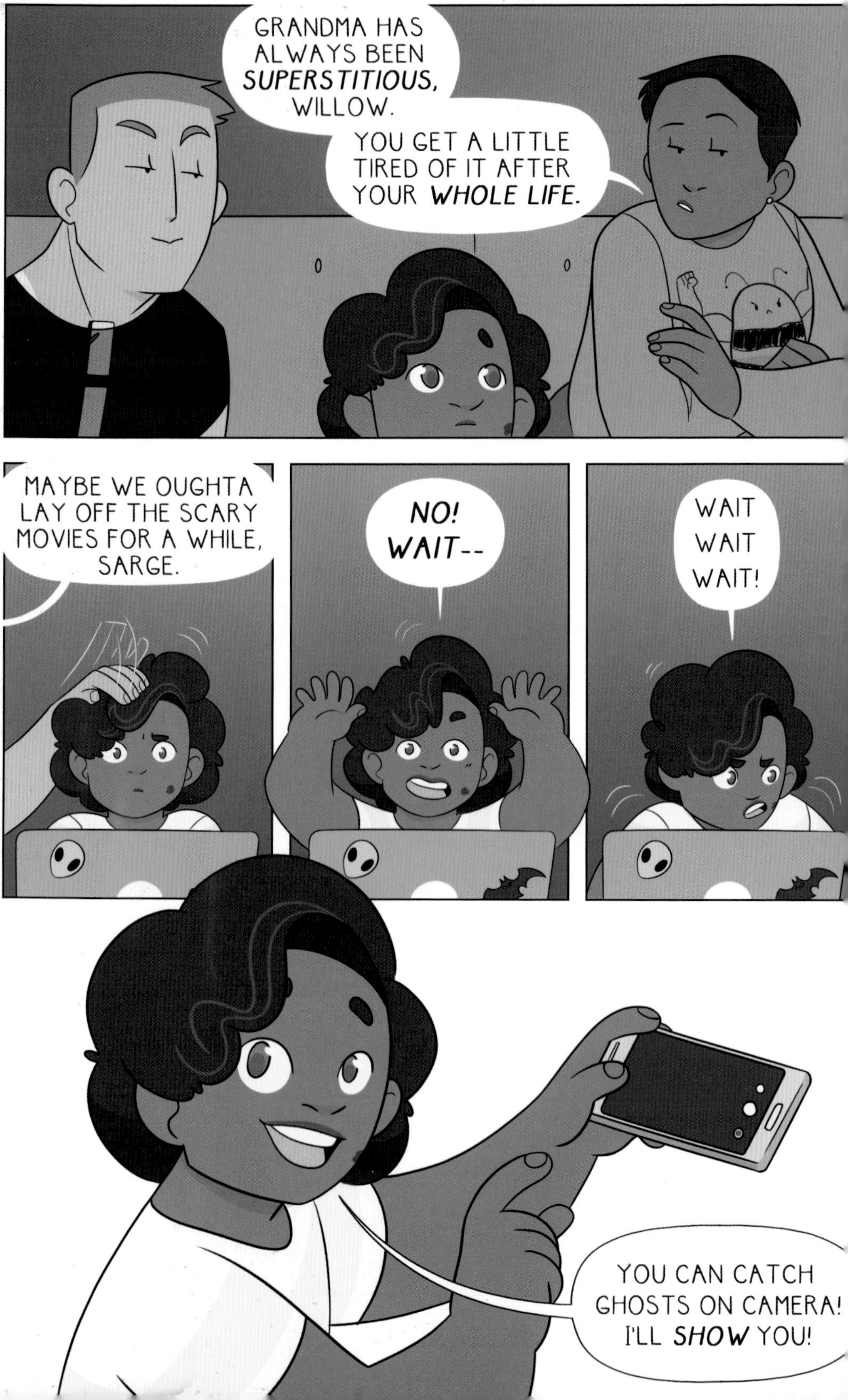
GRANDMA HAS ALWAYS BEEN *SUPERSTITIOUS,* WILLOW.
YOU GET A LITTLE TIRED OF IT AFTER YOUR *WHOLE LIFE.*
MAYBE WE OUGHTA LAY OFF THE SCARY MOVIES FOR A WHILE, SARGE.
*NO! WAIT*--
WAIT WAIT WAIT!
YOU CAN CATCH GHOSTS ON CAMERA! I'LL *SHOW* YOU!

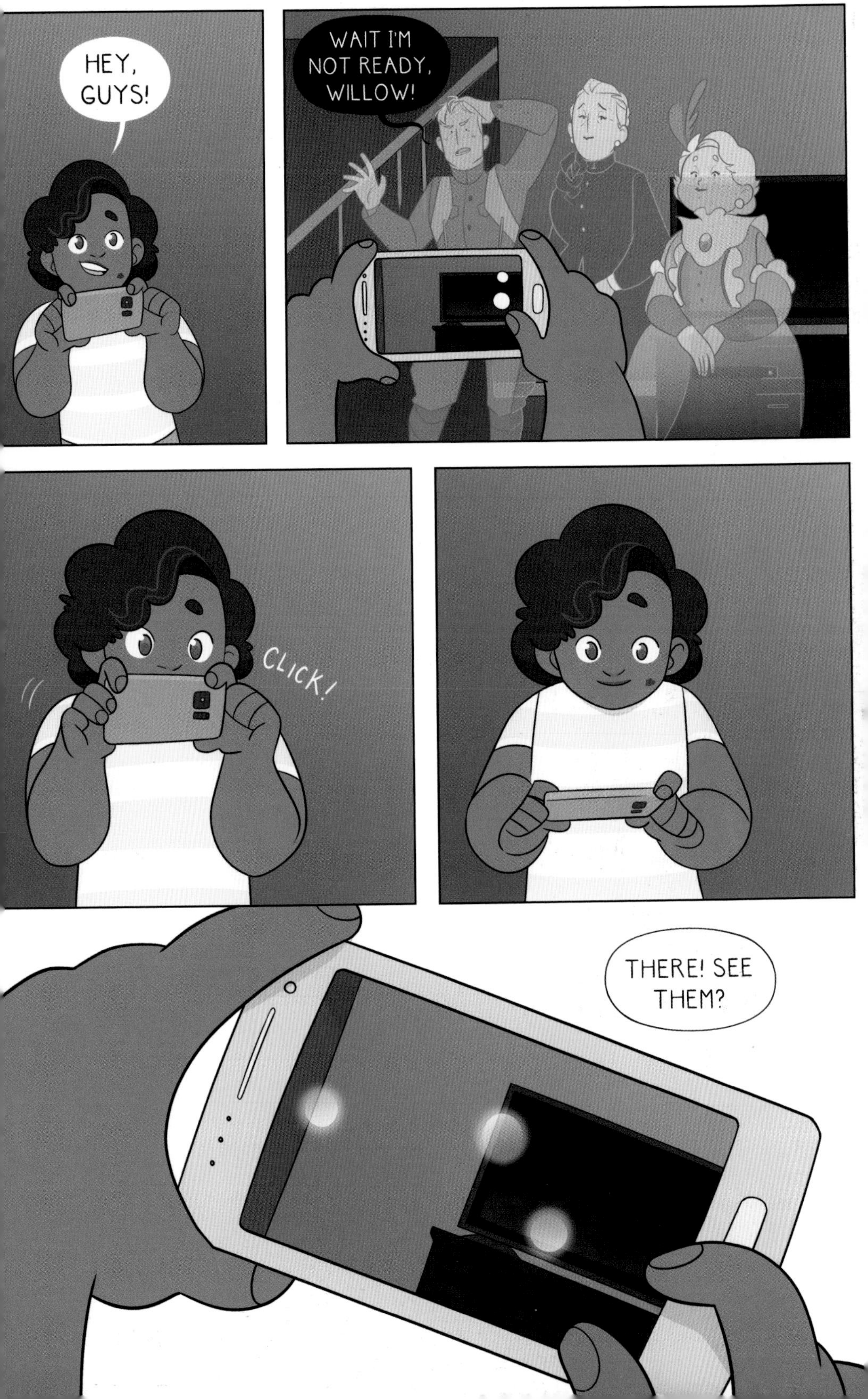
HEY, GUYS!
WAIT I'M NOT READY, WILLOW!
CLICK!
THERE! SEE THEM?

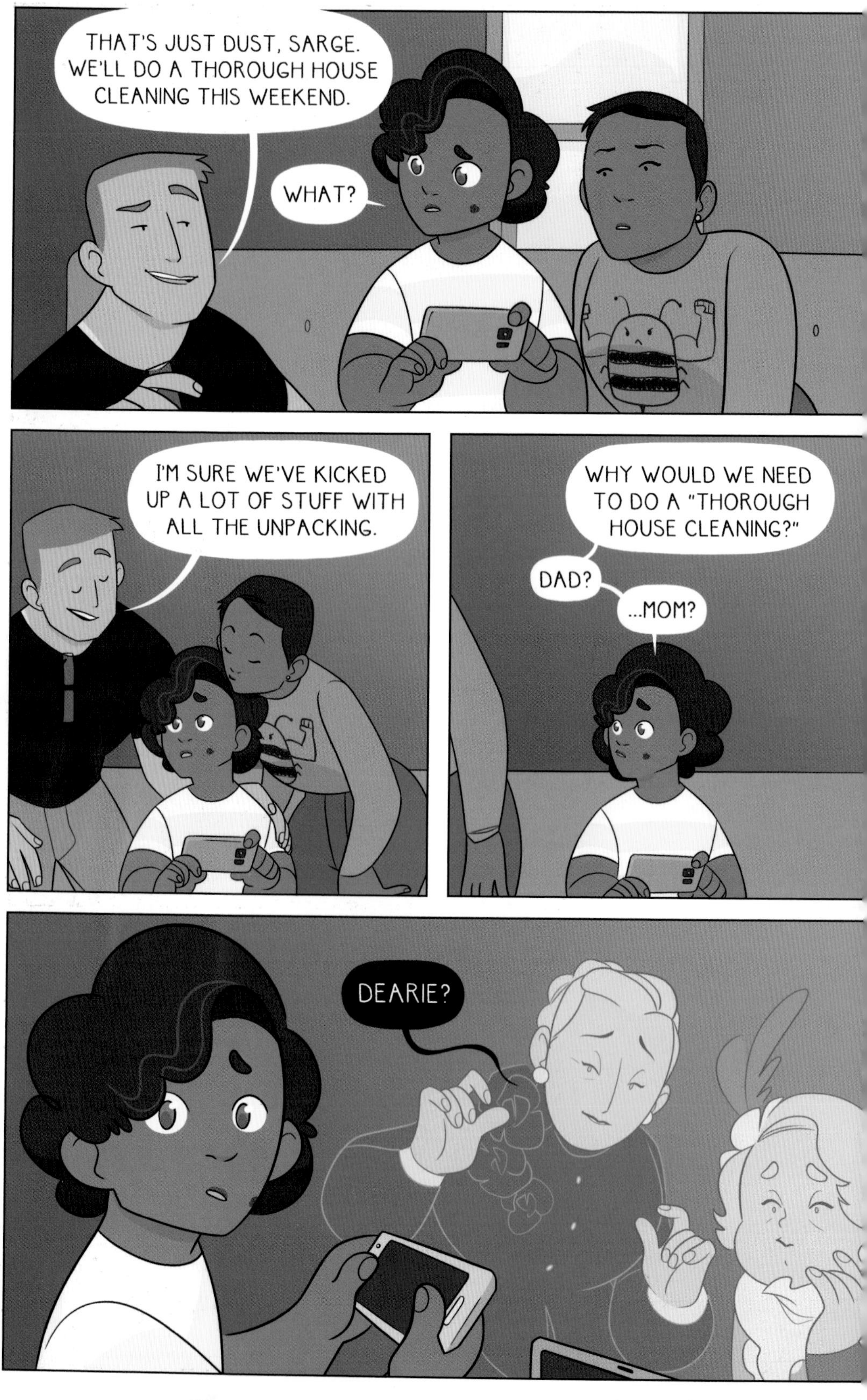
THAT'S JUST DUST, SARGE. WE'LL DO A THOROUGH HOUSE CLEANING THIS WEEKEND.
WHAT?
I'M SURE WE'VE KICKED UP A LOT OF STUFF WITH ALL THE UNPACKING.
WHY WOULD WE NEED TO DO A "THOROUGH HOUSE CLEANING?"
DAD?
...MOM?
DEARIE?

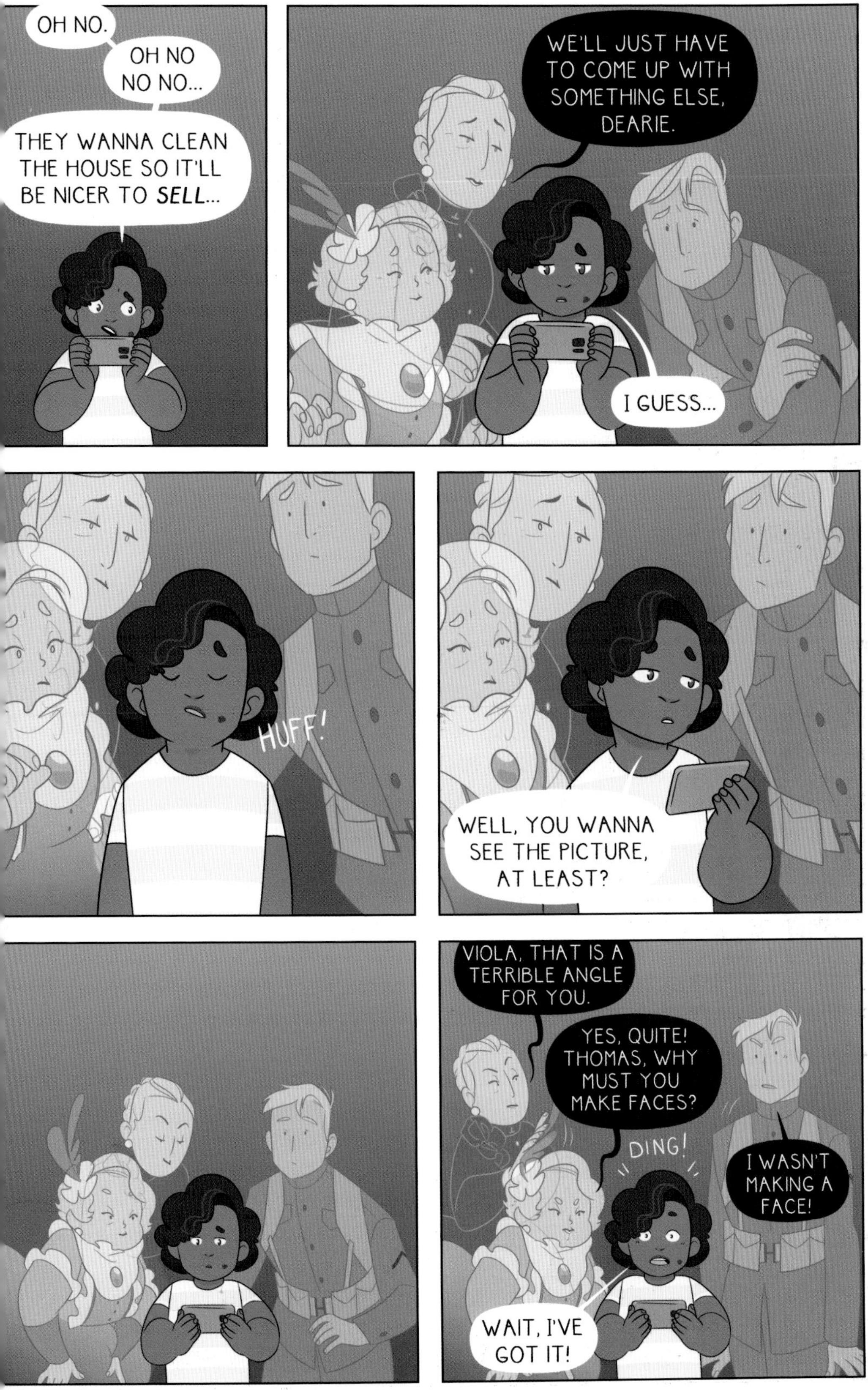
OH NO.
OH NO NO NO...
THEY WANNA CLEAN THE HOUSE SO IT'LL BE NICER TO *SELL*...
WE'LL JUST HAVE TO COME UP WITH SOMETHING ELSE, DEARIE.
I GUESS...
HUFF!
WELL, YOU WANNA SEE THE PICTURE, AT LEAST?
VIOLA, THAT IS A TERRIBLE ANGLE FOR YOU.
YES, QUITE! THOMAS, WHY MUST YOU MAKE FACES?
DING!
I WASN'T MAKING A FACE!
WAIT, I'VE GOT IT!

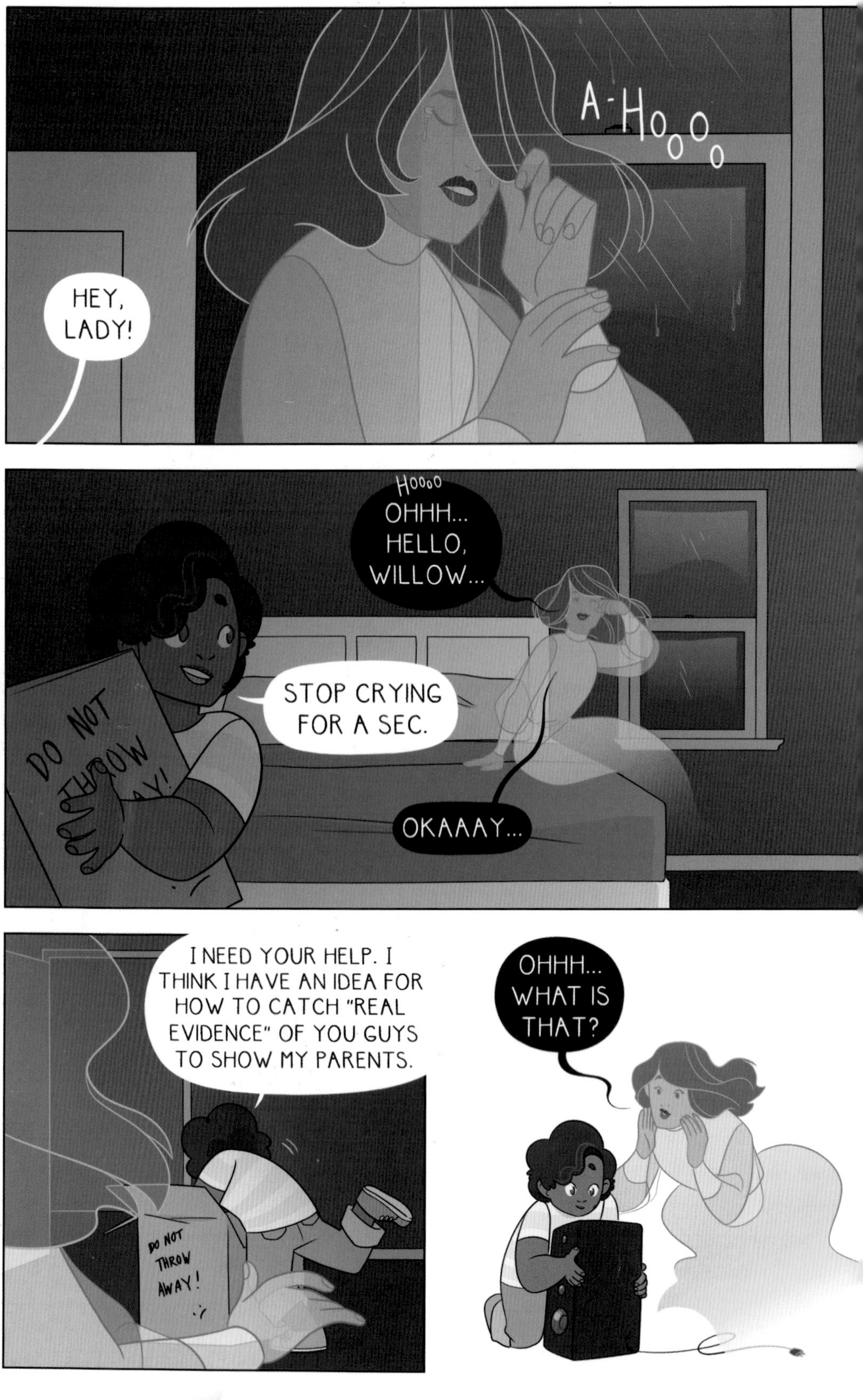
A-HOoooo
HEY, LADY!
HOooo
OHHH... HELLO, WILLOW...
STOP CRYING FOR A SEC.
OKAAAY...
DO NOT THROW AWAY!
I NEED YOUR HELP. I THINK I HAVE AN IDEA FOR HOW TO CATCH "REAL EVIDENCE" OF YOU GUYS TO SHOW MY PARENTS.
DO NOT THROW AWAY!
OHHH... WHAT IS THAT?

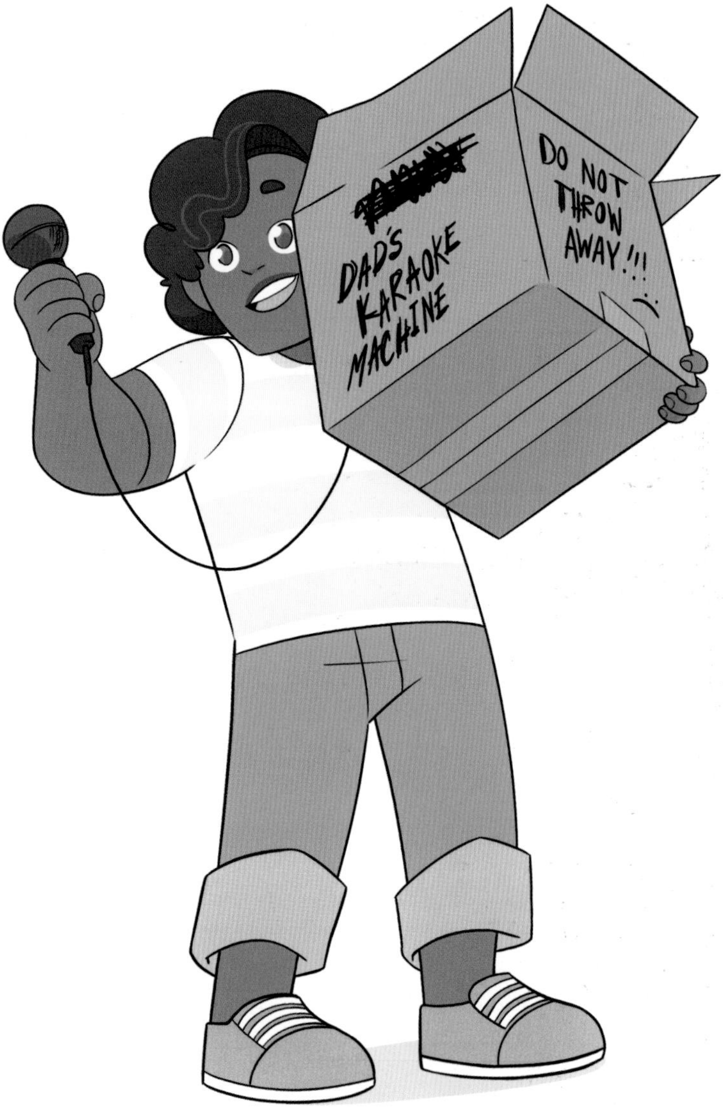
DAD'S KARAOKE MACHINE
DO NOT THROW AWAY!!!

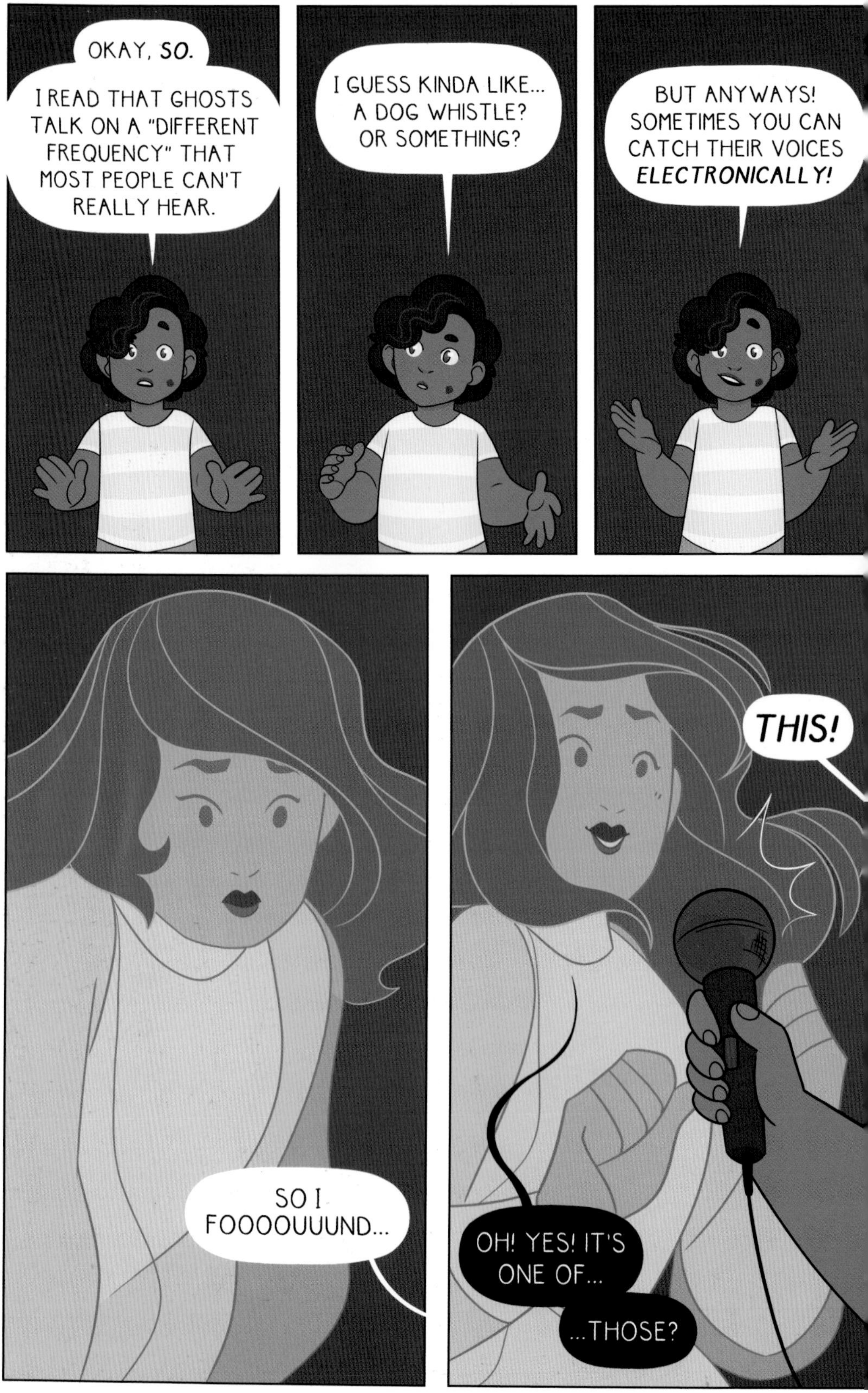
OKAY, *SO.*
I READ THAT GHOSTS TALK ON A "DIFFERENT FREQUENCY" THAT MOST PEOPLE CAN'T REALLY HEAR.
I GUESS KINDA LIKE... A DOG WHISTLE? OR SOMETHING?
BUT ANYWAYS! SOMETIMES YOU CAN CATCH THEIR VOICES *ELECTRONICALLY!*
SO I FOOOOUUUND...
*THIS!*
OH! YES! IT'S ONE OF...
...THOSE?

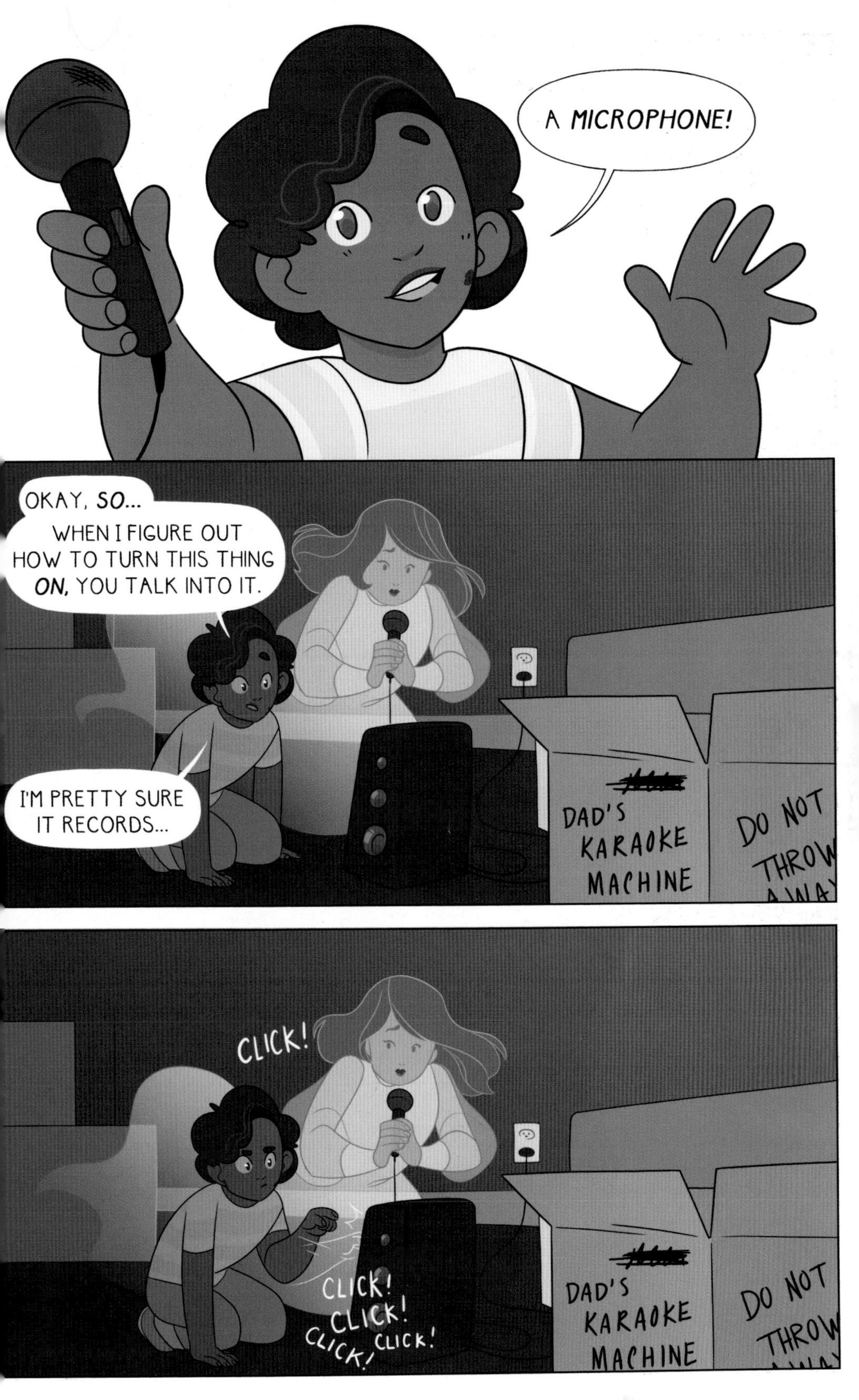
A MICROPHONE!
OKAY, SO...
WHEN I FIGURE OUT HOW TO TURN THIS THING ON, YOU TALK INTO IT.
I'M PRETTY SURE IT RECORDS...
DAD'S KARAOKE MACHINE
DO NOT THROW
CLICK!
CLICK! CLICK! CLICK! CLICK!
DAD'S KARAOKE MACHINE
DO NOT THROW

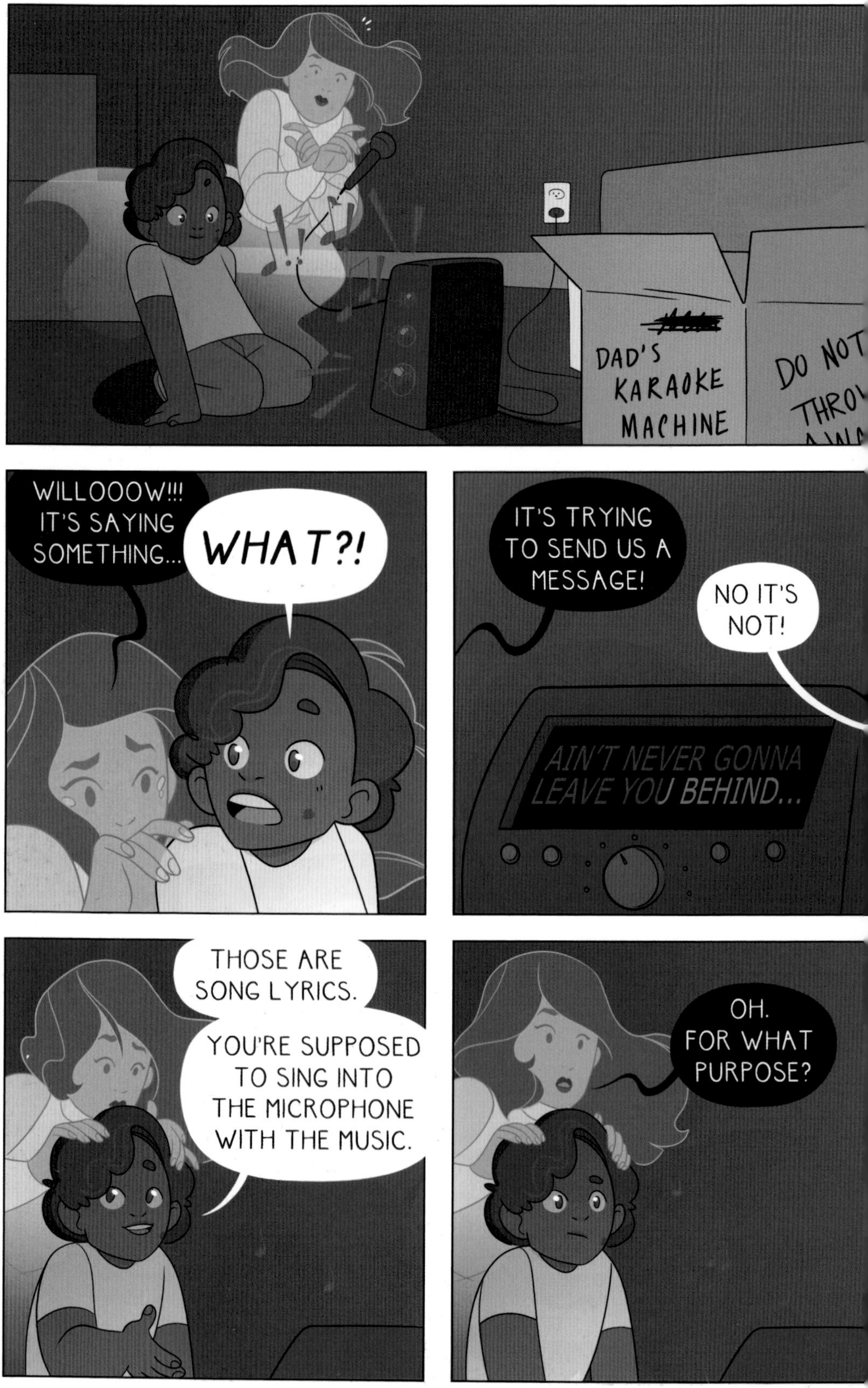
DAD'S KARAOKE MACHINE
DO NOT
WILLOOOW!!! IT'S SAYING SOMETHING...
WHAT?!
IT'S TRYING TO SEND US A MESSAGE!
NO IT'S NOT!
AIN'T NEVER GONNA LEAVE YOU BEHIND...
THOSE ARE SONG LYRICS.
YOU'RE SUPPOSED TO SING INTO THE MICROPHONE WITH THE MUSIC.
OH. FOR WHAT PURPOSE?

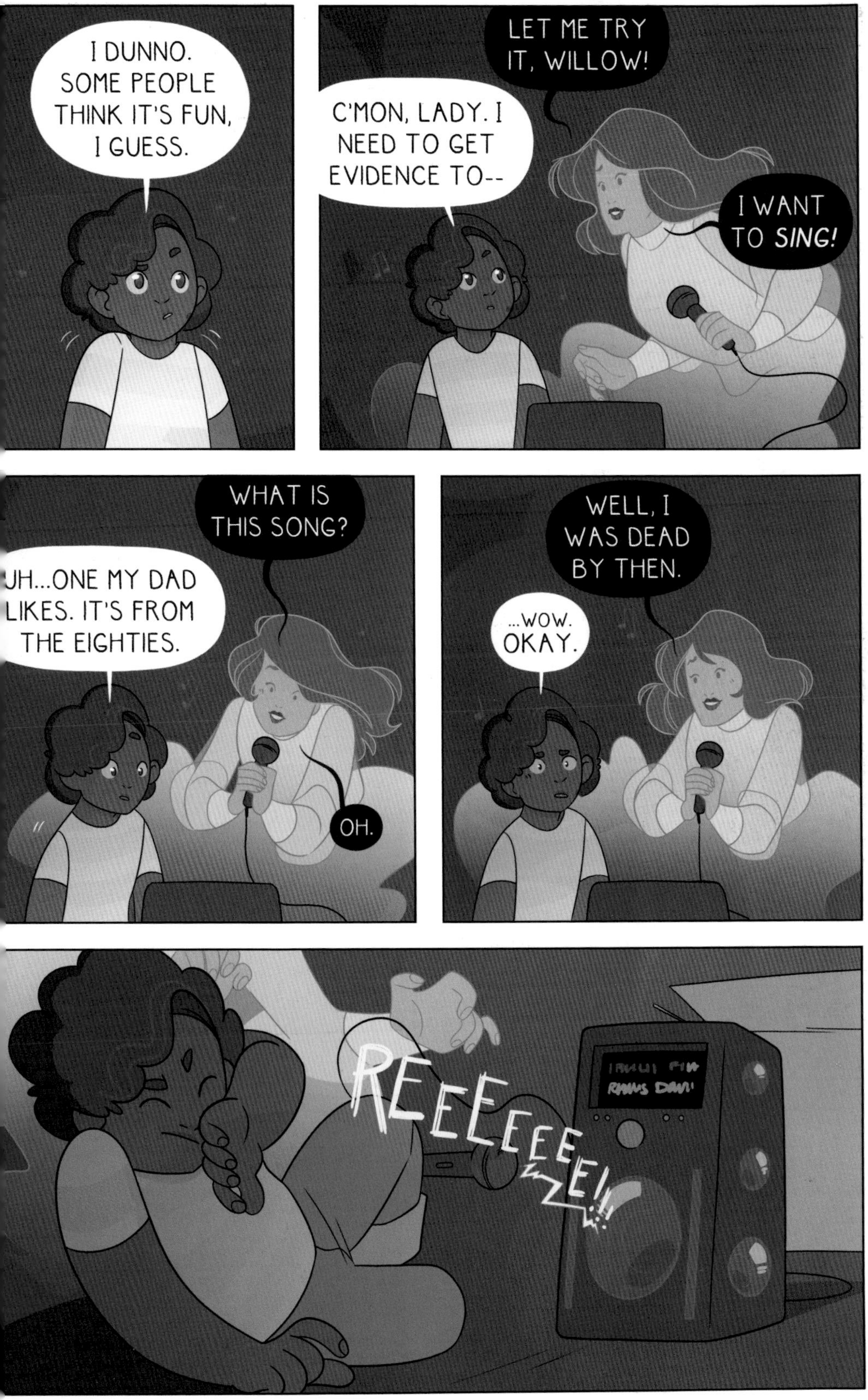
I DUNNO. SOME PEOPLE THINK IT'S FUN, I GUESS.
LET ME TRY IT, WILLOW!
C'MON, LADY. I NEED TO GET EVIDENCE TO--
I WANT TO *SING!*
WHAT IS THIS SONG?
UH...ONE MY DAD LIKES. IT'S FROM THE EIGHTIES.
OH.
WELL, I WAS DEAD BY THEN.
...WOW. OKAY.
REEEEEEE!!

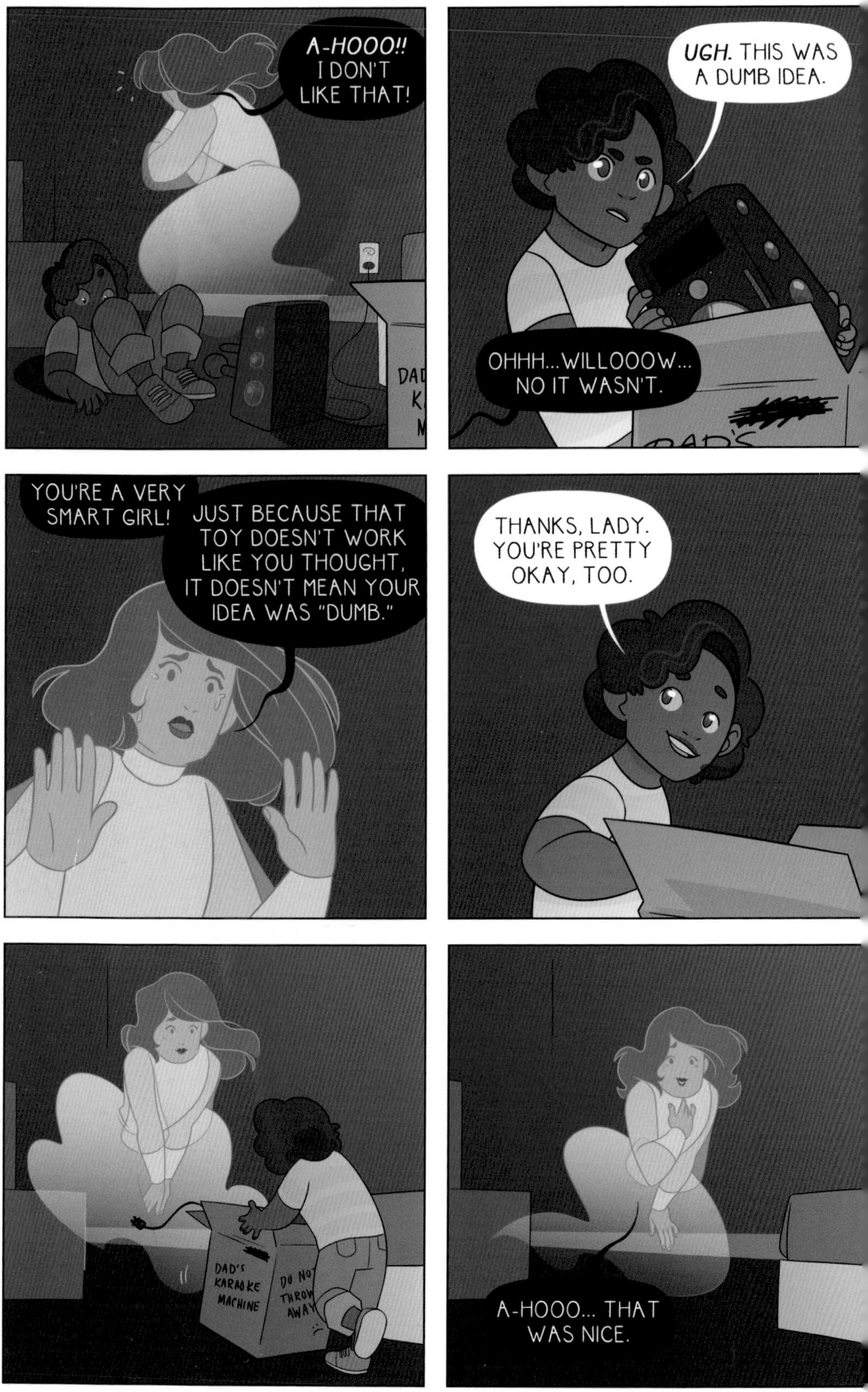

A-HOOO!! I DON'T LIKE THAT!
UGH. THIS WAS A DUMB IDEA.
OHHH...WILLOOOW... NO IT WASN'T.
YOU'RE A VERY SMART GIRL!
JUST BECAUSE THAT TOY DOESN'T WORK LIKE YOU THOUGHT, IT DOESN'T MEAN YOUR IDEA WAS "DUMB."
THANKS, LADY. YOU'RE PRETTY OKAY, TOO.
DAD'S KARAOKE MACHINE
DO NOT THROW AWAY
A-HOOO... THAT WAS NICE.

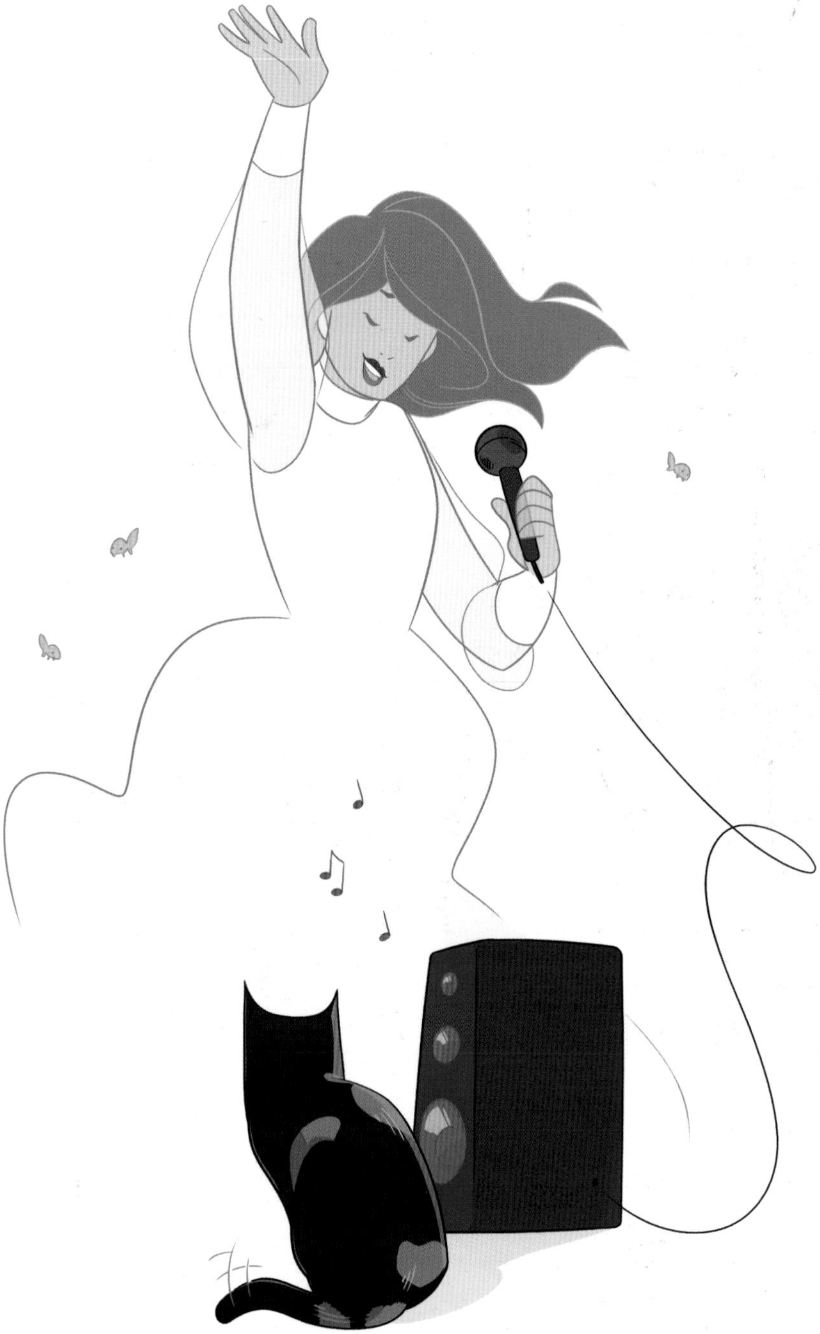

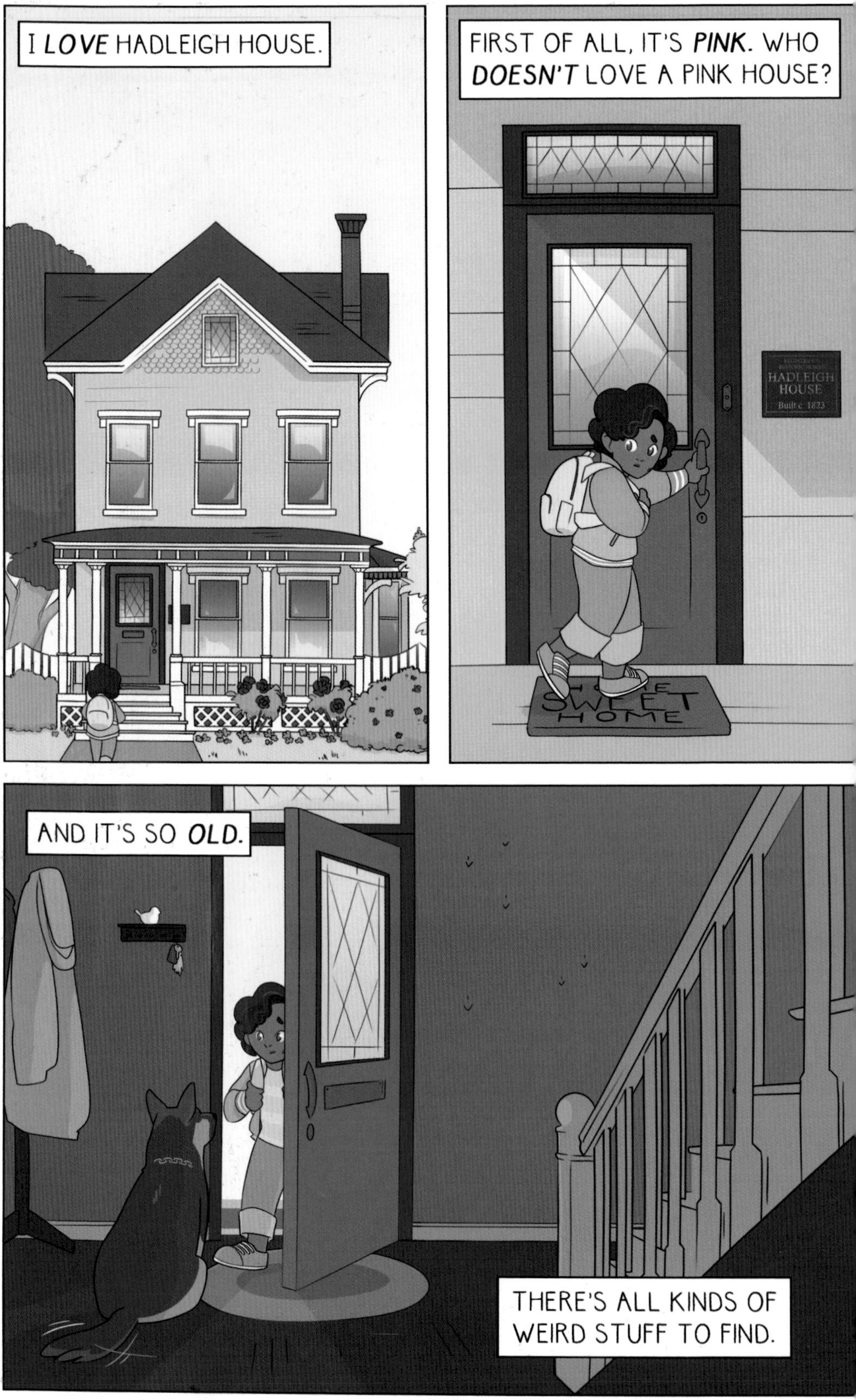
I *LOVE* HADLEIGH HOUSE.
FIRST OF ALL, IT'S *PINK*. WHO *DOESN'T* LOVE A PINK HOUSE?
HADLEIGH HOUSE
Built c. 1823
AND IT'S SO *OLD*.
THERE'S ALL KINDS OF WEIRD STUFF TO FIND.

ESPECIALLY IN THE *ATTIC*.

THE OLD OWNERS LEFT A *BUNCH* OF STUFF UP THERE.

THERE'S STUFF ALL THE WAY BACK TO THE WALL...

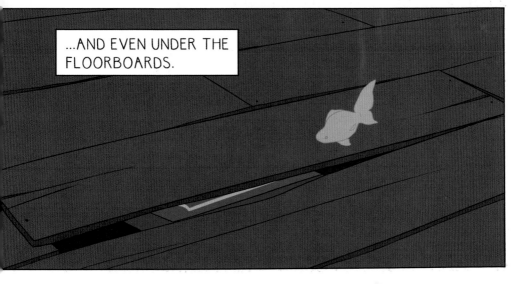

...AND EVEN UNDER THE FLOORBOARDS.

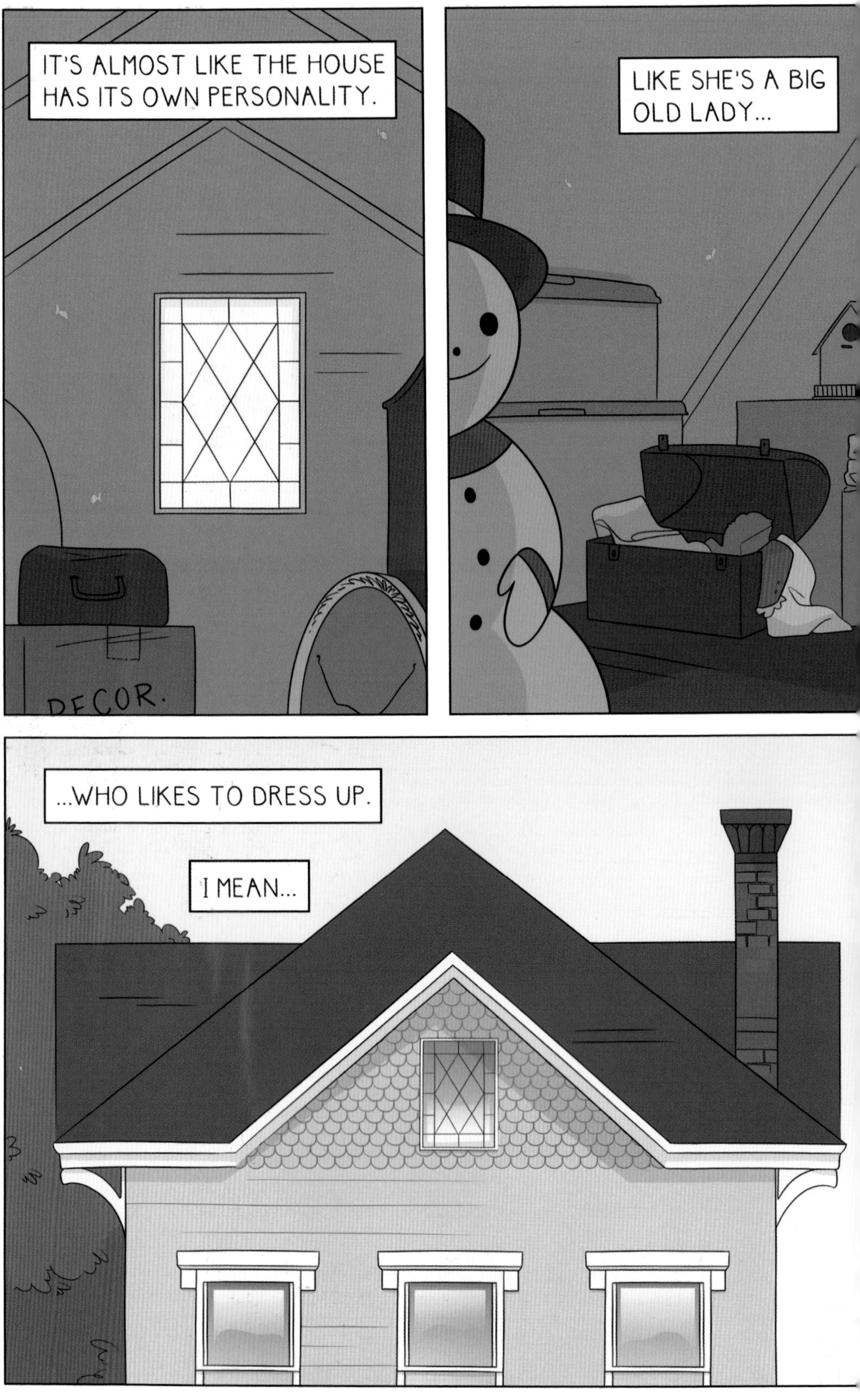
IT'S ALMOST LIKE THE HOUSE HAS ITS OWN PERSONALITY.
DECOR.
LIKE SHE'S A BIG OLD LADY...
...WHO LIKES TO DRESS UP.
I MEAN...

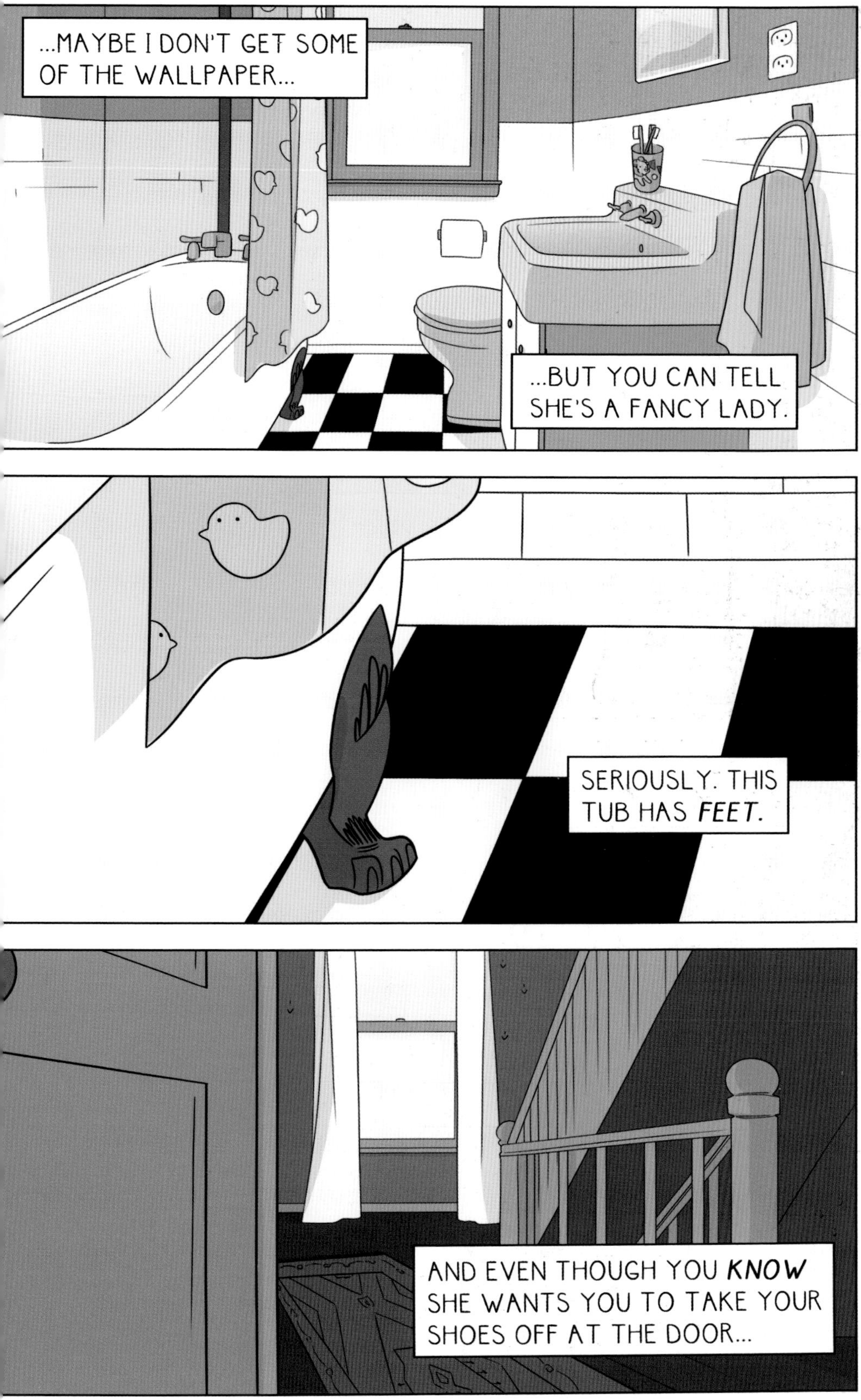
...MAYBE I DON'T GET SOME OF THE WALLPAPER...
...BUT YOU CAN TELL SHE'S A FANCY LADY.
SERIOUSLY. THIS TUB HAS *FEET.*
AND EVEN THOUGH YOU ***KNOW*** SHE WANTS YOU TO TAKE YOUR SHOES OFF AT THE DOOR...

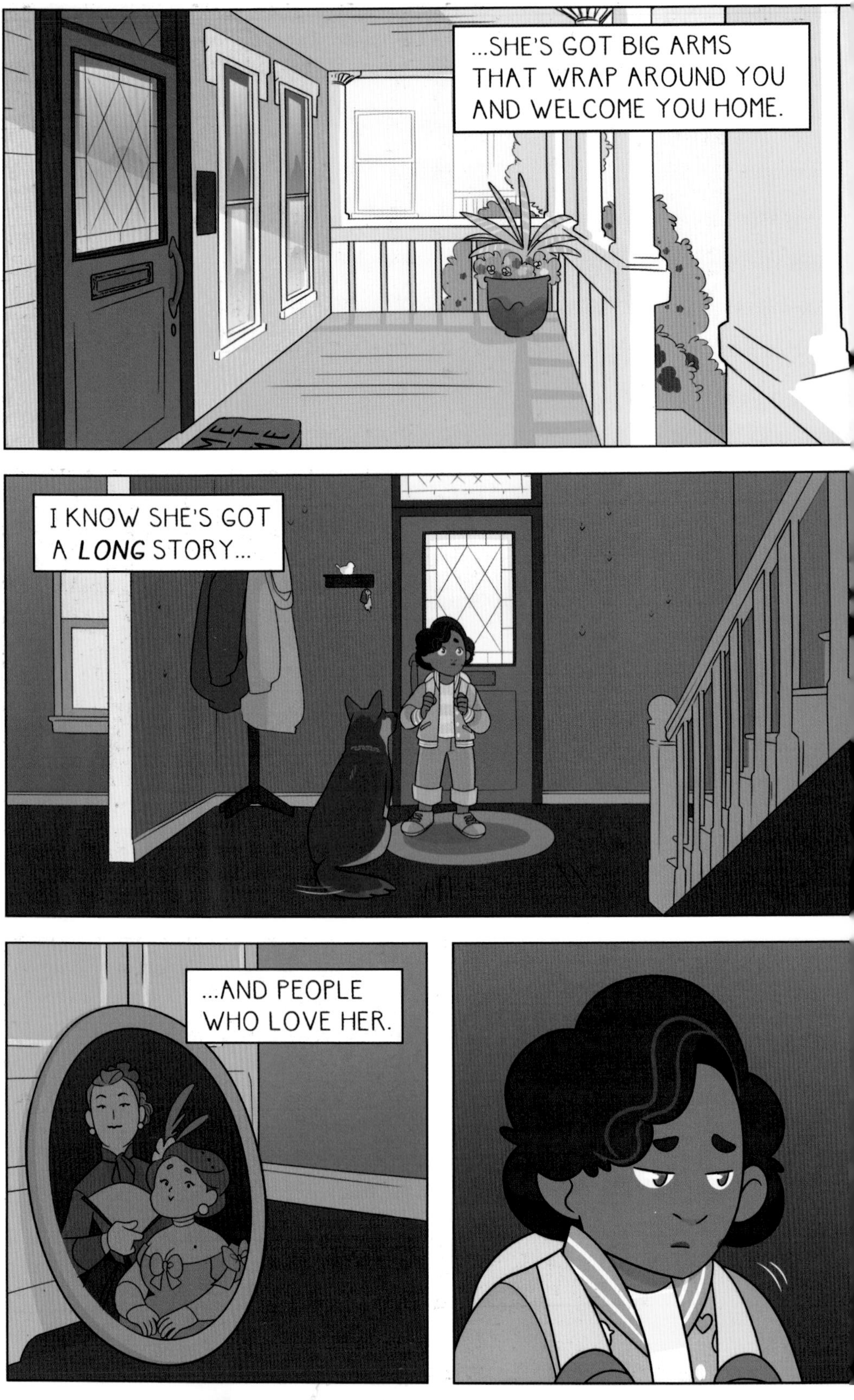
...SHE'S GOT BIG ARMS THAT WRAP AROUND YOU AND WELCOME YOU HOME.
I KNOW SHE'S GOT A *LONG* STORY...
...AND PEOPLE WHO LOVE HER.

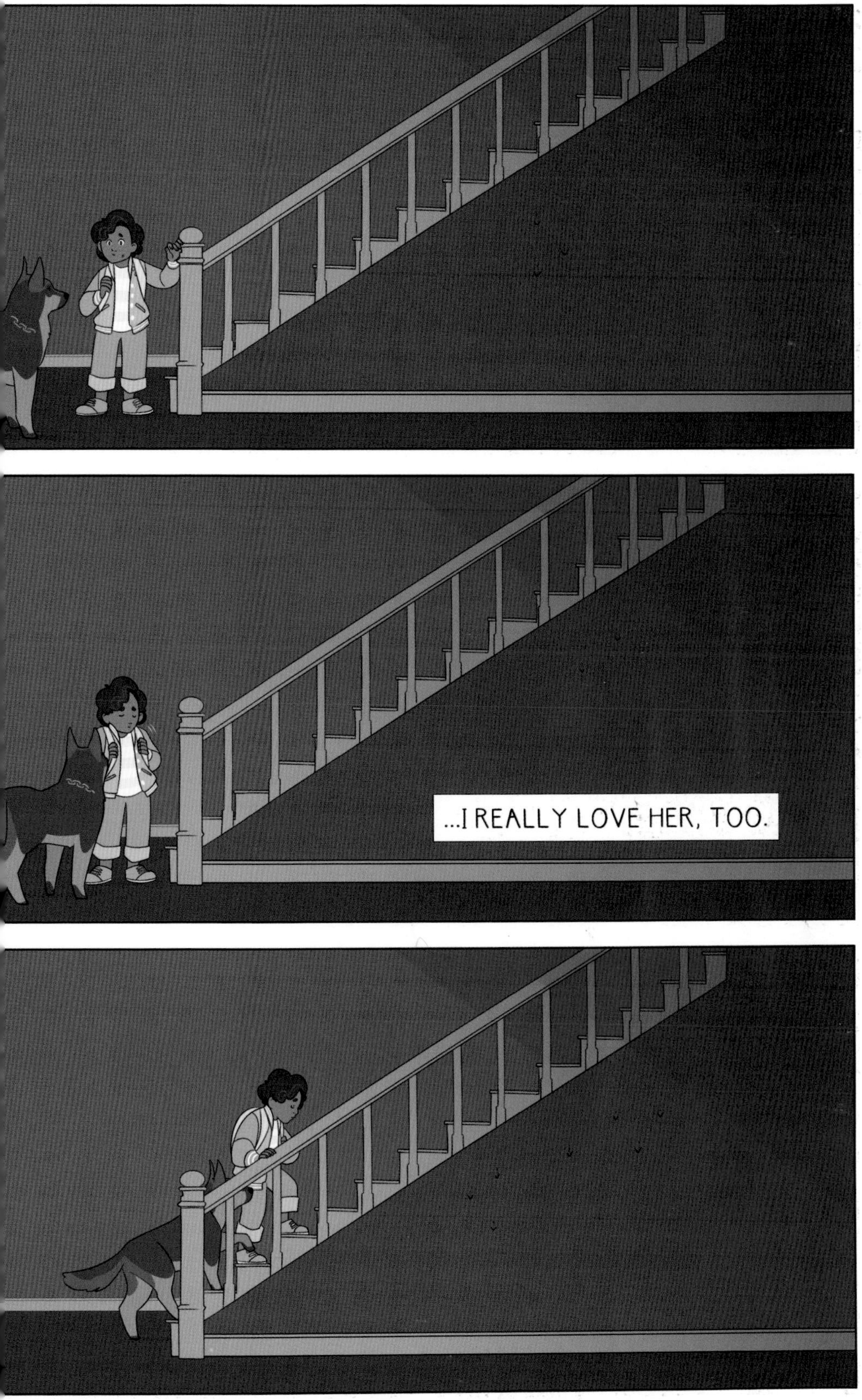
...I REALLY LOVE HER, TOO.

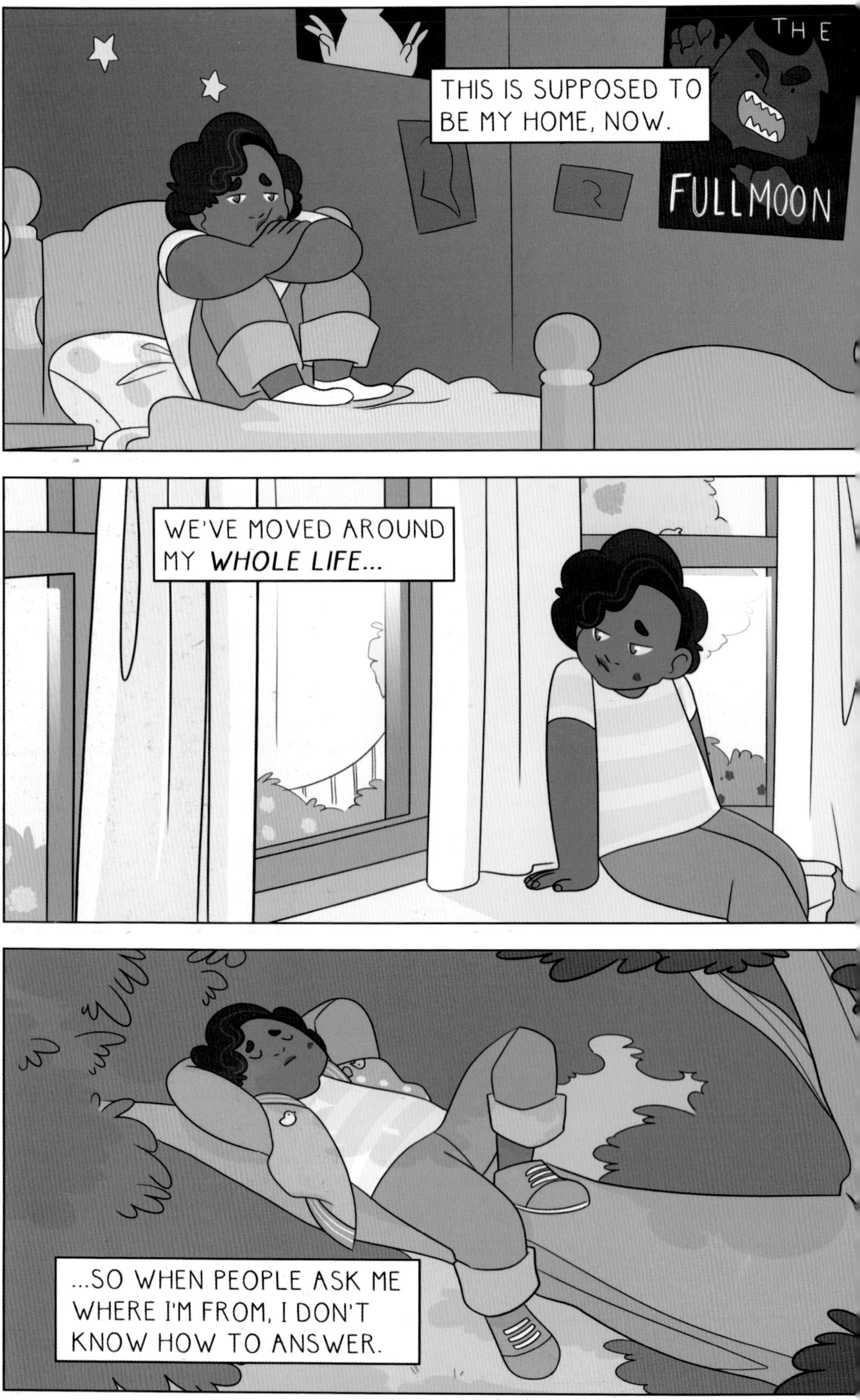
THE FULLMOON
THIS IS SUPPOSED TO BE MY HOME, NOW.
WE'VE MOVED AROUND MY *WHOLE LIFE*...
...SO WHEN PEOPLE ASK ME WHERE I'M FROM, I DON'T KNOW HOW TO ANSWER.

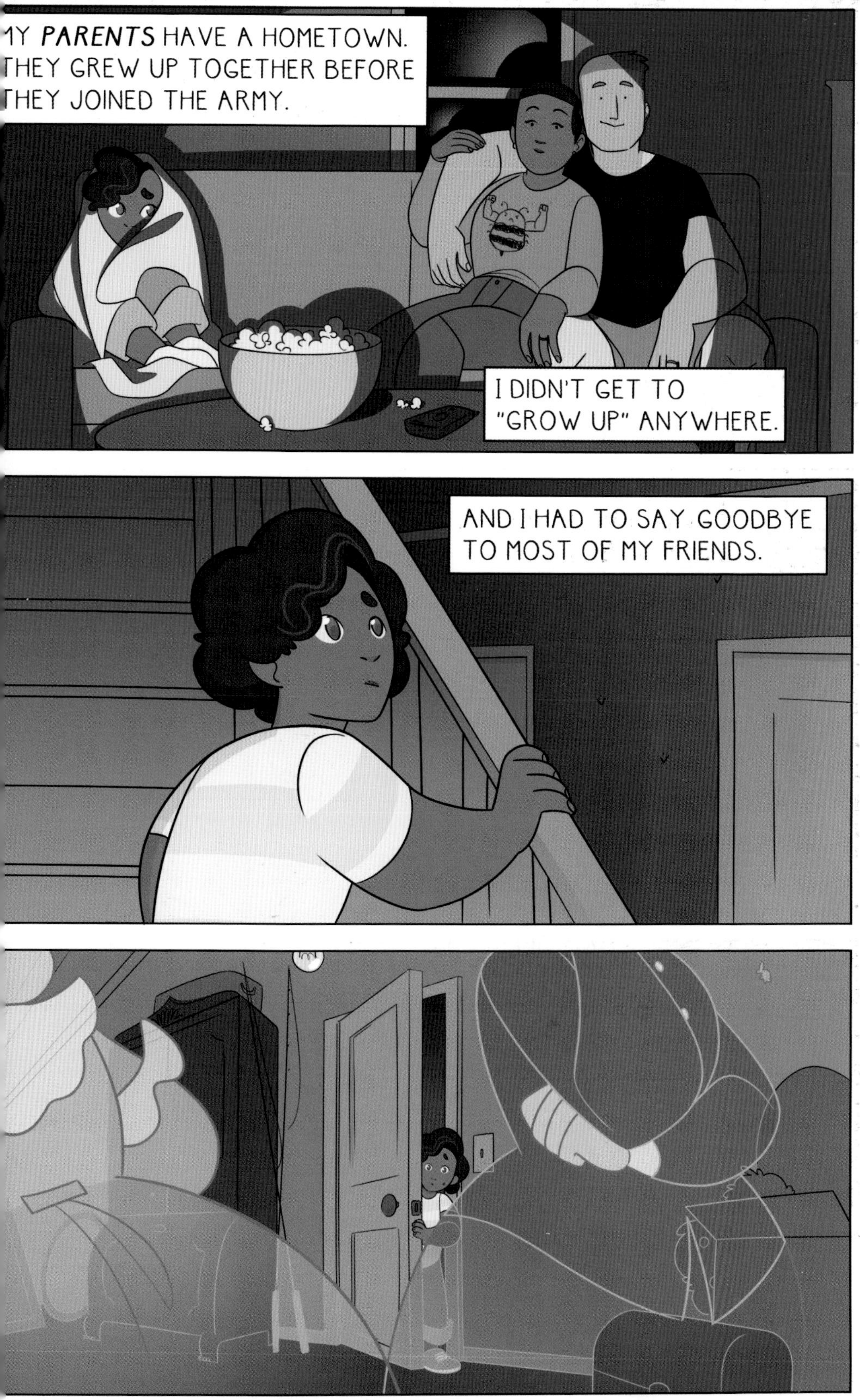
MY *PARENTS* HAVE A HOMETOWN. THEY GREW UP TOGETHER BEFORE THEY JOINED THE ARMY.
I DIDN'T GET TO "GROW UP" ANYWHERE.
AND I HAD TO SAY GOODBYE TO MOST OF MY FRIENDS.

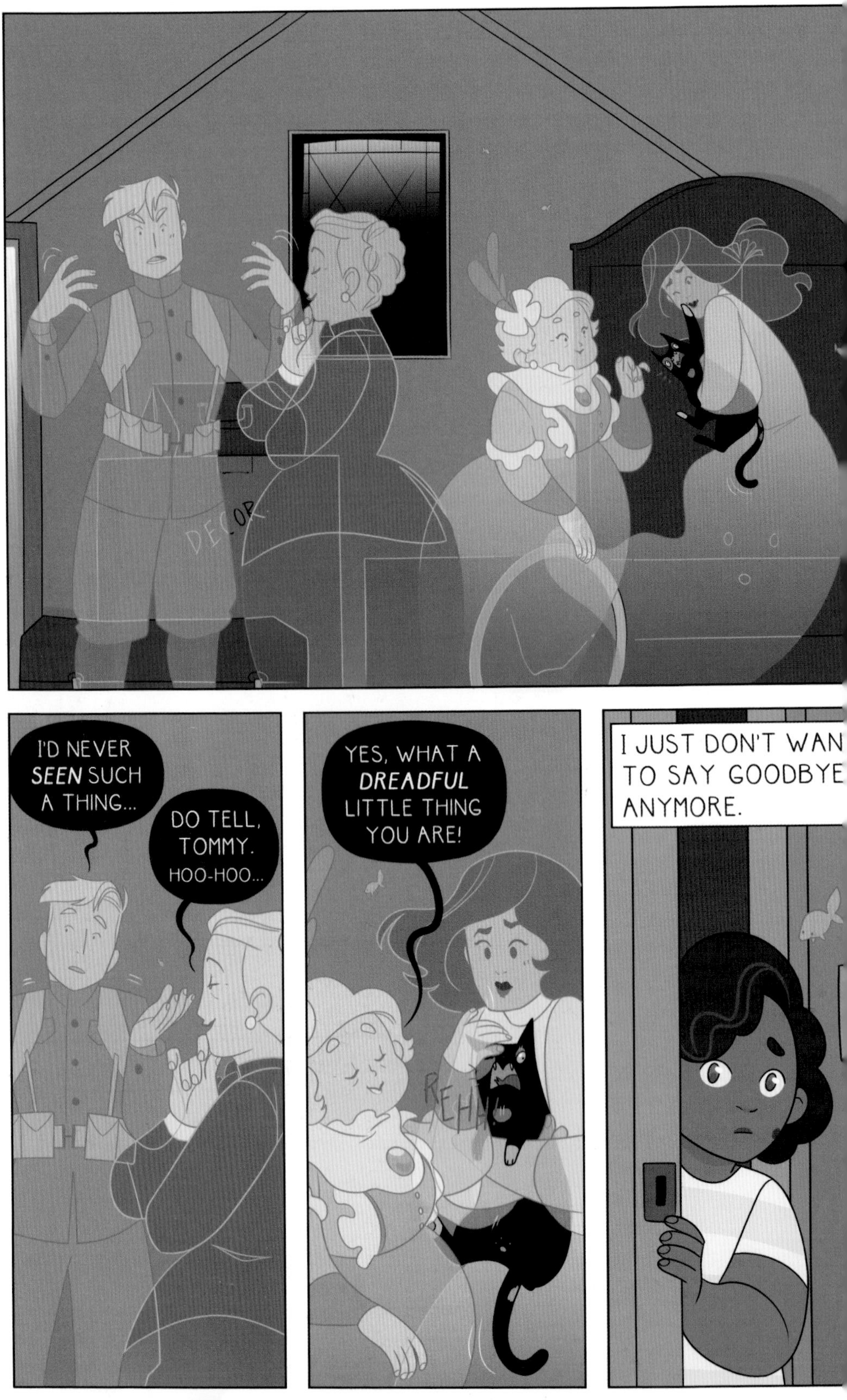
DECOR
I'D NEVER SEEN SUCH A THING...
DO TELL, TOMMY. HOO-HOO...
YES, WHAT A DREADFUL LITTLE THING YOU ARE!
I JUST DON'T WAN
TO SAY GOODBYE
ANYMORE.

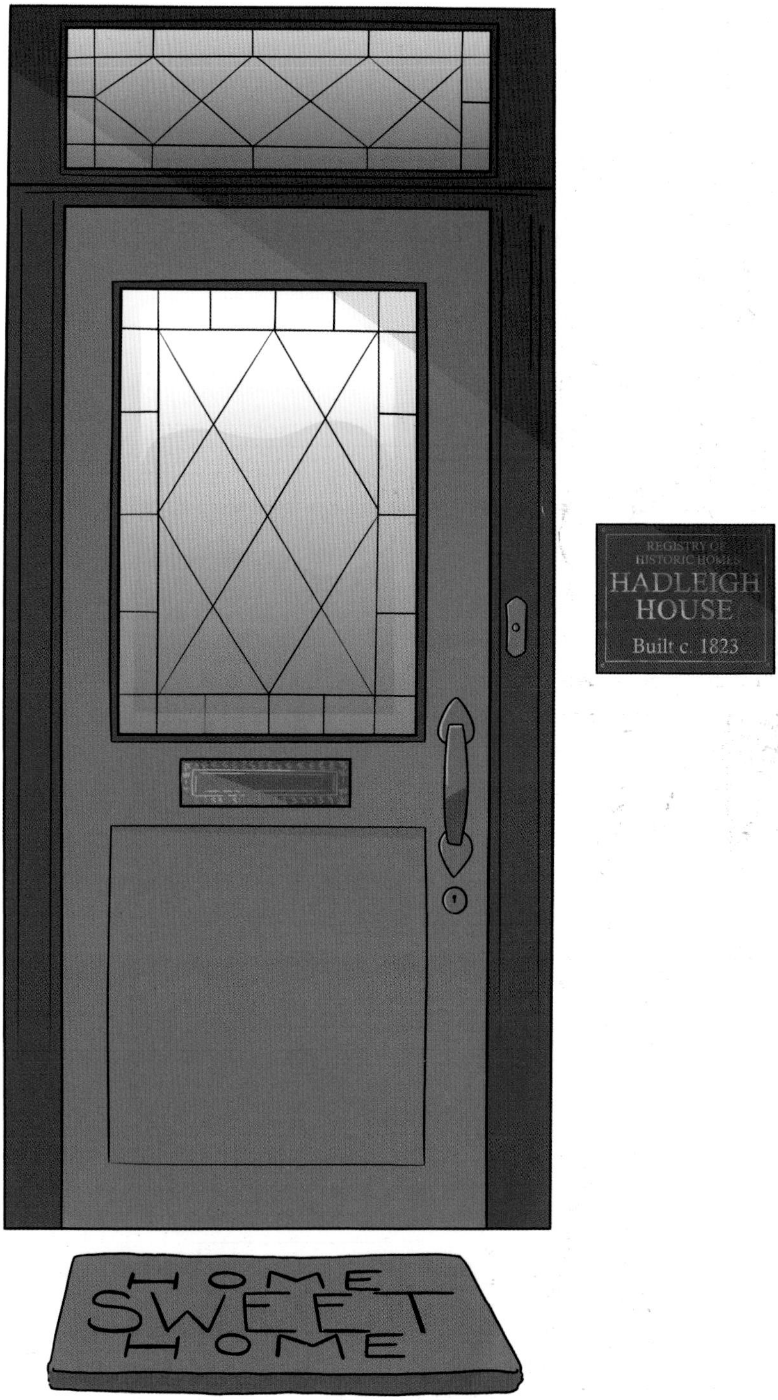
REGISTRY OF
HISTORIC HOMES
HADLEIGH HOUSE
Built c. 1823
HOME SWEET HOME

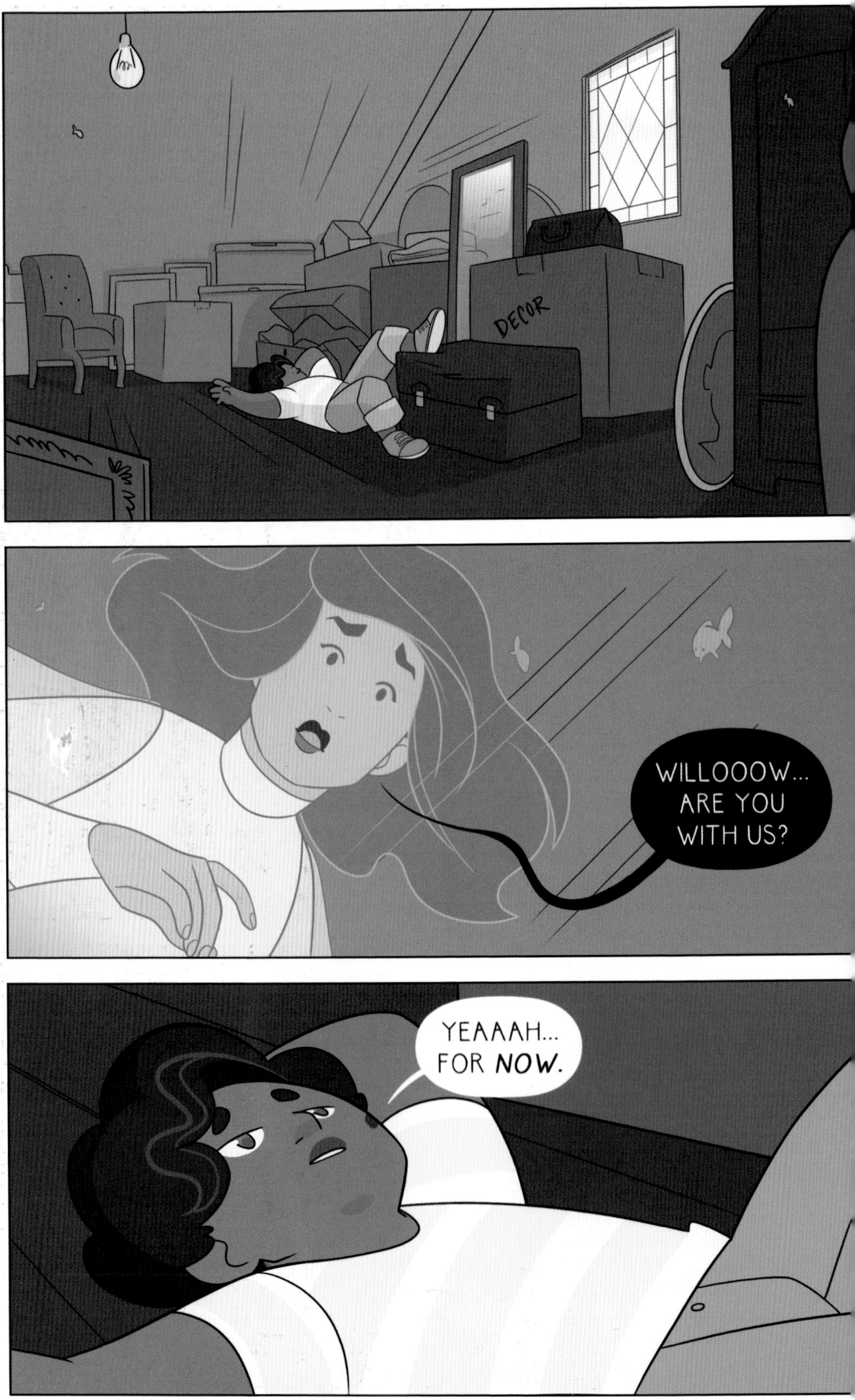
DECOR
WILLOOOW... ARE YOU WITH US?
YEAAAH... FOR NOW.

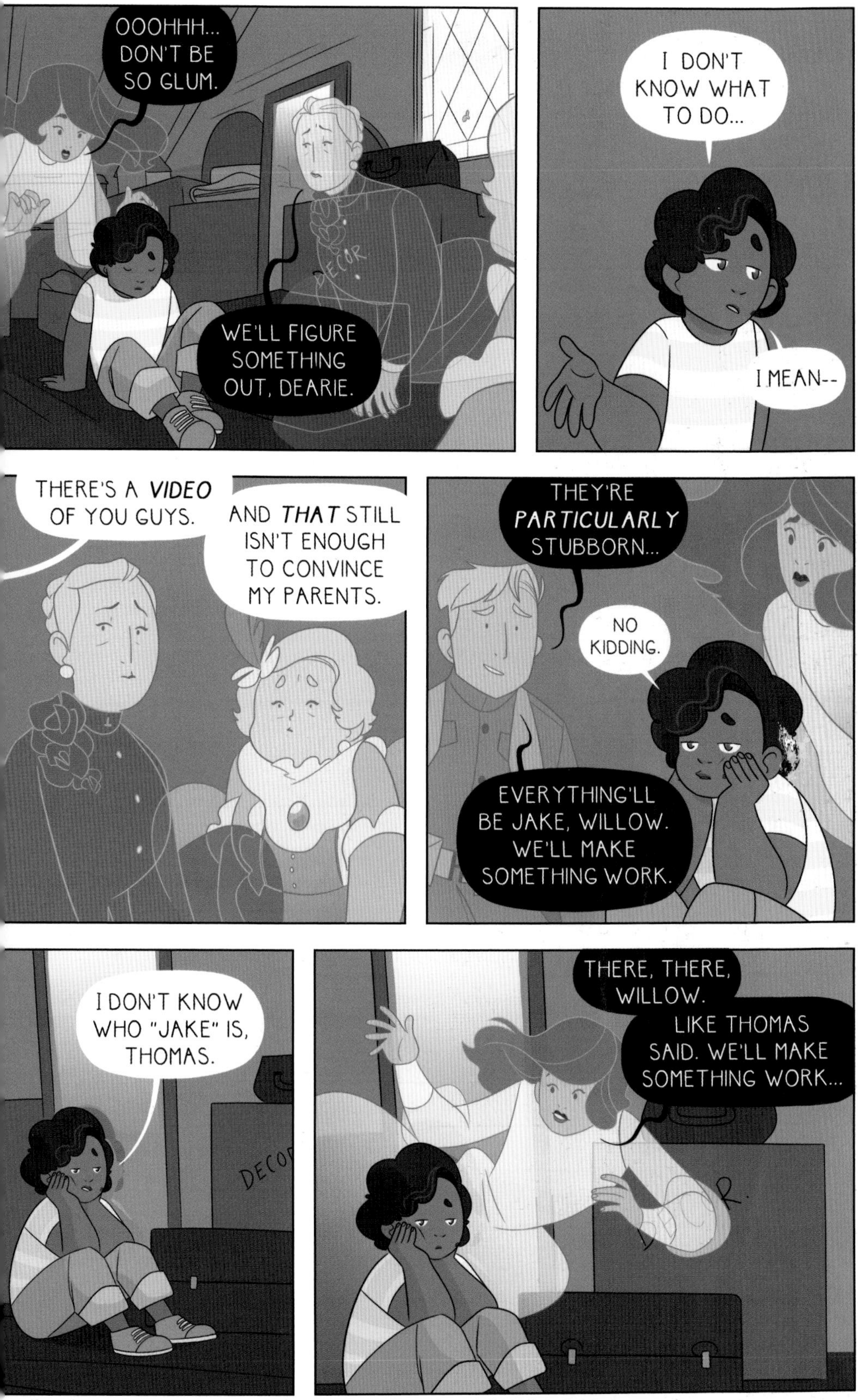
OOOHHH... DON'T BE SO GLUM.
WE'LL FIGURE SOMETHING OUT, DEARIE.
I DON'T KNOW WHAT TO DO...
I MEAN--
THERE'S A *VIDEO* OF YOU GUYS.
AND *THAT* STILL ISN'T ENOUGH TO CONVINCE MY PARENTS.
THEY'RE *PARTICULARLY* STUBBORN...
NO KIDDING.
EVERYTHING'LL BE JAKE, WILLOW. WE'LL MAKE SOMETHING WORK.
I DON'T KNOW WHO "JAKE" IS, THOMAS.
THERE, THERE, WILLOW.
LIKE THOMAS SAID. WE'LL MAKE SOMETHING WORK...

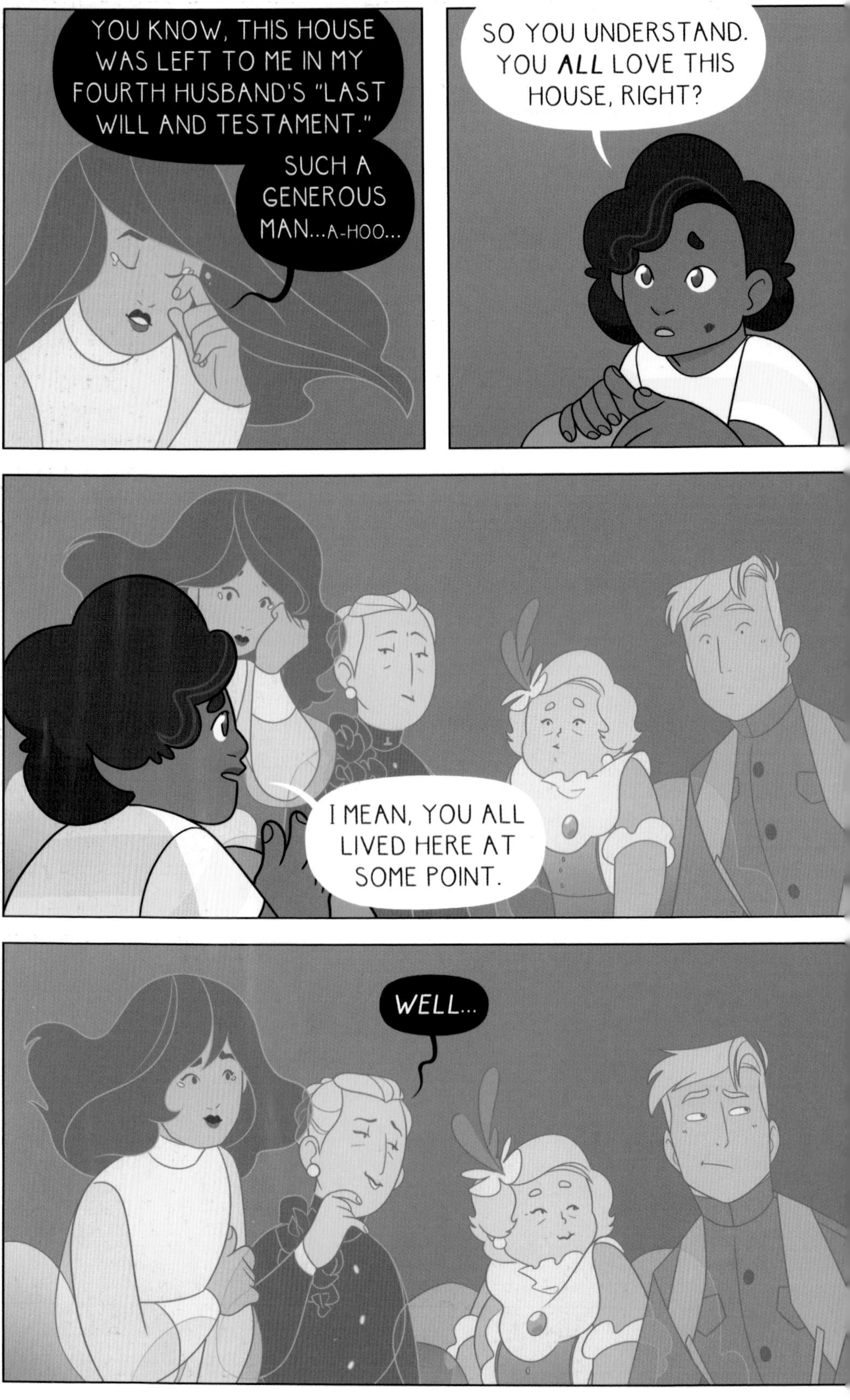
YOU KNOW, THIS HOUSE WAS LEFT TO ME IN MY FOURTH HUSBAND'S "LAST WILL AND TESTAMENT."
SUCH A GENEROUS MAN...A-HOO...
SO YOU UNDERSTAND. YOU **ALL** LOVE THIS HOUSE, RIGHT?
I MEAN, YOU ALL LIVED HERE AT SOME POINT.
WELL...

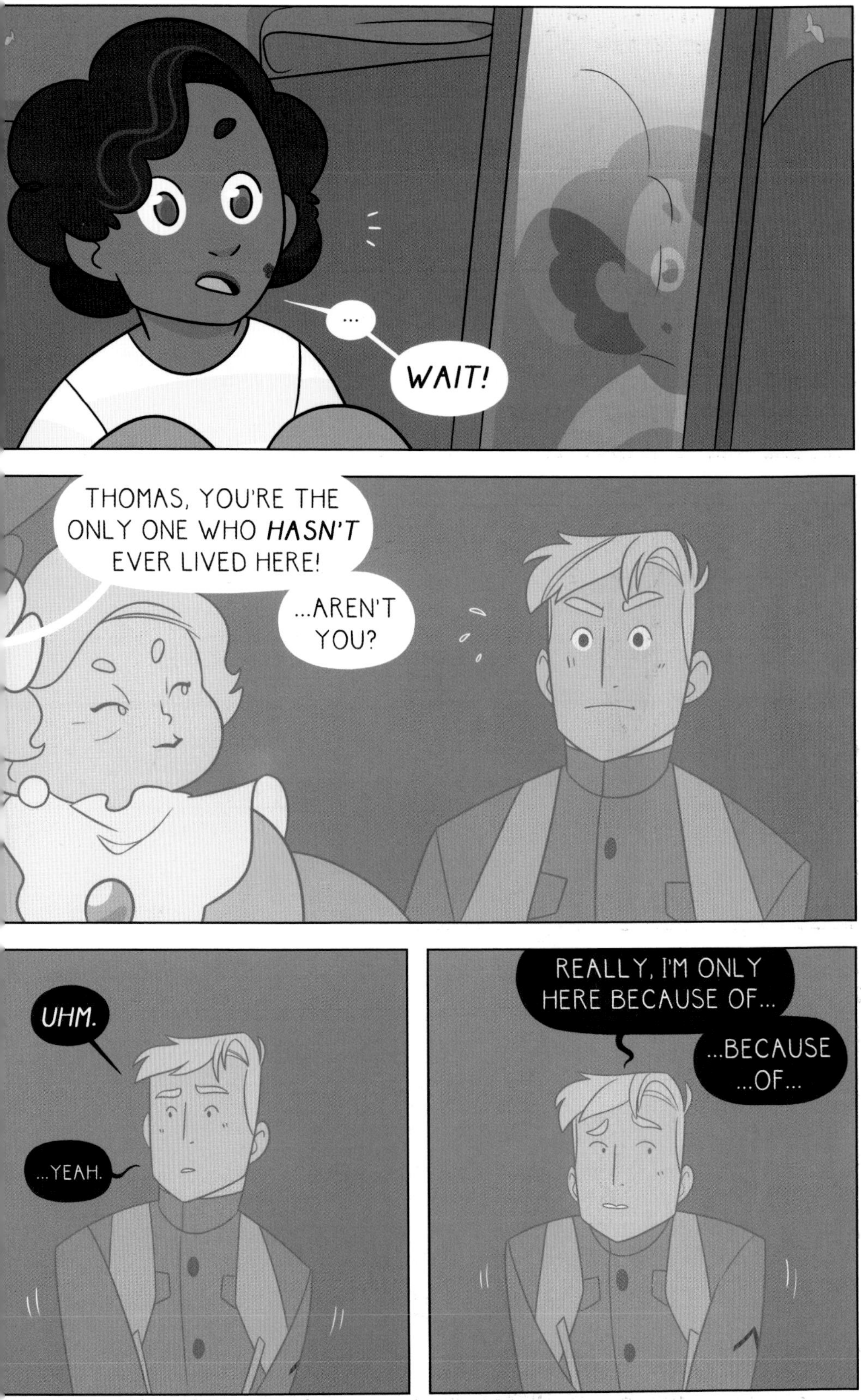
...
WAIT!
THOMAS, YOU'RE THE ONLY ONE WHO *HASN'T* EVER LIVED HERE!
...AREN'T YOU?
*UHM.*
...YEAH.
REALLY, I'M ONLY HERE BECAUSE OF...
...BECAUSE ...OF...

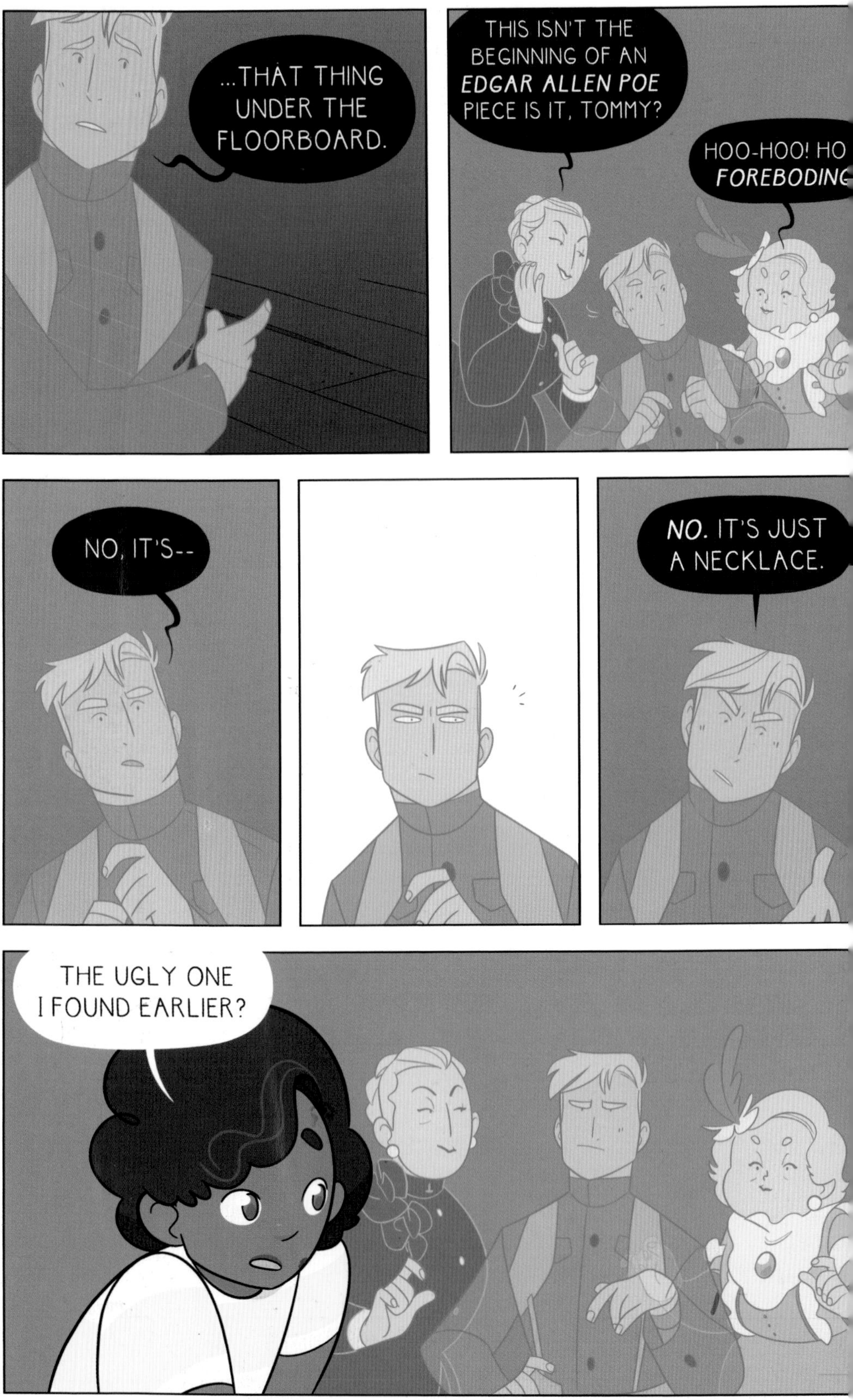
...THAT THING UNDER THE FLOORBOARD.
THIS ISN'T THE BEGINNING OF AN *EDGAR ALLEN POE* PIECE IS IT, TOMMY?
HOO-HOO! HO
*FOREBODIN*
NO, IT'S--
*NO.* IT'S JUST A NECKLACE.
THE UGLY ONE I FOUND EARLIER?

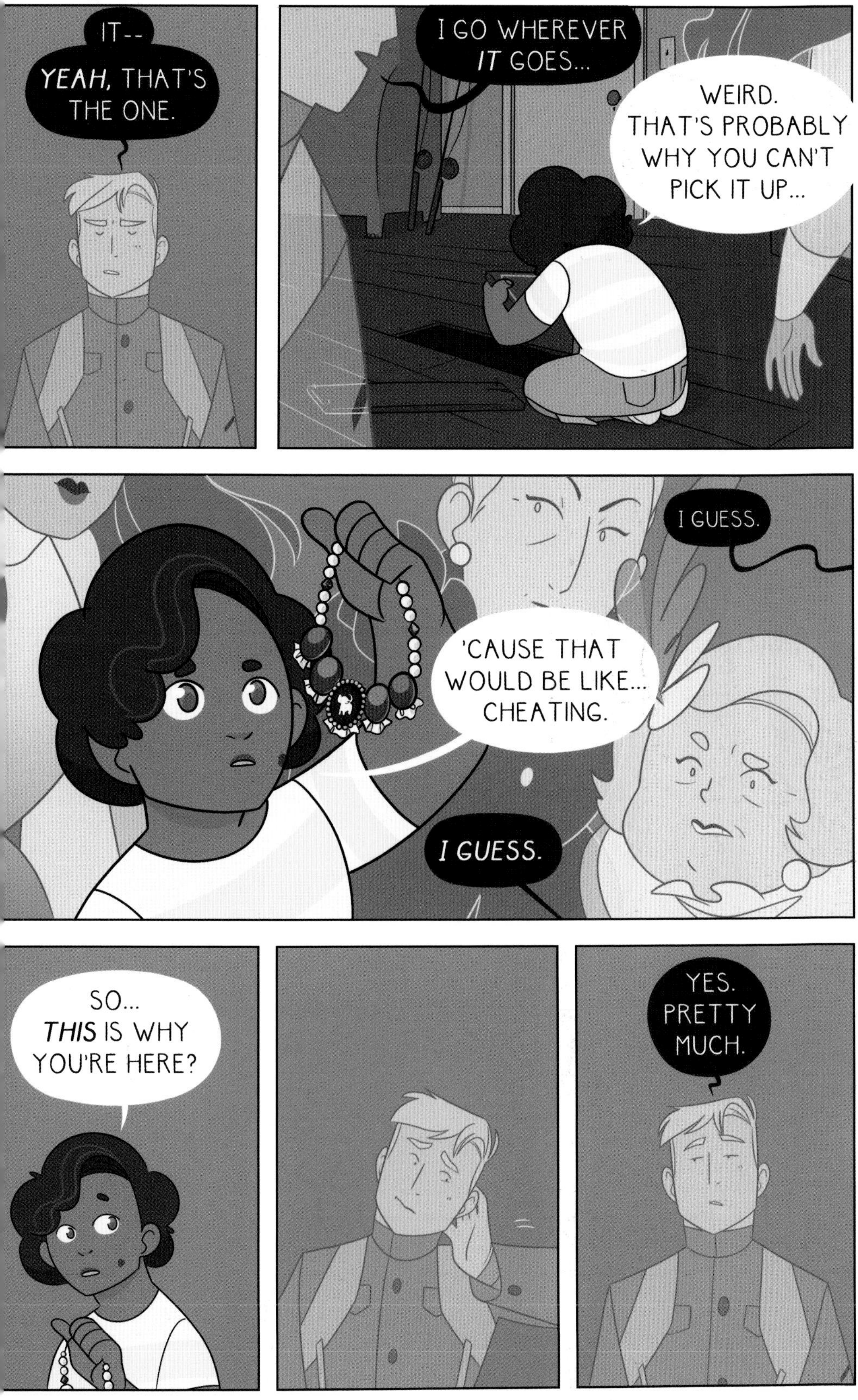
IT--
YEAH, THAT'S THE ONE.
I GO WHEREVER IT GOES...
WEIRD. THAT'S PROBABLY WHY YOU CAN'T PICK IT UP...
I GUESS.
'CAUSE THAT WOULD BE LIKE... CHEATING.
I GUESS.
SO... THIS IS WHY YOU'RE HERE?
YES. PRETTY MUCH.

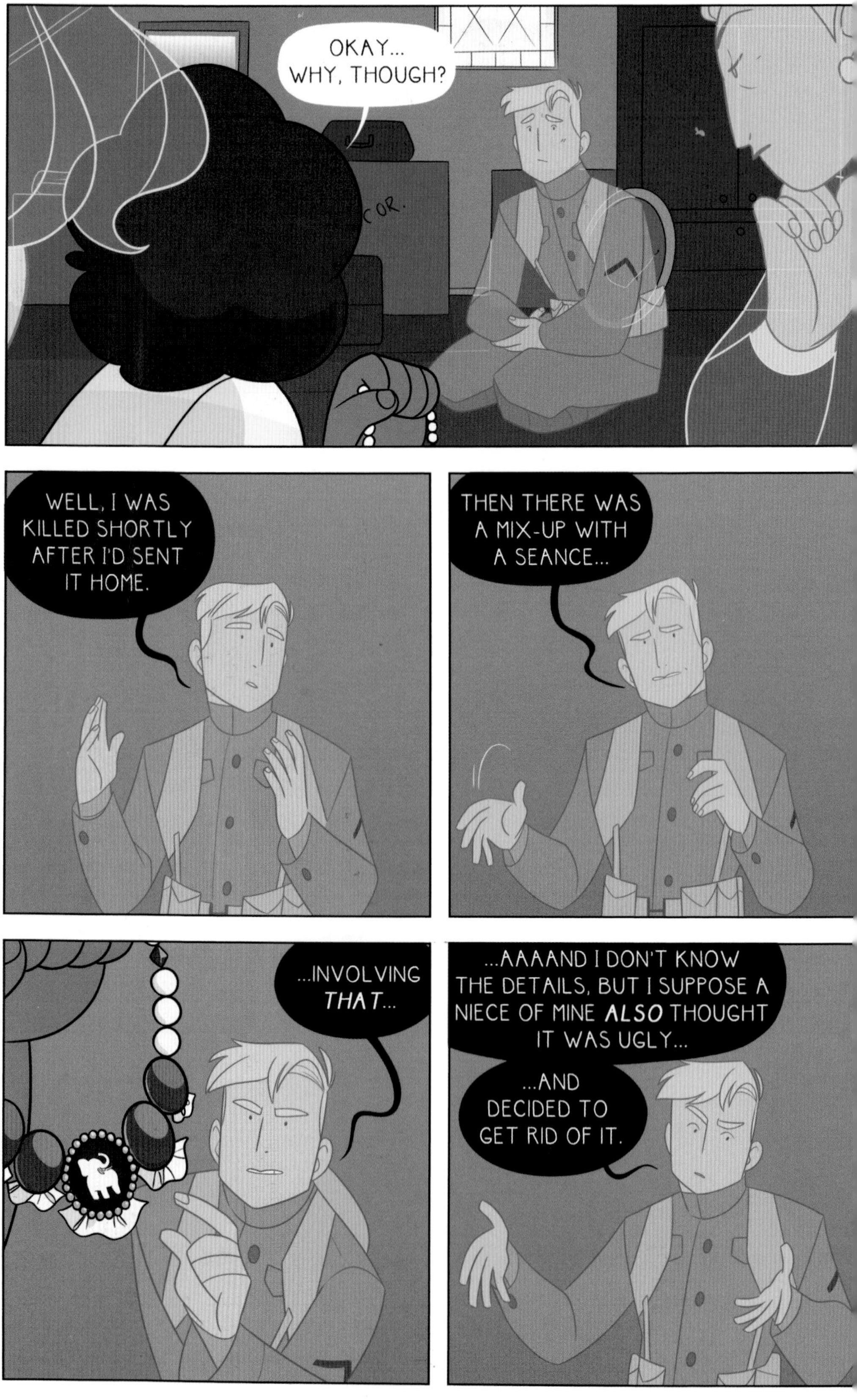
OKAY... WHY, THOUGH?
COR.
WELL, I WAS KILLED SHORTLY AFTER I'D SENT IT HOME.
THEN THERE WAS A MIX-UP WITH A SEANCE...
...INVOLVING *THAT*...
...AAAAND I DON'T KNOW THE DETAILS, BUT I SUPPOSE A NIECE OF MINE **ALSO** THOUGHT IT WAS UGLY...
...AND DECIDED TO GET RID OF IT.

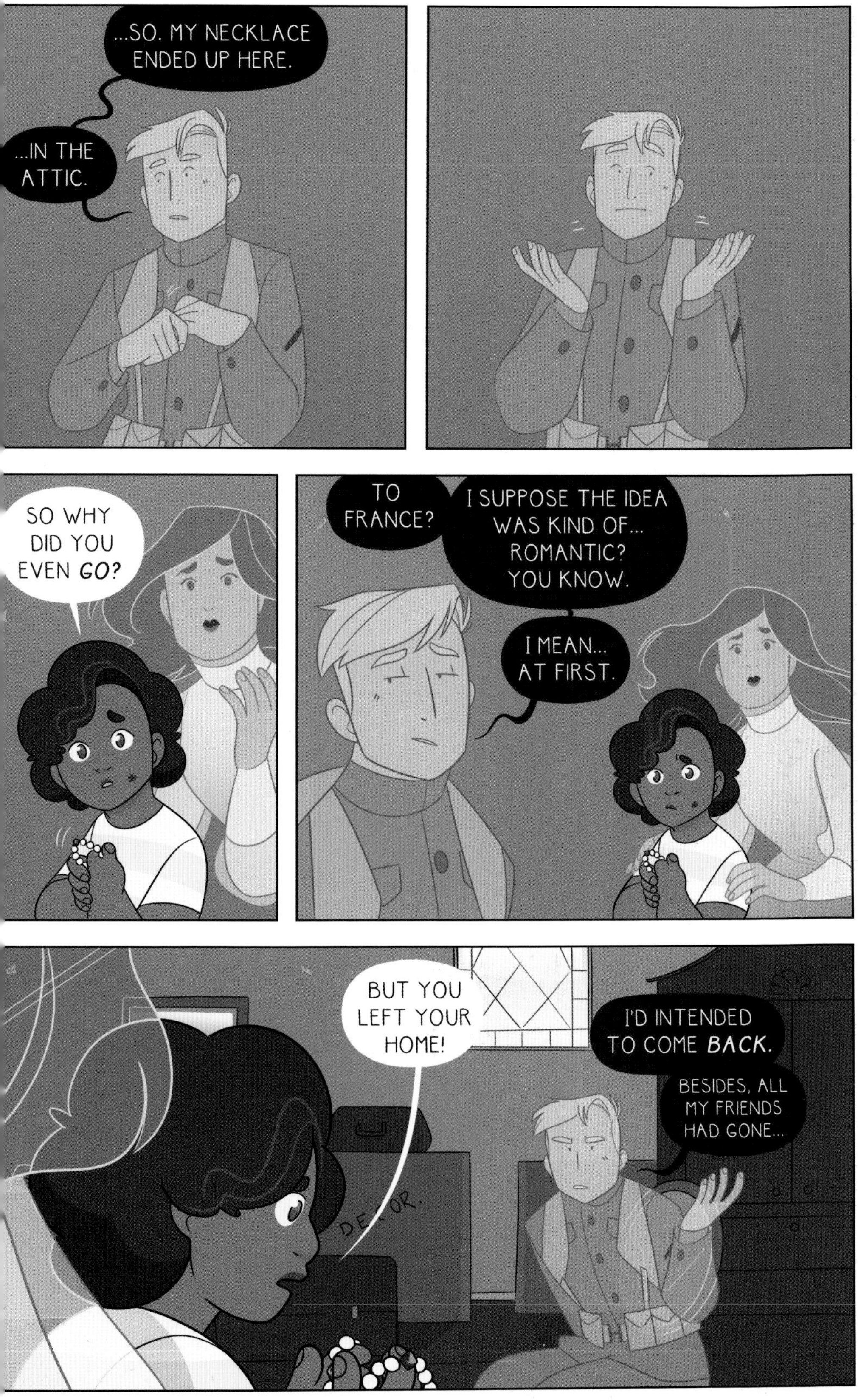
...SO. MY NECKLACE ENDED UP HERE.
...IN THE ATTIC.
SO WHY DID YOU EVEN *GO?*
TO FRANCE?
I SUPPOSE THE IDEA WAS KIND OF... ROMANTIC? YOU KNOW.
I MEAN... AT FIRST.
BUT YOU LEFT YOUR HOME!
I'D INTENDED TO COME *BACK.*
BESIDES, ALL MY FRIENDS HAD GONE...

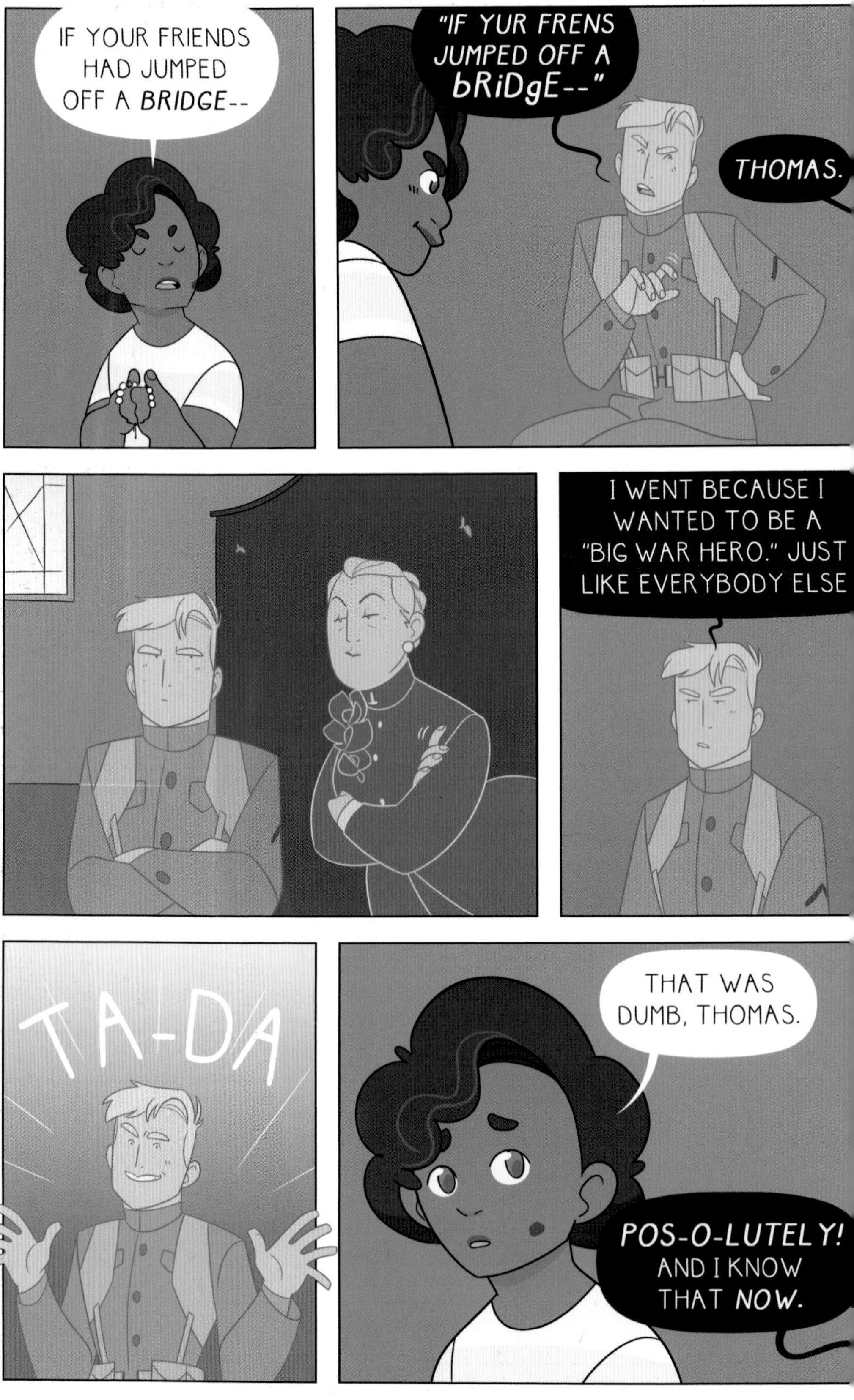
IF YOUR FRIENDS HAD JUMPED OFF A *BRIDGE*--
"IF YUR FRENS JUMPED OFF A bRiDgE--"
THOMAS.
I WENT BECAUSE I WANTED TO BE A "BIG WAR HERO." JUST LIKE EVERYBODY ELSE
TA-DA
THAT WAS DUMB, THOMAS.
*POS-O-LUTELY!* AND I KNOW THAT *NOW.*

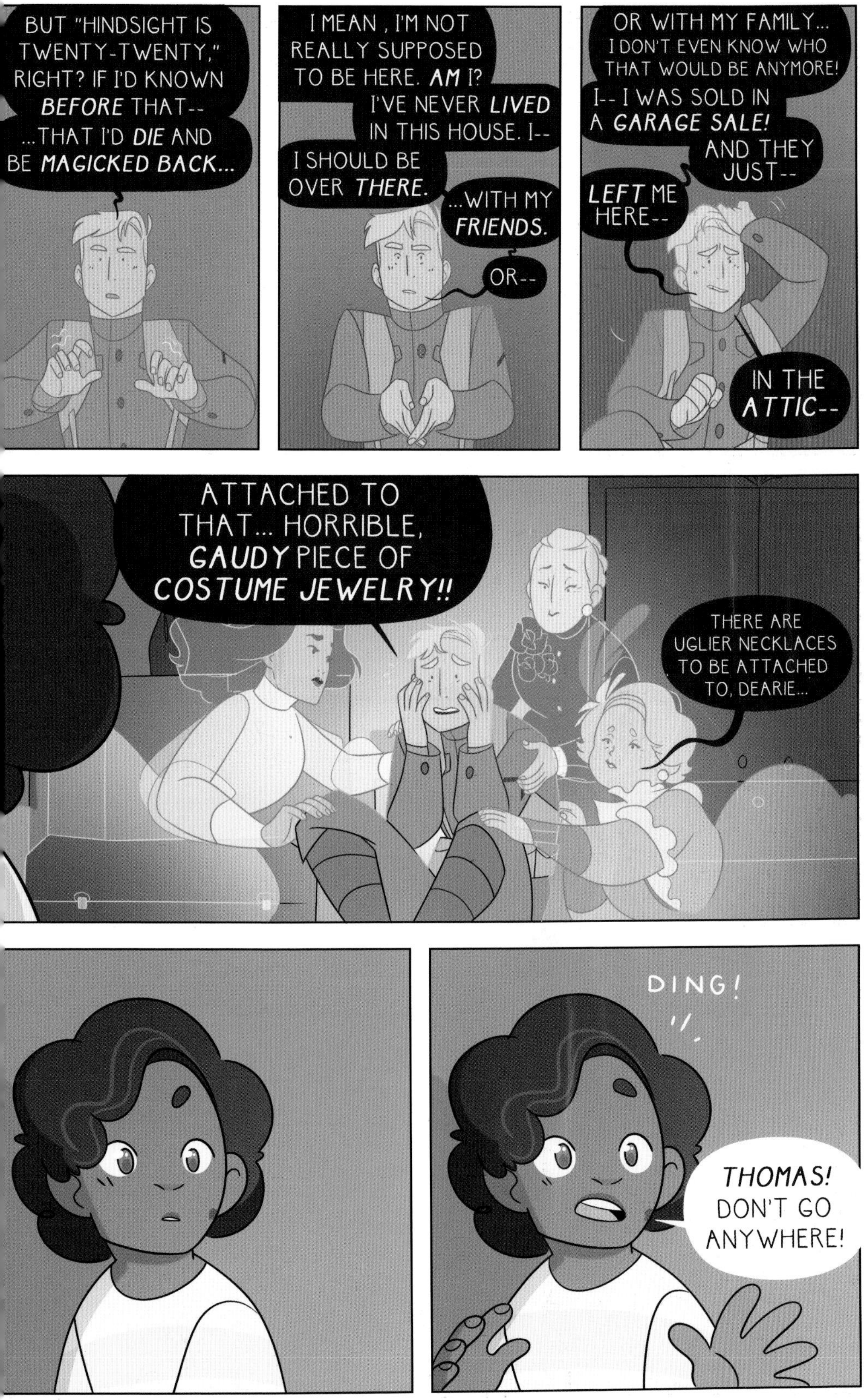

BUT "HINDSIGHT IS TWENTY-TWENTY," RIGHT? IF I'D KNOWN *BEFORE* THAT--
...THAT I'D *DIE* AND BE *MAGICKED BACK*...
I MEAN, I'M NOT REALLY SUPPOSED TO BE HERE. *AM* I?
I'VE NEVER *LIVED* IN THIS HOUSE. I--
I SHOULD BE OVER *THERE*.
...WITH MY *FRIENDS*.
OR--
OR WITH MY FAMILY... I DON'T EVEN KNOW WHO THAT WOULD BE ANYMORE!
I-- I WAS SOLD IN A *GARAGE SALE!*
AND THEY JUST--
*LEFT* ME HERE--
IN THE *ATTIC*--
ATTACHED TO THAT... HORRIBLE, *GAUDY* PIECE OF *COSTUME JEWELRY!!*
THERE ARE UGLIER NECKLACES TO BE ATTACHED TO, DEARIE...
DING!
*THOMAS!* DON'T GO ANYWHERE!

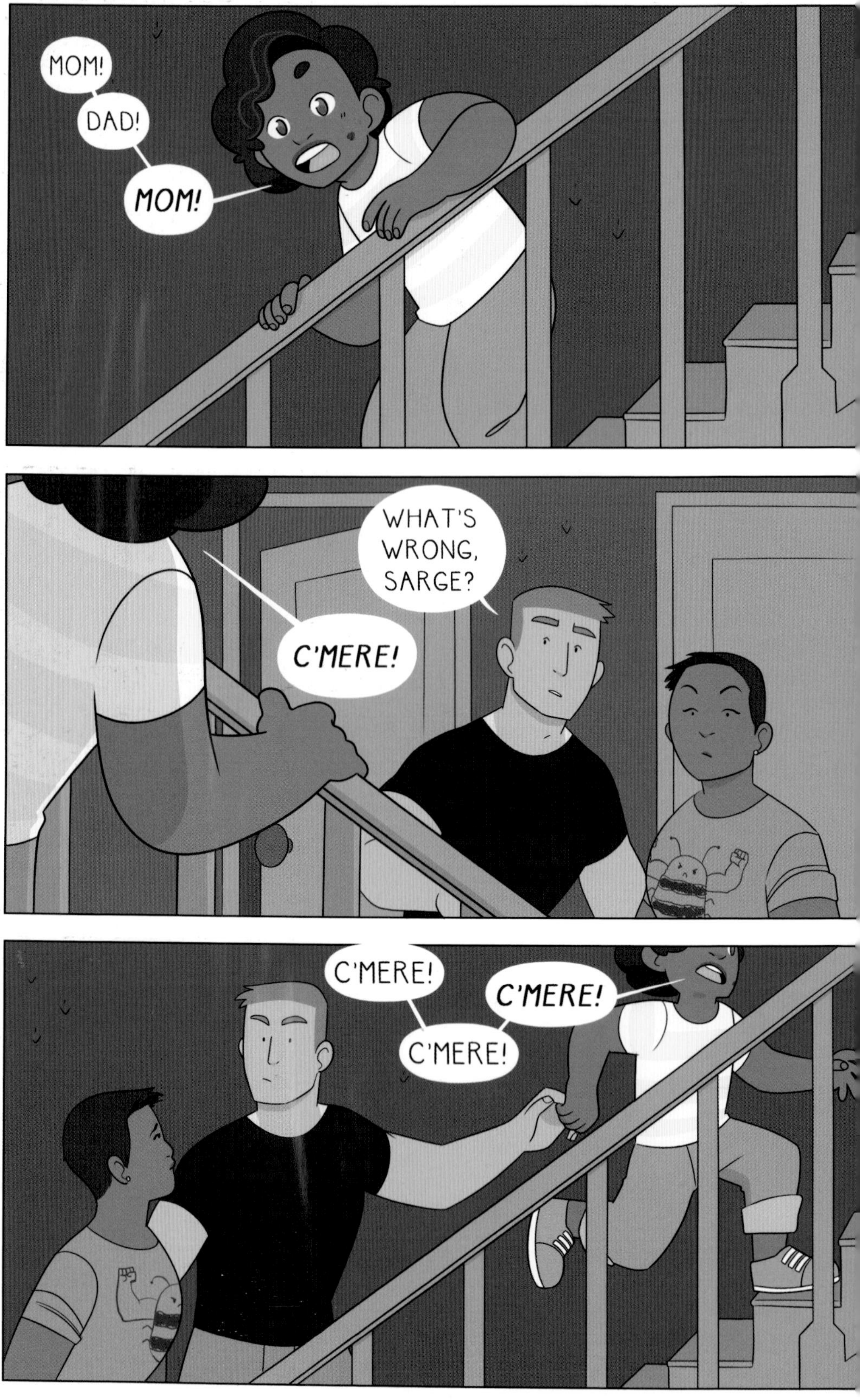
MOM!
DAD!
MOM!
WHAT'S WRONG, SARGE?
C'MERE!
C'MERE!
C'MERE!
C'MERE!

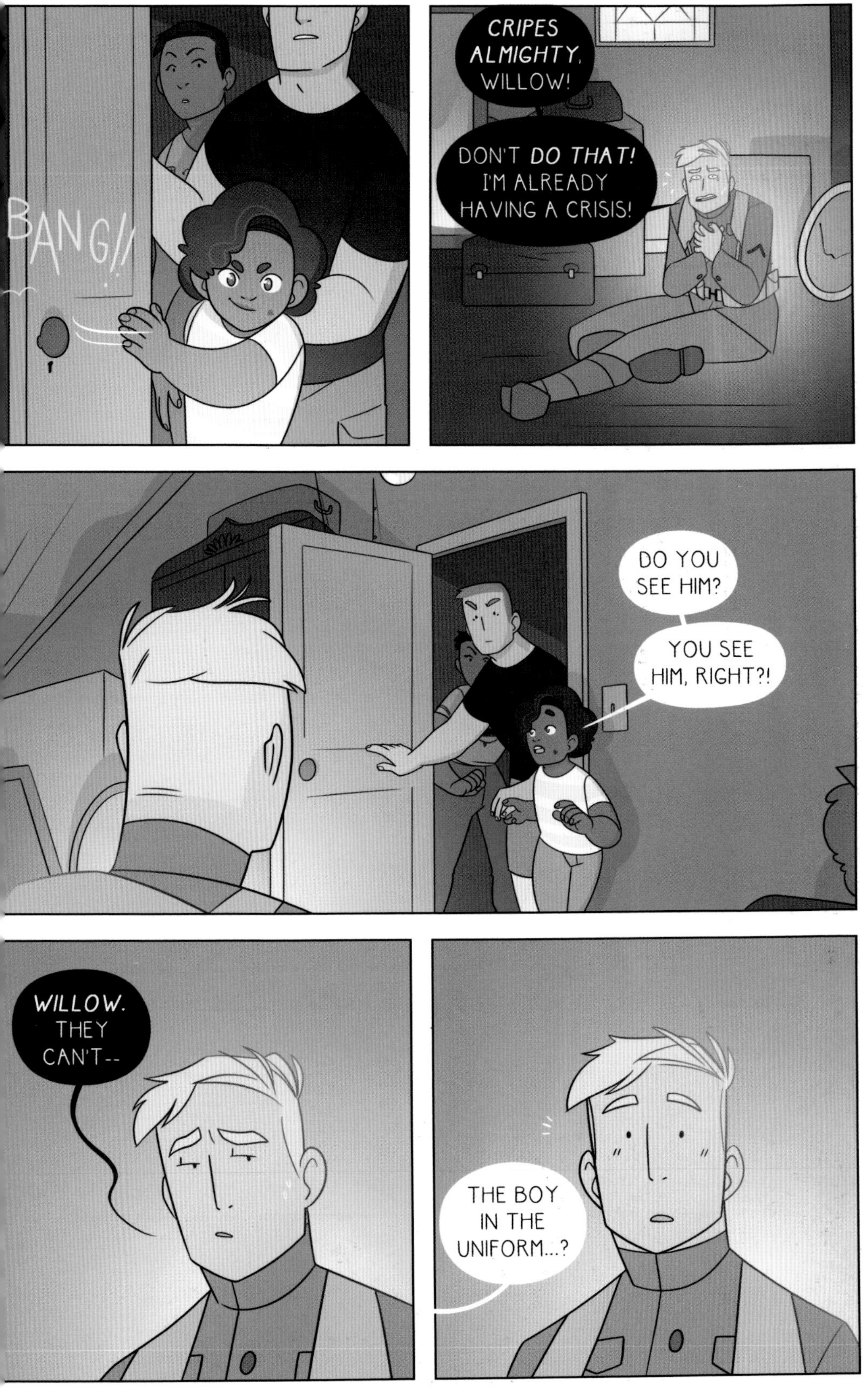
BANG!!
CRIPES ALMIGHTY, WILLOW!
DON'T DO THAT! I'M ALREADY HAVING A CRISIS!
DO YOU SEE HIM?
YOU SEE HIM, RIGHT?!
WILLOW. THEY CAN'T--
THE BOY IN THE UNIFORM...?

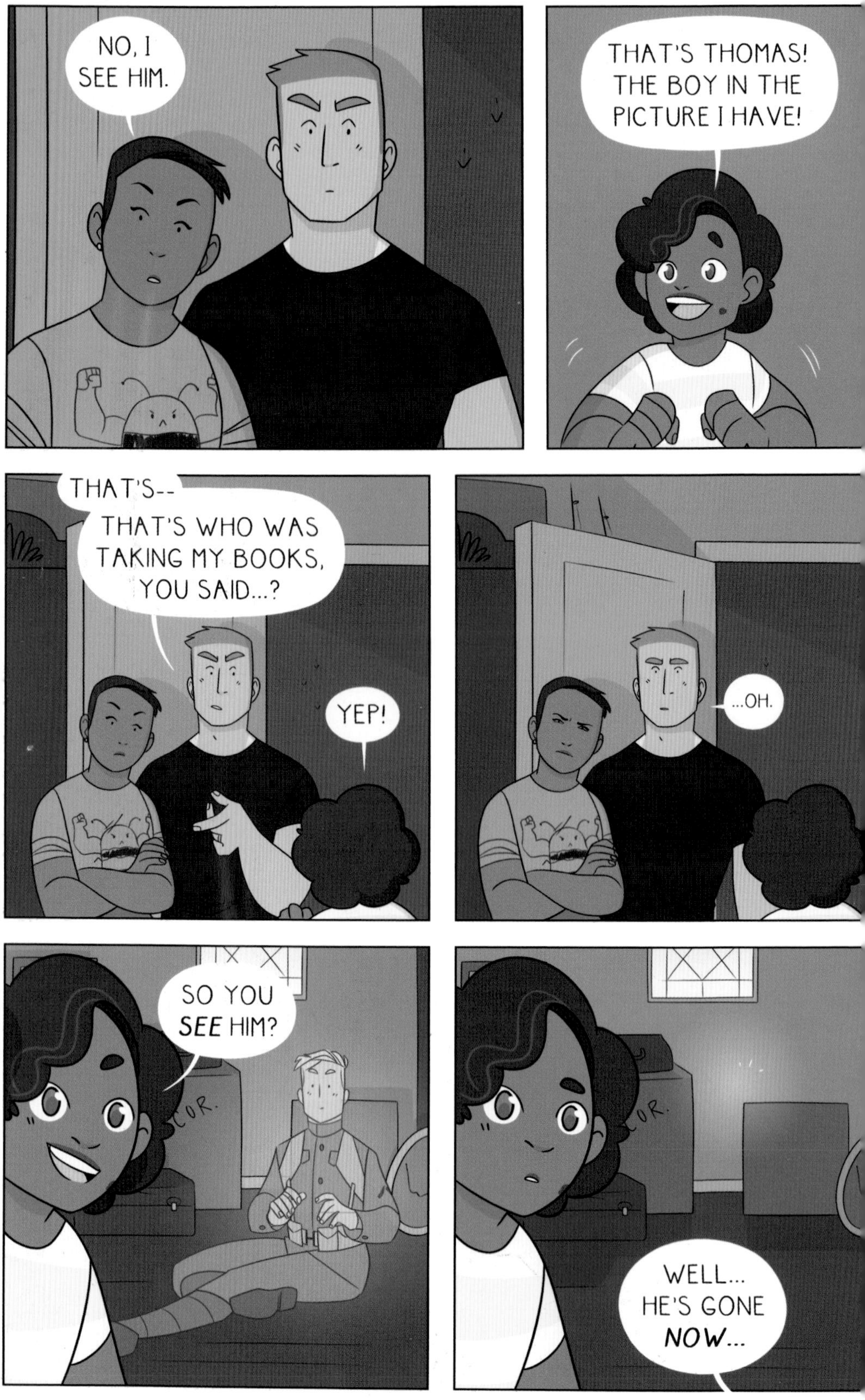
NO, I SEE HIM.
THAT'S THOMAS! THE BOY IN THE PICTURE I HAVE!
THAT'S--
THAT'S WHO WAS TAKING MY BOOKS, YOU SAID...?
YEP!
...OH.
SO YOU SEE HIM?
C.O.R.
WELL... HE'S GONE NOW...

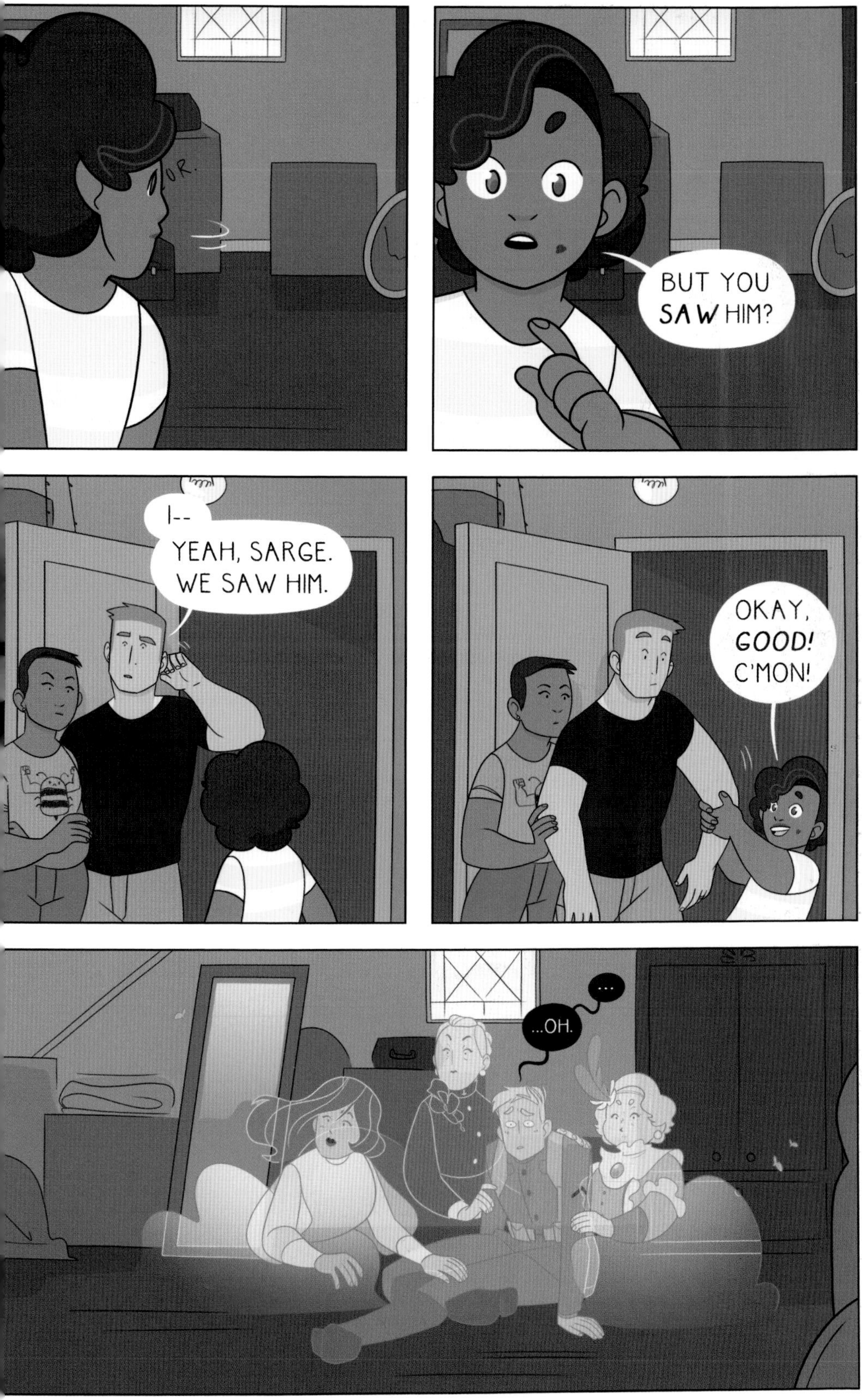
OR.
BUT YOU **SAW** HIM?
I--
YEAH, SARGE. WE SAW HIM.
OKAY, ***GOOD!*** C'MON!
...OH.
...

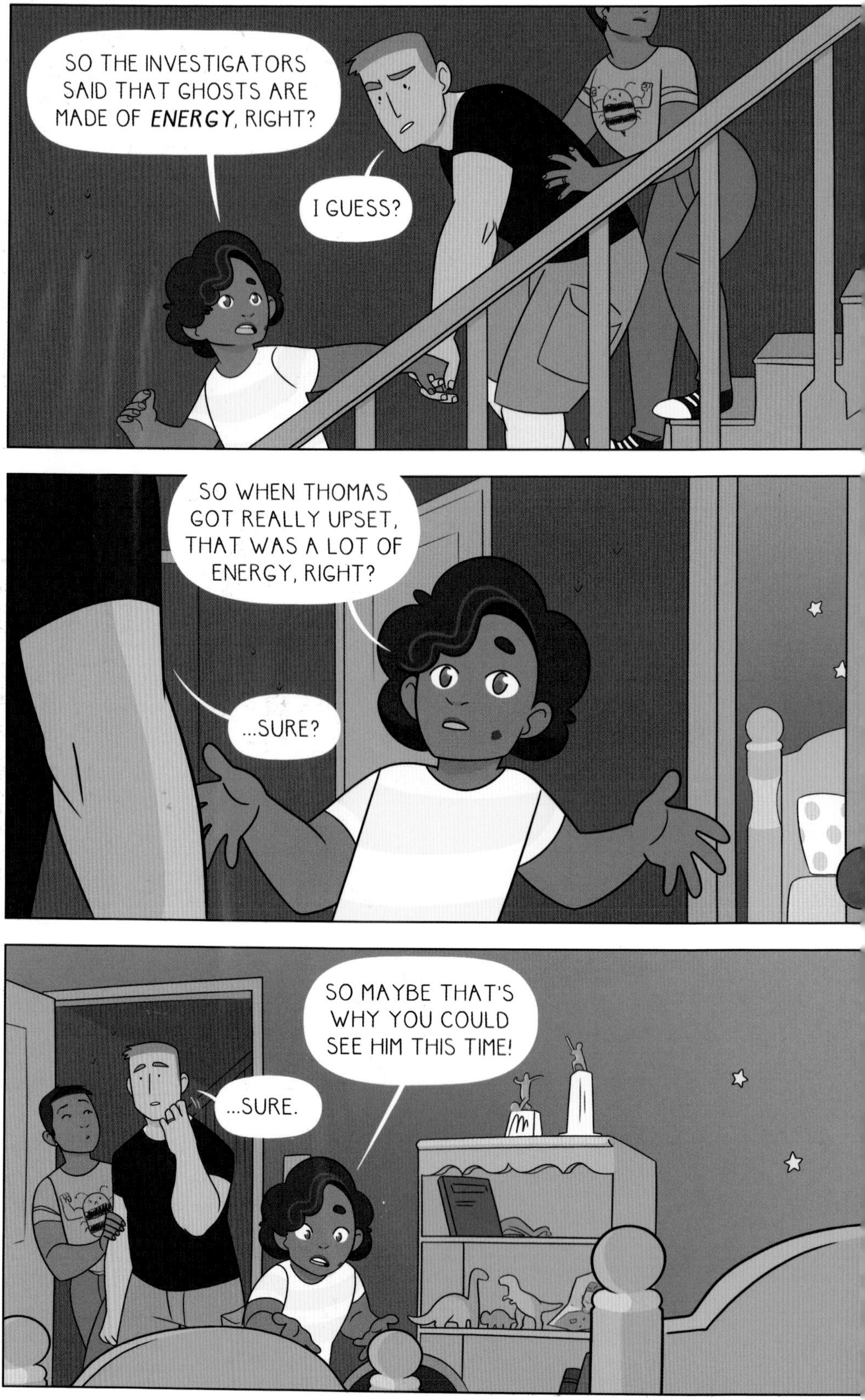
SO THE INVESTIGATORS SAID THAT GHOSTS ARE MADE OF *ENERGY*, RIGHT?
I GUESS?
SO WHEN THOMAS GOT REALLY UPSET, THAT WAS A LOT OF ENERGY, RIGHT?
...SURE?
SO MAYBE THAT'S WHY YOU COULD SEE HIM THIS TIME!
...SURE.

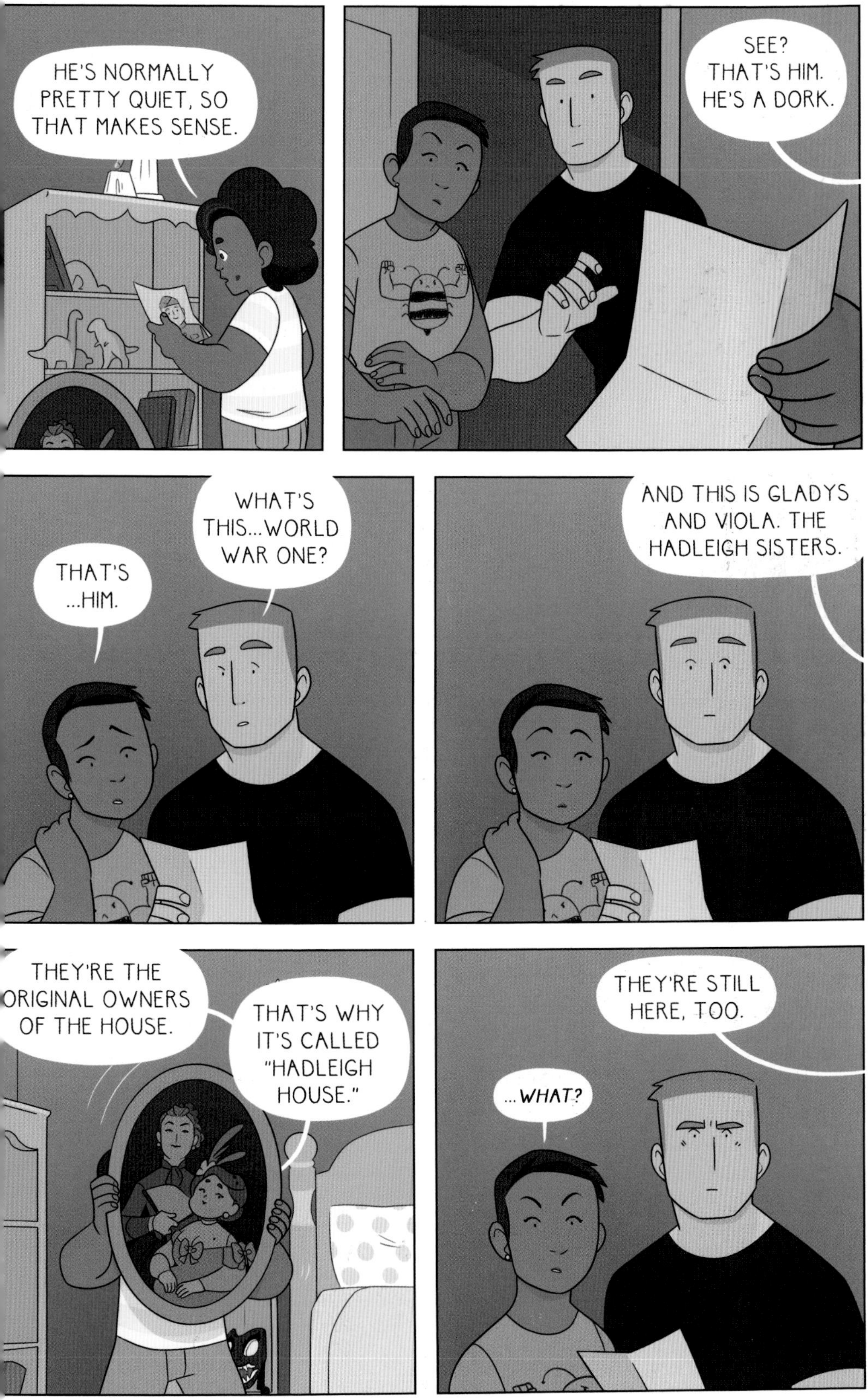
HE'S NORMALLY PRETTY QUIET, SO THAT MAKES SENSE.
SEE? THAT'S HIM. HE'S A DORK.
WHAT'S THIS...WORLD WAR ONE?
THAT'S ...HIM.
AND THIS IS GLADYS AND VIOLA. THE HADLEIGH SISTERS.
THEY'RE THE ORIGINAL OWNERS OF THE HOUSE.
THAT'S WHY IT'S CALLED "HADLEIGH HOUSE."
THEY'RE STILL HERE, TOO.
...WHAT?

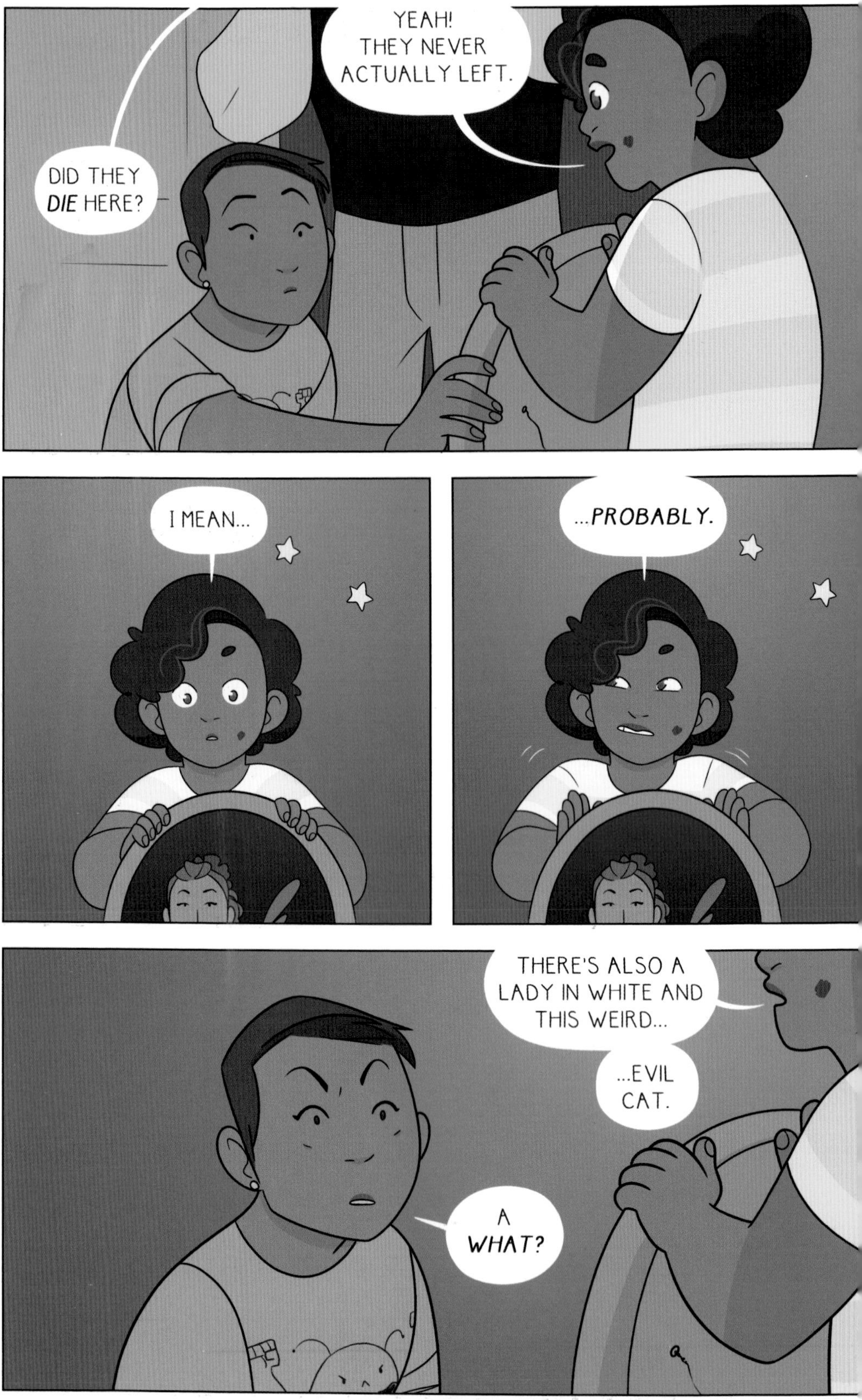
YEAH! THEY NEVER ACTUALLY LEFT.
DID THEY *DIE* HERE?
I MEAN...
...*PROBABLY.*
THERE'S ALSO A LADY IN WHITE AND THIS WEIRD...
...EVIL CAT.
A *WHAT?*

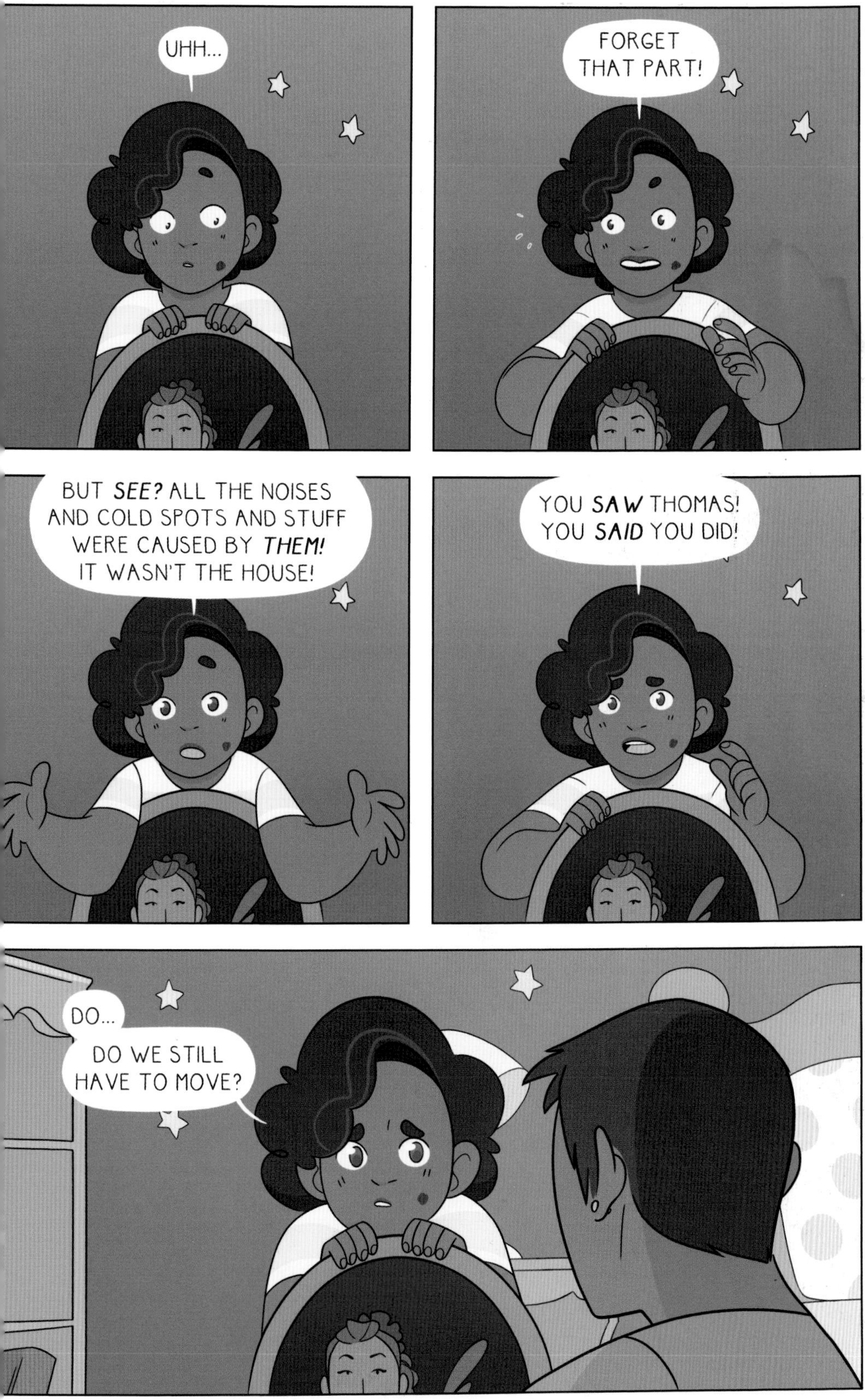
UHH...
FORGET THAT PART!
BUT SEE? ALL THE NOISES AND COLD SPOTS AND STUFF WERE CAUSED BY THEM! IT WASN'T THE HOUSE!
YOU SAW THOMAS! YOU SAID YOU DID!
DO...
DO WE STILL HAVE TO MOVE?

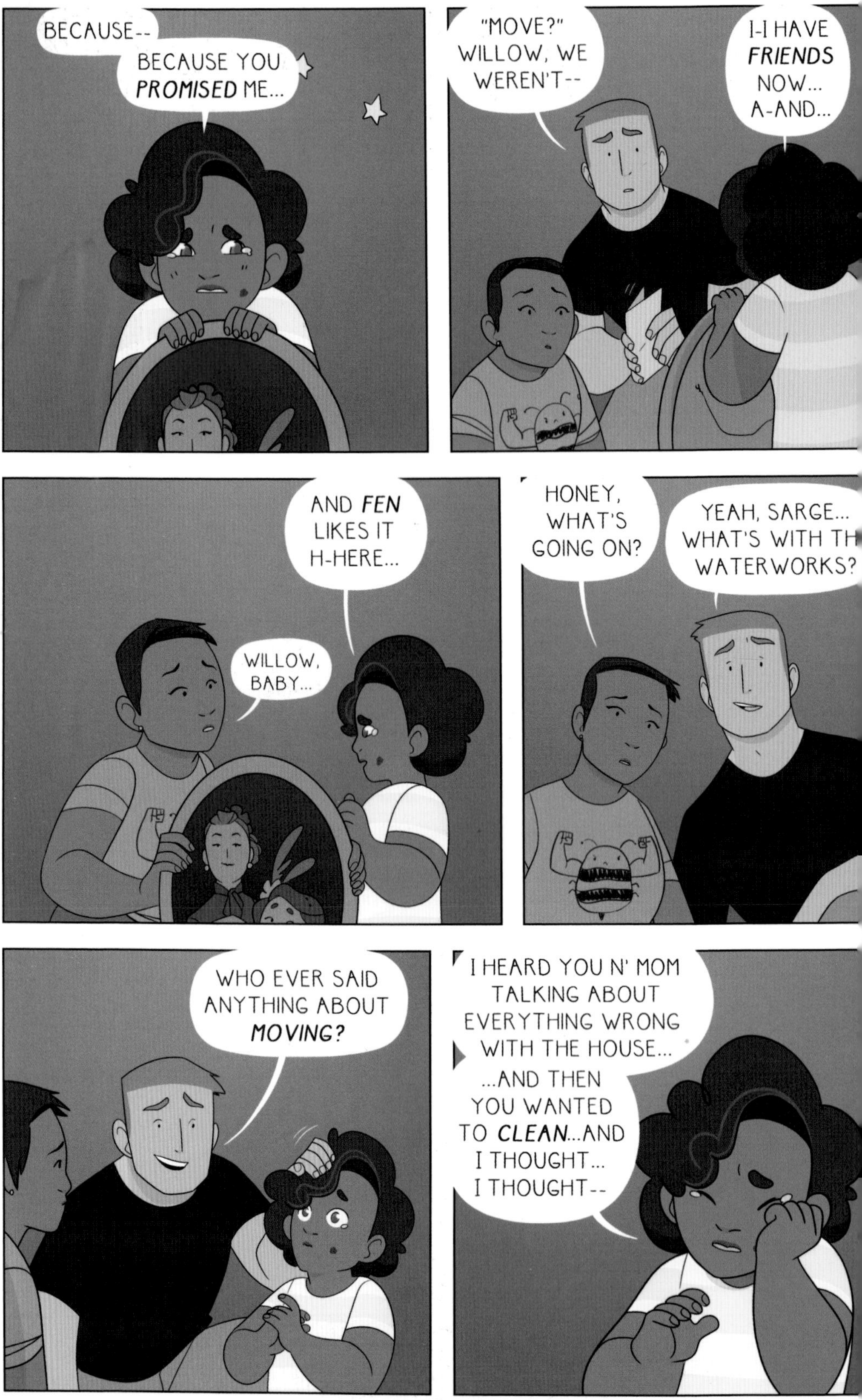
BECAUSE--
BECAUSE YOU *PROMISED* ME...
"MOVE?" WILLOW, WE WEREN'T--
I-I HAVE *FRIENDS* NOW... A-AND...
AND *FEN* LIKES IT H-HERE...
WILLOW, BABY...
HONEY, WHAT'S GOING ON?
YEAH, SARGE... WHAT'S WITH TH WATERWORKS?
WHO EVER SAID ANYTHING ABOUT *MOVING?*
I HEARD YOU N' MOM TALKING ABOUT EVERYTHING WRONG WITH THE HOUSE...
...AND THEN YOU WANTED TO *CLEAN*...AND I THOUGHT... I THOUGHT--

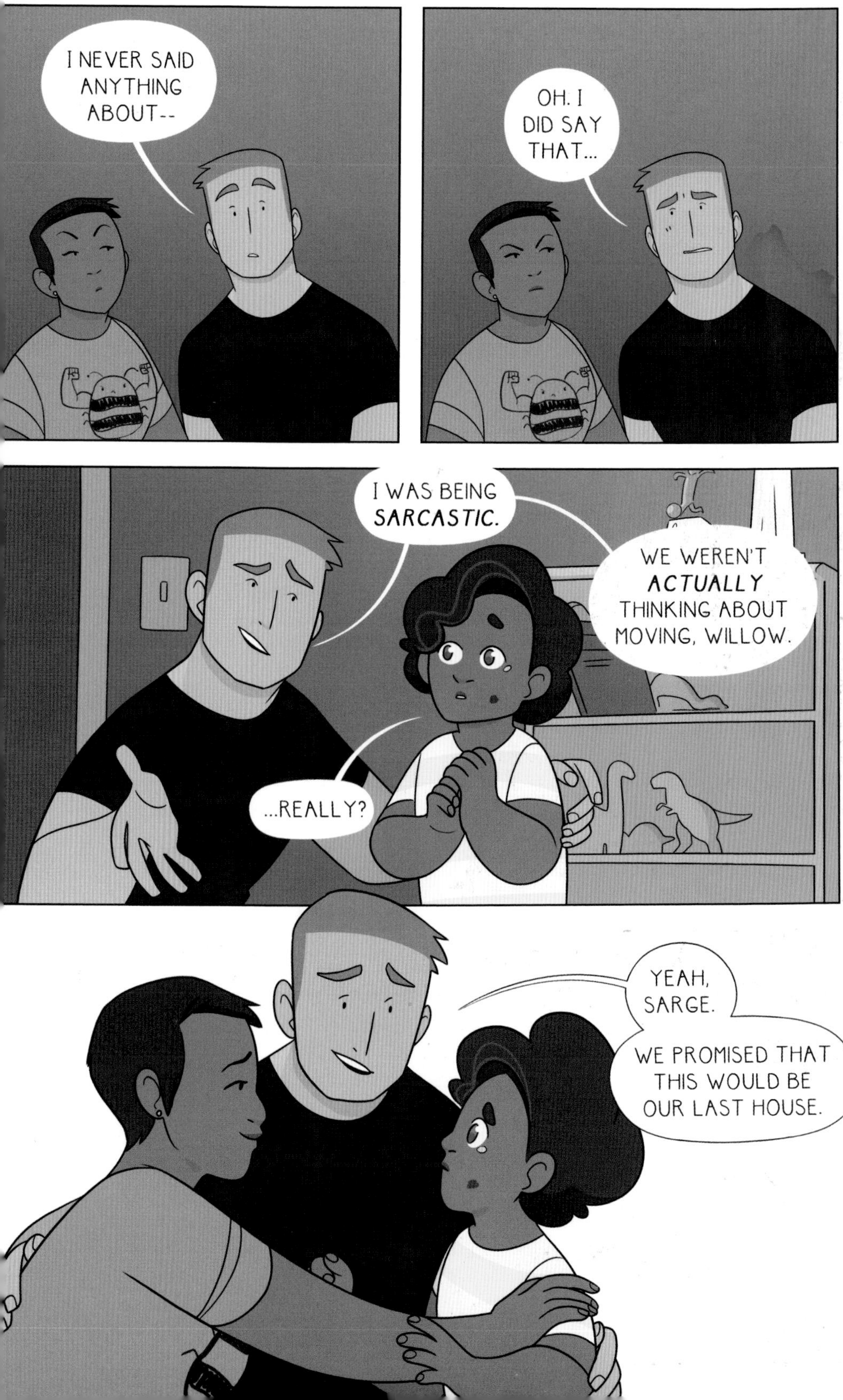
I NEVER SAID ANYTHING ABOUT--
OH. I DID SAY THAT...
I WAS BEING *SARCASTIC.*
WE WEREN'T **ACTUALLY** THINKING ABOUT MOVING, WILLOW.
...REALLY?
YEAH, SARGE.
WE PROMISED THAT THIS WOULD BE OUR LAST HOUSE.

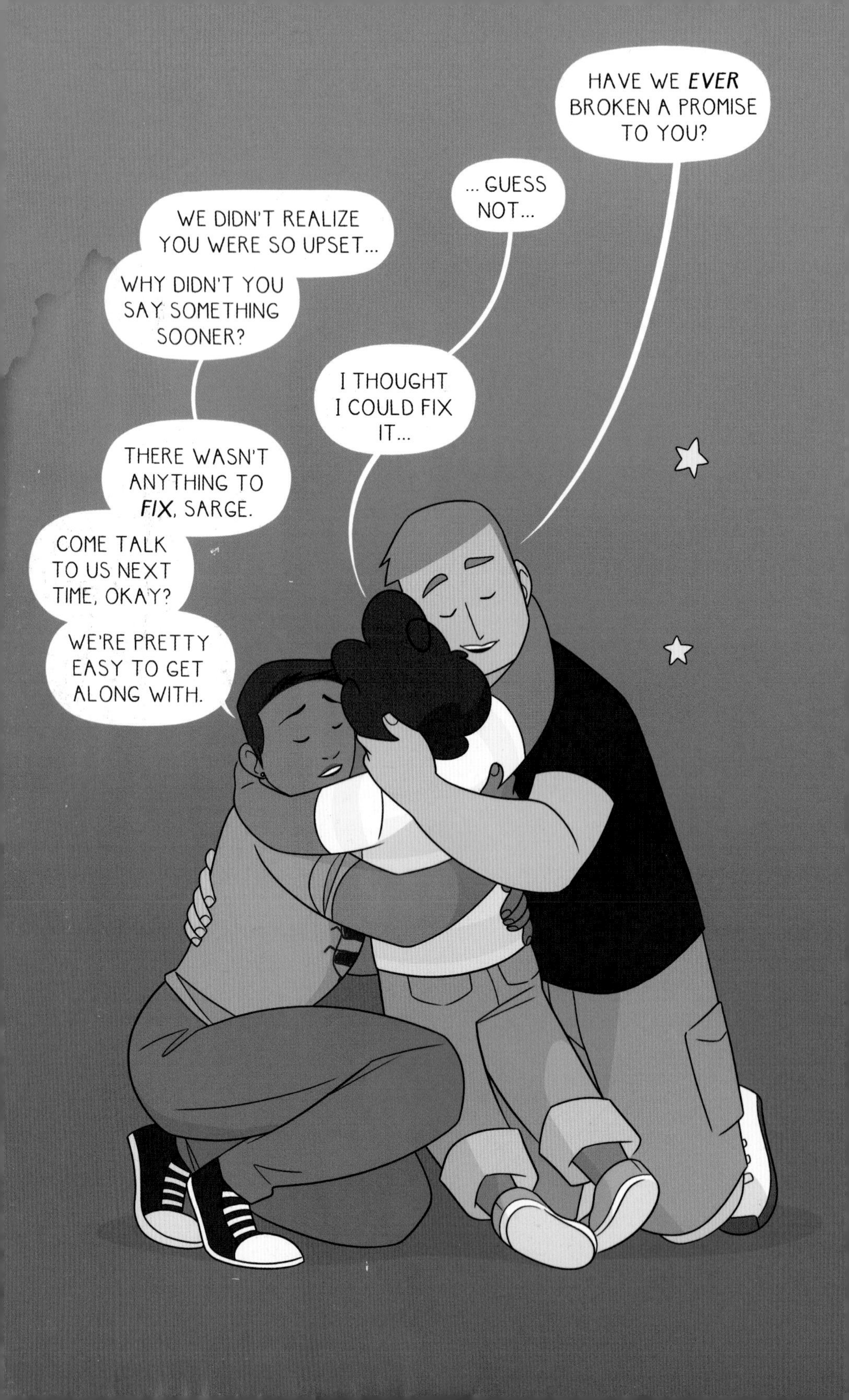
HAVE WE EVER BROKEN A PROMISE TO YOU?
... GUESS NOT...
WE DIDN'T REALIZE YOU WERE SO UPSET...
WHY DIDN'T YOU SAY SOMETHING SOONER?
I THOUGHT I COULD FIX IT...
THERE WASN'T ANYTHING TO FIX, SARGE.
COME TALK TO US NEXT TIME, OKAY?
WE'RE PRETTY EASY TO GET ALONG WITH.

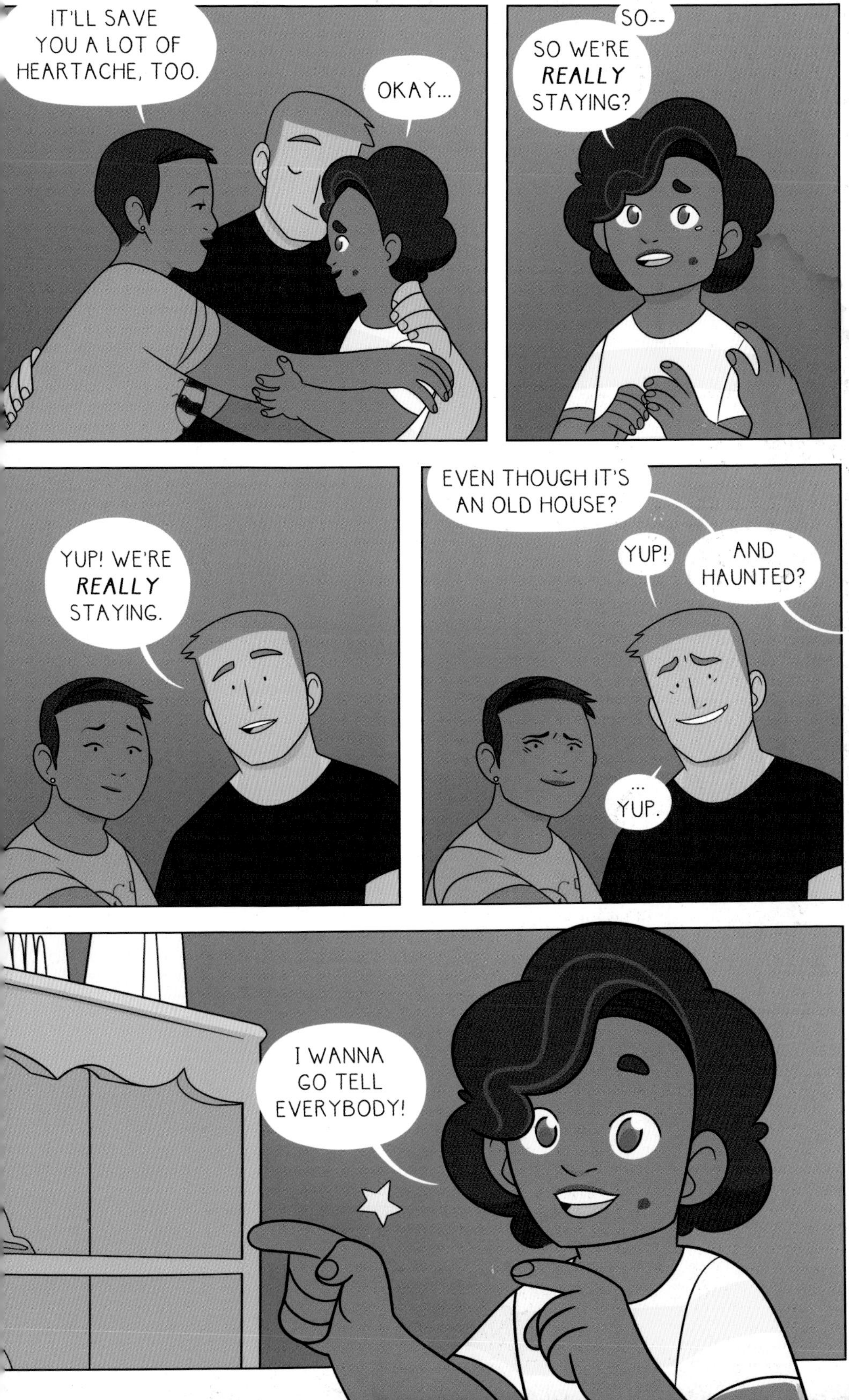
IT'LL SAVE YOU A LOT OF HEARTACHE, TOO.
OKAY...
SO--
SO WE'RE *REALLY* STAYING?
YUP! WE'RE *REALLY* STAYING.
EVEN THOUGH IT'S AN OLD HOUSE?
YUP!
AND HAUNTED?
... YUP.
I WANNA GO TELL EVERYBODY!

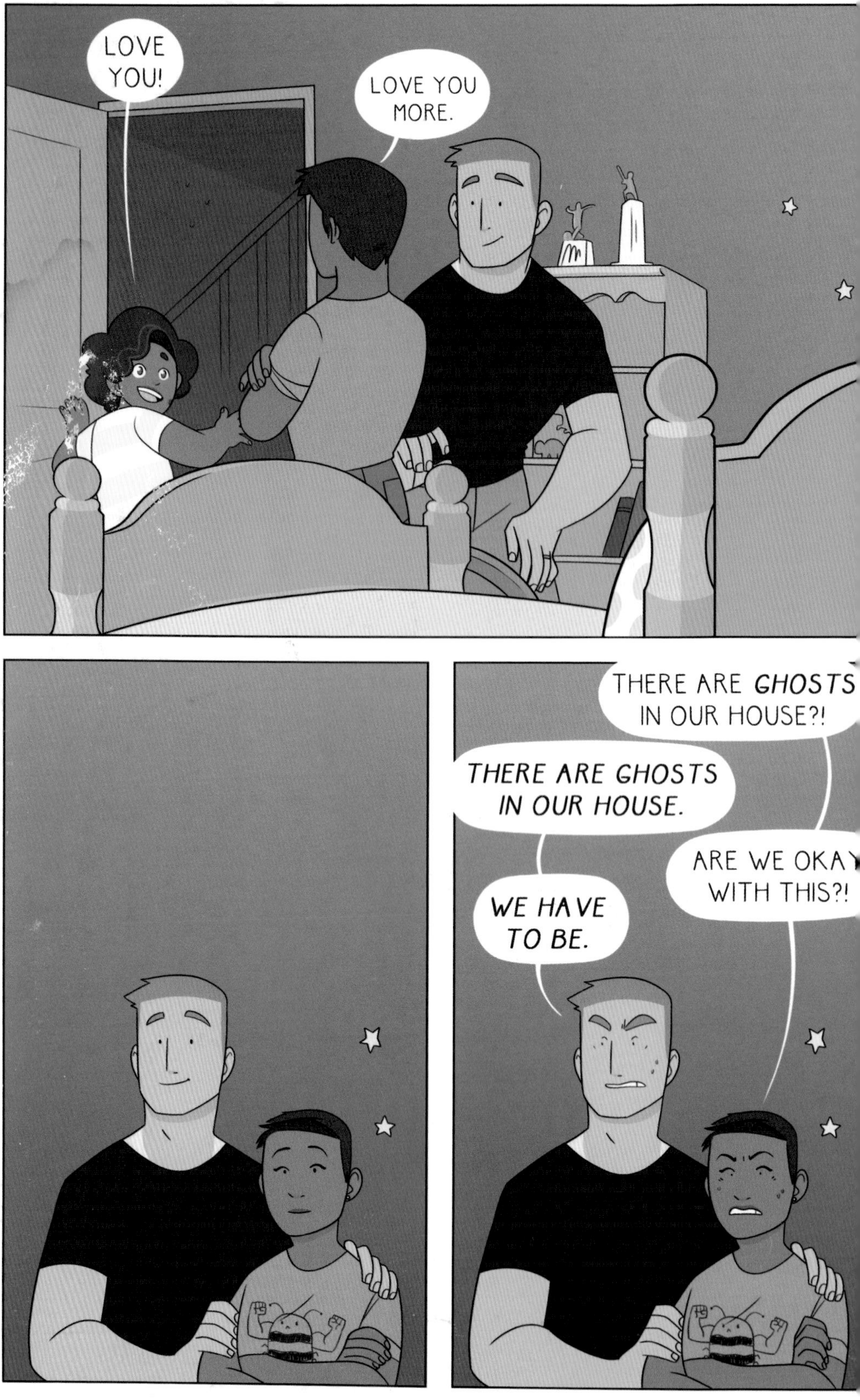
LOVE YOU!
LOVE YOU MORE.
THERE ARE *GHOSTS* IN OUR HOUSE?!
*THERE ARE GHOSTS IN OUR HOUSE.*
ARE WE OKAY WITH THIS?!
*WE HAVE TO BE.*

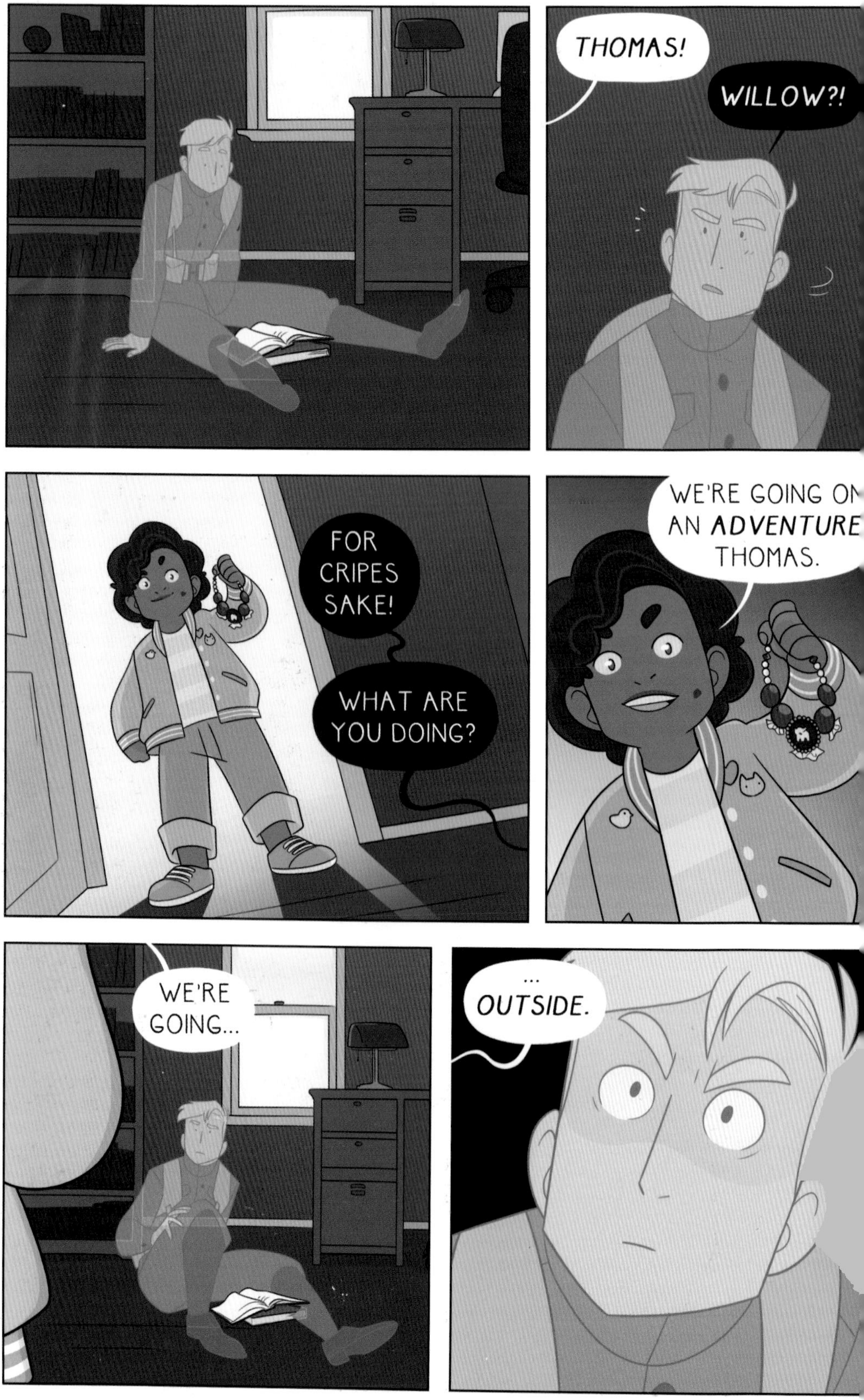
THOMAS!
WILLOW?!
FOR CRIPES SAKE!
WHAT ARE YOU DOING?
WE'RE GOING ON AN ADVENTURE THOMAS.
WE'RE GOING...
... OUTSIDE.

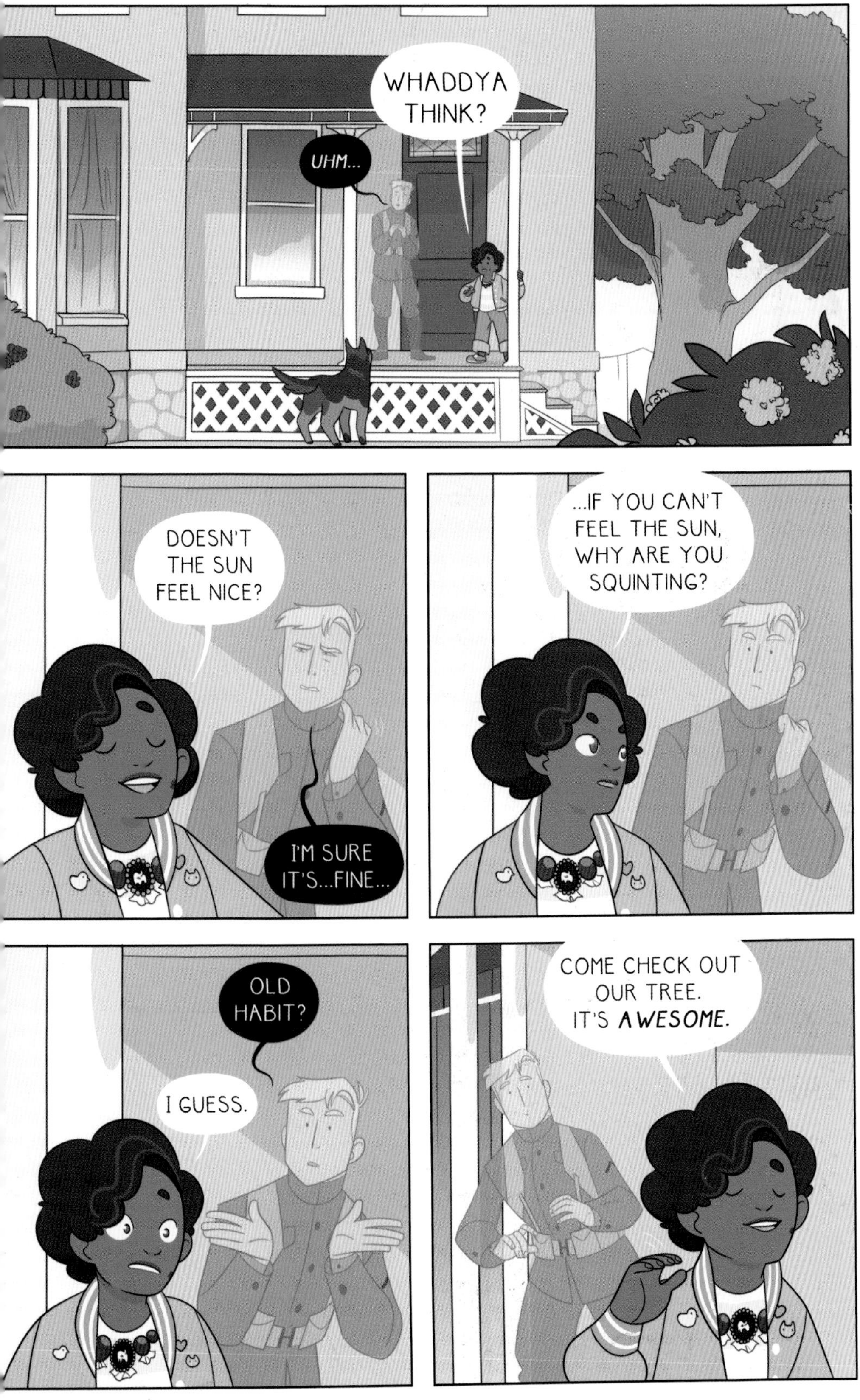
WHADDYA THINK?
UHM...
DOESN'T THE SUN FEEL NICE?
I'M SURE IT'S...FINE...
...IF YOU CAN'T FEEL THE SUN, WHY ARE YOU SQUINTING?
OLD HABIT?
I GUESS.
COME CHECK OUT OUR TREE. IT'S **AWESOME.**

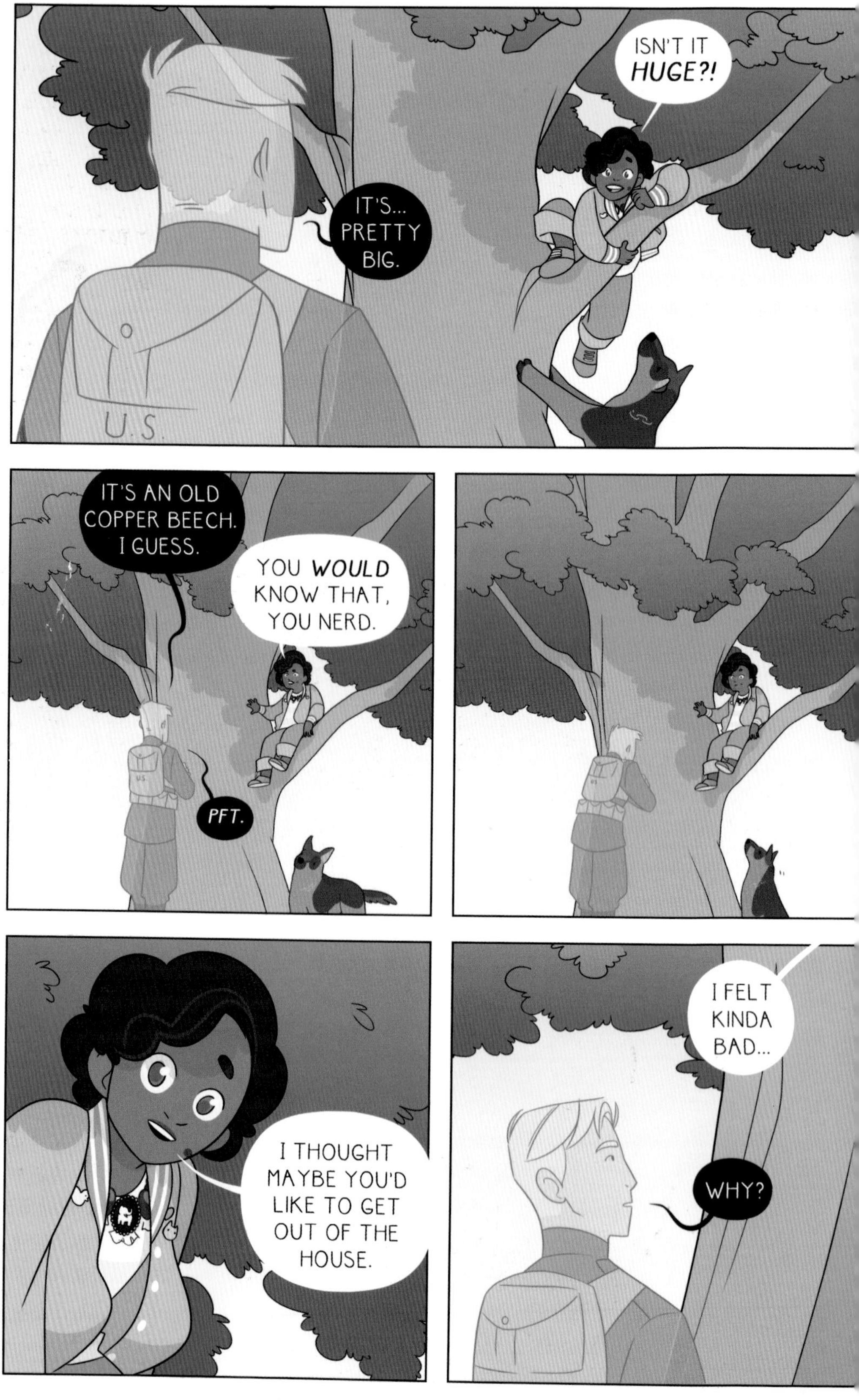
ISN'T IT HUGE?!
IT'S... PRETTY BIG.
IT'S AN OLD COPPER BEECH. I GUESS.
YOU WOULD KNOW THAT, YOU NERD.
PFT.
I THOUGHT MAYBE YOU'D LIKE TO GET OUT OF THE HOUSE.
I FELT KINDA BAD...
WHY?

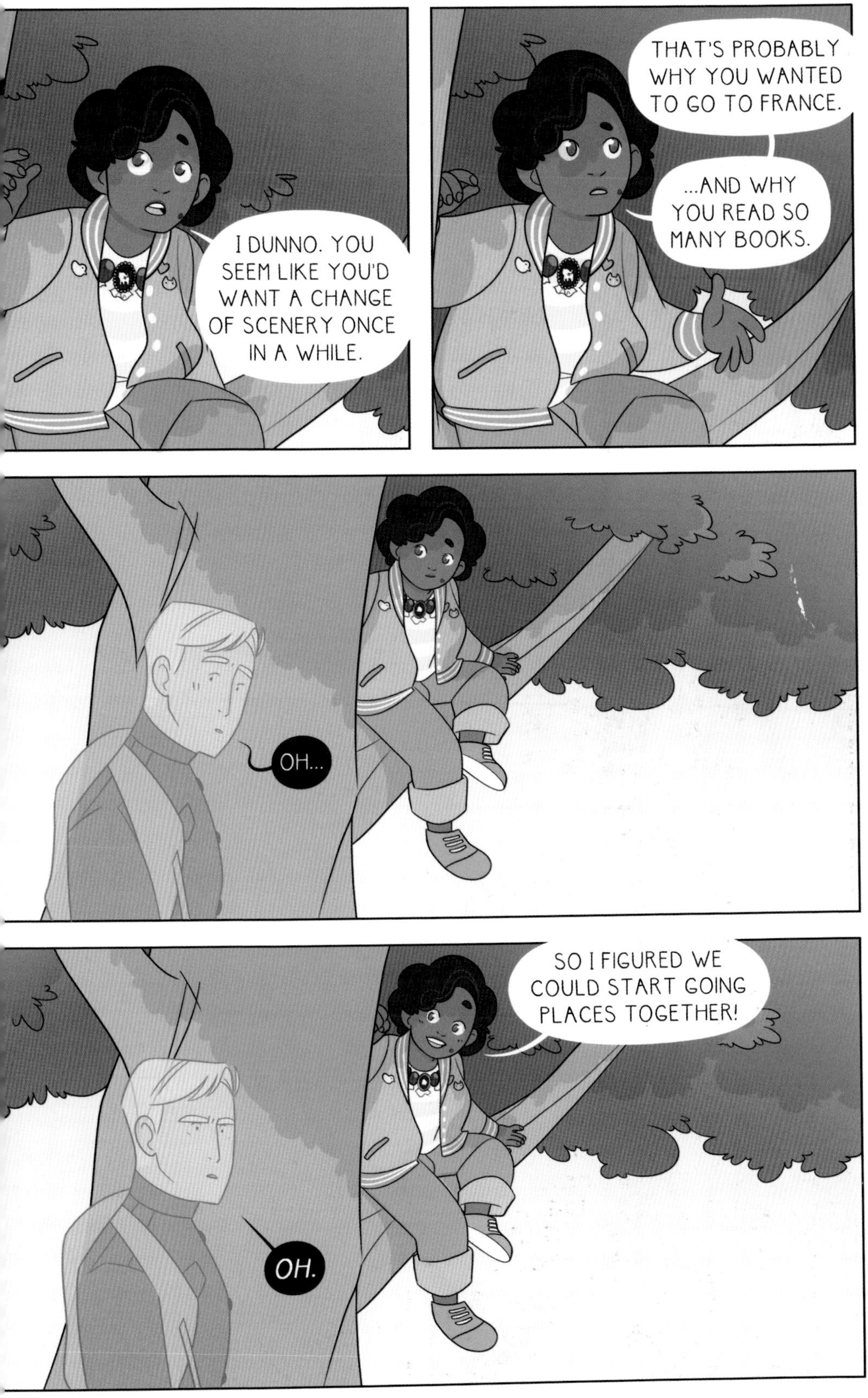
I DUNNO. YOU SEEM LIKE YOU'D WANT A CHANGE OF SCENERY ONCE IN A WHILE.
THAT'S PROBABLY WHY YOU WANTED TO GO TO FRANCE.
...AND WHY YOU READ SO MANY BOOKS.
OH...
SO I FIGURED WE COULD START GOING PLACES TOGETHER!
OH.

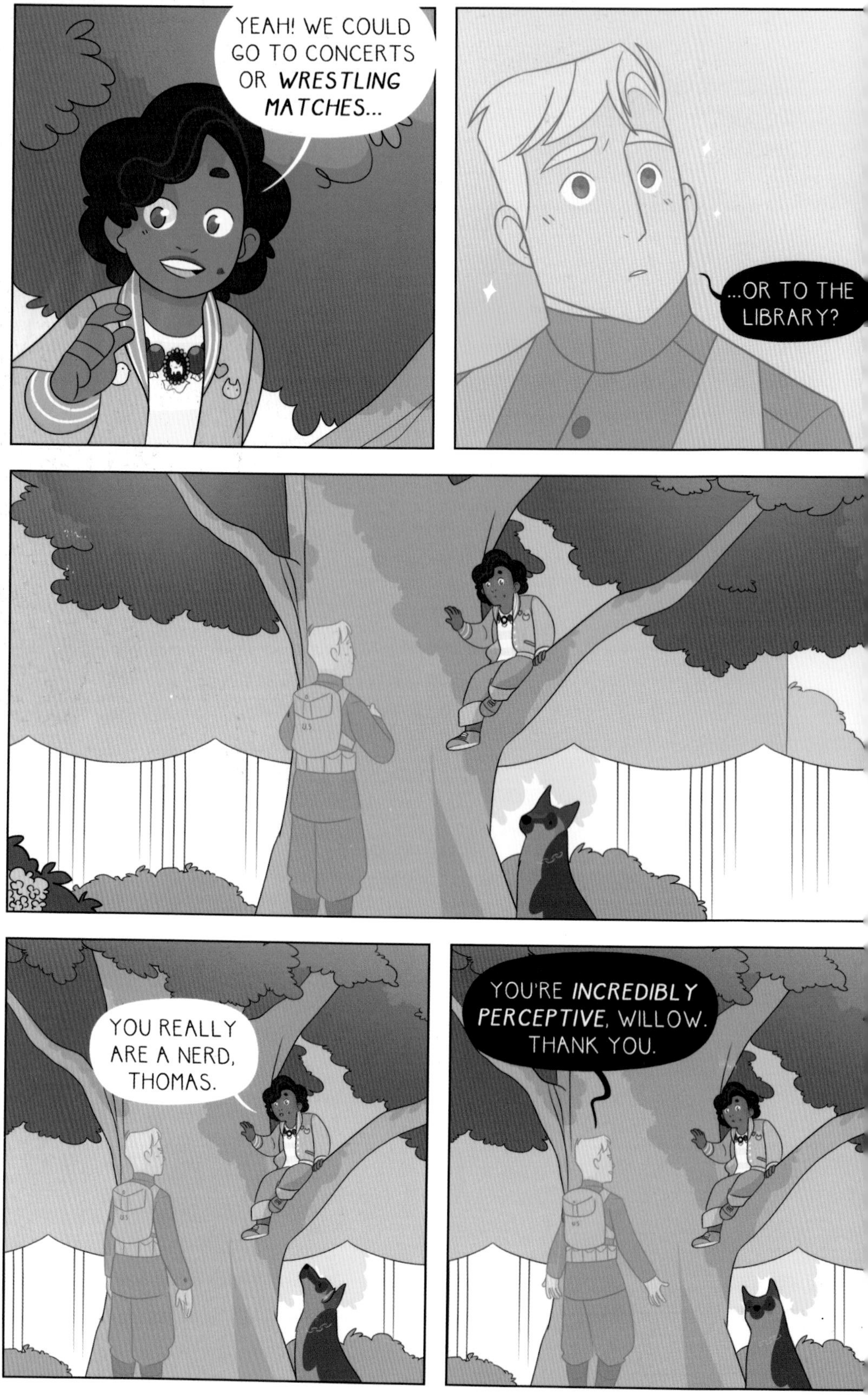
YEAH! WE COULD GO TO CONCERTS OR *WRESTLING MATCHES*...
...OR TO THE LIBRARY?
YOU REALLY ARE A NERD, THOMAS.
YOU'RE *INCREDIBLY PERCEPTIVE*, WILLOW. THANK YOU.

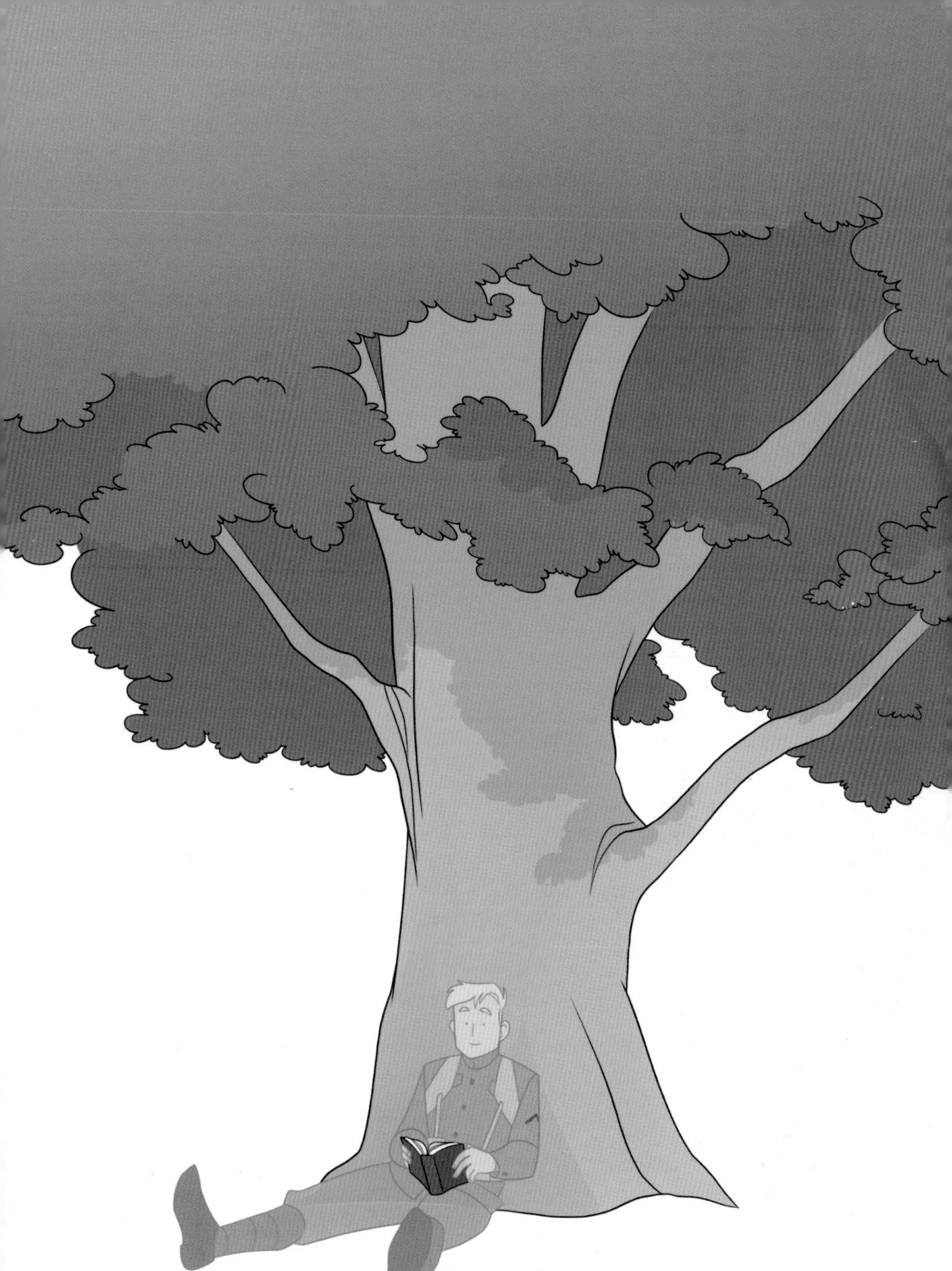

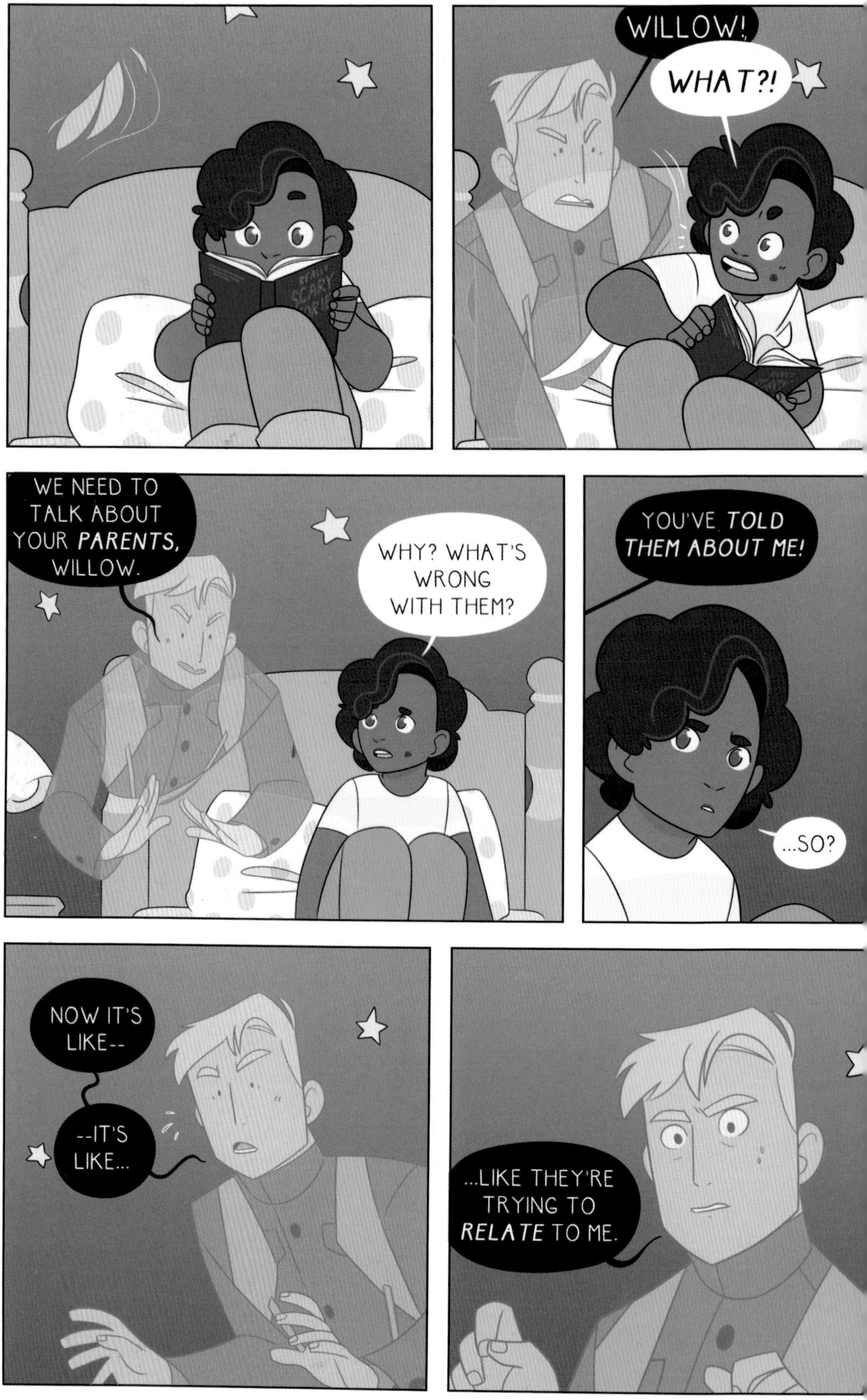
WILLOW!
WHAT?!
WE NEED TO TALK ABOUT YOUR PARENTS, WILLOW.
WHY? WHAT'S WRONG WITH THEM?
YOU'VE TOLD THEM ABOUT ME!
...SO?
NOW IT'S LIKE--
--IT'S LIKE...
...LIKE THEY'RE TRYING TO RELATE TO ME.

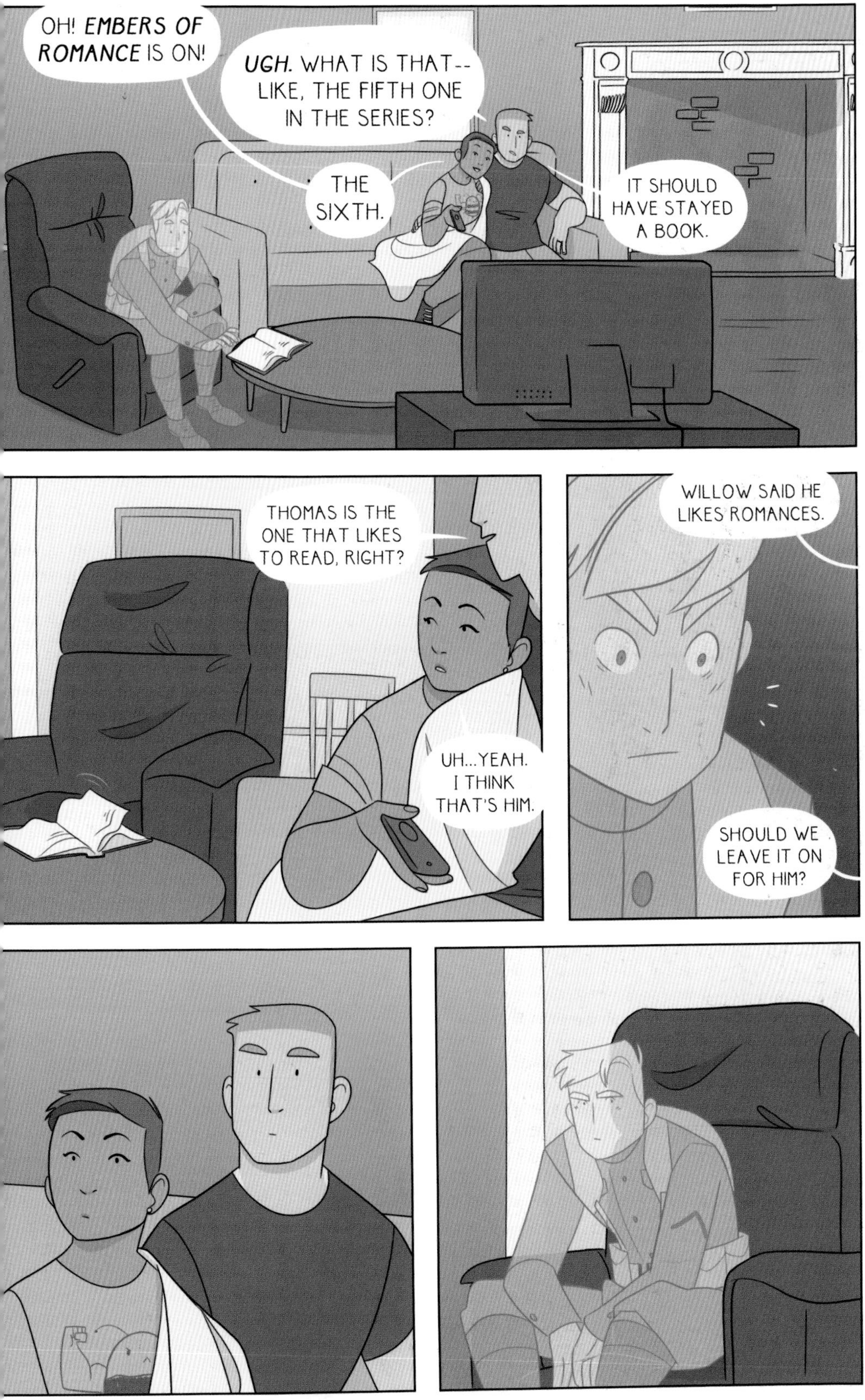
OH! *EMBERS OF ROMANCE* IS ON!
*UGH.* WHAT IS THAT--LIKE, THE FIFTH ONE IN THE SERIES?
THE SIXTH.
IT SHOULD HAVE STAYED A BOOK.
THOMAS IS THE ONE THAT LIKES TO READ, RIGHT?
UH...YEAH. I THINK THAT'S HIM.
WILLOW SAID HE LIKES ROMANCES.
SHOULD WE LEAVE IT ON FOR HIM?

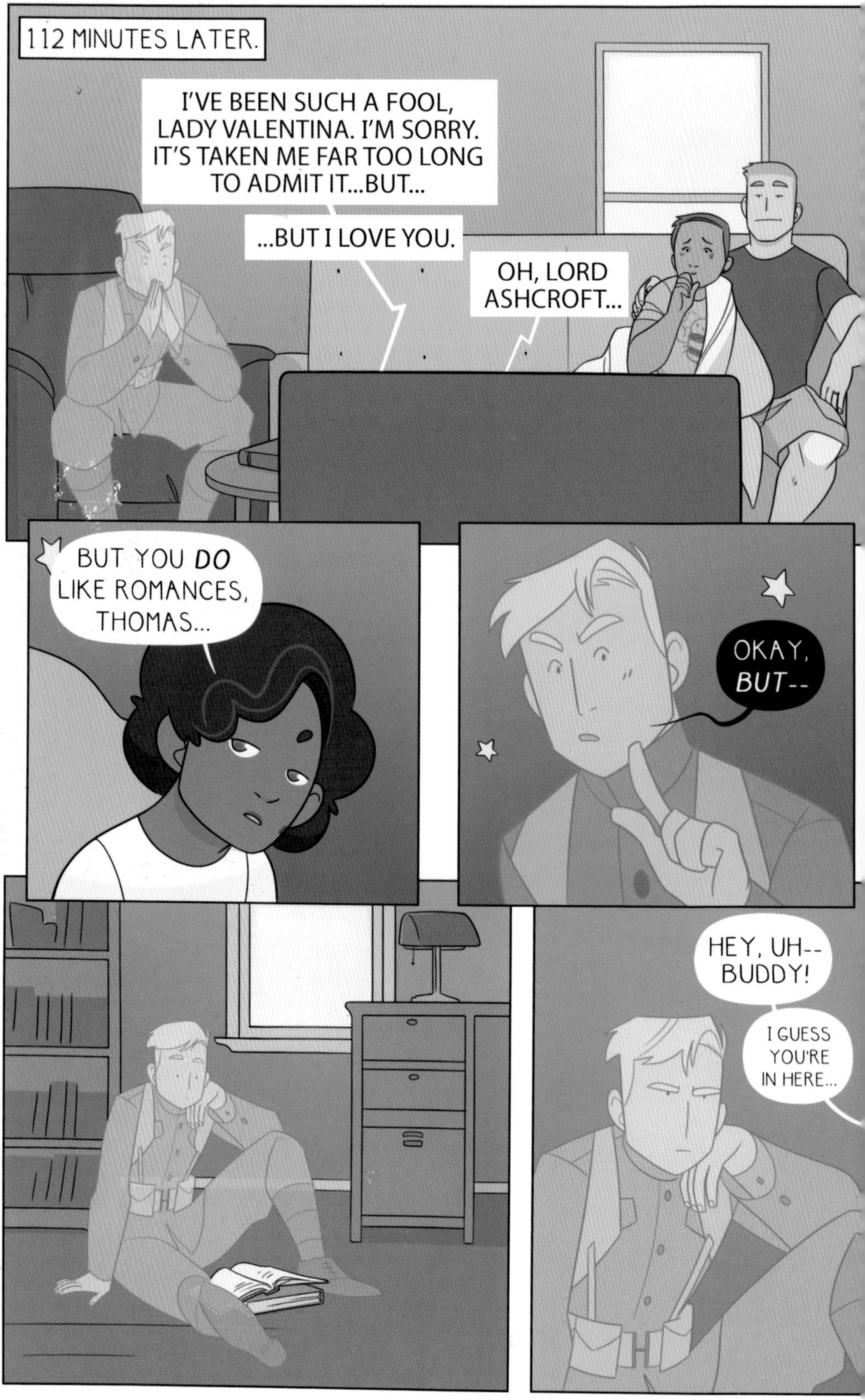
112 MINUTES LATER.
I'VE BEEN SUCH A FOOL, LADY VALENTINA. I'M SORRY. IT'S TAKEN ME FAR TOO LONG TO ADMIT IT...BUT...
...BUT I LOVE YOU.
OH, LORD ASHCROFT...
BUT YOU *DO* LIKE ROMANCES, THOMAS...
OKAY, *BUT*--
HEY, UH-- BUDDY!
I GUESS YOU'RE IN HERE...

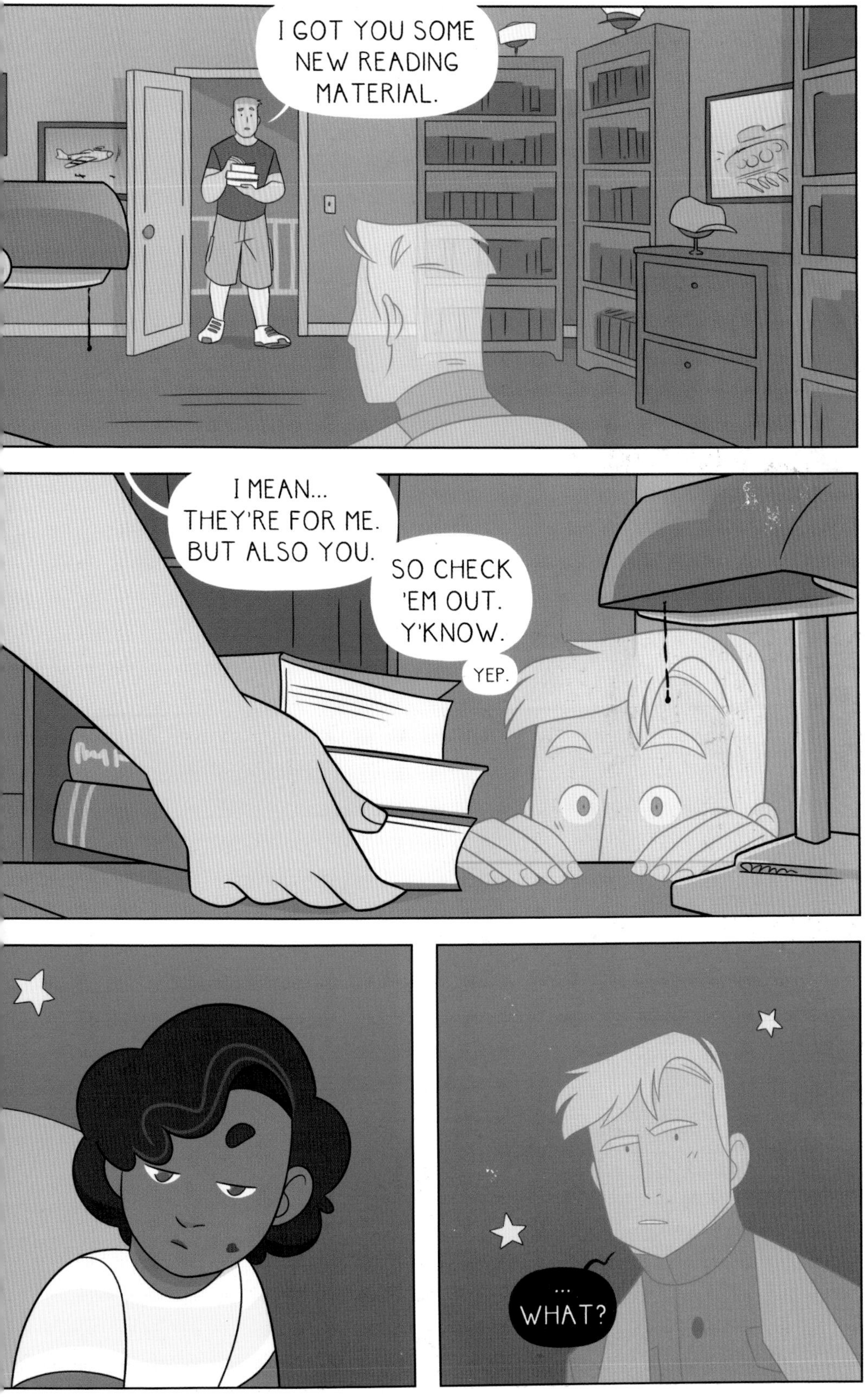
I GOT YOU SOME NEW READING MATERIAL.
I MEAN... THEY'RE FOR ME. BUT ALSO YOU.
SO CHECK 'EM OUT. Y'KNOW.
YEP.
... WHAT?

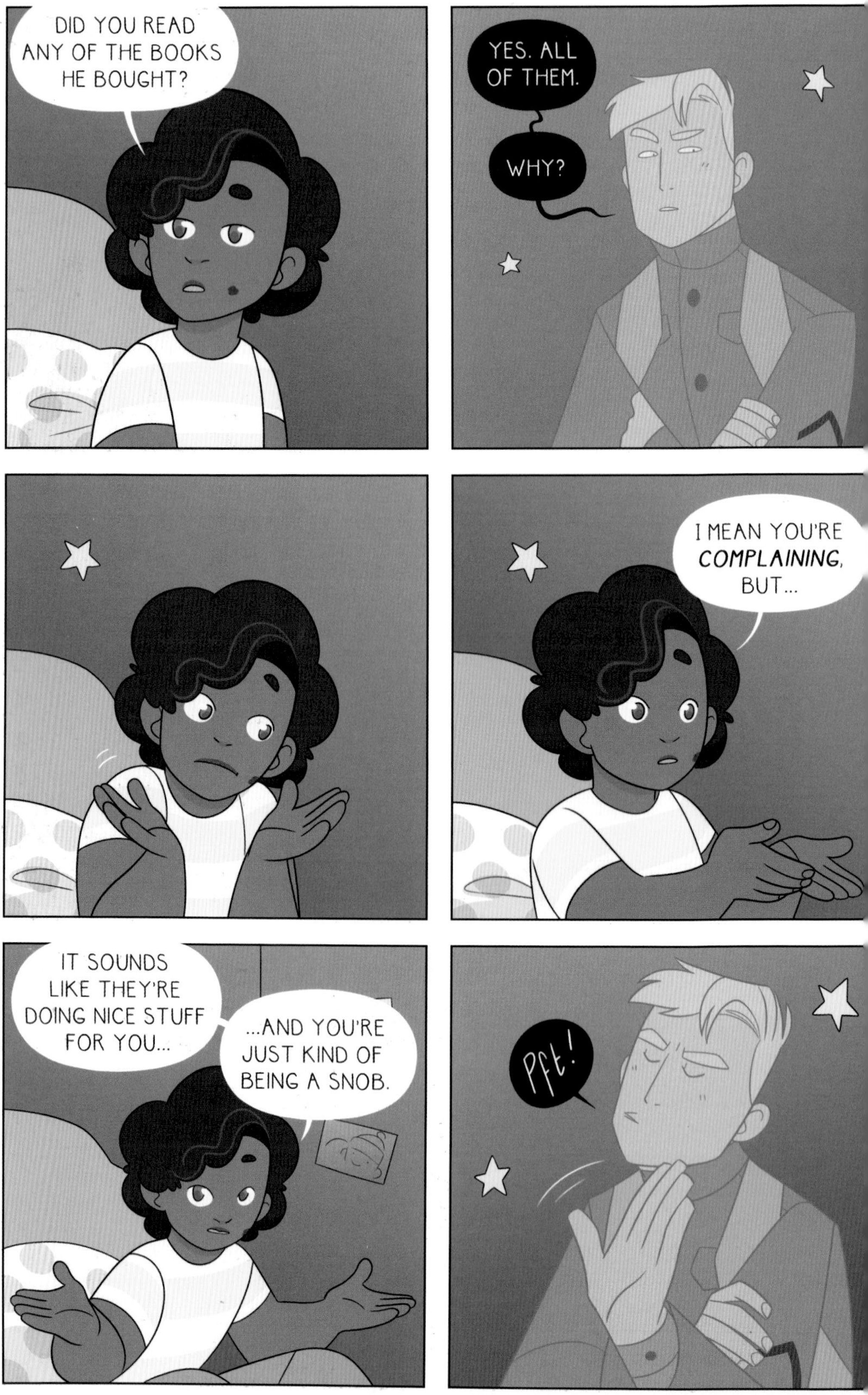
DID YOU READ ANY OF THE BOOKS HE BOUGHT?
YES. ALL OF THEM.
WHY?
I MEAN YOU'RE COMPLAINING, BUT...
IT SOUNDS LIKE THEY'RE DOING NICE STUFF FOR YOU...
...AND YOU'RE JUST KIND OF BEING A SNOB.
Pft!

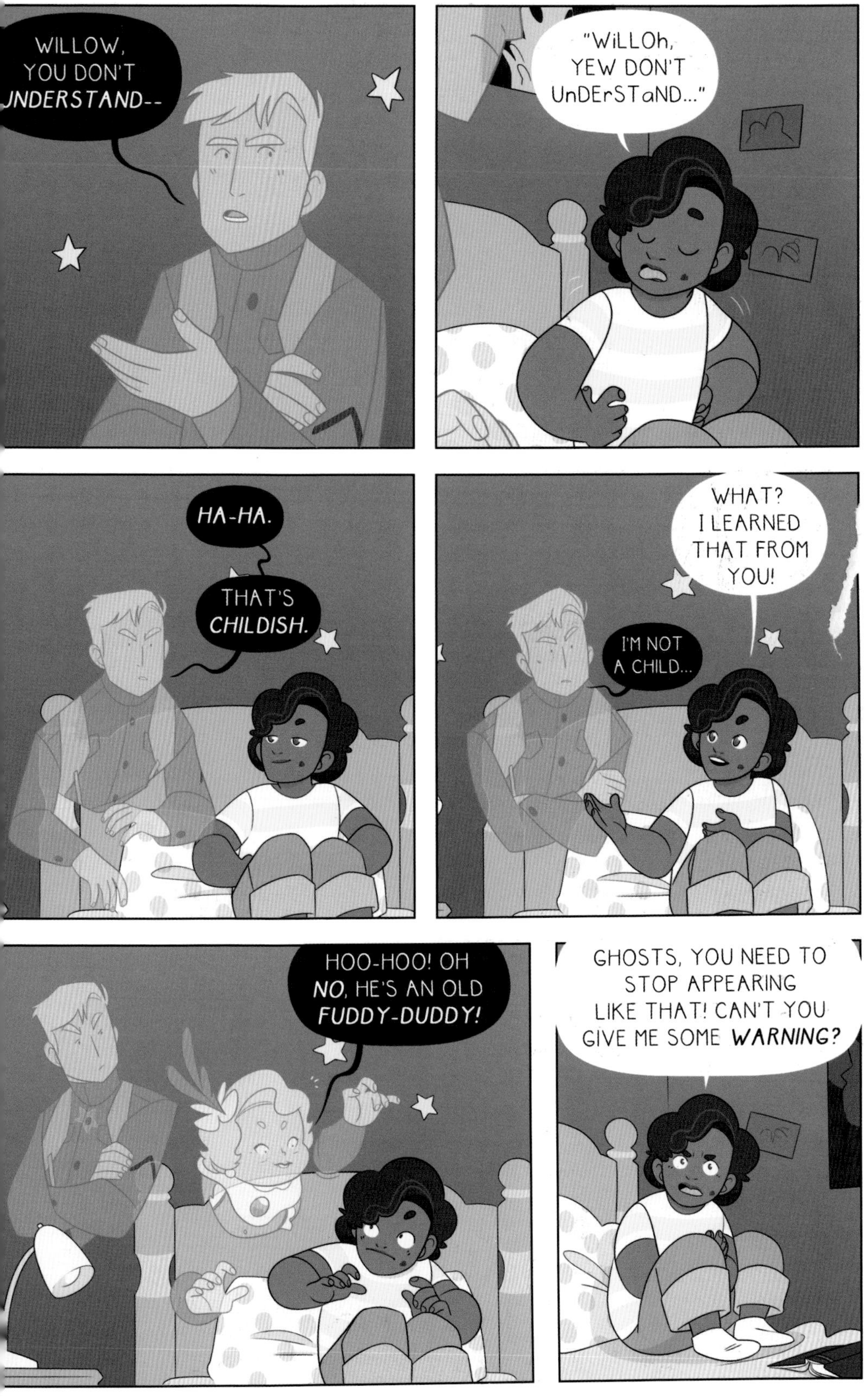
WILLOW, YOU DON'T UNDERSTAND--
"WiLLOh, YEW DON'T UnDErSTaND..."
HA-HA.
THAT'S CHILDISH.
I'M NOT A CHILD...
WHAT? I LEARNED THAT FROM YOU!
HOO-HOO! OH NO, HE'S AN OLD FUDDY-DUDDY!
GHOSTS, YOU NEED TO STOP APPEARING LIKE THAT! CAN'T YOU GIVE ME SOME WARNING?

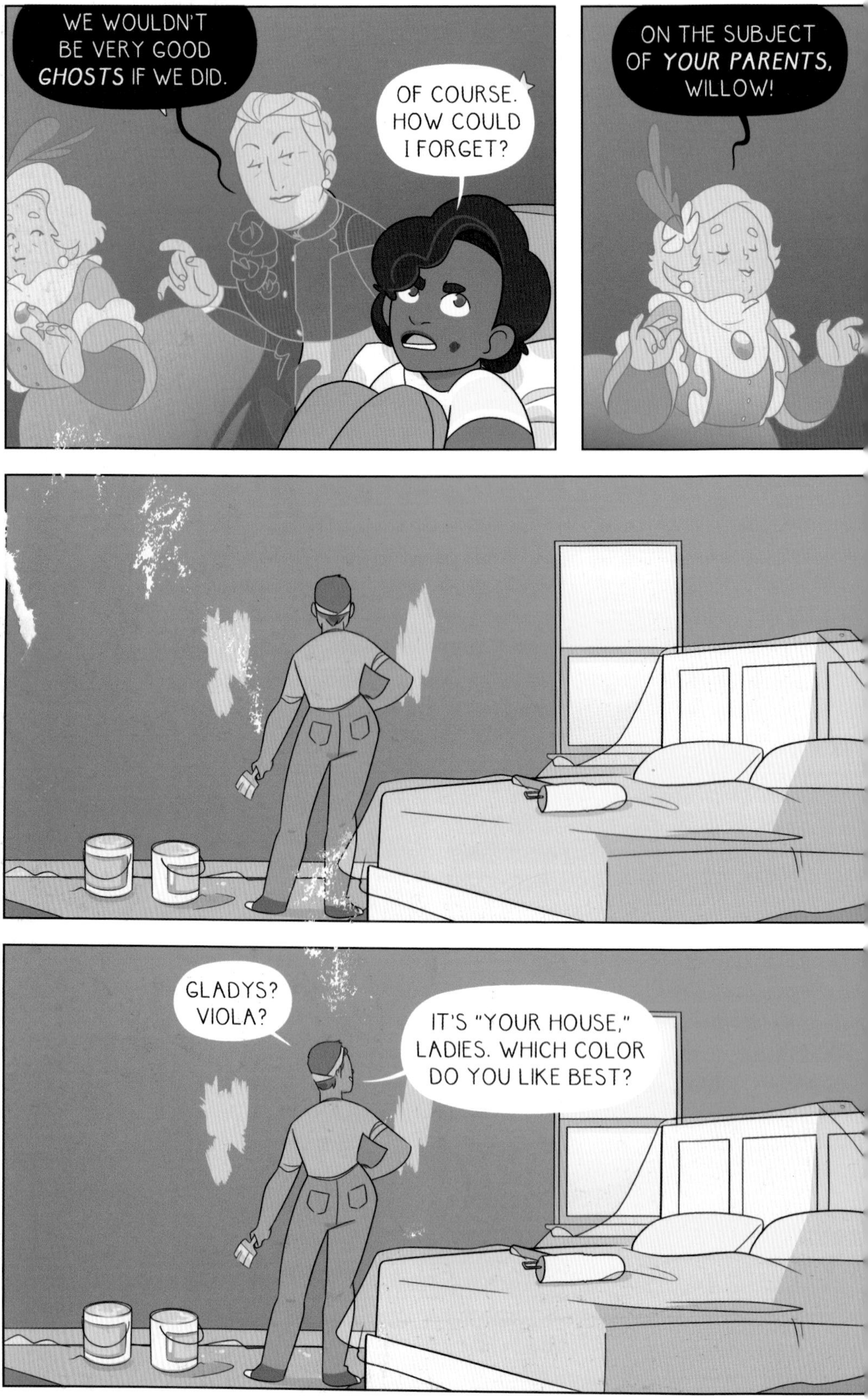
WE WOULDN'T BE VERY GOOD *GHOSTS* IF WE DID.
OF COURSE. HOW COULD I FORGET?
ON THE SUBJECT OF *YOUR PARENTS,* WILLOW!
GLADYS? VIOLA?
IT'S "YOUR HOUSE," LADIES. WHICH COLOR DO YOU LIKE BEST?

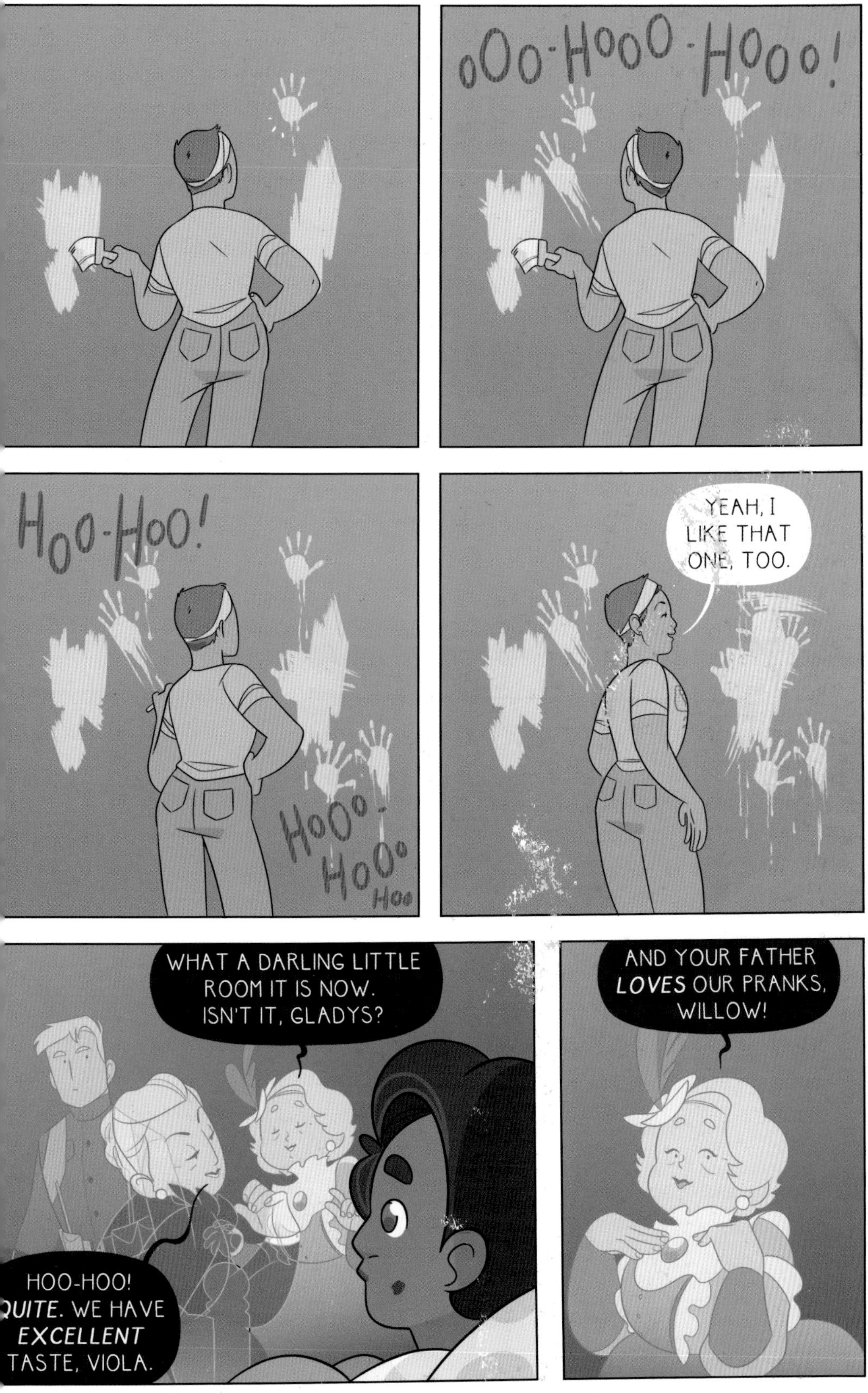
OOO-HOOO-HOOOO!
HOO-HOO!
HOOO-HOOO
HOO
YEAH, I LIKE THAT ONE, TOO.
WHAT A DARLING LITTLE ROOM IT IS NOW. ISN'T IT, GLADYS?
HOO-HOO! QUITE. WE HAVE EXCELLENT TASTE, VIOLA.
AND YOUR FATHER LOVES OUR PRANKS, WILLOW!

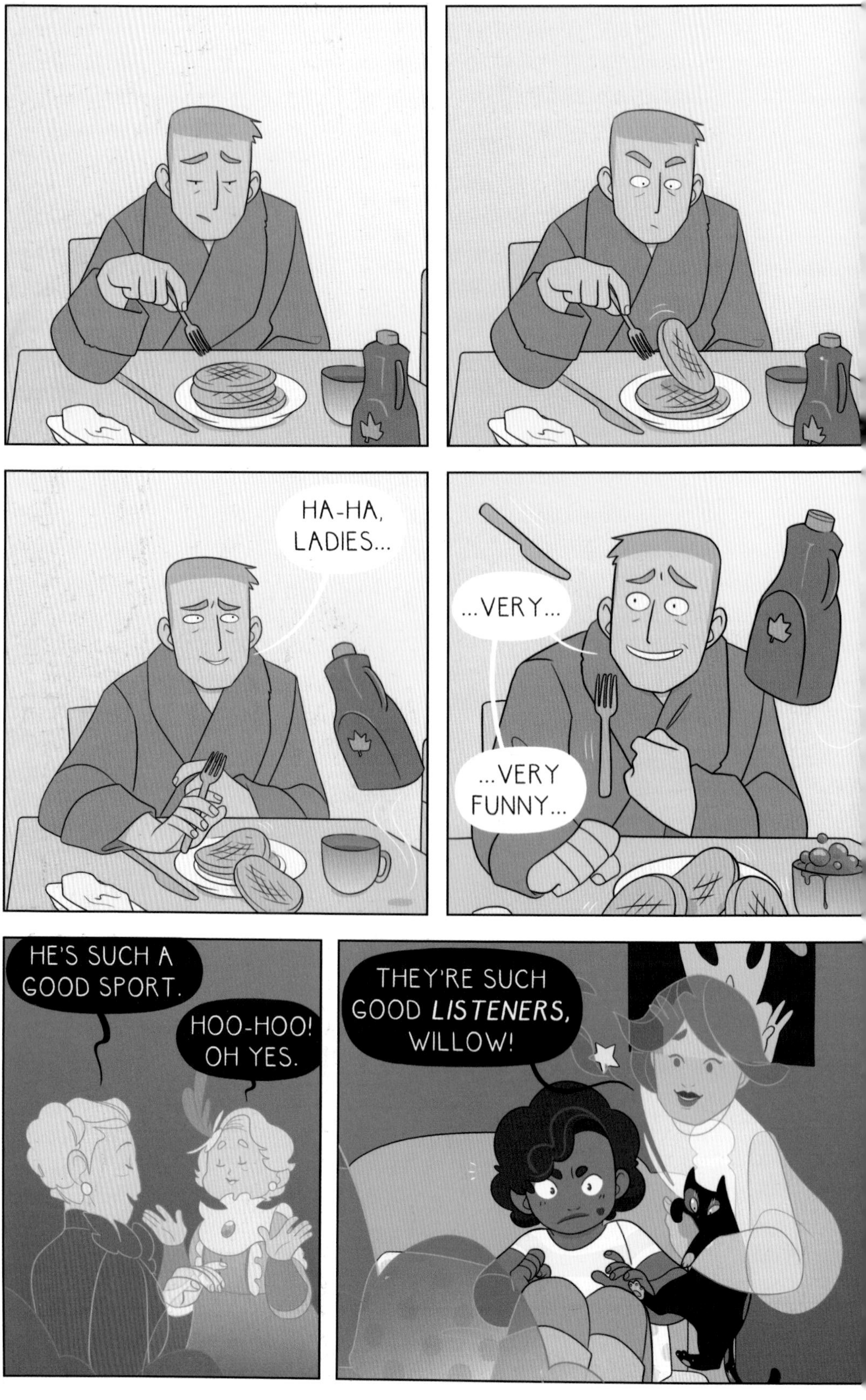
HA-HA, LADIES...
...VERY...
...VERY FUNNY...
HE'S SUCH A GOOD SPORT.
HOO-HOO! OH YES.
THEY'RE SUCH GOOD *LISTENERS*, WILLOW!

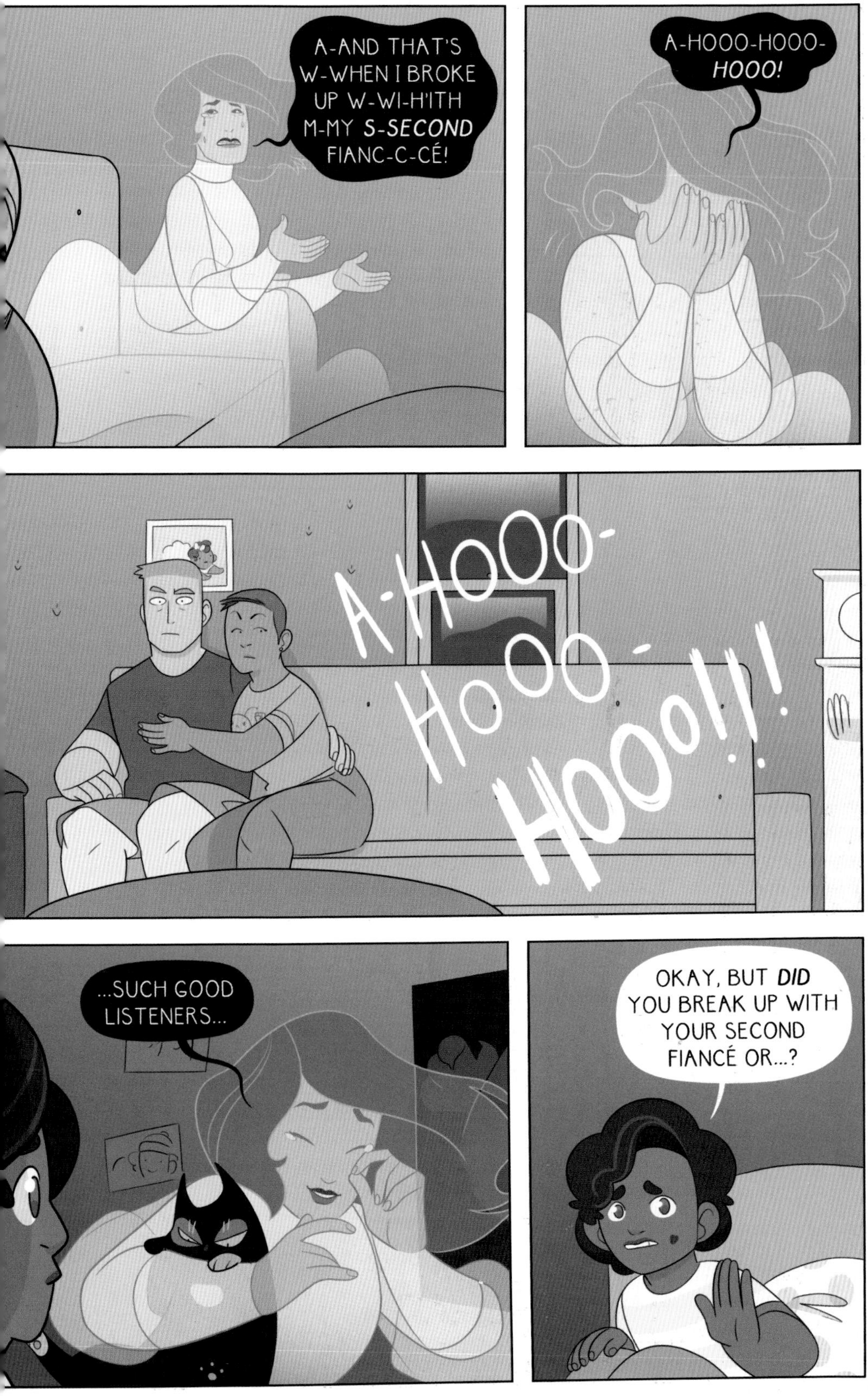
A-AND THAT'S W-WHEN I BROKE UP W-WI-H'ITH M-MY **S-SECOND** FIANC-C-CÉ!
A-HOOO-HOOO-**HOOO!**
A-HOOO-HOOO-HOOO!!!
...SUCH GOOD LISTENERS...
OKAY, BUT ***DID*** YOU BREAK UP WITH YOUR SECOND FIANCÉ OR...?

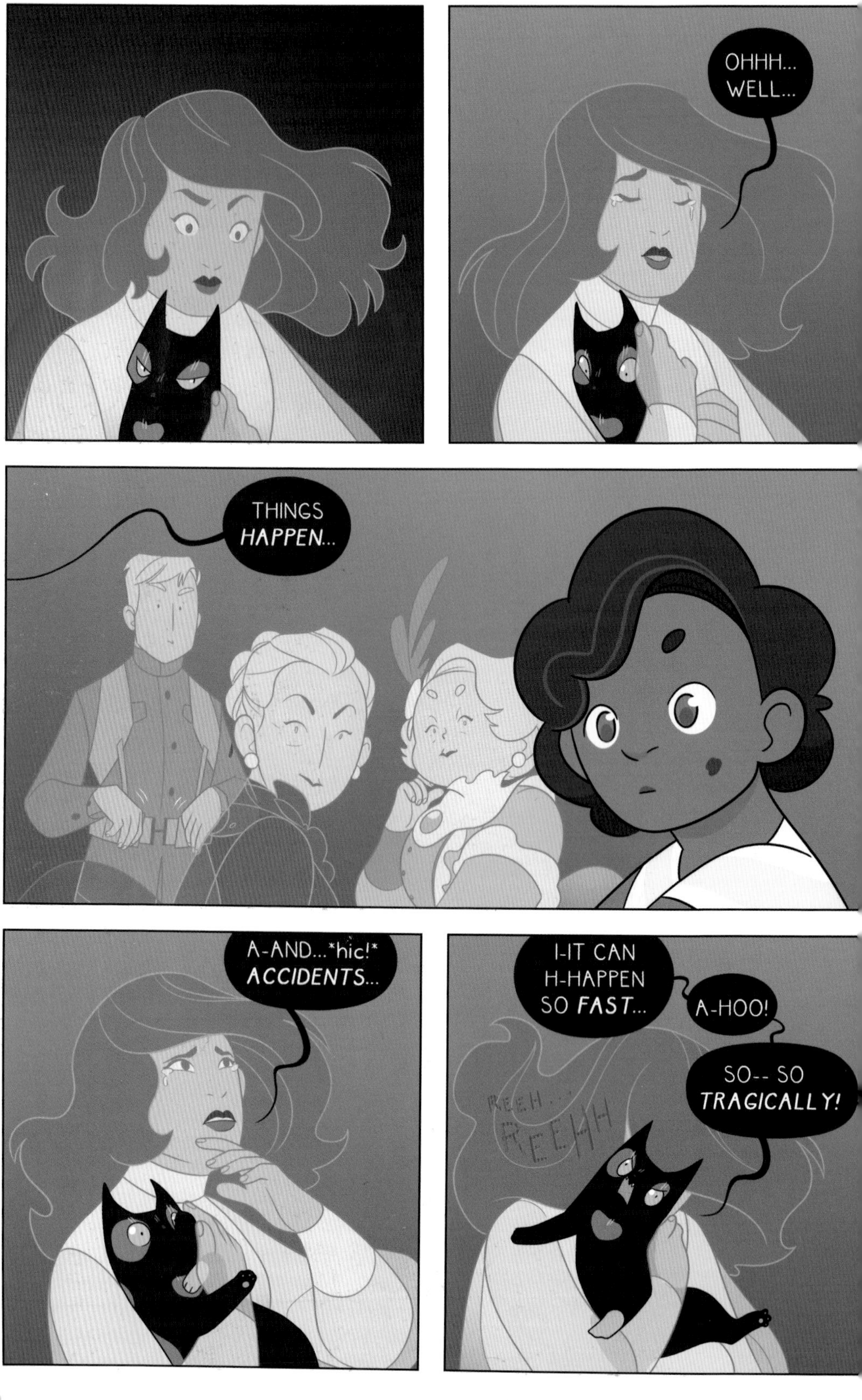
OHHH... WELL...
THINGS HAPPEN...
A-AND...*hic!* ACCIDENTS...
I-IT CAN H-HAPPEN SO FAST...
A-HOO!
REEH... REEHH
SO-- SO TRAGICALLY!

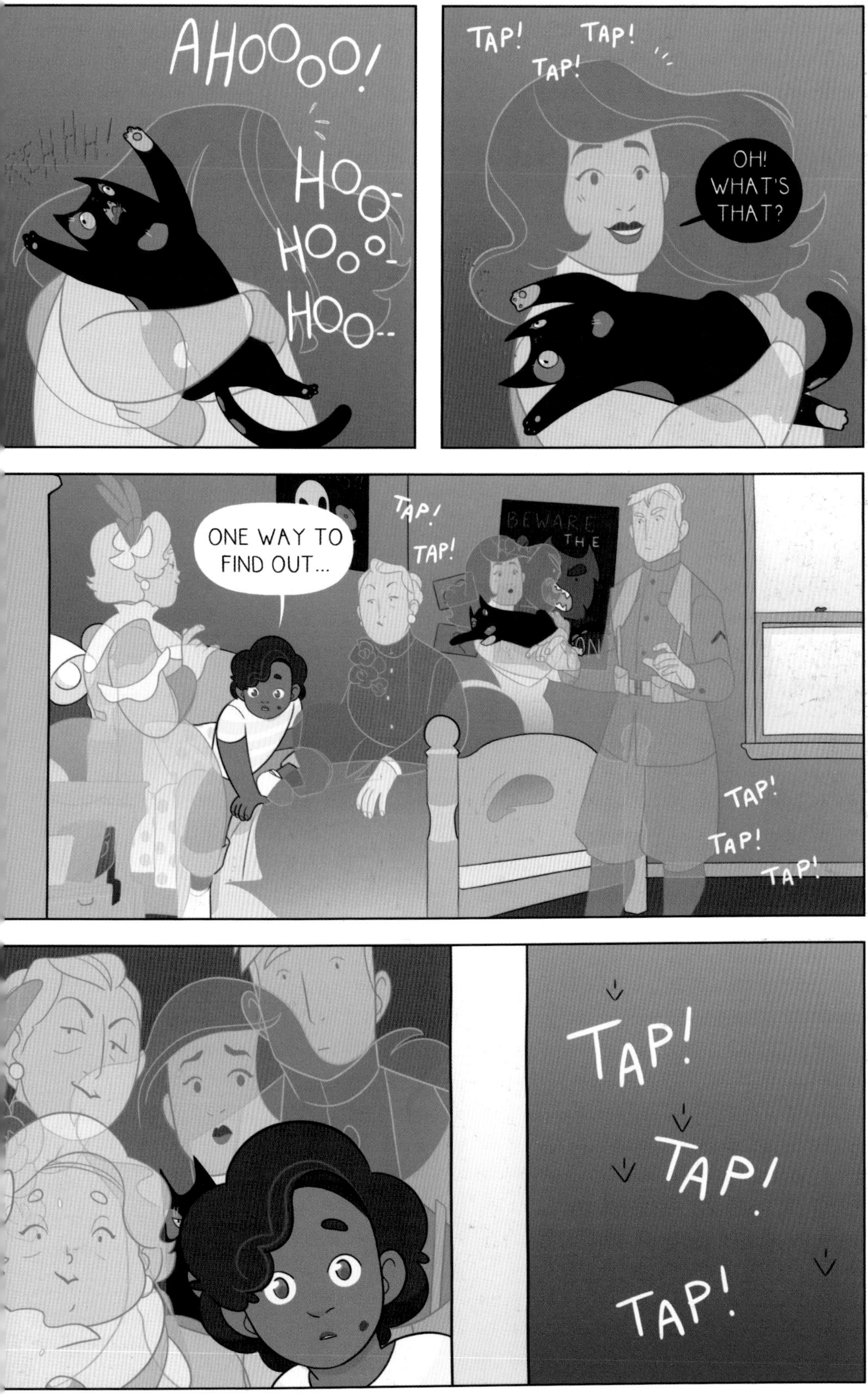
AHOOOOO!
HOO-
HOOO-
HOO--
TAP! TAP! TAP!
OH! WHAT'S THAT?
ONE WAY TO FIND OUT...
TAP!
TAP!
BEWARE THE
TAP!
TAP!
TAP!
TAP!
TAP!
TAP!

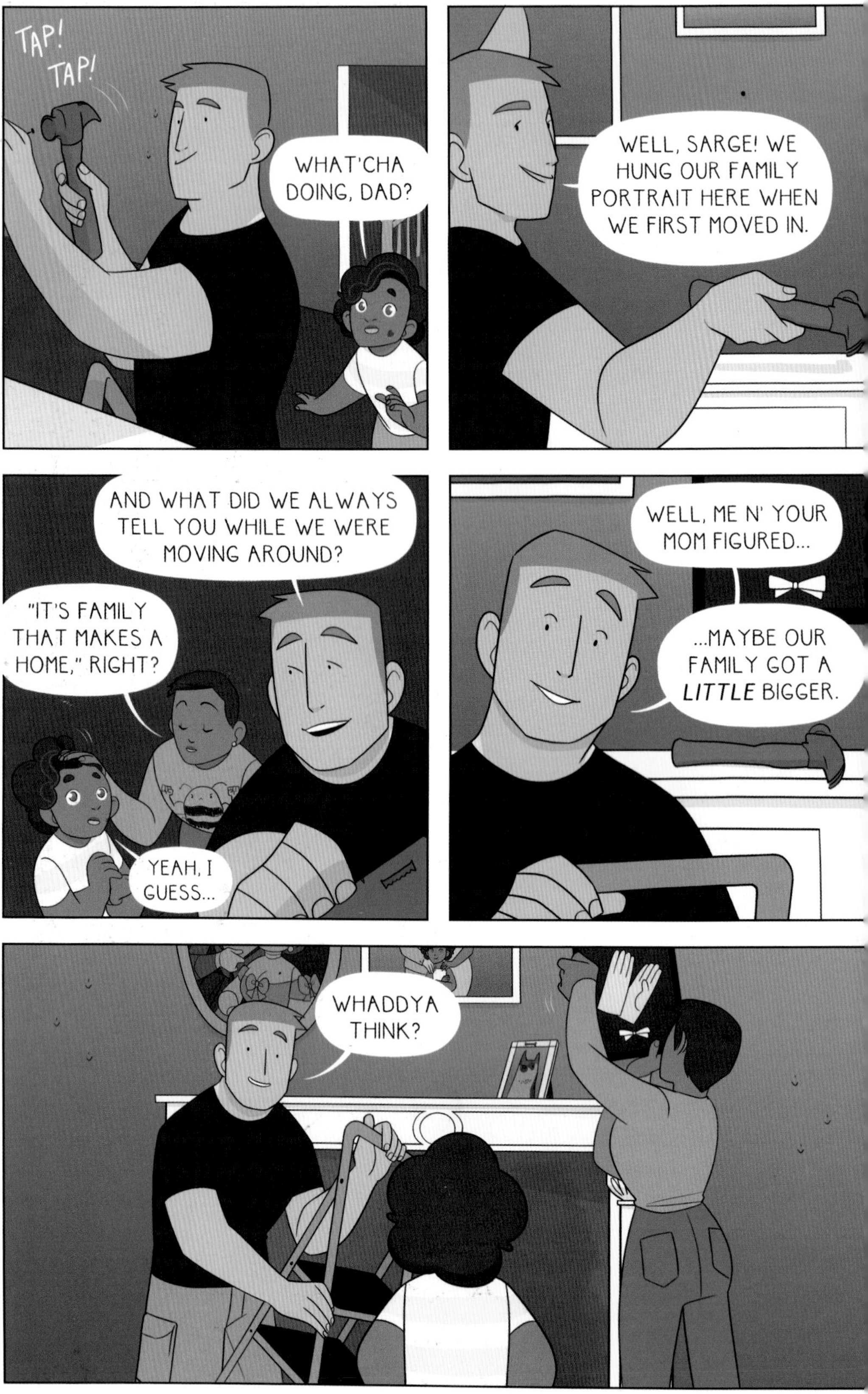
TAP! TAP!
WHAT'CHA DOING, DAD?
WELL, SARGE! WE HUNG OUR FAMILY PORTRAIT HERE WHEN WE FIRST MOVED IN.
AND WHAT DID WE ALWAYS TELL YOU WHILE WE WERE MOVING AROUND?
"IT'S FAMILY THAT MAKES A HOME," RIGHT?
YEAH, I GUESS...
WELL, ME N' YOUR MOM FIGURED...
...MAYBE OUR FAMILY GOT A LITTLE BIGGER.
WHADDYA THINK?

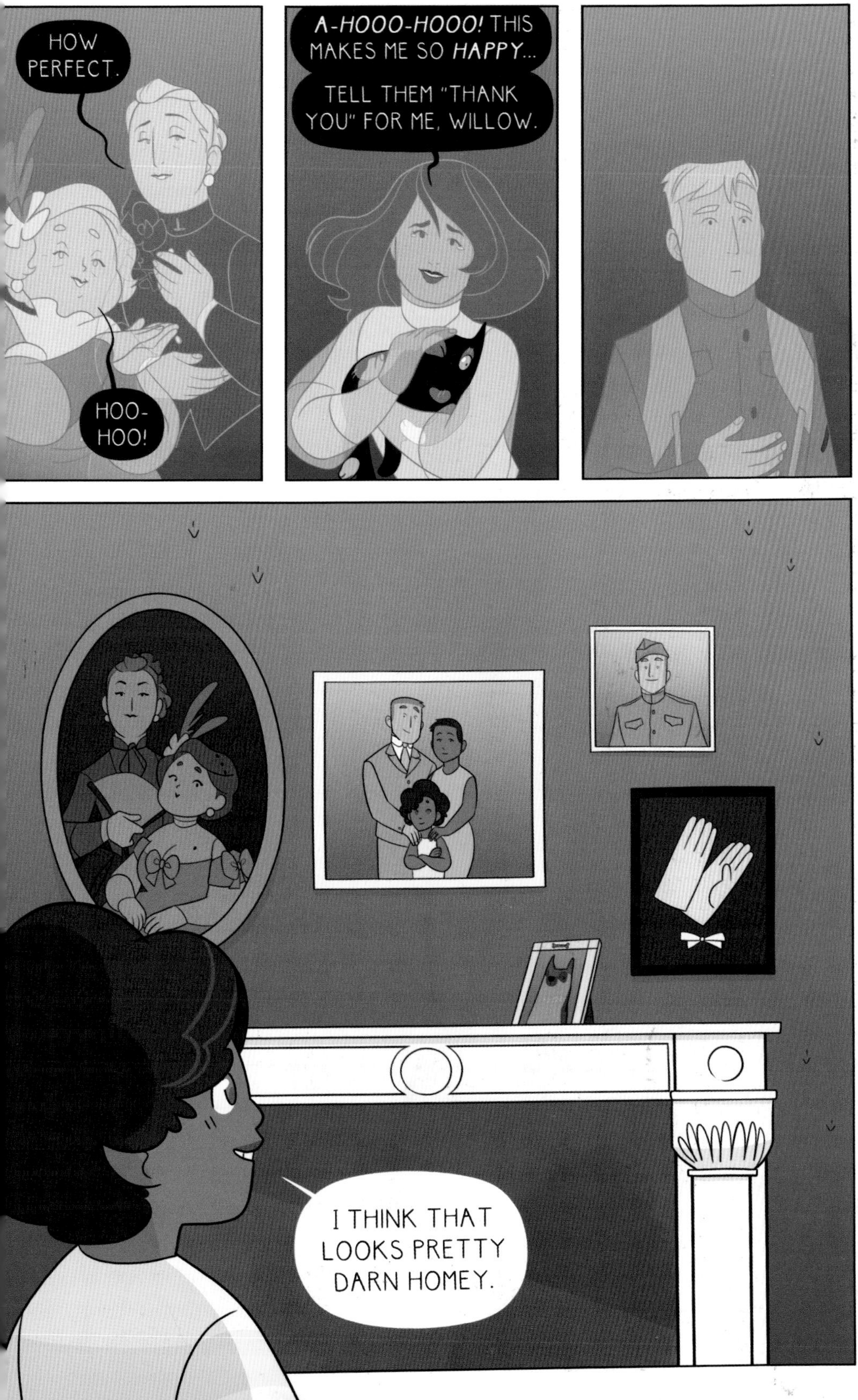
HOW PERFECT.
HOO-HOO!
A-HOOO-HOOO! THIS MAKES ME SO HAPPY...
TELL THEM "THANK YOU" FOR ME, WILLOW.
I THINK THAT LOOKS PRETTY DARN HOMEY.

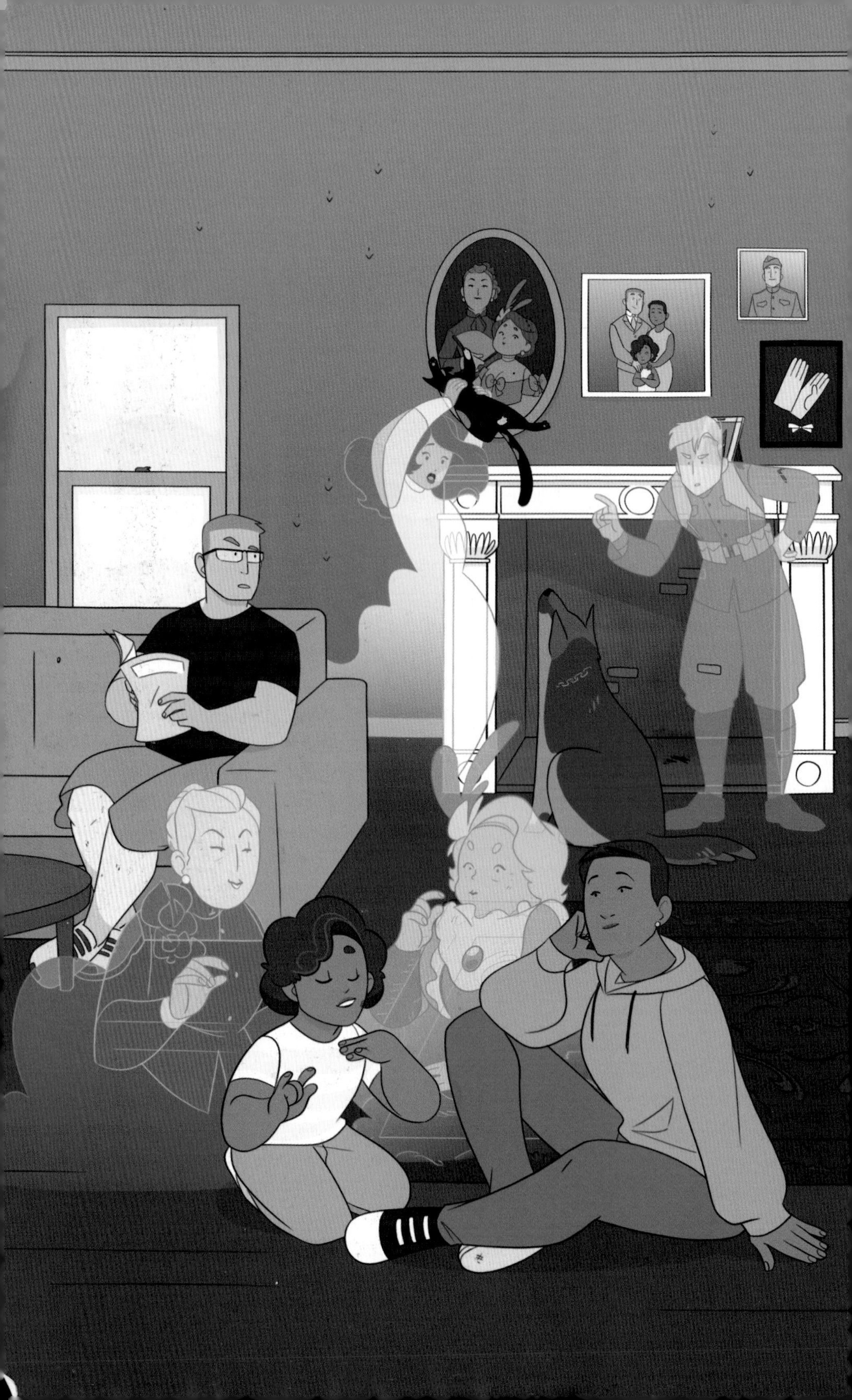

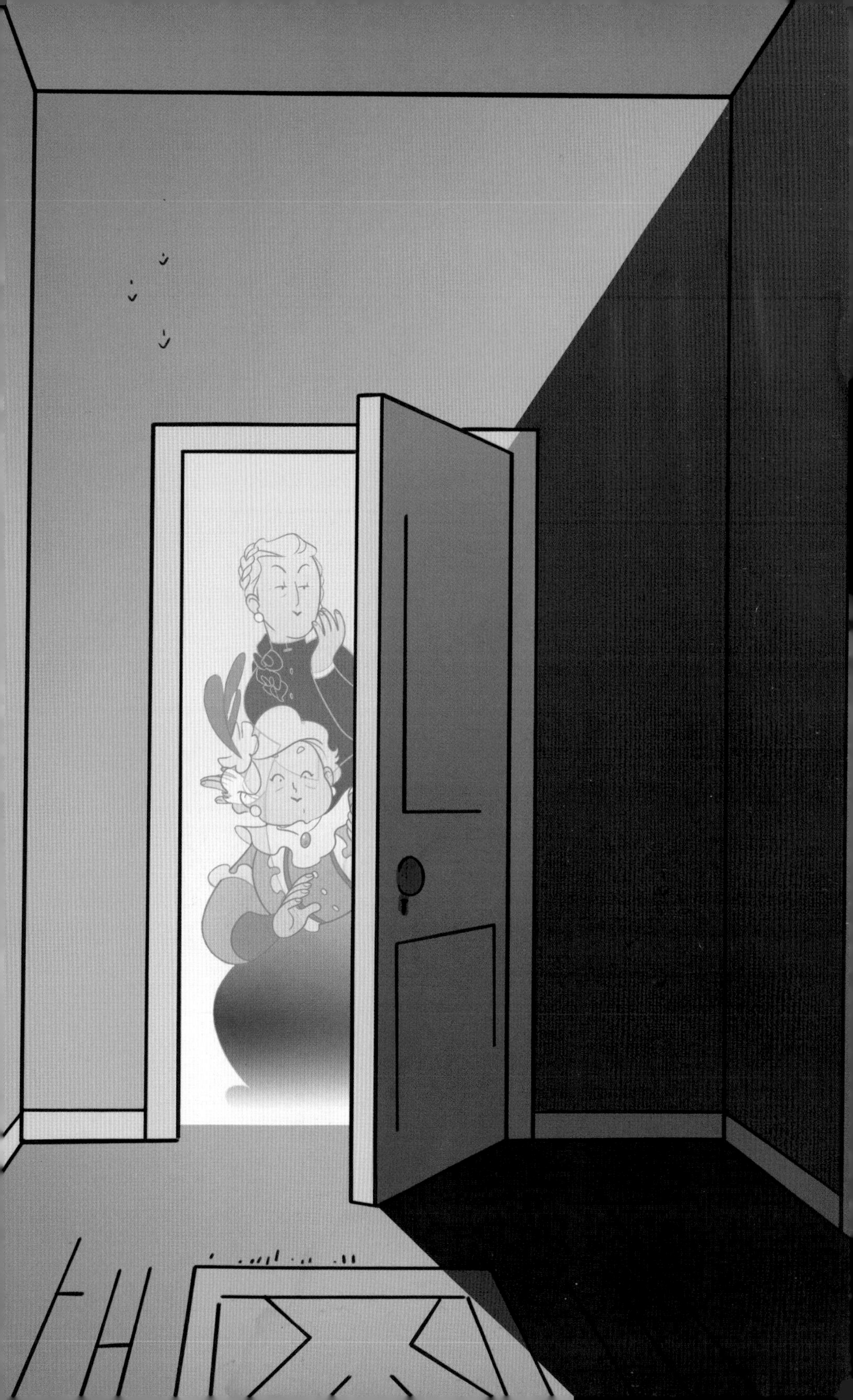

# FOReVeR HoMe™
# Teaching Guide

## Learning Standards

The questions and activities in this teacher Guide correlate with the following Common Core English Language Arts Standards (www.corestandards.org) for Grades 4-8:

ELA Reading: Literature Standards
- Key Ideas and Details RL.4-8.1, RL.4-8.2, RL.4-8.3;
- Craft and Structure RL.4-8.4, RL.4-8.5, RL.4-8.6.

ELA Reading: Informational Texts Standards
- Key Ideas and Details RI.4-8.1, RI.4-8.2, RI.4-8.3;
- Craft and Structure RI.4-8.4, RI.4-8.5;
- Integration of Knowledge and Ideas RI.4-8.7, RI.4-8.8.

ELA Writing Standards
- Text Types and Purposes W.4-8.1, W.4-8.3;
- Production and Distribution of Writing W.4-8.4, W.4-8.5;
- Research to Build and Present Knowledge W.4-8.8, W.4-8.9.

ELA Speaking and Listening Standards
- Comprehension and Collaboration SL.4-8.1;
- Presentation of Knowledge and Ideas SL.4-8.4, SL.4-8.5.

## A General Approach

It is highly recommended that you read Scott McCloud's *Understanding Comics*[1], specifically pages 60-63, which deal with closure, pages 70-72, which deal with panel transitions and 152-155, which deal with word/picture combinations. Depending on the needs of your class, you can have students learn these specific terms and use them to identify the different transition and combination styles. Alternately, you can utilize your understanding of them to guide discussion, when examining specific panels or pages.

---

1. McCloud, Scott, 1960-. *Understanding Comics : the Invisible Art.* New York: HarperPerennial, 1994.

Highlight individual panels and or pages, and ask the following questions:

- What is going on in this panel or on this page?
- What is the purpose of the specific pictures in telling the story? How do they enhance the words?
- Why did the creator choose to put these words and pictures together in this way?
- How does color affect the scene?
- What do we learn about the character from the images?
- What mood is being set and how?

Examine the specific sequence of panels:

- Why did the creator put these panels in this particular order?
- What's happening between the panels?
- How does the transition between these panels indicate things like mood and character?
- How do the panel transitions affect the speed of the scene?
- Why did the creator choose this speed?

### Let's get active!

A great exercise is to have students act out a short scene in the book, getting them to fill in the action occurring between the panels. This demonstrates to them that the gutter (that space between panels) is just as important as the other storytelling elements in the book.

Pre-Reading Activities

What does the cover tell you about the story? What do you think the relationship is between these characters? What do you think the young girl is thinking or feeling?

Read pages 1-5 (until "The Next Morning..."), and answer the following questions:

- What is the story about?
- Does this make you want to keep reading?
- What do you want to learn about the characters or story?
- What do you know about the ghosts?
- Do you believe in ghosts?

3.

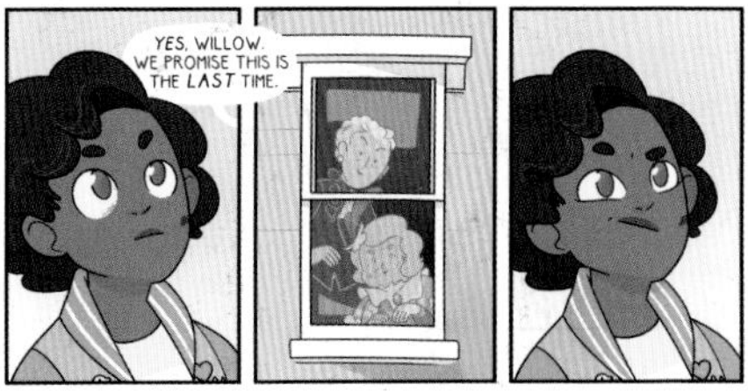
YES, WILLOW. WE PROMISE THIS IS THE *LAST* TIME.

## Discussion Questions

Questions about specific pages:

1. Look at the top two panels on page 3. What is different about the panel layout? How does the font effect the story? How do the backgrounds impact the reader?

2. On page 6, the first two panels are very different. Describe each panel. Why are they placed side by side? Describe the house. How does it meet or differ from your expectations after reading the first 5 pages?

3. Do you think Willow sees the ghosts on page 7? If so, what is her reaction to them?

4. What makes page 9 seem like it should be scary? Why is it not scary in the end?

5. What is happening on pages 22 and 23? How do you as a reader feel? Who do you sympathize with?

7.

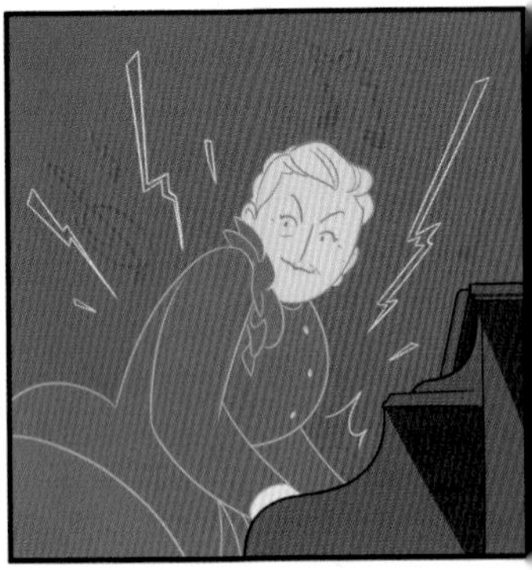

6. Look at Willow's room on page 44. What does it say about her? Compare it with the room on page 46. Describe the room and the mood it creates.

7. On page 52, what do you think the music sounds like? How do you know it sounds like that?

8. Based on the splash page on page 72, what do you think the sisters were like when they were alive compared to as ghosts?

9. On page 77, there are lots of emanata (those little white marks; imaginary visual elements that tell you something without words). What are they communicating in the various panels?

10. Does Willow understand the cat on pages 86-89? How is that demonstrated in the visual elements? What is the nature of the malevolent spirit now that it's a cat?

11. Page 113 is probably the "quietest" page in the book. Describe the various elements and how they contribute to the story: eg. lack of dialogue, color, placement of Willow and Fenrir, amount of action between the panels.

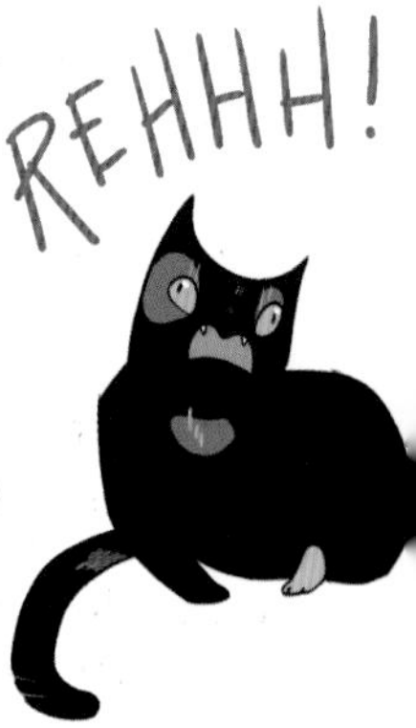
REHHH!

12. On page 135, why does Willow say "Forget that part!"?

13. On page 137, why does Willow's dad say "I was being sarcastic"? Do you believe that? Why or why not?

14. Page 138 is the only splash page with dialogue. What makes it different from the other splash pages? What is the effect of using a splash page here?

15. Why does Tommy pretend to hide from the dad on page 151?

16. How does each ghost react on page 161? What significance does it have to hang everyone's portrait? Why do you think Lady has no picture? Why the gloves and bow instead?

17. Based on the last page, how does everyone feel about each other now?

## General Questions:

1. Find examples of different facial expressions used to indicate the following emotions. What are some of the characteristics of the different expressions?

    - Happiness
    - Anger
    - Sadness
    - Frustration
    - Shock
    - Awkwardness
    - Fear

1.

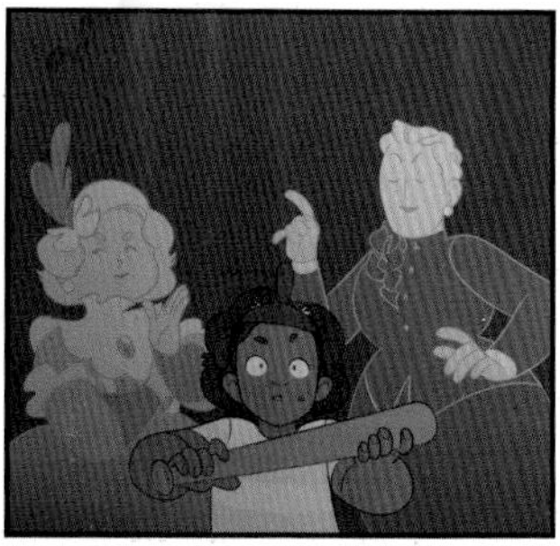

2. Look at the speech bubbles. What elements change the tone and sound of the dialogue? Find some examples of unusual speech bubbles and describe the sounds they make.

3. There are several splash pages throughout the book. What is the purpose of these pages?

4. Why do Willow's parents call her Sarge? Do you think this nickname suits her?

5. Willow doesn't seem to find the ghosts scary at any point, except for the malevolent spirit. Why is that one different for her? Why does she not find the other ghosts scary? What do you find scary?

6.

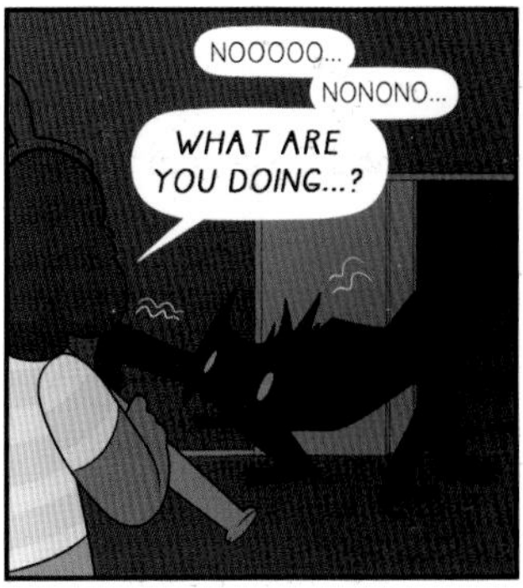
NOOOOO...
NONONO...
WHAT ARE YOU DOING...?

6. How would you describe the ghosts visually? How does this compare to the malevolent spirit? What makes it malevolent?

7. In what ways are the ghosts able to effect the world around them?

8. Why is Willow so adamant to stay in the house, even though it is haunted?

9. Different people react to the ghosts differently. Why do you think it takes so long for for Willow's dad to realize there are ghosts in the house, even though he witnesses some very strange things? Why is the plumber so blasé about the fact that the walls are bleeding?

10. Willow's parents disagree about the existence of ghosts. Willow's mum believes, but she often acts like she doesn't. Why does she pretend she doesn't believe in ghosts? Have you ever modified your beliefs to appease others?

11. What is Willow's relationship with each of the ghosts (the Hadleigh sisters, Thomas, Lady) at first? When does each relationship change? Why and how does it change?

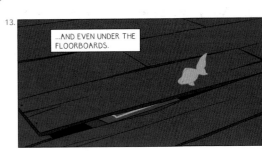

12. Describe Willow's mask. Why does she wear it?

13.

...AND EVEN UNDER THE FLOORBOARDS.

13. Find the instances of ghost goldfish in the book. Why are they there? What might they represent?

14. After her parents find out about the ghosts, how do they feel about the ghosts and their activities? How do you know?

15. Is it important for your family to hang family pictures on the walls? Why or why not?

16. What do you think about the ending of the book? Is it satisfying? Why or why not?

15.

## Post-Reading Activities

### Reading

1. After reading the whole book, summarize the book and describe the main characters. Take a look back at the questions you answered during the pre-reading activities, based on just the first few pages of the book. How did your ideas change after reading the whole book?

2. Describe the characters by selecting 3 panels that reflect different aspects of those characters.

3. Pick 3 panels with backgrounds and 3 panels without backgrounds and explain why these choices were made. It is better to have backgrounds or not? Or is it driven by what's happening in the story?

### Writing

1. Lady's story is never really explained. Write a story about what you think Lady's life was like.

2. Why does Tommy go to war? Write a letter as if you are Tommy, when he was stationed in France.

3. If you were a ghost, what would you do to keep busy? Write a diary describing your life as a ghost. Include at least 3 entries.

4. Provide captions for one or more of the wordless splash pages located throughout the book.

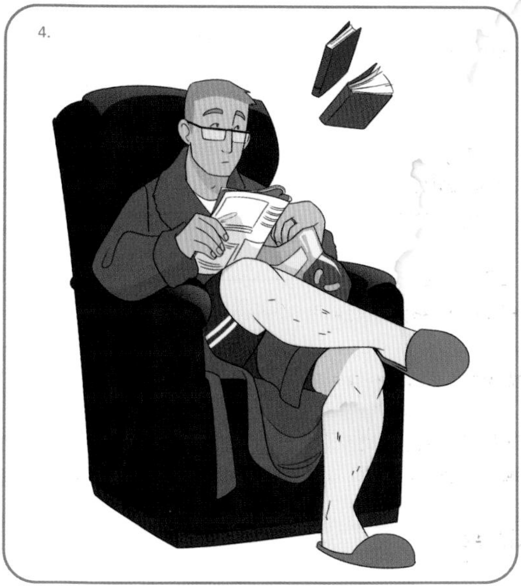
4.

## ntegrating

1. Hadleigh House is a historic building. Are there historic buildings in your city? Find a historic residence (in your city or elsewhere) and research the people who used to live there. Present a biography of one of those residents to your class.

2. Do you know any ghost stories? Discover and examine a ghost story. What makes it scary? How does it compare to this ghost story?

3. On page 122, the Hadleigh sisters mention Edgar Allan Poe. Research Edgar Allan Poe. Why is he being referenced in this scene? What is his relationship to this story?

4. Do you have a nickname? Create a portrait of yourself as a representation of your nickname.

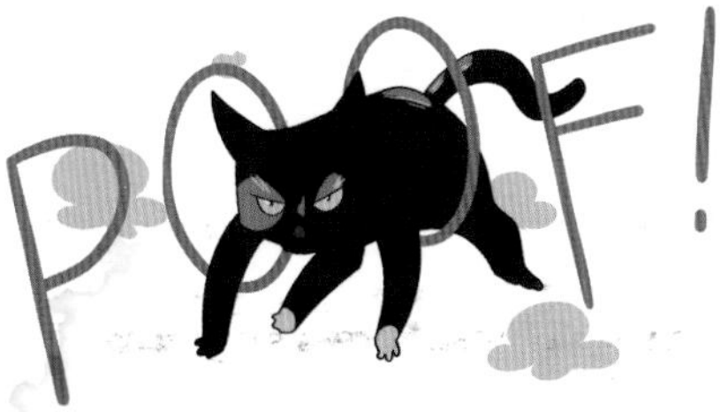
POOF!

# Author Bio

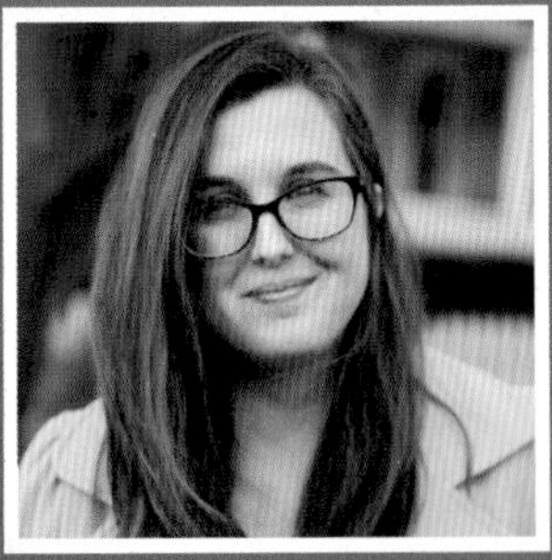

Jenna Ayoub is a comic artist and writer who spent her childhood seeing the world, providing an upbringing that has greatly influenced her love of stories and history. Beginning her career as an inker, she has since illustrated comics under titles like *Adventure Time*, *Regular Show*, and *The Amazing World of Gumball*.

She has an affinity for period pieces and character-driven stories, often with time-travelers as a recurring theme. Jenna also draws from her own adventures for inspiration.

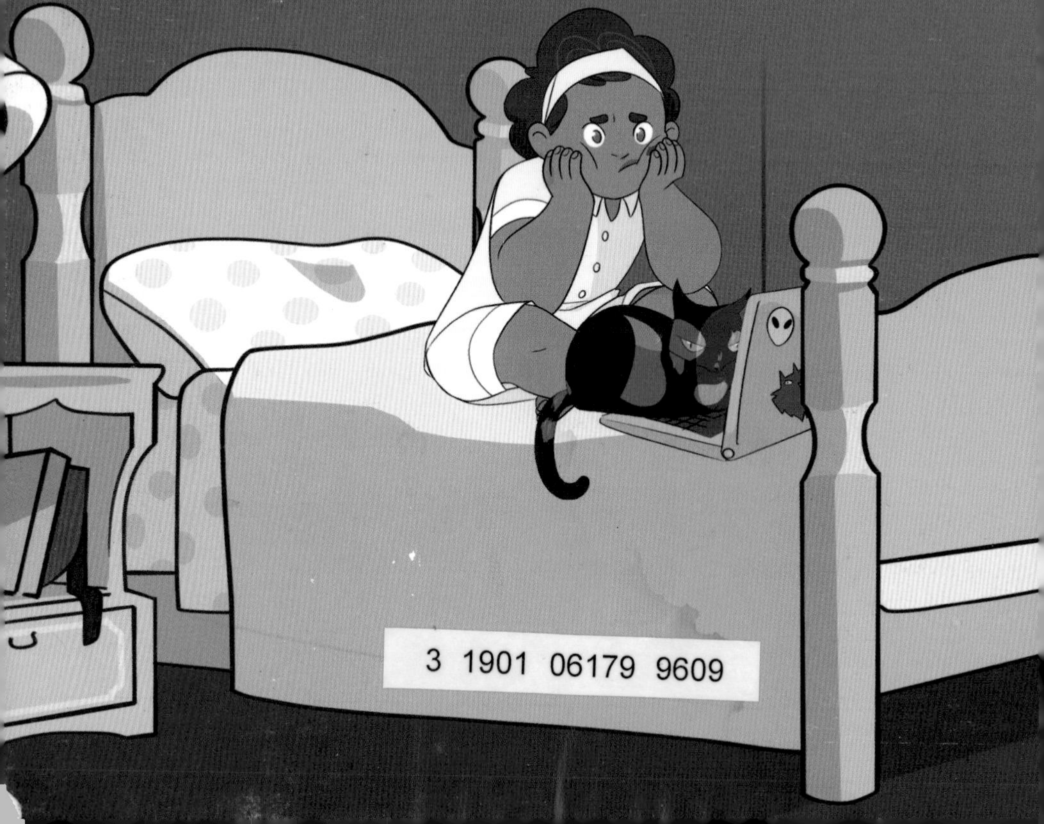